Come a Little Closer

KAREN PERRY

MICHAEL JOSEPH

an imprint of

PENGUIN BOOKS

MICHAEL JOSEPH

UK | USA | Canada | Ireland | Australia
India | New Zealand | South Africa

Michael Joseph is part of the Penguin Random House group of companies
whose addresses can be found at global.penguinrandomhouse.com.

Penguin
Random House
UK

First published 2019
001

Copyright © Karen Perry, 2019

The moral right of the author has been asserted

Set in 12.5/14.75 pt Garamond MT Std
Typeset by Jouve (UK), Milton Keynes
Printed and bound in Great Britain by Clays Ltd, Elcograf S.p.A.

A CIP catalogue record for this book is available from the British Library

ISBN: 978–0–241–34812–3

Nobody sees him. A small boy cutting a line through parked cars towards the green. He is alone and, from a distance, there is nothing extraordinary about him. Nothing to draw attention, nothing to cause alarm.

Heat shimmers above scorched grass although it is not yet noon. The air is filled with noise – laughter, the sound of a child's temper tantrum, a mother admonishing him. Coloured flags flutter on lines of bunting strung between the streetlamps and trees of Wyndham Park. By mutual agreement, all dogs have been left at home and the occasional muffled bark reaches them. There is the bleat of a distant ringing, music from a beat-box, a crowd of teenagers sitting cross-legged around it. Two barbecues have been set up in the middle of the green – big ones, Weber, top of the range – and the men take turns flipping burgers and browning sausages, discussing the football.

The adults have split along gender lines, the women making a ring with their deckchairs, sipping from paper cups. A younger woman – a tenant of one of the basement apartments on the east side of the park – slips off her shirt to reveal a black bikini top. She lies stretched out on the grass some distance from the others, the soft hills of her breasts rising above the mound of her ribcage. The men glance over, and the women's talk drops.

Perhaps it is because of this distraction that they don't notice the small solitary boy coming out of Number 14, the plum-coloured heavy door closing behind him. They don't notice his steady pilgrimage towards them.

One of the mums has brought face-paints with her, and a queue of children has formed, waiting to be transformed into cats and lions and butterflies. She is painstakingly sweeping black paint – tiger whiskers – over a child's cheeks, when the little girl's eyes widen, the pucker of a frown appearing on her brow.

'You all right, sweetheart?'

The little girl opens her mouth to answer, eyes still fixed on something in the distance, but she doesn't get a chance to speak.

A scream rises from the crowd followed by an instant hush while everyone looks around. Mothers scan the green for their children. Teenagers look over with casual disinterest. Only the rhythmic blare from the beat-box disturbs the air.

'Jesus,' a man says, as the boy steps towards them.

It's as if he's dropped out of the sky.

Small and slight, no more than six years old, his bare legs and arms and the insignia on his Batman T-shirt are smeared with blood.

The meat sizzles on the grill, beginning to burn, but no one cares about that now. The park continues to bake in the sun, a hot wind blows through the trees, but everything else is different. They stare at him aghast.

He does not appear to be injured or in pain, and yet there is blood on his legs, on his bare feet. He looks up at the men, his eyes heavy-lidded and staring at them, as if from behind a pane of glass, screened off in his own world of terror. He raises his little hands, the blood already caked into his fingernails, turning rust brown.

'Help me,' he says.

June

I

Leah

When they turn the corner on to Wyndham Park, Leah instinctively squeezes Jake's hand. Excitement, a shimmer of nerves, goes through her as they hurry along the pavement. Jake's hand gives an answering squeeze and, without having to say it, she knows he feels it too: how unbelievably lucky they are.

The flat they have come to view is in the basement of Number 14 and, from what they understand, it is theirs if they want it. Two days have passed since Jake's breathless phone-call. Leah had been at work, going through the painstaking bureaucracy of filing a patent for one of the firm's regular clients, when he had called with the news. Some guy Jake had met through a work colleague was looking for tenants to occupy the basement flat in his father's house. Although it hadn't been lived in for some time, it was spacious and clean, and the rent was cheap for the area.

'What's the catch?' Leah had asked, an instinctive wariness rising inside her.

'There isn't one!' Jake had said, laughing like a delighted schoolboy, and she had found herself caught up in the slipstream of his excitement, his infectious optimism.

All day, the heat in the city has been stifling. But here on Wyndham Park the air holds a rarefied coolness, the houses caught in the pinkish glow of early-evening sun-light. From the nearby courts come the pocking sounds of tennis balls being struck. The distant drone of unseen traf-fic comes from the main street beyond. Dogs bark and strain on their leads, sniffing around the oaks and syca-mores, the chestnut trees that punctuate the green, while kids scoot over the asphalt that splits the park in two. Leah takes it all in – the park, the noise, the lush greenness of summer – and feels an unfamiliar jolt of happiness.

Fourteen Wyndham Park East. She turns the address over and over in her head, feels it humming hopefully inside her as they walk quickly, their footfall sounding on the pavement.

The owner, Mark, is leaning on the railings outside the house. He plucks the cigarette from his mouth as they approach. 'All right, mate?' he asks Jake, the two of them shaking hands.

'Yeah. Good to see you. Mark, this is my girlfriend – Leah.'

Mark doesn't shake her hand, merely nods at her. She's too excited – too grateful to this man – to take offence. He's tall and thin, as Jake described, mid-twenties, slightly stooped, as if trying to diminish his height. Despite the heat, he's wearing a scuffed leather jacket over a black T-shirt, jeans that hang low from his hips, greyish Converse trainers that might once have been white. It brings their own more formal clothing into sharp relief. Both she and Jake have dressed up for the occasion, as if it were an interview they were about to attend, not the viewing of a flat.

His scruffy clothing aside, there's something dark and serious in the quick glance Mark gives her and she sees that he's attractive in a raffish sort of way. Long eyelashes. Liquid green eyes.

The men talk about work and their mutual acquaintance – Ian – the vital link in the chain that led Jake and Leah to Mark and this house. As they talk, Leah's attention drifts, her eyes drawn to the house. One of the terraces flanking three sides of the park, it has all the imposing grandeur of the age in which it was built. Sash windows, a fanlight in a sunburst pattern, stone steps leading up to the threshold. The front door is painted a deep purple, the paint peeling in places, but Leah can imagine that at one time it was bright and glossy, the brassware shining bright.

Jake is giving an account of all the weeks they've spent looking, the dispiriting queues they've joined outside houses in Ranelagh, flats in town, only to be knocked back again and again.

Mark nods, staring down at the pavement where he's dropped his cigarette butt, crushing it beneath his trainer. It's clear he's not really interested. He probably has no understanding of how odd this feels for Leah and Jake, turning up outside a building with no line of people form-ing, knowing that without ever having set foot inside the place, it's already theirs. Or maybe he's embarrassed by their presence here on the street, awkward about the arrangement made between them. Leah is surprised by the feeling that comes over her now of something illicit passing between them – as if the agreement that's been reached is unlawful or underhand. She glances across at the houses on the opposite side of the street – the long row of sash windows, intermittently open to the evening air. The last house is smaller than its neighbours – a newer addition, perhaps, more modest in scale. For just a second, she thinks she sees the ghostly oval of a face peering down at her through an upstairs window. But then she blinks and her vision clears, revealing only a blank space, the swathe of a curtain half hidden from view.

'Right, then. Shall we go in?' Mark asks, before turning and taking the run of steps that descends to the basement at a clipped speed, Jake and Leah following.

It's different down here. There's a dank smell in the air, and the long shadow cast by the path and stone steps lends a chill. Mark fiddles with the lock – it's clearly one that requires a knack – and, for a moment, Leah and Jake stand there, watching him tugging and probing with the key, then casting their eyes around at the broken concrete beneath the window, the rise of brackish moss up the wall to the sill. One of the window panes has a fine crack running through it. Her optimism begins to dip. But then Mark pushes open the door and they file in after him, Leah's eyes trying to take it all in at once.

Mark is brisk as he leads them through. 'Bathroom. Bedroom. Living area,' he announces, with a perfunctory air, while opening doors on to these rooms.

Quickly, she glances into the small bathroom, tucked into the space beneath the steps that lead up to the front door of the main house – cramped but clean. Then the bedroom at the front with an unmade double, the new mattress still encased in plastic wrap, a small wardrobe standing open, a rug, pattern faded, laid over bare wooden boards. The living area is at the back, a large space dominated by French windows opening on to a patio, a hint of the garden beyond in the skirting of lush greenness above the patio wall.

'What's in here?' Leah asks, opening a door to the side, which reveals a small dark room.

When Mark flicks the light switch, it illuminates a space hardly big enough to fit a single bed.

'It can be Matthew's room,' Jake says excitedly, running his hand over the walls as if considering what colour to paint them.

'Who's Matthew?' Mark asks.

'My seven-year-old. He lives with his mother, but he stays with me sometimes.'

As Jake says this, Leah feels Mark glancing at her with new interest. She can tell he's making fresh calculations about her and Jake, about their relationship. She wonders how much he knows about them, what Ian has told him.

Jake is checking the little window at the far end to see if it will open. It makes a cracking sound as it unsticks. She watches him as he stands back, his eyes busily travelling over the room, and she knows he's making silent designs – Matthew's bed there under the window, a chest of drawers here by the door, some posters on the walls, balsawood aeroplanes dangling from the ceiling, a shelf for Lego master-builds skirting the wall. She knows that he is reconstructing the place in his mind, a room for his son that will be cosy and welcoming – safe – and there's something so guileless about him, the obvious need he has to shelter and protect his child, that she feels her heart constrict with love for this man, for the depths of warmth and need within him.

'There's no drier, I'm afraid,' Mark says, drawing their attention back to him, 'but you can use the washing line in the garden.'

He opens the French windows, and a waft of warm air comes in, carrying the scent of lavender and grass. They follow him outside, taking the opportunity to glance at each other while his back is turned in a bid to gauge their reactions to the place. Jake raises his eyebrows, the hint of a smile at the corners of his mouth, and Leah meets it with her own look of approval. She knows they share the same thought: that this is more than they had hoped for. It's true that the flat is somewhat starved of light, and it has an empty feel of neglect from having been unlived in for some years. But it's spacious and quiet, and the neighbourhood is far better than anything they'd hoped for. Compared with the long list of cramped and dingy flats they've traipsed through over the last few weeks, it seems generous and opulent in comparison.

'So this here is yours,' Mark tells them, indicating the patio that has been carved into a space tucked between the garden wall and the steps that lead down from the big house. 'It doesn't get that much sunlight, to be honest, but it's a place to sit in the evenings, I guess.'

'Would it be all right if we put a barbecue here?' Jake asks.

Mark shrugs and says: 'Knock yourselves out.'

He's already turned and stepped up on to the grass, so Jake leans in and whispers to Leah: 'He's really selling this place, huh?'

She smiles and digs him in the ribs, but he's touched on something that she's been feeling too: the sense that Mark is not altogether happy with the situation. He's already a few yards away into the garden, which is overgrown and nettled, a tangle of briars strangling whatever shrubs are there.

'So the washing line is down here. You can hang your laundry, but otherwise keep to the patio, yeah? The old man is fussy about his garden.'

Leah sees Jake glance around at the tangled mess with a sceptical air but he is too polite to comment, and she says to Mark: 'Your father? Does he live upstairs?'

'Well, kind of. He's been away for a while, but he's coming back now.'

'Has he been travelling?'

'Mmm.'

'And your mother?'

'No. She died when I was a kid.' His gaze swivels away from her to Jake, and he says: 'So? Do you want to take it?'

'Absolutely!' Jake replies.

'Cool.' The two men shake on it.

They are discussing the rent, the setting up of monthly payments, but Leah is distracted, her sights drawn to the upper windows of the house, momentarily wondering at the occupant upstairs. Ivy creeps across the rendered wall, snaking into the corners of the windows, which are smeared with dust. There's something lonely about the thought of the widower living there alone. And another thought chases that one: Did Mark's mother die in this house?

'Leah?' Jake asks, and her attention snaps back to him. 'Are you coming?'

She follows Jake through the French windows. As agreed, Jake hands over their deposit as well as the first month's rent – an envelope of cash that Mark casually pockets without checking it first. It comes to her again: the feeling that this arrangement between them is somehow underhand, wrong. Mark's manner unsettles her in a way she cannot put her finger on. She says nothing, just watches as he hands Jake the keys.

'May as well take these, then.'

'We can move in straight away?' Jake asks, excitement again in his voice.

'Sure. Why not?'

Then Mark turns to go, striding out into the little hall. Before he reaches the front door, he stops, remembering something. 'One last thing. That door.' He points to one in the hall that neither Leah nor Jake had spotted. 'It connects to upstairs. It's locked on both sides, so you needn't worry.'

'No, right. Of course,' Jake says.

'He'll keep to himself anyway,' Mark adds. 'He won't bother you.' And something about the way his eyes catch hers gives her pause. 'Right, I'll be off. Call me if there's anything.'

And then he's gone and it's just the two of them alone in their place.

'Why do you suppose he doesn't live here?' Leah asks, as they listen to Mark's footsteps on the pavement above.

'Dunno. He probably has his own place. His own life.'

She thinks again of the look in Mark's eyes, the quick flash in them before he averted his gaze. 'It just seems odd, that's all,' she remarks. 'Perhaps they don't get on — father and son.'

'I'm not really bothered about their filial bonds,' Jake says, not unkindly, as he comes to her.

His arms go around her and she feels herself being gathered up, drawn in. Feels the tender press of his lips against hers. The kiss lasts, and she feels all the hope and love and possibility within it. The difficult weeks are over. They are home.

'Happy?' he asks softly, his eyes searching out hers.

'Happy,' she tells him, and he grins with satisfaction, the now-familiar smile that transforms his face, lights him from within – the smile that drew her to him, the smile that broke down her barriers and finally let love in.

'We should celebrate,' he tells her. 'Stay here.'

'Wait! Where are you going?' He's already heading out into the hall.

'There's an off-licence around the corner. I'll get some Prosecco. Back in a sec.'

She hears the door close after him, and then Leah is alone in the flat, hugging her arms around her chest, walking slowly through the rooms, taking it all in.

Their first home together.

She is twenty-six years old and feels as if her life is finally starting.

In the solitude of the flat, she can hear the echo of her footfall. Her fingertips trail over the walls, the doors, absorbing the feel of the place, registering all its new-ness, its unfamiliarity. This is her home now. Hers and Jake's. She can feel safe here – a conviction that both warms and steadies her.

When she reaches the connecting door in the hallway, she stops and looks at it. There is a brass doorknob in the shape of a rugby ball, and a cast-iron bolt that looks ancient. A thought comes to her. Tentatively, she reaches for the bolt. It makes a rasping sound as she draws it back. Then, putting her hand to the doorknob, she feels her breath held in her chest. Turning the handle slowly, she feels the lock hold, just as Mark had said. She lets go of the handle but doesn't move away. Instead she leans in, presses her ear to the wood panel, listens. Her breathing slows. But she hears nothing, only the swish of blood pulsing through her head.

Just before she moves away, a crazy thought comes over her: the feeling that another person could be standing there, on the other side of the door, and she wouldn't know. Even as she discounts her own foolishness, the image lingers, that at this very moment, he might have his ear pressed against the other side, listening.

2

Anton

Nineteen years since this house has been occupied and he can still hear Charlotte's voice. The rhythmic chant of a nursery rhyme for the children at bath-time. The rill of her laughter spilling down the staircase.

The second day, still disoriented by his return, Anton is standing in the kitchen, trying to get his bearings, when he is sure he hears the clip of a high heel in the hall outside. Quick as a whip, he's out there, his heart going like the clappers, fully expecting to see her standing in her belted raincoat, shaking out her brolly or applying another coat of lipstick in front of the hall mirror. But there's nothing. Not even the drop of post on the doormat.

Still. The fright he gets is enough to fire him out of the house, like a rocket, down the steps, the little gate clanging behind him as he hurries up the street, watchful for neighbours. They'll find out sooner or later that he's back, but he'd rather it was later. He keeps his head down, powering his way past the railings of the tennis courts towards the string of shops just off the roundabout. There's a café he remembers, and he thinks about sitting there with the paper, coffee and a cream bun. But when he arrives, he finds the string of shops has gone. Demolished. In their place stands a giant box of a supermarket – Lidl's yellow insignia across the blue band perimeter. He stares at it, bewildered.

'Are you all right, love?' a voice asks, and he looks down at a woman of his own age, some shopping bags tucked under her arm.

'I'm fine,' he snaps, then catches himself, apologizes for his rudeness and begins to cry. Great sobs pour out of him, the hacking of grief and fear in his chest. It's the unfamiliarity of it all. He hasn't cried like this in years – not counting the private muffled weeping into his pillow some nights – openly bawling on the street.

'What is it? What's wrong?' the woman asks, concern making her shrill. And then she reaches out and clutches his arm, and it's like an electric shock going through him, snapping him back to his senses.

'Nothing. I appreciate your concern. Thank you,' he mutters, and as he walks away he presses one hand to the place on his arm where she touched him, rubs it like it's been bruised.

He buys himself a soft drink and a newspaper in a corner shop, then finds a small, deserted park with a bench and sits down. Litter is strewn in the grass behind him, but he doesn't care. Fresh air is what he needs. Fresh air and to be left alone. Mark had warned him to stay at home that morning – a man would be coming to install the telephone – but Anton is not ready to go back to the house yet. Mark could arrange for the man to come again. And why isn't Mark here, anyway? he thinks, with a flare of disappointment. If he cares that much?

Out by the roundabout, a truck downshifts. Anton sips

his fizzy drink, brings himself under control. He'd talked about it from time to time with the others, what he would do once he was back here.

'Go straight to your local boozer. Get yourself a pint,' Danny had told him.

Jim, Salim, Fat Eric – they'd all agreed. A pint and a slap-up meal somewhere. Steak and chips. A nice curry. Only Nigel had advised keeping himself to himself for a few days. 'Run yourself a hot bath,' he'd advised. 'Relax yourself back into things.'

Of all of them, Nigel had understood him most.

But the house, as well as being his old home, is a receptacle of painful memories. Every room Anton goes into bears some evidence of the life he had once lived there. A picture, a smell, a stain.

At school, there had been a teacher who drove into them the maxim that you cannot step into the same river twice. Heraclitus. Anton has always had a fondness for the Greeks. All is change. Life is flux. And yet in the house it feels like stasis, as if time stopped the day he'd left. The furniture, the clock in the hall, the teacups in the kitchen cupboards, the linen on the bed: all of it preserved, like the charred mummified remains found in Pompeii and Herculaneum. Perhaps he should sell it. Sell it all. Hand over the keys to an estate agent and take himself off to some B-and-B until it's done. But what then? Where could he possibly go?

He finishes his drink, looks at the paper. His eyes pass over the headlines, before he flips to the financial pages. He finds the mutual fund quotation tables, pores over them – an old habit. It had been his one vice, playing the stock markets. A form of gambling, Charlotte had called it, and she had been right. All is flux. The climb and swooping falls of fortunes played out in tiny-print columns. Saturday mornings spent scanning the pages of the *FT*, making calculations in his head, his losses and gains. It was no fun unless you had skin in the game.

He recalls then how she would breeze past him in her dressing-gown, casting a bored glance in his direction as she opened the freezer. It was only after she had wrapped ice in a tea-towel and pressed it to her head that she would breathe: 'Haven't you anything better to do?' The smell of last night's cigarettes clinging to the air.

The pages of his newspaper flutter, but there's no breeze. The air is perfectly still.

It's his hands that are shaking, sweat moistening his fingertips, making the ink run against his skin.

The telephone guy is there when he returns, his van pulled up to the kerb. A young lad, mid-twenties perhaps, not much older than Mark, he carries his bag up the steps to Number 14, following Anton, a stream of conversation coming out of him. There's a sparrow lying dead on the doormat, and the telephone guy peers at it. 'Poor little thing. Must have flown into the window above, cracked its head against the glass.'

'Yes. They do that sometimes,' Anton says.

After he's removed the bird, using a coal shovel to carry it down to the bin, he comes back into the house and closes the door.

'Just moved in, have you?' the young man asks. He's kneeling on the floor in the hallway, running wire along the skirting board.

'Not really. I've been away.'

'You must have been gone a while, by the look of it.' The guy laughs, holding up an old telephone fixture, like some ancient relic. 'I've not seen one of these since my training days!'

Anton smiles like an indulgent uncle. 'Yes. A good while.'

'Where've you been? Anywhere nice?'

He's just being polite, but the blitheness of this young man's manner is unsettling. His presence in the house is disturbing. Too loud, too chatty. Like someone talking on a phone in church.

Oh, if only you knew, Anton thinks, *where I've been. The things I've done.* 'Here and there,' he says, turning away and entering the kitchen.

He busies himself putting away the shopping he picked up on his way home. Two plastic bags of groceries. He moves from cupboard to fridge automatically, as if at a muscle memory – after nineteen years, he still remembers where things go. But, then, he has always been an orderly man. A man who values systems and process. A place and time for everything.

'Do you want a phone upstairs in the bedroom?' The guy stands in the door to the kitchen.

'I . . . I don't . . .'

'It's a big house. People like it. Especially older people. Saves them the bother of coming downstairs.'

'Good Lord. How old do you think I am?' he asks, laughing to take the sting out of it.

The young man grins in the doorway. 'Dunno. Fifty?'

'Fifty-nine,' he declares, with a note of triumph.

Ridiculous to feel so gratified by the error, his vanity coming to the fore. Anton prides himself on his full head of hair, gunmetal-grey. During his long stay at the hotel, he took care to use the gym regularly. His musculature remains firm, no premature hump on his upper back. A woman he once knew told him he had the body of a welterweight boxer. Rose Gleeson it was, he thinks.

He's not some doddery old fool whose knees are about to go. There is still life, still vigour in his meat and bones.

'A phone upstairs would be fine. Thank you,' he says politely, then directs the young man to the bedroom at the front, the one with the bay window overlooking the park.

He listens to the clatter and banging upstairs, wonders why he gave instructions to install the phone in the front bedroom, when he has absolutely no intention of ever sleeping there again. He will take Mark's bedroom, or Cassandra's at the back. But not the front room. He wonders whether Charlotte's clothes still hang in the wardrobe, whether her brushes and cosmetics sit atop the dresser. Does the room still smell of her perfume? Chanel No 5 – the scent of that Nazi collaborator. On his last trip, he had bought it for her in Duty Free, as he always did. Brought it back here to Number 14, placed it on the kitchen table. A week later, she was dead.

Upstairs, a drill is going, buzzing through the wall. It reminds him of another time when Charlotte had had the bedroom redecorated. New linen, new carpets, new wallpaper. Tradesmen wandering through his house for a week. 'We need to spice things up a bit, Anton,' she'd told him, and he knew she wasn't just referring to the furnishings. He remembers her leaning over the railings to chat with the tenant downstairs, saying: 'I've got three men in my bedroom right now, would you believe?' and then the gale of her laughter. She had been fond of innuendo.

The flat downstairs had been their rental property. 'A little bit of extra income,' Charlotte said. 'Keep the wolf from the door.' Young couples, newly married. The odd family. People biding their time until they could buy in the area. It had that second-rate look of a rental – bland and inoffensive, lacking any character. There had been the occasional tenant who made a stab at personalizing the place, a few pot plants out the front, some fairy lights strung up over the patio at the back. 'There's no point in making the effort,' he used to say to Charlotte when she'd glide downstairs with a bottle of wine and some welcome roses from the garden, eager to make new friends. No point getting to know people who will move on in a year.

And now Mark has found new tenants. 'You need the money, Dad,' he'd told Anton firmly, overriding any notion that Anton just wanted to be left alone. 'You won't even know they're there.'

He hasn't seen anyone come or go yet. Hasn't heard any noise travelling up through the floor. Not that he's been listening out for it. If anything, he feels the opposite. Anton wants to forget all about the flat downstairs. If he had his wish, it wouldn't be there at all.

He is asleep when the phone rings, stretched out on the bed in Mark's old room at the back of the house. A few seconds of panicky fluttering in his chest before he realizes where he is. The phone keeps bleating from the other bedroom, and dizzily he crosses the hall.

It is one of those cordless jobs – grey, sleek. It takes another few seconds for him to figure out how to answer it. Already he is overwhelmed, exhausted. The light in the bedroom has grown dim. He has no idea how long he has been asleep.

'Dad?' he hears Mark say. 'You all right?'

'Fine. Fine.'

'You got the phone in, then?'

'Demonstrably.'

He shuffles back out on to the landing with the phone clamped to his ear, crosses back into what is now his room.

'So, how you doing? Happy to be back in the house?'

The question startles him. Is that really what Mark expects?

'Oh, yes. Settling in. I'd been looking forward to seeing you, though, more than the house.'

'Yeah. Listen, I'm sorry, I meant to be there when you got home but then this work thing came up.'

'That's all right. So, when do you think you'll come over? I thought perhaps we might go out. Maybe play a round of golf. My clubs are still –'

'I don't know, Dad. Golf? It's not really my thing. Besides, I'm kind of tied up at the moment with this ad we just shot – they need me in the editing suite.' There's something in his son's voice, a straining. 'You understand, don't you?'

'Of course.'

'I know you need help –'

'I'm not a baby, Mark,' he responds, with some irritation, immediately regretting it.

He catches the hesitation at the other end of the line. Mark was always sensitive as a boy.

'Well, I hope you're finding the house okay,' Mark says, sounding a little defensive. Then, as if to justify his absence, he continues: 'I came down last week and cleared out a few things. Got the gas and electricity back. I meant to do the phone, too, but there wasn't time . . .'

On and on it goes, the stream of justifications, of excuses, when, really, what does it matter now? Standing in the back bedroom, listening to Mark, Anton's eye is caught by movement outside. Down below, stepping up from the patio. The top of a woman's head – dark hair caught up in a messy knot at the crown. A solitary figure, he watches her progress up into the garden, the rest of her form coming into view as she picks her way through the long grass. White T-shirt, bottle-green skirt, flip-flops on her feet.

'I'll be a week in the editing room, maybe more,' Mark goes on. 'And there's this thing I've got to do at the weekend – helping a mate move house . . .'

A basket is held to the flare of her hip and she stoops now to set it down in the grass. White sheets billow and flap in the breeze, and she stretches to unpeg them, half turning so he can see her in profile – slender arms, the swell of her breast, grace in her movements and a sort of containment to her, as if she is utterly lost within her own thoughts.

'Dad?'

A change in his voice. A dip of seriousness.

The sun on her head.

'You will watch yourself, won't you? You won't do anything . . . stupid?'

The delicate stalk of her neck.

'*Don't you dare*,' Charlotte says, her voice finding him by the window, the low threat of her words curdling inside him.

But Charlotte is dead, and Anton has done his time. Nineteen years in the hotel. The crime punished. The debt paid. Charlotte's words can't touch him now. He is a free man.

He pulls back from the window but does not move away entirely. Half hidden by the shadows, he watches the young woman come. The movement of her hips, the dreamy grace of her expression. As he follows her with his eyes, the breath catches in Anton's throat.

3

Hilary

Hilary and Greg are in the car on the way into town when he breaks the news to her.

She's peering into the little mirror behind the sun-visor, dabbing at her eyelashes with the mascara wand, when she hears him clear his throat in that particular way of his and say: 'Look, Hil. There's something I need to tell you.'

She feels a little inward sigh at his words and the tone they are said in. After twenty-five years of marriage, she's used to this. Used to having small disappointments broken to her in this manner: a school commitment that prevents him from going on that weekend away they'd planned, some error in their tax return that has just been discovered, a translation offer for his first book that has failed to ma-terialize. The slow burn of life's disappointments, always heralded by that sombre warning tone of his.

He doesn't take his eyes off the road, and she keeps dabbing at her lashes, steeling herself for whatever new negative is about to come at her.

'It's Anton,' Greg says. 'He's out.'

She lowers the wand, turns her head and stares at him. 'What?'

Greg keeps his eyes on the traffic ahead, even though a

bombshell has just gone off in their car. She finds herself staring at the side of his face, the sprinkling of white through the red of his trimmed sideburns, his inflamed cheek, which she notices now he'd nicked while shaving.

'How?' she asks.

'I don't know. I suppose he's done his time.'

'No, I mean how do you know this?'

Her thoughts are coming at her in a rush, messy and confused. It's like suddenly finding herself at the centre of a swarm of bees – noise and panic in her head. How did Greg find out about this before she did? How could she have missed such a thing?

'I saw him.'

'When? Where?'

All these single-word questions she's firing at him. What? How? When? Where? Like a child, or someone in shock. And she realizes that she *is* in shock.

'On the street, down by the crescent. A few days ago –'

'A few days ago?' There's a shrillness in her voice and she tries to rein it in. 'You've known this for a few days and you never told me?'

She stares at him, waiting for his response, but his jaw is set in the fixed, stubborn way that makes her want to scream at him. 'What if I'd met him? What if I'd turned a corner and bumped into him?'

'That's why I'm telling you now, in case,' he explains, some passion of his own leaking into his voice.

She draws her gaze away from him and stares blankly out of her window. The sun is still beating down even though it's evening, heat making the streets unrecognizable – little seating areas outside cafés and pubs thronged with people in summer clothes. Grey buildings, smog-stained brickwork, all of it transformed by the brightness of the glare. It's like a foreign city, she thinks, Athens or Madrid instead of Dublin, everything unfamiliar.

'It could just be temporary,' Greg is saying. 'You know – some sort of parole. Day release or something.'

'But how do we know? How do we find out?'

A gnawing feeling is growing deep in her gut. She'd skipped lunch – her appetite diminished by the heat – and now regrets it.

'I don't know. I suppose I could go over there, talk to him –'

'Don't you dare!'

'It's not that I have any desire to talk to the man but –'

'I mean it.'

They have stopped at the traffic lights and she watches the tram trundle past in front of them, wonders how she will get through this event, making small-talk with strangers, while carrying this news inside her. *Anton is out.* Then she feels the weight and pressure of Greg's hand upon her knee.

'Hil,' he says again, in a soft voice that makes her suddenly tearful. She can feel his concerned gaze on her face, but can't bring herself to look at him.

Instead, she glances at her reflection in the sun-visor mirror. Eyelashes sticky with mascara, beneath them her pale, pale eyes.

She flips the sun-visor closed, slots the mascara wand back into its tube. 'You can drive home later,' she tells him, in a flat voice. 'I need a drink.'

They walk into a storm of noise.

The launch, held on the first floor of the bookshop, is

already heaving, guests spilling down the staircase and squeezed into the narrow aisles between the shelves and the display tables. Hilary pushes single-mindedly through the throng until she reaches the catering table and helps herself to a glass of white wine. It tastes acidic but she doesn't care – in fact, she welcomes the bite.

She feels a little giddy – a slug of cheap booze on top of the adrenalin rush of Greg's news swirls around inside her, loosening her emotions. She can cope with the news. Hilary is one of life's great copers. Robust. Determinedly optimistic.

So Anton is out. So what?

She surveys the room, the clusters of people she knows or half knows – always the same faces mingling at these events. 'Cliques', Greg calls them, with disdain. 'The literary scene is too cliquey,' he complains. Whereas Hilary wishes to God he would just find himself a clique and join in. Socialize. Even now at this party, where he must know at least half a dozen people – she can see his editor standing right there in Health & Living, for pity's sake – Greg is standing off to one side, alone, leafing through a book.

I wonder what Anton looks like now.

The thought sneaks up on her from nowhere. Hilary blinks and swallows, then thrusts her glass out for a passing member of staff to refill.

She should mingle. Or go and rescue Greg. She owes him that much. After all, it's Hilary's fault they're here. Her fault, because it was her idea – her actions – that had turned Greg into a writer when he might have been perfectly happy sticking to his day job teaching geography to the teenage sons of south-east Dublin's middle classes. But he hadn't been happy – in fact, he had been depressed. At least they had his teacher's salary and hers, she used to tell him, the long holidays, the summers off. While friends and neighbours were losing their jobs, their businesses, during the recession, Hilary and Greg were permanent and pensionable. They were lucky, she used to tell him. It became a refrain of hers, a bulwark against the black tide of his depression.

But it wasn't enough, and when Evelyn at work suggested he should try something creative to draw him out of his mood, Hilary had gone out and signed him up for an evening course at the Irish Writers' Centre. An outlet to release his pent-up frustrations – that was all she'd intended it to be. Something to get him over the hump of his depression until they could return to the normality of their ordinary lives. It had never been part of the plan for him to write a novel and for it to be published. That was a boon, she'd told him – a serendipitous side-effect. What Hilary hadn't anticipated was how writing would, in itself, become a source of anxiety for Greg. He worried when the book met a tepid reception. He fretted over the modest sales. Entering a bookshop, once a source of such pleasure to him, now involved an agonized, and frequently disappointing, search for the presence of his own work. He dreaded people asking him about the next.

Greg hadn't wanted to come to the launch this evening, but Hilary had coerced him. And now she feels a dash of fierce regret, watching her husband as he stands on the outer rim of the throng encircling the celebrated author, the latest sure-fire bestseller pressed to Greg's chest as he waits to get close enough for a signature. There is something so craven about him. The man is hopeless. He will always be hopeless. Hilary's anger flares in her chest.

What is wrong with me? she wonders, as she knocks back the rest of her wine. Her husband is a good man – loyal, kind, faithful. And yet the anger seeps through her brain, like some bitter herb infusing her thoughts with vitriol. But of course she knows what's wrong with her. She has enough self-awareness to realize that the news of Anton's return is at the root of her turmoil. Depositing her empty glass on a stack of books piled high on a table, she pushes through the crowd, recalling another time, another party. Another summer evening, the sway of her hips, and the cruelty of Charlotte Woodbury's amused smile looking her up and down, saying, 'My God, Hilary, whatever are you wearing?'

'Everything all right?' Greg asks, as she takes hold of his elbow.

'Can we go home?'

His eyes flicker over her, confused. He's usually the one nagging her to leave.

'A sudden headache,' she explains.

He doesn't question her further, merely pats her hand and follows her out of the shop.

They don't speak in the car. Hilary keeps her eyes closed, her head leaning back against the rest. Hot air gusts through the open window and swirls around them, reminding her of another time – another summer – but it's so long in the past now she can hardly believe that the memories she has are hers. That she actually was that person – younger, less burdened by respectability, less concerned by what people thought. And now it's about to begin – the second act she has been waiting for. The fact that it's upon her is almost overwhelming. She is impatient to be home, to be sitting in her garden with a G-and-T and a cigarette, her feet stretched out and bare, away from people, where she can think things through properly. She needs to make a plan.

A van is double-parked in the street, blocking access to their house, and Greg pulls the car to a halt behind it.

'Oh, for the love of God,' Hilary mutters, as beyond the windscreen two people struggle to lift out what looks like a piano through the vehicle's open doors. A man and a woman. Young.

'New neighbours,' Greg remarks.

The woman pauses and lets go of her end of the piano – an upright in dark wood, battered and worn – while she climbs down from the van. Small and slight, dark hair and pale skin, a slightly anaemic look about her. She is wearing a smock-like dress in charcoal grey, black ballet flats on her feet. Hardly suitable clothing for carrying furniture, Hilary thinks. It's the kind of garb that architects favour, she has noticed, or graphic designers.

'We should give them a hand,' Greg says.

'No, don't –' But he is already out of the car, the door shutting behind him. Hilary watches, silently furious, as he approaches the van and the woman turns to him, shielding her eyes from the sun.

Greg shakes her other hand, then that of the man emerging from the van. Hilary watches him coming into view. A boyish face, though she guesses he must be thirty or more, wire-rimmed glasses lending him an intellectual look, despite the garish zippered jacket he wears, some sort of sports clothing. From where she's sitting, she can't make out what the three of them are saying, but when Greg gestures towards the car and the couple turn in her direction, she shifts in her seat with discomfort. Both strangers wave to her, the man turning it into a little comedy routine by ducking down and peering myopically at the windscreen. The others laugh, and Hilary knows she should get out of the car. It would be rude otherwise. But something holds her back. She can't explain her hesitation. A cold instinct that keeps her sitting there, clenched in her seat.

She watches as Greg picks up one end of the piano and between the two men, they carry it down into the house. Number 14. Anton's house.

The woman stands back so they can pass, tucking a lock of stray hair behind her ear. There is a sort of dreamy self-absorption about her – a distracted quality – that makes Hilary rethink her initial architect/graphic designer conclusion. And something else – a familiarity, as if she's someone Hilary might already have met. But before she can figure it out, the young woman picks up a chair from the pavement and disappears down to the basement, and Hilary is left alone.

The street is empty. No one there to witness the deep, cold stillness that has come over her.

It's just a house, she tells herself, forcing her eyes to gaze up at it.

Concrete paving slabs, long given over to moss and weeds, lead to the stone steps. The front garden, which had once been carefully clipped and manicured, is choked with bindweed and briars, any semblance of order lost in the mists of time. The lower part of the house is being consumed by Virginia creeper. The upstairs windows appear fastened, the shutters open, curtains half drawn. Hilary's mind travels to the rooms beyond, wonders at the cool, airy spaces inside, all that heavy furniture now shrouded in dust. The rooms crowd her memory, making her head ache, and then a voice whispers in her ear, 'I just came to say I'm sorry,' so close and so real, it raises goose-bumps on her skin.

When the car door opens, she jumps with fright.

'You all right?' Greg asks, sitting in the driver's seat, the car rocking a little beneath his weight. 'I thought you'd come in to say hello.' She feels him watching her expectantly. But she keeps her eyes fixed on their own house a little further up the road on the opposite side. A more recent addition to this otherwise Victorian street, in the lengthening shadows of evening, it looks small and squat next to its more imposing neighbours.

'Another time,' she says wearily. 'Please, love. Let's just go home.'

'Jake and Leah,' Greg tells her, as she puts together a salad, salmon fillets baking in the oven.

'Are they married?'

'I don't think so. I get the impression they're not together very long,' he remarks, unscrewing the Riesling and pouring her a glass.

'Do you indeed?' Hilary says drily, teasing him. 'And how did you reach that conclusion?'

'The way they looked at each other. The excitement between them. Remember that? The excitement at being together?' He comes to stand behind her and she feels his chin rest upon her shoulder as she checks the boiling potatoes with a fork. He feels too close, and she turns her face, pecks him quickly on the cheek. 'Here, help me with these plates,' she instructs.

Over dinner, Hilary is mostly silent. The headache she had faked has sprung to life, as if she had tempted it into existence. The heat has killed her appetite, and she is aware of how quickly she is getting through the wine. Greg talks while they eat, filling her in on his observations. 'The flat hadn't changed much. Still the same old magnolia walls, the same little kitchen with the peeling linoleum. But it felt different.' He spears a potato and pokes it into his mouth, his eyes on his plate the whole time he speaks.

'How so?'

'I don't know. The passage of time, I expect. And it's clear no one's been living there for ages. You'd think he'd have given it a lick of paint or something, cheered the place up a bit for them. You should have come in. You'd have been interested to see the place now.'

'I had a headache, remember?' She glances up at Greg then, checking to see if he'll remark on the slight tremor in her voice.

But he just forks spinach into his mouth, keeping his eyes on the food in front of him as he goes on: 'I think Jake is a friend of Mark's. You know – the son. Thought I saw him around a bit lately. That's how they got the flat. Still, I'm sure they'll spruce it up themselves, make it nice with all their own things. Looks like they had plenty to fill the place with. That piano, for a start. Boxes and boxes of stuff lying around the place. Even a kid's trampoline.'

On and on he continues with his monologue until finally his cutlery clatters on his emptied plate, the sound reverberating painfully in her head. It is only then that he looks across at her almost untouched dinner and says: 'Are you not eating?'

She considers her response; feels herself drawing a breath. Tentatively, she broaches the subject, the real heart of her discomfort: 'You don't think we should tell them, do you?'

His gaze sharpens.

'About what happened in that house?' she continues. 'About Charlotte?'

Her name hangs between them. The silence surrounding it seems to tighten. She sees her husband's eyes flicker over her face, a look that bristles with unspoken questions. Such an eloquent look – twenty-five years of marriage distilled and poured into that one expression.

'No,' he answers, getting to his feet.

'But they're bound to find out eventually.'

'Just leave it, Hil.' He speaks softly but she hears the warning there all the same.

Unhurriedly, he opens the dishwasher and puts in his plate. He flips its door closed, then pauses to pick up his book – the new one that has just been launched – from the countertop. Hilary watches while he scans the dust-jacket, then clutches it to his chest with one hand, the other slipping casually into his pocket.

'Better give this a try, then,' he says, and smiles at her,

as if nothing has passed between them in this room. Nothing at all.

She listens to his step on the stairs, then the creaking floorboards overhead, the sigh of his office chair as he drops his weight on to it.

The saucepans need to be scoured, but instead she takes out her cigarettes, sits at the kitchen table exhaling smoke towards the windows, open on to the garden. Shadows draw across the lawn, shrubs and bushes squatting darkly beyond it as light drains from the sky. And as she sits there, she thinks of all the times they might have left here. Sold this house and moved away. All the times she'd tried to persuade Greg that they should move, but always he'd held firm, adamant in his refusal. And now it is too late.

A feeling of unease comes over her, like the cool surface of still water being broken, unearthing something murky in the depths.

4

Leah

She wakes with a jolt, her heart still racing from the dream. As her breathing steadies, Leah takes in the room around her – the walls and furnishings, the stacks of books on the floor, the green glow of the alarm clock through the early-morning gloom. For a moment, the old panic comes tumbling up inside. It's the unfamiliarity of her surroundings coupled with the streaked memory of her dream. But then Jake's arm snakes around her and she remembers.

This is home now.

'Tell me we have a few more minutes,' he mumbles against her neck. She feels the warmth of him, the heaviness of his arm against her ribs, and realizes that she will wake next to him like this each morning now, possibly for the rest of her life.

The thought rises and threatens to overwhelm her, a giddy feeling starting in her chest. After all these years of being alone, after resigning herself to the fact and inevitability of her aloneness, now to feel the warm bustle of possibilities in this life they're sharing – this love – it feels green and new and invigorating, like the sap rising in spring. No more sneaking around, no more withstanding the irritated sighs of her flatmates at his presence, no more eking out their weekends away in B-and-Bs from Wexford to Cork to Belfast. Their own place. Their own home, with no one to bother them. She turns over and folds herself into him, savouring the sweetly stale smell of his early-morning skin, the tickle of his chest hair against her nose. He begins to wake, desire stirring, and she feels him reaching for her thigh, drawing her leg up over his hip. When he moves inside her, it feels natural and intimate and right. She clasps her legs about him, pushing him deeper, needing him to touch her very core. The bed creaks beneath them, and overhead she thinks she hears a floorboard groan.

Afterwards, they sit at the new kitchen table, and sip coffee with the French windows open on to the patio, breathing in the morning air. The room is littered with cardboard boxes, some still waiting to be opened. They'd gone a little mad in Ikea. 'Everyone does,' Jake had assured her, after they'd returned home and her buyer's remorse had set in.

Her salary is due on Friday, and when Jake's shoot ends, there will be more money. Leah knows from experience how fragile her optimism can be. But she is determined not to let their new life together be spoilt by worrying over their finances. She has her position at the patents firm, and Jake's getting work. There is always the option for him to pick up the odd courier job. They will be fine. We're lucky, she tells herself. And then, because she has committed to being more open with him, she says it aloud: 'We're so lucky.'

Jake's putting their cups on the draining-board, and wipes his hands quickly on his jeans. 'Don't I know it,' he tells her, and grabs his bag from the sofa, looping the strap over his head and fixing it on his shoulder. 'I'd better get going.'

He kisses her quickly, with a promise to call her later. He wheels his bike outside and she hears the front door closing behind him and knows she is alone.

There's a sort of relief to the silence in his wake. Not that she doesn't welcome the warmth and noise of Jake's presence, but somehow Leah, so used to living a solitary life, feels more authentic – more at peace – when she's alone. In the bathroom, she stands in the bath, and listens to the pipes gurgling as the shower above her splutters to life. She washes her hair, then combs it, and dresses for work. She is small-framed – like a bird, Jake says – and her work wardrobe consists of an assortment of plain dresses in muted colours. A light dusting of face powder and a dab of lip-gloss, before she slips on her shoes and checks her bag.

She has a few minutes to spare, and decides to use the opportunity to hang out the laundry. In the time it has taken her to shower and dress, the clouds have cleared and the sun is beating down, even though it's only ten past eight. The wet clothes tumble out of the drum into her basket and she hurries outside, stepping up into the grass and through the garden to where the washing line is strung between two trees. She works quickly, pegging the things to the line, conscious all the time of the house behind her. She cannot resist taking small glances up at the windows.

They haven't yet met or even glimpsed the occupant of the upstairs rooms, although there have been noises. The old plumbing of the house echoes down into the basement, and both Leah and Jake have been disturbed in the night by the rattling of pipes, the odd creak in the floorboards. Yesterday, when she was sitting at the piano, struggling through the opening chords of 'Clair de Lune', a dragging sound overhead made her stop suddenly and withdraw her hands from the keyboard. The suggestion of a listening presence upstairs had made her shy. She had closed the lid and stepped away.

Now, she hurries to finish so that she can retreat into her own space. It's hard to escape the feeling of trespass. But as she picks up the basket and turns quickly towards the house, her shin strikes an obstacle hidden in the grass and she cries out in pain. Dropping the basket, she stoops to examine the offending article, and sees a child's tricycle long-abandoned to nature, rusting amid the weeds. Her leg is bleeding from a deep gash, bright red rivulets rushing towards her ballet flat. Half hopping, she hurries now towards the sanctuary of her kitchen where she slips off her shoe and raises her leg so that her foot is in the sink, cold water rushing over the wound. A hurried search of still-packed crates in their bedroom turns up a box of plasters with a Winnie the Pooh pattern. She patches herself up as best she can, then grabs her bag, conscious now of being late.

She is locking the door when she hears the voice above her, at the top of the stone steps. A man's voice, but not one she recognizes.

'Come on, Anton. Open up. Just for a few minutes?'

She hasn't mastered the knack of the fiddly lock yet and struggles with it for a moment, all the while aware of the one-sided conversation upstairs.

'Look, I know you're in there,' the man says. 'If you open up we can have a quick chat and I'll leave you in peace. Five minutes, that's all. An opportunity to give your side of the story.'

The lock clicks. She puts the key into her bag and hurries up the steps, glancing quickly to where the man leans into the closed door, his mouth held close to the letterbox.

'I'm not going away you know. I'm just going to keep on coming back,' he warns.

He has his back to Leah, but when the gate clangs shut he turns and looks down at her. Fifty-ish, she guesses, in a summer shirt and nondescript slacks. His face has the reddish-purple hue of a drinker.

'Oh, hello,' he says, when he sees her, and there's interest in his voice.

But she just nods and hurries away, troubled by the incident on the doorstep, wondering what the man upstairs is being hounded about. The image that comes to her is of an elderly man sitting still and quiet in his own house while his heart flutters with nerves, waiting for the voice to go away.

By the time she reaches work, the image has dissipated. The morning is busy, and she welcomes the well-worn familiarity of the tasks before her. Since leaving school eight years ago, she has worked for Castle and Maine Patents and Trademarks Attorneys, starting off in the post room before being promoted to an administrative role upstairs. She has a reputation in the office for being quiet but efficient, reserved but dependable. 'Whatever would we do without you?' the senior partners sometimes say to her.

One of them, more recently, had taken her aside and asked if she would consider studying towards the trademark attorney exams. There was a professional career path if she wished to pursue it. No doubt it would be a big commitment, he had warned her, several years of study and exams. But the rewards would make it worthwhile when she eventually qualified, he'd said, adding that he had every faith in her ability and that she would receive full support.

Leah can recall the flash in his eye when she had told him that she had no wish to go down that path, preferring to stay where she was. He hadn't pushed her much, instead accepting her decision graciously, but she could see it in the look he gave her, the way his eyes lingered on her face, speculating, no doubt, on what lay behind her lack of ambition. And she knew he could see it in her: the fear. It is, after all, the commanding emotion in her life. It was hard to explain to a man like him, a man who had striven and studied and pushed his way up the career ladder to reach the fruit hanging ripe on the tree, that for someone like Leah it was necessary to stay small and safe, to remain within the confines of the familiar. To go outside – to push herself – meant the risk of exposure, and she couldn't countenance that. What she had was enough.

'I'm happy where I am,' she had told him.

It wasn't a lie. Not really.

At lunchtime, the girls from the office head out into the sunshine and walk to the pizzeria in Ranelagh – a pay-day tradition. Mostly, Leah joins them, but today she takes her sandwiches and goes to sit alone in the railed park beside the office. There's a small bench there where she can take out her phone without risk of being disturbed.

She dials the number and listens to the ringing tone, imagines the sound of it echoing around the house, up through the hall to the bedrooms above. She imagines her mother in the kitchen, hurriedly wiping her hands on a tea-towel, or her father sitting up in bed and putting down the newspaper, listening. As always when she makes these calls, she feels a murmuring of sadness deep in her chest, the pull of something painful.

'Hello?' Her mother's voice, breathless with enquiry.

'Mum, it's me.'

'Leah.' The name breathed out with something like relief. This is chased with instant anxiety: 'Is everything all right?'

'Yes. Everything's fine. I'm fine. How are you? How's Dad?'

What follows is her mother's cheerfully brisk monologue about her father's continuing health woes – complications from a heart attack some years ago keep him largely an invalid – before moving on to fill Leah in on various pieces of gossip that currently permeate the small town where they live. Leah listens, trying to picture it all, but sometimes the descriptions are lost on her. Her recollections of home have faded in the past eleven years, although some things remain stark and vivid. Not everything can be erased.

'And how are things in the office?'

Leah can hear in her mother's voice the effort involved in keeping this conversation light. Trying to act normally. What hard work it must be for her mother, trying not to frighten her away.

'Fine. Good.'

'Dad wants to know are you playing?'

The thought of her father concerned about her music threatens to bring on emotion, so she says quickly: 'Actually, the piano has found a new home.'

'Oh?' Sharpness in the question, yet she knows her mother is trying to hold back. These phone-calls between them are delicate.

'I've moved, Mum. I'm in a new flat. In Dún Laoghaire.'

'Well. That sounds lovely, sweetheart,' she says cautiously.

'The thing is,' Leah says, arriving at the real purpose of the call, 'I've met someone. His name is Jake. We've moved in together.'

She waits, and into the silence that follows she reads her mother's pain and disappointment and anxiety. The distance between them – the necessary distance – is bearable, but at times like this, she must wonder at Leah, at why she shuts them out, punishes her parents, when, really, they don't deserve it.

'This is all very sudden.'

'Not really. We've been together for a while now,' Leah says, deliberately vague. She doesn't tell her mother that it's a whole five months since she met Jake. Five months since she fell head over heels.

'Is he a good man?' her mother asks then, her voice softening. 'Is he kind to you?'

'Yes. He is, Mum. He really is. He's kind and warm and open.'

'And you? Can you be open with him?'

The question feels pointed, and Leah hesitates before answering: 'I love him, Mum.'

She senses her mother absorbing this careful response.

'I'm happy for you, sweetheart,' she tells Leah, and the words are quietly warm and heartfelt. 'Does he make you feel safe?'

'He does.'

When I'm with him, the demons go away, she thinks. But she doesn't say this to her mother. Doesn't want to frighten her.

'We love you, Leah – Dad and me. You do know that, don't you?'

'Yes, Mum.'

'All we want is for you to be happy. For you to find peace.'

'I know. I'm trying to.'

They talk for a few minutes more, and while it is companionable and pleasant, neither suggests a visit. Neither mentions meeting up.

'Take care, sweetheart,' her mother tells her, just like she always does.

For a few minutes after the call ends, Leah sits still with her eyes closed, turning her face up to the sun.

Later that evening, when she gets home, she finds a business card has been fed through her letterbox. She carries it into the kitchen, puts her groceries on the counter before scanning it quickly. On one side is printed the name Ed McDonagh, *Daily Mail*, and on the back in a spidery crawl are the words: 'Sorry if I startled you this morning. I'd appreciate it if you'd give me a call. Ed.'

Her heart gives an involuntary kick, an old feeling of deep unease coming over her.

She shoves the card far down into the kitchen bin, then scrubs her hands under the tap, wishing Jake would come home soon.

Clouds are gathering in the evening sky and the

washing remains outside. The gash on her shin is healing –
she can feel the tightness of the skin gathering there, the
itch of it knitting together as she hurries out into the garden. She reaches for the clothes, plucks them from the
line, working quickly as she drops them into the basket. It
is only when she retrieves the basket and holds it to her
waist that she looks about in the grass and sees that the
rusting tricycle is gone. A bald patch in the weeds is
the only indication of its recent presence. Her eyes snap
up towards the windows of the house. She scans them
quickly, her pulse quickening, looking for a face. There is
nothing but the panes of glass reflecting back at her the
milky-white bank of clouds.

5

Anton

Anton wakes to the snapping sound of his letterbox closing. He blinks in the new day, feels the weight of heat in the air already bearing down on him. For a few moments, he just lies there, feeling the emptiness of the house, the hours of the day stretching ahead of him.

The ceiling above him shows cracks running through the plasterwork from one side of the room to the other, snaking right through to the cornicing. Anton thinks of the materials of this house standing solidly for more than a hundred and fifty years. A century and a half enduring winters and summers, expanding and contracting with the seasons, the elements taking their toll. No wonder there are cracks. No wonder the edifice is crumbling. He feels a bit like the house. In need of some support. A bit of underpinning.

In the bathroom, he assesses his reflection in the mirror. Not bad, he thinks, parting his lips to examine his teeth, still strong, still whitish. His eyes – always his best feature – are a little bleary this morning, but after rinsing his face with water some of their clarity returns, the irises a muddy green. 'Like looking into a deep pool,' Janice had once told him – or was it Helen? He towel-dries his face, which in recent days has started to tan. Perhaps he should dig out some of his old summer clothes, if the moths haven't ravaged them. He needs a haircut. Today might be the day for it. His birthday. He is sixty years old.

Downstairs, he picks up the post. No birthday cards, no surprise packages, just a postcard from an estate agent and a begging letter from a charitable organization, the envelope adorned with photographs of little African children, their bellies swollen, flies crawling around their eyes. In the kitchen, he throws the post into the bin, then changes his mind and fishes out the estate agent's card. He sits at the kitchen table contemplating it.

Dear Property Owner,

Thinking of moving? We have clients in the area who would love to make an offer on your house! Don't delay. Contact us today on blah, blah, blah . . .

Perhaps he should give it some thought. Maybe Phil might have an opinion – he'll ask his advice when he sees him this evening.

They were golf partners back in the day – Anton's handicap was four while Phil had played off scratch, but even though they were unevenly matched in their abilities, the friendship between them compensated for it. He had called Phil yesterday, suggesting they meet for a small birthday celebration in Finnegans. Anton had heard the surprise in his voice, the hesitation before acceptance of his offer, and it reminded him of how Phil had barely ever visited him in the hotel. Once or twice a year for the first couple of years, but after that nothing. Still, Anton won't hold it against him. He resolves not to bring it up when they meet for pints. Let sleeping dogs lie.

The doorbell rings, startling him from his thoughts. Perhaps it is Mark, he thinks hopefully, come with a present or a cake. He finds himself hurrying to the door full of happy expectation, but when Anton opens it, he finds that it is not his son, but a man who is short and blocky, his torso encased in a striped short-sleeved shirt. A clipboard is slipped casually under his arm, both hands in his pockets.

'Hello there, Anton,' the man says loudly, a broad smile pushing the flesh of his cheeks upwards to make narrow slits of his eyes.

'Yes?'

'Jim Buckley.' He takes a hand from his pocket now and offers it to Anton, who accepts it gingerly. 'Your parole officer,' Jim clarifies. 'Okay if I come in?'

Anton's hand hurts from the other man's crushing grip. He rubs it, pushing the metacarpals back into their places, turning away from the door so that Jim Buckley can follow him into the kitchen. 'Tea?' he asks, over his shoulder.

'Smashing.'

Anton fills the kettle, takes down the cups, and tries to quash the disappointment that it wasn't Mark at the door. Perhaps he will call later, he thinks. He's a good lad, a dutiful son. Yes, Anton thinks, yes, he's sure Mark will be here.

'Nice place you got here, Anton,' Jim remarks. 'Big enough for you?'

His large house seems to shrink with Jim's presence in it. The new voice is too loud – it shatters the silence. The corpulent bulk of him fills the room in a way that's intrusive. Anton tries to concentrate on making the tea, white noise buzzing in his brain.

'Milk, no sugar,' Jim instructs.

There's a small fireplace in the kitchen, the mantelpiece a magnet for the detritus Anton is unsure what to do with. Old postcards, bowed with age, still sit there, twenty years after they were sent. Postcards from a different age, a different life. Jim is sniffing around them now, plucking the occasional one out with his fat fingers, squinting to read the words tooled on the back.

'Bit of a hoarder, eh, Anton?' he says, with a chuckle. 'Would you not clear some of this stuff out?' His eyes roam the cluttered surfaces with barely concealed horror. 'You'd fill a good few bin bags in this room alone.'

Anton puts the tea on the table, doesn't answer.

'Ah, don't mind me,' Jim says. 'I can't stand clutter, that's all. More of a minimalist. The bare essentials. Still. Each to their own, eh?'

On another day, Anton might have been tempted to fling the tea into the big dog-like grinning face, watch with pleasure as the cup bounced off the meaty snout. But he has been lonely since his release, the deep silence of the house making his days seem long and empty. It's good to have some company, even if it's only his parole officer. He sips his tea while Jim Buckley takes a seat at the table opposite him and consults his clipboard, slurping from the cup.

'Let's run through this, shall we?'

'If we must,' Anton says. He gives the man the bare minimum of his attention, just sufficient to oblige the bureaucracy. He wonders a little at Jim Buckley, at his life.

A small two-bed semi in Blanchardstown or Tallaght, he surmises, a few paltry sticks of furniture, a big-screen TV, no clutter – the minimalist look he so reveres. No ring on his finger so let's assume no girlfriend or family. Lives near to his mum. A few older sisters with families close by. Spends his Sundays alternating between their houses – roast dinners and playing with the kiddies. Their favourite uncle. Such a cheery disposition – but what lurks beneath it? Anton wonders. He knows how fractured things can be once you peel back the happy surface.

'Given any thought to employment, Anton?'

'Not really.'

'I see here you're a numbers man. A bit of a whizz at the old accounting.'

'If you say so.'

'Why don't you let me put you in touch with a recruitment agency we use from time to time? See if they have a position that would suit a man with your background?'

Anton doesn't know if by 'background' Jim is referring to his previous career as an accountant or his criminal record. He doesn't seek to clarify because it's not relevant. He has no intention of contacting any recruitment agency. Not now. Not ever.

What kind of person becomes a parole officer? He's had the same thoughts about the screws in prison. As little boys, did they answer, when asked by a teacher or a relative what they wanted to be when they grew up, 'I want to work for the prison service'?

Mark wanted to be a vet. Anton remembers a painting coming home from school, some rudimentary daubs in primary colours that they were supposed to interpret as their six-year-old son with his animal patients. Charlotte had held it in one hand and laughed. 'Mark? A vet?' She had shaken her head, mystified. 'The poor little pet's frightened of his own shadow.' Right there at that sink. Anton half turns his head to look, as if he might expect to find her there still.

'How's the social side of things?' Jim Buckley asks. 'You been getting out much, Anton?'

'A little.'

'Any old friends you been catching up with? Relatives?'

'There's my son, Mark. And I'm meeting a friend later. My old golf buddy.' He hears the optimism in his voice, realizes how much he is looking forward to seeing Phil.

'Good, good. And the neighbours – how're they treating you?'

'Oh, they had a big party for me. "Welcome Home" banners strung up all the way down the street.'

'Seriously.'

Mention of the neighbours makes him uneasy. Anton thinks of the steps outside his house, the little packages that have started appearing – small plastic sacks containing dog excrement. The first time it happened, he'd been irritated, thinking it was some random dog-walker passing his gate, too impatient or lazy to find a bin to dump their dog's leavings. Anton had picked up the little baggie and thrown it into his bin with breezy disgust. But then when he came out of his house the next day and found two more on the same step, his suspicions were aroused. Every time he opens his door now, he finds some. He has begun to dread exiting the house.

'I'm keeping to myself,' he answers.

'That's natural enough at the start. But no man is an island, Anton. You can't turn this house into your own private prison. You've got to make an effort to integrate with the community.'

Anton stares at him, amazed at his naivety, and despite his gratitude for the man's company breaking up the solitude of his birthday, a small gust of anger whips up inside him.

'Pardon me, Jim, but you haven't a fucking clue,' he says, then gets to his feet and leaves the room.

In the living room, he takes the newspaper from the arm of the couch, carries it back into the kitchen. Jim watches him warily, as if he might have fetched a gun or some other lethal weapon.

Anton opens it to the middle page, folds the paper neatly and puts it down in front of Jim. The headline screams from the table.

WIFE KILLER RELEASED

Jim Buckley leans forward to read. It's only one column, along with a picture of Number 14's exterior, an inset photograph of Anton from twenty years ago, and another of Charlotte – the tragic victim.

'Now tell me how you think I can integrate with the community,' Anton says, 'when I'm dealing with that.'

Nineteen years he's served. Longer than the Trojan War. His anger simmers beneath the surface.

'They call here, you know,' he tells Jim. 'These so-called journalists. Hacks. Bloody vermin they are. Shouting through the letterbox, trying to get me to cooperate with their interview requests. It's harassment. And look! Let me show you.' He hurries to the dresser and shuffles through one of the drawers. Then, returning to the table, he places the cards in front of Jim. 'They drop these in my letterbox – their business cards. Can you believe it? As if I'm going to call them up and invite them in. Vermin. Parasites, that's all they are.'

'Just ignore them,' Jim says, flicking through the cards with casual disinterest. 'Keep your head down. They'll soon get bored.'

'I ought to sue the bastards.'

Jim looks up. 'For what?'

'For what? For libel, that's what.'

'Still maintaining your innocence, are you?' Jim asks, in a flat, disbelieving tone.

'Of course I bloody am!' he snarls, leaning forward with some force of feeling so that his face is right up close to Jim's, veins bulging in his neck.

As Jim recoils Anton realizes he has gone too far, revealed something of his nature that he had not intended to. He straightens, waits for the heat in his face to dissipate. Then, in a calmer, more reasoned voice, he says: 'Look, I know you have your job to do, and I know it must make it easier for you just to accept a man's conviction on the face of it, but you don't know the facts. You weren't there. You don't know what went on. I did *not* kill my wife. It was an intruder – a man the police never found. I went to jail because of their incompetence.'

Jim watches him coolly. He flips the paper to the front page, points to the tabloid header. 'It's a rag, Anton. I can't imagine many people round here even read this sort of newspaper.'

'Oh, they've read it. Don't you worry about that.'

'Look, it's to be expected at first that there'll be a little . . . atmosphere. That relations will be a bit awkward, a bit chilly. But in a few weeks it'll die down. I'm telling you. People have other things on their minds besides you and your past misdemeanours. In the meantime, just keep your head down. Carry on as normal.'

Normal, Anton thinks, whatever that might be. He'd like to know.

Jim is rolling up the paper into a tube or a truncheon, preparing to leave. 'You know, you're in a much better situation than a lot of the blokes I see,' he tells Anton. 'You've got your own place, your son's nearby.'

'I should count my blessings, should I?' Anton asks caustically.

'That's the ticket.' Jim grins and taps the rolled newspaper on the edge of the table.

Anton follows him out into the hall, watches as Jim looks at the staircase, the ancient mouldings, the corbels beneath the arch. And then he stops and turns, as if picking up a strange scent, and says: 'What's that?'

'What?' Anton asks.

'That sound. Is someone playing the piano?'

Anton feels the colour creeping up his neck. He's been aware of it all along, the low melody from downstairs seeping up through the floorboards. He's surprised it's taken this long for Jim to hear it.

'It sounds like it's coming from your basement,' Jim says, suspicion creeping into the look he gives Anton.

'Friends of my son's,' Anton explains. 'They're staying in the flat downstairs at the moment.'

Jim frowns. 'You never mentioned that.'

'You never asked.'

'Listen, Anton, you know as well as I do that, under the terms of your parole, you are obliged to inform me if –'

'It's my son's flat,' Anton replies firmly, though his nerves are fizzing under the surface. 'It's none of my business who he has living there.'

'So these people – your tenants – are they aware of your situation?'

'They're not my tenants. They are nothing to do with me. It's Mark's flat – it's completely separate from this house. And who he has staying there is really not my concern.'

'All right, all right. Keep your hair on.'

He objects to the term but says nothing, embarrassed by the rise in feeling within him.

Softening his tone, Jim says: 'I'm just looking out for you, mate. It's your welfare I'm concerned with, as well as that of the community.'

At the door, Jim takes his leave, calling, 'Be good now,' as he saunters down the steps, which, for once, are mercifully free of plastic baggies. When he closes the door, Anton leans against the wall, listens for the music again – the slow air of some Scottish lament, its plaintive chords travelling up from below.

The visit from his parole officer has left him feeling flat and exhausted. The house is otherwise quiet. He needs to go out to do some shopping. But the spaces beyond the perimeter walls of his house frighten him. Even a trip to the park across the street seems beyond him. His world has narrowed to this house and all the memories within it.

He crosses to where the phone sits on the hall table.

Mark's number is jotted on the notepad and he punches in the digits.

'Dad,' Mark answers, surprise in his voice.

'Hello, son. I'm not disturbing you, am I?' In the background, he can hear the noise of traffic, people talking, a loud hiss like steam.

'Is everything all right?' Mark asks, concerned.

'Fine, fine! I just wanted to see if you'd like to call over today.'

'Well, I have work –'

'Oh, yes, but maybe after work. I could cook dinner or we could go out. I'm meeting Phil Doyle later, but we'd have a few hours still.'

The pause that follows feels awkward, and Anton rushes to fill it. 'Only if you're not busy, though.'

'Listen, I'd love to but I've got this thing on –'

'No, that's fine! Not to worry –'

'Sorry, Dad. I'll try to call over at the weekend, okay? We'll go for a walk. Get a pint somewhere.'

'All right, son. I'll leave it up to you.'

He lays the phone down in its cradle and raises his fingers to pinch the bridge of his nose. How craven he must have sounded to his son. How desperate.

It has not gone well with Mark since his release. Absurd to suppose it would. But somehow, over the years, through every awkward encounter in a prison visiting hall, every letter received that made him want to bang his head against the wall with regret, Anton always told himself that once he was out it would be different. They would be able to have a real relationship. Maybe not as close or as normal a bond as other fathers and sons – he wasn't expecting intimacy or shared confidences – but he would like a little access to his son's world. A very small window would do.

As he stands in the hall, massaging the tension from his forehead, Anton becomes aware of sounds – occasional small cracking noises from outside the house. He listens for a moment. There's a brief interval and he hears it again, this time from higher up the wall, somewhere above the fanlight over the hall door. A sharp tap and then nothing. Perhaps he imagined it. But when it happens again, this time on the bay window in the sitting room, he rushes in to see egg yolk sliding down the pane, fragments of shell adhering to the window.

'Bastards,' he mutters, hurrying to the front door.

The sun glares down on the doorstep. He has to squint against it. But there, across the road at the edge of the park, he sees two boys – barely teenagers – facing his house and laughing. One is already poised to throw another missile, and Anton shouts: 'Hey!'

He ducks but the boy's aim is true. Anton feels the shock of it pelting his shoulder, horrified by the gluey mass running down his shirt. Fury rushes up his throat.

'You little pricks!' he roars, coming down the steps, but they are off, racing over the green, and by the time Anton is halfway across the road, they are already past the tennis courts, disappearing out of sight.

For a moment, he stands there, drawing breath in and out of his lungs, a pain in his chest that has nothing to do with his fitness and everything to do with the deep sense of grievance lodged within him. Turning back, he surveys the front wall of his house spattered with raw egg, yolk and albumen running over the masonry and glass. The front door next to his has also opened, and his neighbour in Number 16, an elderly widow, comes out. She closes the door behind her and descends the steps with her shopper.

'Look at this,' Anton says to her, as he approaches, still incensed. 'Did you see those boys? See what they did?'

She casts a glance up at his house, then turns to continue down her steps.

'If I catch them again,' Anton says, 'I swear I'll –'

She looks up at him sharply. Her face is aghast. In a voice that is hoarse and exasperated, she tells him: 'I don't know why you came back here. I just wish you would go!'

The wheels of her shopper rattle and scrape over the pavement as she hurries away.

The anger in his chest is still there, but it mixes now with a rising sense of shame. The judgement in that look she gave him, the annoyance in her words . . .

He climbs the steps to his house, and sees his front door running with the congealed yellow slime. Inside, he fetches a basin of water and a cloth. He's back outside on his hands and knees, picking up pieces of eggshell from his front step, when a young man on a bicycle stops at the gate, dismounting in one fluid movement. A small, thin-nish man, his face open with interest as he wheels his bike with one hand, unclipping his helmet strap with the other. It's a surprise to see him come through the gate, nodding hello and glancing up at the house flecked with egg, then looking back at Anton with an expression of curiosity behind his glasses.

'Hello,' he calls. 'You must be Mark's dad.'

Anton nods briefly, then turns his attention back to his cleaning. He has no wish to make conversation with this young man, no desire to explain the mess on the walls and windows. There is an awkward moment of silence, before the young man seems to give in, saying, 'Well, nice to meet you,' with an air of bemused resignation, then carries his bike down the steps to the basement. Anton takes another glance at him, sees a round coin of scalp beginning to show through the hair at the crown of the young man's head, and feels a stab of envy at the thought of what awaits him downstairs – the music, the dreamy enchantment of the woman he's seen in the garden.

He scrubs the steps for a few more minutes before going back inside. A light is flashing on the phone in the hall. He must have missed the call when he was outside. He presses the button and hears Phil's voice coming through the speaker: 'Hey there, Anton. Happy birthday. Listen, just giving you a call about this evening. I'm sorry, I'm not going to make it.' Anton listens with a heavy heart, hears the somewhat sheepish tone of apology creeping into Phil's voice as he continues: 'I could make up an excuse, but the reality is I just don't think it's a good idea right now. It's too soon after you've been out, and, well, people are still upset. It's kind of brought it all back. Jane's been crying again over Charlotte, and it just doesn't seem fair that . . .' The sound of him taking a deep breath. 'Anyway. It's best if we leave it. Hope you understand.'

The voice dies away, the message ends. Heaviness takes hold of him.

The house is quiet now. He realizes that the piano in the basement has fallen silent. Disappointment is filling out inside him, and his thoughts snake downstairs, wondering at the young couple there, what they might be doing.

He recalls how he'd heard her crying out in pain the previous morning when she had hurt herself in the garden, felt the shock of something old and forgotten going through him as he had watched her crouching in the grass, the way she had drawn up the hem of her dress to examine the wound. Imagines again the pale smoothness of her leg.

A door underneath the staircase leads to another run of steps — narrower and meaner than the grand sweep that ascends to the bedrooms. He hasn't set foot here in years. When he flicks the switch, the light bulb casts a greyish meagre light on dusty steps. He slips off his shoes, takes the stairs in his socked feet, wincing at every slight creak and groan of the boards against his weight.

The air down here is dense and dank, a stale smell filling his nostrils that makes him think of mouse droppings and decades of balled-up lint. In that cramped dark space, he leans into the door, presses his ear against the painted timber, and listens.

6

Leah

'Guess what?' Jake says.

Leah tucks the stool back into its place against the piano. 'What?'

'I just saw him.' Jake's eyes dart in her direction as he dumps his bag and helmet on the couch and crosses the room to where the little stereo speakers sit. He slips his phone into the receiver and instantly the space is invaded by the music he's been listening to – some upbeat funk that jars with the mood she'd fallen into while practising the Nyman pieces.

'Who?'

'*Him*,' Jake repeats more firmly, his eyes flicking with amusement to the ceiling above them. 'The old man upstairs. He was at the door when I came in.'

She watches him rummaging in the fridge until he finds a can of beer and snaps it open. 'What's he like?'

'I only got a glimpse of him cowering there on the step. But he looked grizzled.'

'Grizzled?'

His expression changes, his mouth downturns into a comic mask of ill-favour, hunching his shoulders forward to appear disfigured.

'*Grizzled*,' he snarls, in his mock-frightening voice.

She laughs at him. She's seen him do this before – his Caliban, his Henry V, his Frankenstein's monster.

She moves towards him and he drops the act, kisses her swiftly, then offers her his beer but she declines. She's been feeling out of sorts since lunchtime.

'Did you talk to him – introduce yourself?' she asks.

'I said hello but he didn't respond. Too busy picking bits of eggshell off his house.'

'Eggshell? What do you mean?'

'The house. Someone's pelted it with eggs.'

'Who?' she asks, a note of surprised indignation in her tone.

'I dunno. I didn't see them doing it. But the house is dripping in raw egg, and he's outside on his hands and knees, cleaning it up.'

'That's awful. Should we offer to help him?'

'No! Why would we?' Jake is rummaging in his bag, and when he finds his script, he throws himself into the armchair and starts looking through it.

'Because he's an old man. It doesn't seem right.'

'He's not that old.'

'What age do you reckon he is?' she asks, curious now. She hasn't seen him yet, their landlord, although she's heard him. The creak of floorboards, the gurgling pipes. Sometimes she thinks she catches the low melody of him singing. Or maybe it's just the radio she's hearing.

'I dunno. Younger than my dad. He looked fit enough. I wouldn't feel obligated.'

She feels the smallest rise of annoyance inside her at the way he's loafing on the armchair with his beer and his script.

'Well, I'll check on him, if you won't,' she says.

But when she goes outside and looks up towards the front door, she finds it closed and the step empty. There are marks on the walls where the egg has started drying in the sun, and it makes her uneasy, the randomness of the act. None of the other houses seem to have been picked out for this abuse.

'Any sign of him?' Jake asks, when she comes back inside. She tells him no, and he remarks: 'Scuttled back into his lair, has he?'

'Perhaps he's shy.' Being shy herself, she feels a duty to defend him.

'Perhaps he's a weirdo. Some mad recluse who only comes out at night and spends the rest of his time dressing in the dead wife's clothes.'

She moves past him to the kitchen to make a start on dinner. 'I'm sure he's perfectly nice,' she says.

'If you say so.'

The atmosphere between them has grown slightly strained since his arrival home. This is not how she wants it to be – not how she envisaged it. So she lifts her mood, and adopts a more cheerful tone. 'I got fish,' she tells Jake.

He makes a noise of approval. 'So this guy I met on the shoot today – Dara – he was telling me about a new round of funding the Film Board are putting out. Reckons I'd have a shot if I send in the short I've been working on.'

Leah listens to him talk as she rinses the salad and waits for the oven to heat. She has bought sea bass – Jake's favourite – and there's a bottle of white in the fridge. They're going to eat outside, and Leah wonders whether she should make her announcement before or after dinner.

She is aware of the changed energy in the room since Jake's return, the busy snap of his thoughts as he recounts his day's events, breaking off to follow different tangents, his conversation interspersed with swigs from his can of beer and flipping the pages on the script he is half reading, his phone giving pipping alerts every time a WhatsApp message appears. It strikes her that there has been no transition from the solitary peace of being alone with the slow strains of her delicate piano-playing to the bustle and noise of Jake's presence, the steady insistent beat of music he has put on, the demands on her attention. It is something she will grow used to, she expects – a period of adaptation, a settling in. They are so different from each other, yet it was his busy warmth, his almost childlike prattle and need for attention that drew her to him, saved her from drowning in her own quiet introspection. This is what I need, she tells herself.

'How was work?' Jake asks. Then, remembering, he adds: 'Hey, did you guys go for lunch?'

'Good. Yes, we all went.'

'And how was it? How's Tricia?'

'Fine. The baby's doing great.'

Leah is careful to keep her voice level. She doesn't want it to betray any hint of how she'd felt.

It was a lunch they'd organized for Tricia – one of the girls from the office – to celebrate the recent birth of her baby. A pizza in the Italian on Ranelagh Road – and Tricia had taken her new baby girl, all bundled up in a soft downy Babygro, like a little pink parcel being handed around the table, each of them having a go holding her. When it was Leah's turn, she had sat still and quiet, looking into the baby's squashed face, tiny curled fists held close to the little one's cheeks, Leah trying to quell the thudding of her own heart. She avoided babies as a rule, but on this occasion, she had allowed herself to relax, her defences temporarily down. Absorbed in the peaceful miracle of holding a sleeping child in her arms, she hadn't noticed the waitress approach with the tray of coffees. It was not until Tricia called sharply, 'Hey! Careful there, would you?' that Leah had looked up with sudden alarm, anxiety waking like an angry beast in her chest. The waitress, handing out the coffees, had blithely lifted the brimming cup from the tray and passed it over the child's head before placing it on the table.

'God, I can't stand the way they do that,' Tricia had hissed, once the waitress was out of earshot. 'I mean, haven't they any awareness? Any common sense?'

Leah handed back the baby and excused herself to use the bathroom. None of them had noticed the change that had come over her. Nothing had happened, yet the vulnerability of that infant's head throbbed in her thoughts. In the cubicle, her legs were shaking so hard that she had to reach out and place both hands on the walls, trying to steady her nerves until the trembling stopped.

Those girls have no idea of what she'd done.

'I always liked Tricia,' Jake says, flipping through his script.

He knows all the girls from the office. His courier route meant he was regularly dispatched to the patents firm where she worked. It was how they had met.

It would seem like such a small thing, what had happened to her at lunch. He wouldn't understand her reaction. To explain it, she would be forced to open up the side of her she locks away; she would have to let him into the secrets she keeps hidden and she cannot countenance that. Not now, not this evening when there are other things she wants to tell him. So she says nothing.

Leah slides the fish into the oven and opens the wine.

Because the evening has come on warm and balmy, she opens the doors and carries the little table from the kitchen out on to the patio, returning for the chairs. She sets the table, brings a candle in a jar, clips some stray roses from overhanging branches of the climber next door and pops them into a water glass. She wants the setting to be perfect. She wants them to remember it.

Briefly, she looks up at the house, but the windows are all closed and there is something forbidding about the place. She calls Jake and he carries their plates outside, whistling, while Leah pours wine into his glass.

'To us,' Jake toasts, clinking his glass with hers, and he leans across to kiss her tenderly and happily, then raises the wine to his lips.

All week, she has been waiting for this moment: Friday evening, just the two of them alone together, no distractions, sharing a meal. And it's more perfect than she could have imagined. The taste of the food she has prepared, the privacy of this outdoor space, the scent of roses rising strongly from the little glass between them. Her senses feel alive, a shiver of nerves in her tummy as she waits for the right moment to tell him.

Over dinner, Jake talks about the progress of the pilot he's been filming – a project coordinated by one of his friends, whom Leah doesn't know. She's somewhat amazed by the number of friends Jake has. Her boyfriend is a sociable creature, someone who forges bonds easily – a talent she does not possess. It's because of the openness of his nature – a lack of guile coupled with a genuine interest in other people. She envies him this quality. Perhaps it's one of the things that attracted her to him – as if she might absorb some of his confidence through sheer osmosis. And it amazes her that this gregarious life-embracing man has fallen so completely for a bookish, introverted person like her.

'Ian had another meeting with RTÉ – showed them the latest cut of the pilot,' Jake tells her, between mouth-fuls. 'He says they loved it, that they're giving serious consideration to commissioning a series.'

'That would be amazing.'

'Of course there'll be a few things they'll want to change. I mean, that's inevitable. But they were really posi-tive about it.'

'What things would they want to change?'

'Ian didn't say. He said we don't need to worry about any of that until we get the green light. Anyway, who cares, right? A part in a series, Lee,' he says, reaching over the table for her hand. 'On national TV! And not just any part – the main part! I'd be sorted. I'd be made.'

'When will you know?'

'Ian says they're going to get back to him in the next couple of weeks. And I know I shouldn't get my hopes up,' he adds, perhaps sensing her reserve, her caution, 'but I could tell by the way he was talking that he thinks it's in the bag. And this is Ian we're talking about – he's super-cautious. Almost as cautious as you!'

His excitement is infectious and they both laugh and

she drinks from her water glass, allowing herself, just for a moment, to get caught up in his dream. What would it be like, she wonders, to have her boyfriend a successful actor? Even modest success would be life-changing.

He picks up the bottle and refills his glass. 'Aren't you drinking?' he asks, noting her full glass, and she shakes her head.

'I'm fine.'

'All the more for me,' he replies.

His happiness matters to her, in some ways more than her own, and she thinks of how charged he is these evenings after a shoot, the pump of adrenalin through his veins making him garrulous and full. Distantly, she hears the bleat of his phone from inside the flat, hopes he will ignore it, which he does, and for a few more moments, they talk about the opportunities such a career move would involve, allowing themselves to occupy the fantasy for a little while.

She decides to tell him as soon as the meal is over, after the table is cleared and they're sitting, relaxing, looking up at the moon. But as he's gathering up their plates, she hears the ringtone of his phone start up again, and when he goes inside, she hears the small clatter of the dishes on the counter, followed by Jake's voice saying: 'Hey there, what's up?'

A warm breeze wafts across the patio carrying the scent of cigarette smoke from a neighbouring garden. From a few doors down, she can hear the clink of glassware, laughter, soft jazz in the background – Leah and Jake are not the only couple dining al fresco this evening – and she feels a warm glow of belonging, of community, that is both unfamiliar and welcome. Leah wonders briefly about the other people living on the street. Apart from the first day, carrying their furniture into the house, when that man had got out of his car to help them – Greg was his name – she hasn't met or spoken to another neighbour. She has seen Greg's wife walking past the flat, glimpsed her from the bedroom window. A small stout woman, being pulled along by a big dog on a lead, Leah had caught her glancing up at the house, with a harried look, as she rushed past. Leah remembers the way she had sat in the car that evening, something cold about her, stand-offish.

'I know, but can I just talk to him for a sec?'

Her attention is caught by Jake's rising tone, a whine of impatience in it. She sees him standing by the couch, his back to her, the phone pressed against his ear, and knows that he is talking to Jenna, his ex.

'Okay, just calm down,' he says, and Leah shifts in her seat, listening carefully now, alert to the change in his mood.

'Fine,' Jake says, a note of unhappy resignation there, and adds, 'About fifteen minutes,' then ends the call.

She watches him, the phone in his hand hanging down by his hip, the bend in his neck, before he straightens and turns. When he comes out on to the patio, there is an expression of apology on his face.

'It's Matthew,' he tells her.

'What's happened?'

'I don't know. Some fight at school. He's upset.'

On the occasions she has met him, Leah has found Matthew to be quiet to the point of stubbornness. A shy boy, he averts his gaze from her in a way that feels pointed.

Even his interactions with his father seem strained and tense.

Jake sits down opposite her, reaches for her hand. 'I'm sorry, babe. I hate to do this.'

'It's okay,' she tells him, forcing herself to smile, forcing herself not to betray any disappointment. 'You should go to him.'

'It's probably nothing, just Jenna overreacting.'

'Really, it's fine,' she assures him. 'You should call around there, make sure he's okay. You know you're not going to be able to think about anything else until you do.'

He squeezes her hand, smiles his apology. 'I won't be long. I promise.'

'I'll wait up.'

He kisses her quickly, then he's gone, and the breath Leah has been holding releases. Another puff of warm air into the hot night. Alone once more, she sips from her water glass, fingers the petalled head of the rose, feels a tear roll down her cheek.

'Stupid,' she tells herself.

Stupid to feel this disappointment. Stupid to have allowed the evening to become so freighted with hope.

She shakes her head a little – a quick twitch – masters her emotions. He will be back soon, and she will be waiting with the wine and the soft night air, and then she will tell him. In the meantime she will wait. She goes indoors, into the bathroom where she wets a flannel with cold water and holds it to the back of her neck. In the bedroom, she kicks off her shoes and takes her book from the night-stand – *Old School*, by Tobias Wolff – a favourite that she rereads for comfort whenever she's in need.

Back outside on the patio it seems darker, as if the sun has dipped lower and faster in her absence. She resumes her place, feels the quietness of the garden behind her, and something else – a low, whispery presence.

Quickly, she turns around. Trees and grass, black boughs, the faintest swish in the undergrowth.

The smell of smoke reaches her where she sits. It's absurd, straining through the darkness to see, nerves alive in her throat, so that when she speaks, the words come out strangled. 'Is someone there?'

And through a break in the thinning screen of leaves that separates the patio from the garden she sees the red glow of a cigarette, the brief inflation of it before it recedes into darkness.

Again, she speaks, 'I said, is someone there?' and gets to her feet.

A moment then of dry-mouthed uncertainty.

But then the stillness of the garden fractures, and someone moves towards her.

7

Anton

Her voice crackles through the darkness. It tingles on his skin.

'Is someone there?' she asks again, sounding a little firmer now, as he draws closer.

'I'm here,' Anton replies, keeping his own voice soft and low.

She is standing just beyond him on the patio. There can't be more than three or four feet separating them. But the trees are heavy with rich summer foliage casting thick shadows, making it difficult for her to see him. His heart beats steadily in his chest as he moves towards her, watching the pale orb of her face as he moves into the direct line of her vision.

'I'm sorry,' he says. 'I didn't mean to startle you. I'm Anton. I live upstairs.'

He indicates the house with a nod, and watches her processing this. It's clear that he's frightened her, but now, given his position as landlord, he sees her vacillating on how to admonish him. And yet she doesn't seem the admonishing type. Not from what he's learnt of her over this period of observation.

'That's all right,' she tells him. 'I'm Leah,' she adds.

'Leah,' he says, pleased with the softness of the name on his tongue.

She is standing there, looking awkward, one hand clutching the back of her chair.

'I've only just come into the garden,' Anton tells her. 'I assure you I haven't been lurking here in the shadows,' he says softly, before looking down at his feet. Humility seems the best approach with her. He's given it some thought over the past few days.

'It's your garden,' she says. 'You're entitled to be in it.'

'I met your young man outside earlier this evening. I'm afraid I was a little rude to him.' His eyes flicker past her to the open French windows, the dark rooms inside. 'I wonder, is he home? I'd like to apologize, if I may.'

'He had to go out.'

'Oh dear,' says Anton, making a show of being surprised. He'd heard the front door bang, watched the young man cycling off down Wyndham Park not ten minutes ago, before seizing upon the opportunity. 'Nothing serious, I hope?'

Her forehead creases with suspicion.

'No. Just a family thing,' she answers, cagey. 'He'll be back soon.'

'Well, perhaps you might convey my apology to him when he returns.'

'I'll tell him.'

'Thank you.' He smiles and nods, aware that she's waiting for him to go. But instead of turning and making his way back up the steps to the lifeless rooms of his home, he lingers. It's been such a long time since he's spoken to a woman like this – he's not quite ready for the encounter to end. His eyes flicker over her, coming to rest on her legs. There is a plaster on one of her shins and he gestures to it now. 'Your leg. Is it all right?'

She glances down, then back at him, a guarded expression on her face. 'Yes. It's fine. I cut it in the garden.'

'I'm so sorry. I hope the cut didn't go too deep. The rust –'

'It's fine, really. It was just an accident.'

She shifts awkwardly from one foot to the other, something prickly and defensive about her stance, and he wonders whether he should have said anything about the rust, worrying that he's crossed a line.

'And how are you settling in, otherwise?' he asks her, anxious to change the subject. 'Everything to your satisfaction?'

'Oh, yes,' she says, and *there*, a little twitch of a smile. A glimmering of an opening. 'It's great. We're delighted, and grateful.'

'Good. Good. Nice to have young people living here again. Such a shame for it to be locked up, unused.'

'It's a lovely house,' she offers, her eyes coasting up towards the rooms above.

Has she wondered about those spaces? Have her thoughts been scouring the rooms he occupies? 'We bought it in 1990, my wife and I. Before our children were born. Back then, Dún Laoghaire was quite different. A big drug problem. Very down at heel. Half the houses on this street were full of bedsits. Not like today.' He shakes his head, acts a little baffled. 'When I hear what people today have to pay just to rent in this area, it makes my eyes water.'

He gives her a benign smile, but the implication is there – the favourable rent – and the same thoughts flicker visibly across her face.

'Yes, I know. That's why we're so grateful.'

'Oh, not at all.' He flaps away her gratitude. 'Well, I should leave you to your evening. No doubt your young man will be back soon and you can enjoy finishing the wine together.' He indicates the half-empty bottle, turns as if to leave, then looks back, and adds: 'You know, I think I might take your cue. Go upstairs now and pour myself a glass. I could do with it after the day I've had.'

'Oh?'

Her attention is caught, as he knew it would be.

'A day of trials and disappointments,' he says, smiling to take the note of self-pity from the words.

'Jake said eggs had been thrown at your house.'

'Ah, yes. Some local louts getting their kicks.'

'They didn't throw eggs at any other house – just yours.'

Does he imagine it, or is there a challenge in her voice? Until now, he's had her down as the meek sort, easily led, but perhaps he needs to reassess.

'Well, I can't think what I've done to be singled out for the honour,' he replies, aware of how disingenuous this is, but he's not ready yet to own up to his past. He can't quite face it, after the day he's had. 'Some birthday present,' he remarks, with a brief laugh that dies quickly.

'It's your birthday?'

'My sixtieth. I was supposed to meet a friend for a drink, but I'm afraid he's cancelled on me. Still,' and now he turns as if to leave, 'a glass of wine alone should do just as well.'

'Look, why don't you join me?' she offers, and he has to push back against the smile of satisfaction that threatens to break out over his face.

'Are you sure? I wouldn't want to intrude on your solitude.'

'I don't mind – honestly. Jake will be back very soon, and I'm sure he'd love to meet you properly.'

'Oh, well, then, in that case . . .' He smiles and nods. 'How kind of you. Thank you.'

He takes the chair the young man had been sitting on, while Leah disappears inside for a fresh glass. He can't help feeling pleased with himself at arriving in this position, the way he's turned things around. The smell of fish lingers in the air, and in front of him some salad leaves, limp and damp with dressing, adhere to the sides of an earthenware bowl. Her bare feet pad across the paving – he hears the soft sucking sound they make, feels it tickle the nerves at the back of his neck.

'Thank you,' he says, as she pours him a glass. The wine is tepid, he notes with disappointment as it slips past his lips, not that he should care about the wine. That's not his purpose.

She has picked up a napkin and twists it between her fingers. There's something nervous about her – an uneasiness in company. A silence sits between them, not completely awkward, yet he senses she doesn't know how to break it. Her shyness makes her all the more attractive to him. It reminds him of Janice Simmons – a blonde timid little thing, with grey eyes that wouldn't settle. He'd met her at an office party.

His gaze passes over the paleness of Leah's skin, takes in the small childlike frame, the narrow ridge of her clavicle jutting out beneath the straps of her dress.

'Tell me,' he says, watching as her eyes lift to meet his – soft brown eyes, dusty lashes. 'Which of you is the piano-player?'

An instant flush in those pale cheeks, and she draws her hands back from the table, flustered. 'Oh, that's me, sorry. God, I'm embarrassed.'

'Don't be!'

'No, really, if I'd known you could hear . . .'

'Please,' he says, taking the liberty of reaching forward to tap her wrist – lightly, briefly, but the thrill of her skin beneath his touch! He forces himself to sit back, not to frighten her.

'Charlotte used to play the piano. My wife,' he explains. 'It was a great pleasure to listen to her. I always feel that a house needs music to give it a heart. Do you know what I mean?'

She nods, but tension remains in her shoulders.

'I used to love coming up those stone steps after a day at the office, and hearing the piano before I'd even put the key in the lock!' He smiles and shakes his head, as if it were a fond memory. 'Her piano is still upstairs. A very fine baby grand.'

'My piano teacher had a baby grand. Not in her practice rooms, but in her home. She used to let me call over there sometimes and play. I loved it.'

'Well, you must come upstairs and play my piano sometime.'

'Oh, no, I couldn't.'

'Of course you could,' he says plainly, openly, and he can see the want in her.

It's all about finding the way in.

'I used to say to Charlotte that when the kids had grown up and we were retired, we should move down here to the basement flat, let Mark or Cassandra take the house upstairs. We used to talk about it, Charlotte and I – about

80

how wonderful it would be to have our grandchildren living upstairs, playing in the garden beyond our back door.
And she was insistent that when that day came the piano
would move downstairs with us. That was non-negotiable,
as far as she was concerned.' He laughs, allowing the sound
to trail off wistfully. 'The best laid plans . . .' he says.

'I heard that she died,' she says. 'I'm sorry.'

A coldness lodges in his chest, like indigestion. 'It was
a long time ago now.'

'Even so you must miss her,' she adds. 'Charlotte.'

How strange it is to hear his wife's name on her lips. But
stranger still is the emotion it stokes. It's not expected that
he should miss Charlotte. After what happened. Assumptions were made after the arrest, assumptions that hardened
into fact after the conviction. That he hadn't loved her.
That he had brutalized her. It seemed an aberration to
miss the one you were thought to have murdered.

But he has missed her. At times, over the years. On
lonely days, the reels of their early courtship had unspooled
in his mind as if he was watching them projected on to the
blank wall of his cell. It is harder, now that he's home, to
locate those early happy memories. The later ones carry a
heavier smell, rank with the stench of betrayal.

'Sometimes when I enter a room in my house,' he tells
Leah, 'I'm sure that I can smell her perfume.'

'Today must be especially difficult,' she remarks, and when
he looks at her, confused, she clarifies: 'Your birthday.'

'Oh. Yes.'

'Sometimes it's the days of celebration that can be the
harder ones,' she says, and he knows from the clear manner of her delivery that she speaks from experience.

81

Anton has always preferred the company of women – the way they move, the way they speak. He is more at ease in their company than in that of his own gender. It was one of the aspects of his incarceration that he found hardest to bear – the boredom and brutishness of all-male society. Since his release, he has been aware of women in the street, in the park. He has spoken to them while buying his groceries, or conducting a transaction in the bank. But this is the first time he has been alone with a woman in almost twenty years. It lends the encounter a particular resonance for him, makes him acutely aware of every word spoken, every gesture made.

There is something indefinably gentle about this young woman's presence. What he'd spied from a distance – a languid grace – now reveals itself as a softness, an empathy that is utterly captivating. Something has happened to her, he thinks.

'I'm sorry your friend let you down,' she tells him.

'Thank you. But these things happen.'

'What about your son, Mark?'

She means well, but the mention of this presses against the tender spot of his disappointment. And he realizes, too, that he would rather be here with Leah than sitting in Finnegans with Phil or making awkward conversation with Mark.

'He has his own life to live. And I prefer not to go out of the house, not if I can avoid it.'

'Why not?'

How to explain the wave of nausea that comes over him every time he steps outside his front door? How it is all too much – the unfamiliarity of places he had once frequented, the oppressive clamour of other people's voices, the strangeness of everything from the self-service checkouts at the supermarket to the way the human race now seems inseparable from its mobile phones. He would be ashamed to admit these thoughts and feelings to anyone who doesn't know what it's like. But in a space made possible by the darkness, by the lull of her voice, he says: 'Because I am afraid.'

'What are you afraid of?' There's warmth to her voice, that empathy of hers breaking through again.

'People.'

She doesn't say anything, and he thinks that it is also true that there are things within his house that frighten him: the past, the dangerous drift of memories, his wife's voice ghosting through every room. He remembers again the pelting of eggs against his house, the anonymous gifts of dog faeces left on his front steps. Nowhere is safe. Except here in the garden with Leah.

'I find that I get anxious. That's why I like it here.'

'In the garden?'

'It was always my refuge. You wouldn't think it now, but it was once a beautiful garden.'

He used to devote hours to it, the kids playing on their bikes around him while he knelt there, wrist-deep in soil, coaxing life out of seeds and bulbs.

'Was your wife a gardener too?'

'Oh, no!' He laughs at the thought of it, a deep chortle that gurgles up out of nowhere, surprising him. He can't remember the last time he laughed like that. 'No, Charlotte was more of a house-cat. Always more comfortable indoors.'

His wife had never understood the quiet pleasure he drew from this patch of soil, the way it flourished under his care. She teased him about it at parties, his green fingers. 'He gets down on his knees and takes scissors to the edge of that lawn.' He'd once heard Charlotte say that to a neighbour at a party, a knifish edge to her voice. She'd known he was within earshot.

He doesn't mention this to Leah. He shivers in the darkness, unnerved at the flow of Charlotte's bitterness in finding him out here where he thought he was immune, where he thought he was safe.

Somewhere in the garden there's a rustling sound. Their gaze is drawn away into the undergrowth. In the darkness, you can't see the full tangled mess, the briars and rhododendrons rampaging through what had once been a tidy, orderly space.

'It's probably just a fox,' he tells her. 'The gardens along here always had a lively fox community.'

His wine glass is empty now.

'It's getting late,' she says, and he feels her drawing in. Whatever brief opening there'd been between them is closing.

He wants to keep her there. To say something to draw her in. He has a sudden impulse to thrust out his hand and grab her wrist. Impulses like that can't be trusted, but he understands the need in him that she has called up from the depths. Nineteen years since he has held a woman in his arms, felt her flesh against his bare skin. A conversation in the twilit garden, the wine, the night deepening around them, he can't help but conjure images.

'The first week you're back,' Nigel had told him, 'get yourself to a massage parlour. Or call up one of those escort services. Get yourself laid. Not because you think you deserve it, or because you've been thinking of little else for the past two decades. Sex is like everything else that's on the outside — another bloody link in the chain that shackles you. Do it so that you can rid yourself of it. So that you don't have to think about it any more. Trust me,' and Nigel had given him a long, exacting look, 'you don't want to have that hanging around your neck.'

Advice that was well meant, but for once Nigel had missed the mark. That is not how Anton is made, not how he functions. The thought of approaching a prostitute fills him with a rank fear that he can almost taste. And he suspects that, rather than providing comfort, it would only deepen his loneliness.

But being here in the semi-darkness with Leah fills a void in him, slakes his thirst for companionship.

'There is something about you,' he says, 'that feels so familiar to me.' And then he reaches tentatively for her hand, rests his ever so lightly on hers. 'Like we knew each other in a past life.'

She is visibly embarrassed by this strange display, and quickly he withdraws his hand.

'Goodnight, Leah. Thank you for the wine. And the company.'

She gives him one of her distracted little half-smiles and stands there watching him climb the steps up to the back door that leads into his kitchen. As he reaches for the handle, he casts one last look down at her.

'Happy birthday, Anton,' she calls up softly, and that one salutation – that solitary voice on the warm air – causes something inside him to flutter and hum. A whirring vibration about his heart.

For hours afterwards, he sits at his kitchen table, smoking one cigarette after another, his mind racing.

She will be in bed by now, he thinks, the boyfriend turning over, his arm finding her in the darkness.

Anton pours himself a whisky, hoping it will settle his mind. For years his conversations have been confined to male circles. He feels weirdly agitated after tonight, as if some part of him has been altered. Subtly changed.

He looks at the kitchen window, sees the darkness pressing up against the panes, knows that soon the dawn will seep through the dark – it is never really dark anyway, not at this time of the year.

And now, as the ash smoulders and falls, and he stubs out the cigarette on the saucer in front of him, he sees the shake in his hand, feels it.

He is on his way to bed, still turning over thoughts of Leah in his head, when he sees the envelope on the floor by the front door. The recent assault on his house and the various harassments make him wary as he approaches. But when he picks it up and draws out the letter, a hard little knot forms in his chest at the sight of the familiar handwriting.

He mounts the stairs slowly, tiredness filling his legs, like sand.

He sits on his bed and reads the letter once more. He thinks he catches the whiff of bergamot and lemon – his dead wife's fragrance.

It is a problem he will have to confront. He cannot keep putting it off.

After a moment, he drags the box out from under his bed, stuffs the note inside it, along with all the others. Then he lies back, stretching out. Closing his eyes, he tries to sleep.

8

Hilary

'You're so lucky,' Claire tells Hilary over dinner, 'that you don't have to put up with any of this.'

Hilary smiles and tucks into her beef chow mein while the three other women around the table nod and give sympathetic groans.

'Hormones, hormones, hormones,' Claire continues. 'I'm up to my neck in hormones with Josh. Facial hair, acne, perpetual showering, not to mention the mood swings and the backchat. It's a nightmare, I'm telling you.'

Hilary twists noodles around the tines of her fork and thinks of an afternoon many years ago, all four of them working in the same school, when Claire, who was pregnant at the time, had tripped and fallen in the staff-room. It was she – Hilary – who had put her distressed young friend in the car and driven her to the maternity hospital, staying by her side until the two of them were admitted to an examination room. There, the attending physician had drawn a paddle over the small hillock of Claire's belly and Hilary had stared with wonder and envy at the little waving arms, the kicking miniature legs on the screen. And now to think that the tiny foetus she had glimpsed that day is growing chest hair, snogging girls at rugby club discos and giving his mother all manner of grief. Where have the years gone?

'At least he doesn't hate you,' Anna states, leaning forward to make her point. 'I've lost count of how many times Kelly has told me she detests me. That's what she says! *I detest you, Mother. I loathe you.* Honest to God. Hell is a fifteen-year-old daughter.'

The others laugh while Hilary empties the last of the wine into her glass, then raises the bottle aloft to catch the waiter's attention and shakes it to indicate he's to bring another. Their third bottle of the evening, and the main course has only just arrived, but sod it, Hilary thinks, it's only once a year.

The St Agnes's girls' dinner. Their annual reunion. Although none of them are girls any more, their ages ranging across the upper forties. While, next to her, the waiter fiddles with the cork, Hilary allows her gaze to pass around the table, and tries to see in their middle-aged faces the young women she had first met when the four of them had joined the staff of St Agnes's, the new recruits banding together, a friendship forged between them that has lasted more than twenty years. Only Hilary and Evelyn remain at the school, but these annual summer dinners when the school term finally ends have endured and held them together.

It could be argued that some of them have improved with age. Claire and Anna are better-dressed, more polished versions of their younger selves. Anna, in particular, is unlined and blemish-free, skin stretched taut over prominent cheekbones, a wide-eyed unblinking look. Of them all, Evelyn looks closest to her age. After a battle with breast cancer three years ago, she had stopped dyeing her hair, given up wearing make-up and drinking alcohol, and embraced veganism. Hilary has always felt closest to Evelyn. When the others had left the school, Anna to take up a different position, Claire to stay at home with her children, Hilary and Evelyn had stuck together, sharing their hopes and their discontents. Hilary can feel Evelyn watching her carefully across the table, raising her eyebrows a fraction to check that she is okay. She'll have clocked the speed at which Hilary is drinking, and Evelyn, for all her quiet rectitude, is observant of these signs.

Hilary shoots back a warm, bracing smile, straightens, gives her hair a little shake. The wine is threading through her veins. I can cope with this, she thinks, applying her attention once more to the conversation. I can cope with their chatter about hormones and discos, about hockey matches and gym gear, the financial drain of after-school activities and summer camps. I can cope.

'How is Greg?' Evelyn asks, shifting the conversation with a view to drawing her friend back into it.

'He's good. Working hard.'

'When's the new book out, Hil?' Anna asks, and Hilary tells them August, realizing with a jolt that there's only a few short weeks left.

'Oh, how exciting!' Anna remarks. Claire tells her that she'll add it to her list of holiday reads, and the others agree.

Hilary appreciates their enthusiasm, feels buoyed by their friendship, and for the rest of the main course, she fields their questions about the book, about Greg's writing life, about whether he will quit his teaching post and turn to writing full time.

The conversation runs along pleasantly, aided by the tinkling of wine in her head, and Hilary thinks of all the dinners she has shared with these women over the years, and all the other times, too, when life's difficulties entered the fray, requiring the friendships to step up a little. When Evelyn went through her cancer treatment three years ago, Hilary was on hand, calling her religiously after each round of chemotherapy, taking her for walks along the pier to get some exercise, clear her head, talk. When Anna's marriage went through a rough patch, Hilary arranged for all four of them to head away for a weekend in a spa retreat where they could be pampered, get drunk, cry, do whatever was necessary to bolster Anna's resolve. And when Hilary herself went through her own trial of sorrows – the string of miscarriages and an ectopic pregnancy that led to an inevitable surrender of hope – she had felt supported by the many kindnesses of her friends.

'You know, there's nothing I couldn't tell you girls,' Anna had declared on that weekend away when she had given them chapter and verse on David's affairs, his cruelties and deceits, the shame she felt at having put up with them for so long. 'I feel like I can tell you the deepest, darkest secrets and you still wouldn't judge me.'

The others had loudly concurred, and Hilary had made soft noises of agreement. But, in her heart, she knew differently. Because some secrets are too dark to tell. And people do judge. Even the strongest friendships, in the face of horrors, would balk and break, run for cover.

Inevitably, her thoughts turn to Charlotte, as they so often do. She thinks of an evening long ago when Charlotte had tapped on the patio door with the stone in her ring, a bottle of wine in one hand and some flowers in the other. 'A welcome gift,' she said.

Her voice was throaty, her manner smooth and confident, and she listened to Hilary's effusive thanks – for the flowers, for the use of the flat – while her eyes looked beyond, flickering over the room and taking in the mess of their possessions, most of them still in boxes. Charlotte's dress, her hair, her casual elegance made Hilary feel drab and scruffy in comparison.

'Why don't you and your husband come upstairs later, hmm?' Charlotte had suggested. 'Once you've settled in. Come up and we'll have a little drink.'

It was evening by the time they mounted the steps, tired from their unpacking.

'Just make yourselves at home there,' Charlotte had instructed, while she disappeared into the kitchen to fix their drinks.

Greg collapsed on the sofa, exhausted, legs akimbo, while Hilary sat on the edge of an armchair, alert, looking all around her at the scrolled marble of the fireplace, the cornicing, the ceiling so very far above their heads.

'Now! The bar is open,' Charlotte said, returning with filled glasses. 'You must tell me all about yourselves!' She passed around the G-and-Ts.

There wasn't much to tell, but dutifully they explained the essential details: how they were both teachers, how they'd used a small inheritance to buy the house across the road. Builders would begin work on Monday. Ten weeks, they'd been told.

'And how long have you been married?' Charlotte asked. She'd taken a seat on the sofa next to Greg, sat perched on the edge, like Hilary. She was not relaxed. Something over-attentive about her, eyes a little too wide and glittery.

'Six years,' Hilary said.

'No kids?'

'No,' she answered, offering a tight smile. Without looking, she could feel Greg's eyes on her, knew that she'd see concern there.

'Plenty of time for that,' Charlotte replied. Her own children were nowhere to be seen, although there were occasional thumps and shouts from upstairs. 'But you have a little dog.'

'That's right. Bella,' Hilary said, instantly brightening. She always did when it came to Bella. 'She's a cocker spaniel. A blue roan, to be precise.'

'Lovely,' Charlotte said, but she did not sound sincere. Hilary had the impression that she was not really interested, that her thoughts, in fact, lay elsewhere. And when the front door banged and her husband appeared, her manner seemed to change again.

'There he is. The man of the house,' Charlotte announced, in a way that felt falsely bright.

She disappeared once more to fix a drink for him, while Anton walked slowly into the room, loosening his tie. Dressed in a suit, he'd come straight from work, and it was obvious from his expression that he had not expected to find Hilary and Greg in his living room, and was probably not thrilled about it either, as he dutifully shook their hands, introducing himself.

'Here we are!' Charlotte proclaimed, in her new fake tone. There was a shrillness to it and Hilary caught Anton glancing at his wife – wariness in the swift, assessing gaze – as she put the glass into his hand, resuming her place on the sofa.

In one way, she was easy company, with a gift for moving the conversation along. Peppering them with questions, she never once allowed the talk to flag. Her responses to their offerings seemed effusive and generous, if not entirely heartfelt. The husband, on the other hand, Hilary noted, was watchful and laconic. He preferred to let his wife do the talking. Only once – when Charlotte returned to the kitchen to fix a second round of drinks – was Anton pressed into conversation, exchanging a few sports-related opinions with Greg while Hilary sat there, smiling, and taking in the room.

'God, I can really feel that gin in my legs now,' Greg remarked, laughing, when they were halfway through their second drinks.

They had all loosened up by that stage, their conversation splitting in two. Hilary was leaning forward and listening to Anton describing the history of the street, how the houses had been built in the 1840s by a wine merchant, while Greg and Charlotte sat alongside each other discussing restaurants and pubs, and gossiping about the other neighbours.

'That's one of the wonderful things about gin, I find,' she heard Charlotte say, 'how it wends its way gloriously into all the limbs,' and she put out her hand and touched Greg's leg as she made her point, then left it there.

Until that moment, the atmosphere in the room had been convivial. But now the air seemed to shrink, charged with a new and dangerous mood. All of them were aware of Charlotte's hand resting on Greg's leg, the fingers slowly caressing the tiny hairs peeping out where the cotton of his shorts ended above the knee.

Hilary couldn't quite believe it. Greg was just sitting there, staring now at his drink, frozen to the spot while those fingertips kept gliding up and down his thigh. And when Hilary's eyes passed to Charlotte, she saw with a jolt that Charlotte was staring right back at her, a hard smile on her face, her eyes bright with the challenge. Confusion tangled her thoughts, and her heart was pounding with an unnamed fear. She hadn't a clue what to do, completely out of her depth.

Greg knocked back the rest of his drink, and leant forward quickly, placing his glass on the coffee-table.

'Well, that was lovely,' he declared, getting to his feet.

Hastily, Hilary stood up, too, taking his cue.

They said their goodbyes and hurried back downstairs to the garden and into their flat. The door closed behind them and they fell against one another, elated, delirious in their disbelief, their shared excitement. 'Oh, my God!' they said, clinging to each other. 'Did you see that?' Their laughter and excitement mingled like an aphrodisiac, and it carried them to their bedroom where they abandoned themselves to a new, gleeful lust. But distantly, above them, Hilary was aware of voices raised, sharp words spoken. Sometime in the night, she awoke and heard a woman crying.

'Hilary?'

Her attention snaps back to the table, and she sees Claire leaning towards her conspiratorially.

'Is it true what I heard?' Claire asks, her eyes flaring with ghoulish delight. 'That man on your street – the one who murdered his wife – has he been released?'

Dryness in her throat. She reaches for her glass. 'Yes, it's true,' she says, then takes a gulp and swallows.

'My God,' Anna says, her hand going to her neck. 'And have you seen him? Is he back living in that house?'

'I haven't seen him, no, but I believe he is back.'

'Aren't you freaked?' Anna asks. 'I mean, he murdered someone! Honestly, Hil, I admire your sangfroid, but even you must feel a little twinge. After all, you knew the woman, right? Weren't you friends with her?'

'I wouldn't go so far as to call us friends. But we were . . . friendly.' She says this lightly, but feels the heaviness of the words in her heart. 'She was our landlady for a little while. When the work was being done on our house, before we could move in, we rented the basement flat beneath their house. Just for a couple of months.'

'So, were you guys living there when it happened?'

'No, no. We'd moved out at that stage,' Hilary says, making it sound like they were long gone when, really, they were barely out of the door.

'What was he like, though?' Claire asks, a hungry look entering her eye. Hilary has seen it before, inwardly recoils from it. 'Had you any inkling at all of what he was capable of?'

'No, of course not.' She laughs, but it sounds forced and she's aware of Evelyn watching her from across the table. 'I hardly knew him, really,' she adds, a twist in her gut at this denial. 'He was always polite to me. Well-mannered.'

Anna shakes her head. 'That poor woman. God love her. Had she any idea of what was in store for her?'

Poor woman, Hilary thinks, the words curdling inside her. Not words she would ever have associated with Charlotte. And then it comes at her without warning: a flash of memory. Coming up from the past, the sound of banging on glass. Charlotte with her fox-red hair, wearing a green sun-dress, spaghetti straps carving tracks through her shoulders, standing on the patio. Breasts, not large but shapely – you couldn't miss them under the stretch-cotton. The little boy in tears by her side – Charlotte clutching his wrist and quivering with rage. Greg, inside, calling: 'Hi? What is it?'

A shiver passes through her despite the heat of the res-taurant. She realizes she's drifted into silence, the others staring at her, awaiting her response.

'Who knows what she knew?' Hilary says, her voice dry and scratchy in her throat. 'The things that go on inside a marriage – can you ever really tell when you're outside looking in?'

'That's certainly true,' Anna agrees, with feeling.

'And I think he was misrepresented in the press at the time,' Hilary goes on, a little recklessly. 'Making him out to be some sort of monster. He really was a very nice man. Always very charming.'

'Hmm. They're usually the ones you have to watch,' Claire replies.

'Don't they say,' Anna adds, 'that nine times out of ten, when a woman is murdered it's her husband or partner that's the guilty party?'

'That's right,' Claire agrees. 'You're absolutely right.'

'And yet, growing up, we're always warned about men we don't know, cautioned against walking home alone in the dark or taking a lift from a stranger. My God, it's the same drill I'm giving my own daughters.' She throws down her napkin with an angry little pout. 'When, really, it's the men we share our lives with – the men we share

97

our beds with – who pose the real danger. We should be warning them about that.'

Afterwards, Evelyn drives Hilary home. The two of them are mostly silent in the car, the radio tuned to Lyric FM, some baroque choral music filling the space between them. Hilary has drunk too much and the food she has consumed sits uncomfortably in her stomach – a fat greasy lump lodged in her gut. As the car draws up alongside the kerb outside her house, she unclips her seatbelt, and says: 'Will you come in for a coffee?'

To her relief, Evelyn says no, that she'd best get home. And yet Hilary can sense a lingering within her friend – a hesitation – and when she looks across to wish Evelyn goodnight, she catches the look her friend is giving her: watchful, probing.

'You are all right, aren't you?' Evelyn asks.

'Of course I am!'

'It's just I know how difficult it must be for you, with Anton being back.'

Hilary feels herself stiffen.

Evelyn seems nervous now, as if unsure whether to proceed with this line of questioning, but she continues nonetheless. 'Years ago, I know that you were very unhappy. Things you said back then, the way you were . . . It seemed to me that he offered some sort of consolation. I know you were friends. It must be awkward for you now with him –'

'It's not awkward,' Hilary says sharply.

'Isn't it?'

'I don't see him. I've had nothing to do with him since it happened.'

Evelyn's eyes flicker over her face, as if searching for a chink in the veracity of her statements. 'Haven't you? I thought you had.'

'No, Evelyn. You thought wrong.' Words spoken coolly but firmly. A line drawn under it.

She thanks her friend for the lift, leans in to kiss Evelyn swiftly on the cheek, and then she is clack-clacking up the path in her high heels, inserting the key into the lock, and by the time she turns to wave, Hilary has recovered enough to have a smile of reassurance plastered across her features. Evelyn's pale face shimmers behind the windscreen.

She bangs the door shut, leans against it for a moment, eyes closed, awash with regret.

Foolish woman! The things she'd admitted to back then. Loose thoughts aired aloud. She bangs her head lightly against the door, then pushes herself away. The house is quiet. It hums with a feeling of emptiness, the lights off in the rooms downstairs, no sign of Greg.

In the kitchen, Mona has been sick on the floor. Hilary stares at the small puddle of vomit by the back door and the dog cowering in her basket and feels a surge of angry despair rise within her. Sometimes it's hard to love Mona. Not like Bella, Hilary's first dog, whom she had loved unconditionally. A silly, warm-hearted spaniel with beautiful eyes and silky fur. But Mona is nothing like Bella. As she looks at her, burrowing deeper into the blankets of her basket, casting occasional rueful glances in Hilary's direction, something snaps inside. Rage vibrates through her, and she drags Mona out of her basket, then flings open the kitchen door and the dog flees to the safety of the garden.

Hilary cries as she cleans up the mess, down on her hands and knees, in her Marigolds, scrubbing at the floor with disinfectant and paper towels, great big sobs of self-pity. Afterwards, she sits at the kitchen table, hunched over a notepad, scribbling furiously. The words pour out of her on to the page, and it is only when the letter is written that she looks up, sees the dog's doleful gaze through the glass, and feels ashamed. When she opens the door, Mona slinks back in, eyeing her warily, and silently bearing it when Hilary presses her face to the dog's flank, whispers that she's sorry.

The lead is hanging from the newel post, and once she's fixed it to Mona's collar, they head out into the evening air. Hilary feels sober now, aware of the quiet in the street, the swish of warm air against her bare arms, the dog's claws clicking against the pavement. She hurries to the house, up the steps, not giving herself time to think, to change her mind, opens the letterbox and slips the note through. She presses the doorbell once and then she hurries away, across to the safety of the park where she can hide in the shadows, watching safely from the distance.

In the park, she lets Mona off the lead, appeasing her own guilt by allowing the dog to run loose for a few moments. The trees hulk in dark shadows against the purplish sky. Across the street, the houses glow in the moonlight, and she watches his door – Number 14 – shut firmly against the night, the windows dark upstairs.

He hasn't come to the door – hasn't answered the bell – and that makes her feel twitchy with disappointment and impatience. Curiosity has been nudging at her for some time, but now it builds inside her, pushed by the time she has spent waiting, the endless accumulation of days, and by Evelyn's words – the reminder of past confidences, of secrets told. Hilary thinks of that note waiting for him and feels the draw of that garden, awash with memories. The things that had happened to her there . . .

She clips the lead back on to the dog's collar and, moving with purpose now, she walks down Wyndham Park and out on to the road behind. It's late now, and all is quiet. She finds the entrance to the alleyway easily enough, feels her heart fill with fear and expectation as she hurries along the narrow space, ivy spilling over the high walls. It's been years but she finds the gap quickly. The garden is densely overgrown and it's dark back there. The dog is her cover. If caught, she can claim Mona slipped the lead and ran this way – she was merely coming to reclaim her.

Through the undergrowth, she sees a light and creeps towards it. Catches the scent of cigarette smoke on the air – at once nostalgic and achingly familiar. Halfway down the garden, the house comes clearly into view and she stops. Stares. Grips the dog's lead firmly to her side, feels the animal's warmth against her shin.

Voices in the darkness. Two of them. Her eyes narrow and strain through the gloom.

They are sitting together, Anton and the young woman. Hilary holds her breath, taking him in – the broadness of his shoulders hunched forward a little, a new thinness to his frame. Through the darkness it's difficult to see, but she can make out the contours of his shapely head, the line of his jaw, a pugnacious tilt to his chin – these things have not changed. The dog shifts by her side, looks up at her, confused, but Hilary doesn't move. She is transfixed.

'There is something about you,' she hears Anton say, 'that seems utterly familiar to me.' Watches him reach forward, touch the girl's hand.

Years crash away, all the layers stripped back, old feelings flooding to the surface. Hilary crouches there in the shadows, the blood pounding in her ears, feeling the build of those dark emotions inside her, loud and threatening.

9

Leah

'I don't believe it,' Jake says.

Leah watches him carefully. He is still standing by the door but his face has drained of colour.

'You're sure?' he asks then, and she nods, waiting for him to say something more now that she has finally told him.

They are in the kitchen of their flat on Saturday afternoon. Jake wears his soccer gear, having just come from training with Matthew, who's now flopped on the bed in the little room he has made his own. The mindless electronic drone of music from the Xbox reaches them. Jake closes the door on it before pulling out a chair from the kitchen table and sitting down. He looks stunned.

'I'm sorry,' she says. 'I didn't mean to tell you like this . . .'

'No. No, it's fine.'

Moments earlier, he had found her, hunched over the sink, dry-retching. The nausea came upon her so suddenly. She was going to wait until the end of the weekend, after he had dropped Matthew home to his mother, to break the news to Jake. But once he had discovered her like that, she had no choice other than to make her announcement.

And now he is sitting at the table, not looking at her, his concentration fixed on some inward point she can't see.

'Jake?'

'How far along are you?'

'Not that far. I'm three weeks late, maybe a month.'

'Right.'

She's still by the sink where he found her, her hip pressed against it, the coolness of the stainless steel coming through the thin cotton of her skirt. Outside, she can hear seagulls screaming. The sky is a perfect shade of blue.

His shock is to be expected. This is not something either of them has planned or even discussed. Having a baby had never seemed a possibility for her, the chances of it so remote, given the way she had set up her life, keeping people at arm's length, until Jake came along. He loves Matthew, that much is clear; he is a devoted and affectionate father. But whether he has any desire for further children has never occurred to her. Their relationship is still so new. And it comes to Leah now how precarious their situation is. She loves Jake, but watching him, his hands cupping his cheeks while he scours the wooden surface of the table as if the answer could be read there, it occurs to her that she doesn't really know him at all.

'How did this happen?' he asks, bewildered. 'You've been taking the pill, right?'

He glances up at her, and the nerves she felt about telling him crystallize into something colder and harder. The look he gives her is distrustful. She can't remember him ever looking at her that way before.

'Of course I have.'

'Sorry. I'm sorry – I didn't mean it like that. This is all just a shock.'

She sits at the table with him then, reaching out to take his hand.

'It must have been that tummy bug I had,' she explains nervously. 'A few weeks back – do you remember? It must have interfered with the pill.'

'Christ.' He rubs his spare hand over his hair, the other lying inert beneath her grip.

'Please, Jake,' she says, and something gives way in her voice – the break of emotion. She needs him to be happy about this, but she can't express it: the tears are too close.

Only then does he see how deeply he has hurt her. Immediately regretful, he reaches for her across the table and they hug awkwardly. He strokes her hair and her cheek, kisses her firmly, passionately. 'I'm a thoughtless dick,' he says.

'No, you're not.'

'It's just the shock. Hey, I was the same when Jenna told me she was expecting Matthew. Come here.' He gets to his feet, and pulls her up so that she's standing against him, holding his gaze.

'A baby,' he says, beaming at her.

Reassured that he wants her to be happy, some of the coldness melts away. '*Our* baby,' she tells him, hope beginning to hum inside her.

'Promise me you'll forget my reaction just now?'

'It's forgotten.'

'This will turn out to be the best thing that's ever happened to us,' he says, with warm conviction. 'Right?'

And she laughs away her fears and nods, inwardly turning away from the notion that he's trying to persuade himself. She manages to convince herself that it is enough.

'How long have you known?' he asks, and she shrugs.

'I began to wonder about two weeks ago. I finally did a test last weekend.'

'Last weekend?' He draws back and stares at her. 'You kept it from me for a whole week?'

'I was nervous about telling you. I wanted to wait for the right time.'

Her voice trembles and he seems to read within it the depth of her insecurity. He kisses her then and she feels reassured by his affection.

'You mustn't keep things to yourself,' he says. 'We're together now. We've got to be able to tell each other things, right? No more secrets.'

Now is the moment, she thinks. The opening she's been waiting for, the invitation she's been dreading. This is when she should tell him. The secret buried so deep inside her that unearthing it would feel like an act of violence.

But then his right hand moves around her waist, coming to rest on her tummy. She feels the tentative pressure of it, the tender movement of his thumb across the surface of her skin. There is a queasy pleasure to the newness of this gesture. She is used to the weight of his arm around her shoulders, or the soft pressure of his hand around the curve of her bum, gestures that are sexual and proprietary by nature, but this is different. Tender in a way that makes her avoid his eyes.

She can't tell him. Not now. She just wants to keep him there with his hand on her belly. She doesn't want to break the spell.

But then he pulls away his hand abruptly, as if suddenly embarrassed by the intensity of his tenderness. And there is Matthew behind them at the door, his eyes casting from one to the other, suspicion on his face.

'There's a funny smell in my room,' he says, his nose wrinkling with disgust.

Jake sighs with resignation, the moment over. He ruffles the boy's hair, and says: 'Come on. Let's all go to Teddy's for ice-cream.'

The pavement bakes in the sunlight as they emerge from the flat. Across the road, the green is swarming with people, queues of kids lining up to use the tennis courts. A tent has appeared beneath the tall trees at one end of the park, laundry hanging on a makeshift line strung between the trunks of two sycamores. Jake nods towards it. 'Poor sods,' he mutters, taking Matthew's hand.

She's reminded of how lucky they are to have their own place now.

They walk around to the People's Park, Jake marvelling aloud over an amenity like this only minutes from their front door. The railed-in grounds are thronged on this sunny late-afternoon, picnic blankets spread over the grass, teenagers sprawling in packs beneath the trees, screams rising from the playground beyond. Matthew has gone ahead of them on his scooter. Leah and Jake follow, holding hands, watching him as he weaves his way along the path between jaunty flower beds, the fountains spouting, sending out bright arcs of sparkling water.

A couple walk past, a baby strapped to the man's chest, little legs vigorously kicking, and Leah squeezes Jake's hand. How extraordinary this is! She feels the newness of everything, their secret lending a freshness to the afternoon, the clipped lawns, the blue swathe of the sea in the harbour beyond. A year ago, she could not have imagined this turn her life would take, and the thought fills her with hope.

'You wait here,' Jake says, directing her to a bench in the sunlight, while he takes Matthew around the corner to Teddy's where a queue has formed.

She closes her eyes, feeling the heat on her face as she lifts it to the sun. For just a moment, she feels perfectly relaxed. Untroubled. Serene.

'Hello there.'

She hears the voice and opens her eyes, squints in the bright glare of the sun at the silhouetted figure before her.

'I'm sorry. I've startled you,' Anton says, and she sits up straighter, looks down quickly, smoothing her skirt across her thighs.

'No, that's all right. I was just soaking up the sun.'

'It's a glorious day.'

He smiles down at her, and for some reason Leah feels shy under his gaze. Carrying a plastic bag of oranges, he looks different in the daylight. His clothes for a start – a light blue linen shirt, a white golf-cap that's seen better days. He appears more relaxed, and younger than she remembered. It is only now that the similarities between Anton and his son Mark become apparent to her. It's there in the eyes, the same expressive quality, the direct gaze. Anton, though, is less serious than his son. His smile comes readily, and she feels the warmth of it now as she says, 'It's busy here today,' making small-talk.

He nods. 'It has ever been so. A hint of good weather, and this place is thronged.'

She likes the way he speaks – the occasional old-fashioned formality within it.

'I was going through some things in the house,' he tells her now, 'earlier on today and I came upon some old sheet music of Charlotte's that I wondered if you might like.'

'Oh?' she says, unease creeping in.

'John Field's nocturnes,' he says, with an air of apology. 'Perhaps you'll think them old-fashioned.'

'No, not at all. I love them.'

'I could drop them down to you later. Or perhaps you could call up, maybe even try out the piano. It's been such a long time since –'

'Look, no. I'm sorry, but I don't think so.'

She's not sure why she says no, but it's got something to do with the oddness of meeting him here like this, outside the confines of the garden. In the evenings, she's noticed him sitting on the steps while smoking his cigarette and gazing out over the trees and shrubs – a benign and unthreatening presence. But now, the thought of going upstairs into his house – of being alone with him in a room – makes her feel instinctively nervous. His words from that first conversation linger in her mind: 'I prefer not to go out of the house, not if I can avoid it.' And even though he is standing here among the crowds in broad daylight, she is troubled by his admission. *Why not?* she wants to ask. *What are you hiding from?*

'Yes. Well, that's quite all right.'

'I'm sorry, it's just that –'

'No, no! No need to apologize. I understand.'

He is backing away from her now, about to join the slipstream of people.

'Well, goodbye,' he says, and as he turns, a man walking past bangs against his shoulder and pushes him off-balance.

The bag slips from Anton's hand, oranges rolling around his feet.

'Hey!' Leah shouts after the passer-by, appalled when he doesn't even look back.

Anton is bending to retrieve the oranges, and she hunkers down to help him, feeding the fruit back into the bag.

'Thank you,' he says.

'Are you all right?'

'I'm fine, dear.' But there's something distracted about him, his face serious and intent on his shopping.

'He didn't even stop to see if you needed help.'

Her voice is breathy and indignant, and when she gets to her feet, she sees the way he is looking at her, his expression softening.

'You're lovely,' he tells her, the words spoken so clearly and tenderly as to make her awkward. She has never been easy with compliments, but there is something in the way he is staring at her that makes her deeply uncomfortable.

'I'm not lovely,' she says quietly, her eyes sweeping the pavement in front of her, and when she looks up again, he's still gazing at her in that way.

'Jake will be back in a minute,' she says, and he nods in understanding.

'Goodbye,' he tells her, then breaks eye contact and moves away.

She notes the manner in which he walks, head down and thoughtful, taking his time, sauntering towards the traffic lights. But just as he crosses the road, he puts a hand to his head, lifts his hat, and wipes the sweat from his brow with a hankie. That one gesture gives her pause, reminding her of her father in a way that is painful.

She thinks of how she turned him down about trying out his piano, wishing she hadn't sounded so hard, so unfriendly. He's just a lonely man who had been kind to her. Why had she sounded so mean?

'Is that who I think it was?' Jake asks.

She looks around and sees him standing there with Matthew. Distractedly, he hands her an ice-cream, his gaze still fixed on the dark figure hurrying up the hill towards the church. 'He was just saying hello,' she says, as he settles himself on the bench next to her, untwisting paper from the cone of his Cornetto.

'Oh, yeah?' He licks at the ice-cream. 'I don't know about that bloke. I've heard some things.'

'What things?' She tries to keep her voice neutral, concentrates on the ice-cream's sugary taste on her tongue.

'Something Ian said. They're a weird family, apparently.'

'I thought he was friends with Mark?'

'Nah. They know each other, but I wouldn't call them friends. Ian says Mark didn't grow up with his dad. That he lived with his aunt.'

'I lived with my aunt.'

'Yeah, but that was for school, right?'

She nods but doesn't look him in the eye.

'He and the dad don't get on, apparently,' Jake continues. 'Some kind of trouble there.'

'Well, it must have been hard for him after his wife died. Perhaps he couldn't cope,' she says reasonably, thinking of her conversation in the garden with Anton. How quiet and reassuring he had seemed.

'Yeah, but his kids? I mean, surely he'd hold them closer, not push them away.'

You don't know how it is, she thinks darkly in her head. *You don't know how you'll react when tragedy strikes. You don't know to what lengths you'll go just to cope.*

'And have you noticed the way nobody ever calls to see him, and how he hardly ever goes out? I'm surprised to see him out here in the daylight.'

'He's not a vampire, Jake.'

He smiles at the notion, and says: 'So what were you two talking about?'

'Nothing. Just saying hello. He'd heard me playing piano. Says he's got a piano upstairs.'

'Oh, yeah? I'd better watch out or he'll be luring you up there to have his wicked way with you.'

She shoves against him playfully, her temper dissipating.

'Anyway. Best keep away from him,' Jake says, distracted by the beeping of his phone.

Leah watches as he reads the screen.

'Listen, I've got to go,' he tells her. Then, seeing her confusion, he explains: 'It's Ian. We're meeting to discuss things. Remember, I told you?'

'I thought that was later.'

'He's free now,' Jake says, pocketing his phone and getting to his feet.

'But what about Matthew?'

'You'll be all right with him, won't you?'

Her heart pounds with fear. She's never been alone with Matthew before. The thought of being left in charge of Jake's son – having sole responsibility – shakes her a little. All these years she's spent safeguarding herself against such a situation, and now here she is, desperately thinking of a way out.

'I don't know, Jake. I mean, it's not as if Matthew and I know each other well. You're his dad – he's here to see you, not me.'

He leans forward and kisses her on the mouth, makes it last, and when he draws back he's giving her the grin she finds impossible to resist. He says softly: 'Relax. It'll be fine. Take him home and stick a movie on for him.'

She watches then, as he goes to the boy, bends to speak to him, gives his shoulders a squeeze. Her eyes stay on Matthew, his disappointed slump, the way he keeps his gaze on his father, watching him walk away.

A feeling of dissatisfaction lingers in her mind as they walk home together. Matthew is tired and unhappy now that his father has deserted him. Leah carries the scooter, while the boy trails along behind her. She tries to push down her unease at Jake's decision to leave her for the evening. Since they have moved in together, she has been struck by the blitheness with which Jake flits in and out of the flat, working to his own timetable, his own social obligations. She doesn't mind being alone, but wonders what it says about his commitment to her.

Now, as they stand at the traffic lights, she takes Matthew's hand. In front of her, a woman pushes a pram with a baby in it, another child next to her in the throes of a tantrum. The woman turns her attention to the screaming toddler, bending down to coax him into compliance, but Leah keeps her eyes hawk-like on the woman's unsteady grasp of the pram's handle, the loose, distracted manner with which she holds it.

Something happens inside Leah. Waves of panic threaten. Bile rises up to her throat.

113

'You're hurting me!' Matthew wails, and she realizes she is clutching his hand so hard that her nails are digging into his flesh.

'I'm sorry, love,' she says, her heart beating wildly. But when she looks back, the lights have changed, and the woman is pushing the pram across the road, safely moving her two children along.

Matthew holds his hand to his chest, refuses to let her have it again. Back at the flat, he retreats into his room, claiming not to be hungry. She sits on the patio, tired and unsettled by the afternoon's events. *Why isn't Jake here with me?* she wonders. After the news she has broken to him, surely he should be at her side, celebrating, or at least reassuring her.

Movement at the top of the steps makes her start. She has forgotten about Anton, about the earlier awkwardness, but now as she sees him retreating back into the house, having spied her on the patio, she feels a stab of shame at the hostility in her manner earlier.

'No, wait,' she calls, getting to her feet.

'I didn't mean to disturb you. I'll leave you be,' he says, mustering his dignity in a way that makes her feel remorseful.

'Anton,' she says, coming forward and putting one foot on the step, looking up at him. 'I wondered if I might have those pieces after all – the nocturnes?'

He begins to smile now and, after a moment's hesitation, he holds out a hand to her, and as she presses her foot to the step and starts to climb towards him, she briefly wonders what spark of misplaced intuition had made her so reluctant and nervous. There's no harm in him.

He stands back and opens the door so she can go in.

IO

Anton

He's in the sitting room, eating rashers and eggs in front of the TV, when she comes. On the screen, some scantily clad idiots, their faces impastoed with make-up, foxtrot and tango to the delight of the baying crowd. This is what passes for entertainment, these days. Charlotte would have liked it, he thinks. Anton remembers her rigid schedule of soap operas, her *Changing Rooms* fixation. 'If it was up to you it would be David bloody Attenborough night after night,' she'd sneered at him once. Accusations of cultural snobbery while she leafed through one of her magazines, the trashy ones she liked, with lurid headlines over the featured articles: *Sex-mad Monster Raped Me In Front of Kids!*; *Stepdad Ran Off With Babysitter, Leaving Me With His 100k Debt!* She'd sit at the kitchen table, a cigarette smouldering in the ashtray by her coffee, casually perusing these barbarous accounts, her face blank. 'My little indulgence, Anton,' she'd tell him, whenever he tackled her over it. 'Not doing anyone any harm, is it? My one little weakness.'

A lie, that. There were other weaknesses. He remembers.

He watches the TV with the volume down, and when he hears the scrape of the French windows over the patio paving downstairs, he rises slowly and crosses to the door, taking his time, the negative feelings receding at the prospect of what's to come.

For a moment he stands there, looking down on her as she reads, enjoying this stolen glance at her, before moving backwards with deliberate noise, attracting her attention.

'Anton?' she says, and a thrill goes through him at the sound of his name coming from her lips.

When she asks about the nocturnes, he cannot keep the smirk of satisfaction from rising. And when she steps past him into his house, he breathes in the scent of her, the movement of warm air as she passes, feels the weird impulse to gulp it in.

He keeps the door to the garden open so as not to alarm her. The last thing he needs is for her to feel trapped. She steps into the living room, and he hastily clears away his plate, switches off the telly.

'Sorry about the mess,' he calls, as he carries the plate into the kitchen.

When he comes back into the room, she is gazing around her, eyes drawn up to the lofty ceilings, the cornicing lacy with cobwebs. She runs her hands up and down her upper arms, a mindless gesture of comfort, and offers him a nervous smile.

'I've been wondering about these rooms,' she admits, 'what they looked like. They're very grand, aren't they?'

Her eyes cast upwards again, and it is true that the dimensions are imposing, but he looks at the faded wallpaper, the pall of dust on the wall-sconces, and can think only of how shabby it must all seem.

'I'm afraid I've rather let things go.'

She smiles but doesn't contradict him.

'It's a bit too big for me, to be honest. A single man rattling around in this big old place. These houses were built for families with servants.'

She nods, and he feels awkward, as if suggesting that, living in the servants' quarters, she's beneath him in more ways than one. He could tell her the real truth – that the space makes him uneasy. That he cannot relax in it. Years spent in a cell, his whole life shrunk to an area less than half the size of this room, has made it impossible for him now to feel comfortable within his cavernous house. The way it catches sounds. The gloom of shadows that slide along the wall and clot in corners. And always Charlotte's voice brushing against him. Even now, he can hear her: '*Up to your old tricks again, Anton? Naughty boy!*'

He doesn't want to tell her about his years in a cell although he knows he should – that she will find out in the end. In the park, when he'd suggested the nocturnes, he'd seen the flash of fear in her eyes and, for one horrible moment, he'd felt sure she'd discovered the truth about his past. But now, watching as she steps towards the mantelpiece, raising a hand to touch the candle-holders – Waterford Crystal, dull with dust – he realizes she doesn't know anything of what happened. For the time being, he is safe.

'My wife's,' he explains. 'She was quite a fan.'

He'd bought them for Charlotte – he cannot remember the occasion. A birthday or anniversary, or a gift to say he was sorry.

Behind Leah, in a corner of the room, a glass-fronted cabinet displays the collection of cut glass – the decanters and glasses, the jugs and bowls. Some he'd won in golf tournaments; others had been wedding gifts. He watches Leah studying them now.

'They remind me of home,' she says.

'Oh?'

'My mother shares your wife's taste.'

'And where is home?'

She tells him, and he nods, picturing the small mid-lands town with its single main street dotted with pubs and betting shops, a church rising severely at one end. One of those depressingly grim places where everyone knows everyone else's business; a place you'd drive through with a groan of relief that you didn't have to live there.

'When did you leave?' he asks.

He is surprised when she says: 'I was fifteen. I moved up to Dublin. The schools were better here. I lived with my aunt.'

Something in the way she says it makes him study her closely – her answer feels too practised. And he cannot help but think of his own children. Like Leah, shipped out to an aunt to be brought up. The thought is painful and he pushes it aside.

'And your family?'

'My parents are still there. My father retired some years back – his health's not great. My mother is still active, though. She helps out in the local nursing home, a mem-ber of the bridge club, that kind of thing.'

'Brothers and sisters?'

'No. Just me.'

'An only child, like myself.'

He might have guessed as much. Something in her

solitary nature. The quietness she carries around with her. A beloved only child.

He wonders at how they let her go so young. What was it that drove her away? 'It must have been hard for them, losing you at that age.'

She shrugs, rubs her arms again, this time more vigorously. A nerve touched, he can tell.

'I went to boarding school,' he tells her. 'Sent away when I was twelve. For the first few years I was desperately unhappy but I felt I couldn't show it. That it would be letting my parents down. It was a good school and they'd sacrificed so much to send me there. How could I tell them I was unhappy?'

'What did you do?'

'I kept my head down and got on with it. And by the end, I was happy enough.' He smiles at her with sympathy. 'Not always easy, is it?'

'No,' she says, in that quiet, cautious manner, her eyes sliding back towards the mantelpiece.

'Who's this?' she asks, plucking a photograph of Cassandra from behind one of the candlesticks.

'My daughter,' he tells her. 'One of her baby snaps.'

'She's cute,' Leah says, and he nods.

'Lives in Australia now. She's a nurse, I believe.'

'You believe?'

He shrugs, looks down bashfully. 'I'm afraid my Cassandra is not one for keeping in touch with her old man.'

When he looks up, she is giving him a thoughtful stare, as if considering whether or not to press him on the subject. Then, as if deeming it too delicate, she says: 'Cassandra. That's an unusual name.'

'After the Trojan princess. Actually, when she was born, I wanted to call her Iphigenia, but Charlotte would have none of that.'

Her smile is quizzical, confused, so he explains: 'Iphigenia was the daughter of King Agamemnon and Queen Clytemnestra. She appears as the Greeks prepare for war with Troy. A sacred deer, accidentally killed, enrages the goddess Artemis, who demands that Agamemnon sacrifice Iphigenia to make amends.'

'And does he?'

'In some accounts, yes, to the abiding murderous rage of her mother. In other accounts, she is spared and becomes the goddess Hecate. Others again report her to survive and be awarded in marriage to the great hero, Achilles.'

'Quite different fates,' she remarks, 'depending on which is true.'

'Which you believe,' he corrects her. 'So often in life, everything hangs on what you choose to believe.'

He has spoken with too much conviction, allowing his personal feelings to creep into his voice. Now is not the time, he thinks. Instead, he brightens, and says: 'So, the nocturnes?'

He pulls back the dividing doors, hears the clunk and roll of the ancient mechanism creaking to life, and reveals the front room, with its marble fireplace, the walnut dining-table and chairs, the glazed bookcases with their antique volumes bound in leather and, in the bay window, the piano.

'Oh, how lovely,' she says, with genuine feeling, and she moves past him into the room, her eyes fixed on the instrument.

He watches as she goes to it, touches it tentatively, then trails her hand along it, caressing it. He feels a shimmer of nerves run up and down his spine, as if it were his tired body the hand was stroking. All this time, he's been telling himself that it's her companionship he craves. But this reaction surprises him. For the first time his hopes seem to extend beyond friendship, the glimmer of an old want stirring to life.

'I used to dream of having a piano like this,' she admits, her voice still dreamy, her gaze on the instrument, not on him. 'I used to love playing in competitions, because it meant I got to play on a grand piano. I remember how magical it felt.'

'You played competitively?'

'When I was younger, I used to think one day I might be a professional musician.' She flashes him an embarrassed smile. 'Pretty naive, hmm?'

'Not at all. I'm sure you're very talented.'

She shakes her head in vigorous dismissal. 'I'm not. And even if I was . . .'

'What?'

'It takes a sort of courage to pursue a career like that. To be able to put yourself out there . . . And I just don't have it. I lack the bravery, the drive.'

'You're shy,' he says softly, and is gratified by the blush it brings to her cheeks. 'Why don't you try it out?' he asks, indicating the piano, witnessing her hesitation, but alive to the desire within her, the temptation.

'No. I couldn't.'

'Please,' he says, more forcefully. 'I insist.'

He comes to her, draws out the spindly-legged piano

stool, and taking hold of Leah's shoulders he guides her into place. It's a risk, touching her like this, but she doesn't object and he feels a little tic of pleasure, a flare of optimism.

When her hands go to the piano, he watches, taking in the long pale fingers, the narrow wrists. The skin on her upper arms is slightly mottled, and it endears her to him, makes her flesh seem more real, more alive. He remains standing behind her so he cannot see the expression on her face as she begins to play, his eyes remaining fixed on the bend of her neck beneath the dark hair that she has tied up. Slender. The stem of a flower.

The music that comes from the piano is simple and slow, an old folk tune, a ballad – melodic and plain. A sweet sound, but she is right about her lack of talent. Nothing showy or bravura about her performance. Her reticence comes through in her playing, and yet for him it is perfect. It is what he needs. A salve to all he has endured.

He closes his eyes, gives himself over to the music. He thinks of the lie he had told about the nocturnes. Charlotte wouldn't have been caught dead playing such pieces. The only tunes she ever played came straight from the Andrew Lloyd Webber songbook – bashing out 'Memory' day after day just to torment him. But this . . .

To have her in his home, to hear music filling this room after all the silence, the emptiness . . . He opens his eyes now, looks at the darkness of her hair piled loosely at her crown, so close now he can see the soft down on the back of her neck, the nub of bone at the top of her spine. If he put out his hand, he could touch it.

A crash from below.

The music stops.

'What was that?' she asks.

He holds his breath, startled, confused.

She gasps. 'Matthew!' she cries, and she's off the stool, racing towards the door.

He stands there, leaning against the piano, feeling the weight of his flesh, his fast-beating heart, while from outside comes a hammering, her voice raised in alarm. Slowly, he moves to the back of the house, warily takes a step outside.

She's down on the patio, banging against the glass panes with the flat of her hand, shouting the boy's name over and over.

'Please, Mattie, come to the door. Please let me in.'

Desperation in her voice.

She looks up and sees Anton, her face drawn and tight with anxiety.

'He's locked me out,' she explains, with urgency. 'Do you have a spare key?'

'I might. Let me look.'

He goes back inside, stands in his kitchen for a moment, thinking. His dinner plate is still in the sink. Slowly, he scrapes it into the bin, slots it into the dishwasher, considers the options while the banging goes on outside. When she comes up the steps and into the house, he adopts an expression of concern.

'I've looked through the drawers for a key, Leah. I'm so sorry, but I cannot find one anywhere.'

The hopeful look on her face falls, replaced by deep anxiety.

'Don't worry, dear. I'm sure it's just a little game he's playing. He'll let you back in soon.'

'What if something happens to him? I'm supposed to be minding him.'

Her hand goes to her head, and she stares around unseeing.

'He'll be fine.'

'What if he's not? What if he hurts himself? Children do.'

'If you're worried, why don't you call Jake? I'm sure he'd come back and –'

'No, you don't understand. He trusted me with the boy when he shouldn't have. I should have told him. I should have explained.'

He makes soothing noises, but inside his interest has sparked to life. Something she's been keeping from the boyfriend – a secret.

All her grace is gone, in its stead this rigid panic. She is pacing the room now, mumbling something about being unreliable, incapable. Bad luck follows her, she mutters. It wasn't safe, she knew it wasn't. Her guard was down, she says, otherwise she would never have agreed –

She stops then, points to the door beneath the stairs, which stands ajar.

'That door,' she says, alighting on the word with new hope. 'Does it lead downstairs?'

'Yes, but –'

She hurries into the hallway, Anton following. He sees her pause, a moment's hesitation, before she pulls the door back and plunges down the steps into the darkness. He can hear her down there, banging at the inner door, fiddling with the lock, calling the boy's name over and over. Slowly now, he comes to stand in the doorway, watching.

He can hear voices in his head.

Mark: '*You will watch yourself, won't you, Dad? You won't do anything . . . stupid?*'

Nigel, when they parted ways at the hotel: '*Stay out of trouble, Anton. You don't want to end up back here.*'

Jim Buckley, his parole officer: '*Be good now.*'

But there she is, at the bottom of the stairs, dimly lit, frightened. He could close the door now and she would be trapped, like a butterfly in a jar. For a moment he stands there, wavering, horrified by the thoughts that have come to him, that he might become the monster they always claimed him to be.

But then she turns her face up to him, and something inside him falters.

When she comes up the steps towards him, his knuckles whiten, his grip on the door tightening. A split-second decision, and he catches the look in her eye – the brief realization of all the danger he poses. At the last second he stands aside so she can hurry past. Powered by an urgency he can attribute only to fear, she flings wide the door and then she's outside, down the front steps, lost to him.

His heart is a trapped bird in his chest, fluttering wildly against his ribs. He sinks back against the wall, feeling faint and light-headed. All these years – the caution that has held him in check, abandoned in a fleeting instance.

Through the open front door, sunlight falls on to the carpet, too bright, searing against the headache that has roared to life. There are voices outside, and the sound of a dog barking. Impelled by some confusion inside him, he moves towards the sounds, hears them grow louder.

Outside the sunlight burns his eyeballs. He looks down over the iron railing that flanks the steps, sees the swish of a dog's tail. Two women are standing in the small clearing by the door, working at the lock. Feeling his shadow cast over them, they look up.

Two faces. Both familiar. His heart kicks with sudden fright.

'It's all right, Anton,' Leah tells him. 'We've found the key.'

But Anton is not looking at her. He's looking at the other face turned up to him, feels the shake start in his hands, the surge in agitation. All this time. All these years. Hair brightly coloured. The angle of her head, poised and still. Those pale eyes fixed and steady, avid yet imperious, gazing up at him like a cat.

Hilary.

Her voice cracks through the white noise that fills his head. 'Hello, Anton,' she says.

II

Hilary

Hilary waits until she is past the railings before breaking into a run. The dog, confused by the sudden change in tempo, reacts with enthusiasm, bounding forward, pulling Hilary with her. Crossing the road, her heart pounding high in her chest, she feels the breath catching in her throat as she reaches her house. Her hand shakes as she presses the key into the lock.

She pushes through the front door, hastily shutting it behind her. Mona circles Greg's legs as he emerges from the kitchen.

'Nice walk?' he asks her.

She forces a smile and a nod, moves past him to hang the lead on its hook, hears her voice emerging from her throat to say: 'I bumped into that young woman who's just moved in down the street – Leah. She was locked out of the flat, panicking because of the little boy alone inside. Then I remembered about the key that was hidden outside when we lived there. Well, it was still under that rock.'

'Really.'

'Yes! A little rusty, but it still works.'

'You'd think they'd have had the locks changed since.'

'I know. But she got in. And she was very grateful. Poor

thing, worrying herself sick over the child. And all the time he was fast asleep in his room!'

It's amazing to her how normal she sounds. As if nothing had happened.

'Did you go inside?' Greg asks, something strained in his voice.

'Just for a minute. I didn't stay. She was a bit flustered.'

He stands there, as if waiting for something.

'Think I'll have a shower,' she says then. 'I'm all hot and sticky.'

Greg says, 'Okey-dokey,' and she can feel him watching her as she runs up the stairs.

In the bathroom, she stands with her back to the tiled wall, listens to the slam of the fridge door downstairs in the kitchen, Mona's cheerful yelp as Greg fixes her dinner. She thinks of what just happened, remembers the words she spoke to that woman. 'I feel it my duty to tell you, dear . . .' God, had she really said that? The look in her eyes, the way they had widened with horror and then disbelief. 'It can't be true,' Leah had actually said, and a tremble of unexpected anger had quivered under Hilary's skin.

'Look it up, if you don't believe me,' she had countered, flashing a smile to take any malice from the words.

Wife-killer, she had called him, still thinking of how he had looked at her, how he had hastily withdrawn into his house.

Quickly, she sheds her clothes, and turns the shower to full power. It is as if a rash has broken out all over her body, as if it has wormed its way beneath the layers of skin. She feels the itch communicating itself through her flesh and bones. The jets on her face sting. She keeps her eyes closed and stands perfectly still, enduring it.

And as she stands there, her thoughts leave her body and travel back. Back to the heat of another summer.

'*I came to say I'm sorry.*'

She had stayed when they put her dog to sleep. In a room at the vet's – not the usual surgery. A small room, with just an examining couch for the dog and a chair for the owner. She had stroked Bella's soft muzzle and wondered how many animals' lives had been extinguished in this room. How many other people's hearts had been broken there?

Charlotte had insisted upon it. Hilary remembers the shrill vehemence of the woman, the wild flight of her fury.

'Your bloody dog tried to savage my son!'

Still Hilary had resisted. It was a little nip. A mild tussle in the garden. The boy had been driving poor Bella crazy with a stick. She had held on for as long as she could.

'That child's arm,' Greg eventually said, driven to exasperation. 'We have no choice, Hilary. She must be put down.'

After two days of fighting it, refusing to have the dog destroyed, finally she had succumbed. She recalls now how Bella's heavy head had lowered to the black rubber surface of the table, her features more droopy, her eyes more mournful than Hilary could ever remember them being. A low whinnying sound emerged from the dog's throat, and Hilary put her arms around the warm body, rested her face against Bella's velvet ears, and something ruptured deep inside her.

Afterwards, she felt numb. Greg made the arrangements with the vet for disposal while Hilary sat in the car and waited. He was kind to her on the journey home, speaking words of sympathy and reassurance but it all washed over her. She was miles away, unreachable. And when the car pulled up at the kerb, and she got out, the first thing she heard was Charlotte Woodbury laughing.

Hilary stood stock still in the street and looked up. An upstairs window in the Woodburys' house was open. She could see Charlotte up there, standing with the phone held to her face, the other hand clutching a lit cigarette, talking and laughing as if nothing had happened. As if only two days before she hadn't stood on Hilary's doorstep, shaking with rage, thrusting her little boy's bleeding arm forwards, spouting accusations, demanding that the dog be destroyed.

Hilary might have got over it, if it hadn't been for that laughter.

That was a Saturday, and when Monday morning came around, she rang the school and informed them that her dog had died so she wouldn't be coming in. She read the headmistress's disapproval in the brief pause before she responded, but Hilary didn't care. She had gone beyond that. The depression that came over her was worse than anything she had experienced before. Years later, she would pay for a therapist to tell her that the grief suppressed with each miscarriage had come gushing upwards at the death of her beloved pet. But at the time all she could do was walk around the rooms of the basement flat, feeling something clawing at her insides, the dreadful injustice of it, the senseless waste. It was a silent internal kind of grief, one she couldn't communicate to or share with Greg, who was at a loss as to how he could help her.

Then one day, late into the week after Bella's death, Hilary stood at the French windows, watching the Woodbury kids outside in the garden. An inflatable paddling pool had been filled with water, and the little boy and girl were in their swimming costumes, kicking water at each other and squealing with delight. Nearby, their father stood with a garden hose, laughing and spraying them as they jumped and splashed. The way the sun hit the water, the obvious joy of the children – it was such a perfect scene. Love and summer. Happiness and innocence. It rose up at Hilary, like a rebuke, and the thing that had ruptured inside her flew to the surface. She let out a scream full of wildness and rage and despair, bent double with the force of all that emotion.

The children didn't hear. They kept on laughing and playing. But their father looked around. She saw his face, the smile falling away, replaced by something more thoughtful and grave.

She had drawn away and lain down on the couch, sobbing so loudly she almost didn't hear the tapping at the door.

'I came to say I'm sorry.'

There he was, standing beyond the French windows. His low voice, his gentle eyes.

Caustic words backed up inside her, questions snapping about his bitch of a wife, and whether she was sorry too. But there was something so simple and plain about his presence there, something genuine in his offer of sympathy, that those bitter feelings slid away. She turned from him, leaving the door open for him to follow, and went to the kitchen.

It was dark and cool back there, shadows cast by the house and the trees outside.

'It was a hard thing to ask of you,' he said, 'and I'm sorry.'

Outside, the children's voices continued to rise. Hilary wondered, vaguely, who was watching them while their father was with her. She brushed the tears from her cheek and turned to him.

'Did you ever have a pet?' she asked, and he shook his head. Immediately, she felt embarrassed, looked down at her bare feet, the dirty lino beneath them. 'You must think I'm mad,' she said.

'I know what it is to love,' was his reply.

She met his gaze and had to chew her lip to stop the tears returning. A shriek from outside drew their gaze to the window for an instant, and when she looked back he was staring at her again. It was peculiar, being there with him. She felt calmer than she had all week.

'I can't have children,' she told him. It seemed appropriate to share this information. The childish voices in the garden were voluble, a chattering stream, as if they were right there outside the window. She needed to impart this information so he would understand just what Bella had meant to her. So that he would comprehend the depth of her loss.

She could see from the expression crossing his face that he did.

'Oh, Hilary,' he said, and a jolt went through her to hear him say her name. A pleasurable ripple beneath her skin.

She smiled at him. He would go back to the children

he'd left unattended and she would feel — because of his visit — a little better.

But he crossed the room to her and touched his lips to hers.

His mouth felt smooth and dry. She didn't draw away, didn't express surprise or indignation. Instead she felt compelled to wait, and when she felt his mouth opening to hers, his hands moving to her hips, something leapt inside her, the thump of her heart, as if it had suddenly been brought to life. Outside the children screamed and the sun beat down, but there in the kitchen it was quiet and still, every fibre of her being concentrated on the touch of his hand, the press of his body against hers, this contact at once intimate and strange. She knew it was wrong. She knew she didn't want it to stop.

She forgot about Greg. She forgot about the children outside. She even forgot about the grief that had been ravaging her. All of it fell away as he leant into her, the kiss going on and on, like a long, slow, cool drink of water on a hot, hot day. Nothing else mattered. They knew so little about each other beyond the bitter skirmish with his wife. And yet it was as if, in that moment, they were one person.

In her whole life, nothing has rent her heart as much as what happened that summer.

And now he is back. She thinks of him leaning over the railings, looking down at them, the flash of recognition when his eyes had locked on hers. The sudden dizziness she had felt at being in his orbit once more, after all these years . . .

'Why? What did he do?' Leah had asked, and Hilary

133

had watched her eyes widening with horror as she had told her of his crime.

White-faced and silent, she had stared in amazement, and Hilary had felt a sharp twinge of guilt.

Now she pushes it away. It's important that she remains patient. She will not lose control again. If she holds on a little longer, if she sticks to the plan, nothing will come between them.

Hilary stands under the shower, allowing these thoughts and memories to pour down through her until the hot water cools and eventually turns cold.

July

12

Leah

Leah waits in the car. She wishes Jake would hurry, feeling conspicuous and uneasy out here on her own.

The window is rolled down but there's no air wafting through. Heat shimmers over the bonnet, making the vista beyond it wavy and blurred. There hasn't been rain for weeks, and the grass of the field, around which the housing estate sprawls, is tawny and bald. A gang of boys shoot past on bicycles, their wheels kicking up dust. They peer through the window at her and hoot with laughter.

Leah shifts in her seat, and watches them pass. The cotton of her skirt sticks to the underside of her legs. In a garden a few doors down, two women are sunbathing, rolls of fat beneath their bikini-tops, cans of Budweiser in their hands. She glances at the white uPVC door that had shut behind Jake, the house swallowing him. Net curtains obscure the windows. Paint blisters on the walls outside. In the small garden, there's a set of miniature goalposts, two bins stuffed so full the lids won't close. It's hard for her to imagine that Jake once lived here. There was a time when he called that house his home. A place where he built a whole other life without her – Jake and Jenna, fresh from their summer romance, scrabbling to adapt to the news of a baby on the way. Leah looks at the bins, imagines she can smell the refuse from here. Putrefaction. Filth. Her stomach turns.

Her sensitivity to smells and tastes has grown stronger with each week. Looking down at her waistline beneath the seatbelt, she pinches the band of thickened flesh between her thumb and index finger. It astonishes her, the rapid advance of her pregnancy, changes discernible on an almost daily basis. That morning, she had been woken by the press of her bladder, as if she had downed a few pints before retiring for the night. And several times in the office that week she had felt so overcome with weariness that she might have lain down on the floor beneath her desk and fallen fast asleep.

She hasn't told anyone yet about the baby. None of the girls in the office know, or her old school friends, with whom she has kept in touch sporadically. Definitely not her parents – she cannot begin to think how she will handle that conversation. Briefly, Leah wonders whether Jake is telling Jenna. Perhaps that is the reason he is taking so long. But she knows he won't. They have agreed to keep it a secret, just between the two of them, at least until the first trimester has passed. Thinking of Jake alone in there with his ex inspires some anxiety within her, even though she knows there is nothing to be fearful of. On the calendar of her phone she has marked in the date of her first hospital appointment – less than four weeks from now. A date she leans towards, impatient, excited. But, until then, she is reliant on websites for information, loitering in chatrooms, pitting her own symptoms against the experiences of others.

The sun is getting high in the sky and, while she waits

for Jake, she takes out her phone, looking to google the latest symptom. Is it normal to feel this level of exhaustion so early in her pregnancy? And the weight she is putting on – surely it's not possible for her to start showing yet. But when she opens the browser on her phone, she's confronted with the results of a previous search – Anton's full name slotted in the search engine. In the early hours of the morning, when she couldn't sleep, her thoughts had turned once again to what Hilary had told her. The occupant of the house upstairs, his troubled history. Her thumb hovers over the screen.

She can still feel it – the shock of that word: *killer.* The sour plunge it brought about in her tummy. Sitting in the car, turning the word over in her head, she thinks of Anton, the soft timbre of his voice, the gentleness of his expression, and tries to marry this image of him with her recently acquired knowledge of his violent history. It seems incongruous. For the past two weeks, she has kept returning to the facts, trying to parse them to make sense of what she's learnt, but still she can't quite believe it. Two weeks of careful avoidance, the attendant guilt deepening every time she hears the creak of a floorboard overhead or catches the scent of cigarette smoke on the air through the open French windows.

In the evenings, sometimes, she can hear him out there in the garden, waiting for her. And yesterday a letter was pushed under the door.

There are many different versions of the truth. Just because something is reported doesn't make it fact. Remember our conversation about Agamemnon and Iphigenia? Was she

139

sacrificed for the sacred deer or did she change into a goddess?
Different accounts, different outcomes. What matters is what you
choose to believe. I did not do that of which I am accused . . .

Her head hurts thinking about it. She looks at the list of
Google results, the lives of all the other Anton Woodburys
scattered around the world. Tentatively she scrolls down the
page until she finds him. She selects a result, clicks on it.

EVENING HERALD
25 MAY 2000

Behind Façade of Happy Marriage Was Violence and Betrayal

To the casual observer, Anton Woodbury and his wife Charlotte had it all.

He was 41, a successful businessman, and she was six years
his junior, attractive and sociable. They lived with their two
young children in a plush Victorian terraced house in Dublin's
upmarket Dún Laoghaire.

Neighbours included former Attorney General N_____,
and the acclaimed theatre director D_____.

But the social life, the material success and veneer of happiness were merely a façade concealing a 'shell marriage', full of
bitter recriminations, infidelities and violent rows.

In the early hours of 2 August last year, it also turned into a
recipe for murder.

Leah reads on, riveted, and as she reads, the brightness
of her disbelief begins to cloud, as the details emerge in

print before her eyes: the marriage gone awry, the terrible revenge, all of it enacted in the rooms above her home. Her thoughts go to that afternoon when he had brought her upstairs. She remembers the hallowed sense of reverence she had felt, seated at that piano, the smooth coolness of the keys beneath her fingertips. Hard now to think of those rooms, knowing the dark history held within them. A woman met a violent death there. Another image comes to her: she is standing at the bottom of the stairs, pushing her weight against the door, hammering and calling to Matthew to open it. And when she glanced back up the stairs, there was Anton looking down. His expression was lost to her – he was a silhouette against the sunlit hall beyond. But for just a second or two she had sensed it – some dark hesitation within him – and in that moment, she had felt afraid.

The door to the house opens. Leah switches off the screen of her phone, puts it away. She watches Matthew come out, Jake behind him carrying his bag. Jenna stands on the doorstep, watching them leave. She is small, with short-cropped hair, but there is nothing boyish about her. Leah does a quick appraisal: white T-shirt, denim cut-offs, tennis shoes, tanned limbs. It's easy to see why Jake had fallen for her. An involuntary spasm of envy passes through Leah, of which she feels immediately ashamed.

She raises her hand to wave, but Jenna is already withdrawing back into the house. The white plastic door closes firmly. Leah sits there, feeling the missed opportunity. Perhaps she should have gone inside with Jake.

'Hey there!' she says to Matthew, craning around to smile at him as he climbs into the back seat.

'Hiya.' He looks flushed, anxious to get going.

'You got everything?'

'Yep.'

'Everything okay?' she asks Jake, as he shuts the driver's door. The muscles of his face look stretched and tight.

'Yeah, fine.' He buckles his seatbelt. In the back, Matthew does the same.

'You sure?'

'Let's just get home and eat.'

He starts the engine, rolls the windows fully down. Hot air buffets the back of Leah's head, and as the car pulls away, one of the boys who has been circling on his bike tosses a can at the vehicle. They feel the metallic clink of the impact and Jake sticks his head out of the window. 'Get fucked, you little prick!'

And then he draws his head back in through the window, slams his foot on the accelerator – Leah's hands grip the seat beneath her – and the car roars away.

She waits until they are home, lunch finished, the dishes put away, before she asks him.

'Did something happen?' They are in Matthew's bedroom where Jake is painting the walls a bright green. Leah has brought in pints of iced water, and she holds hers against her cheek. 'With Jenna,' she nudges him. 'You seemed tense afterwards.'

He drains his glass, puts it on the floor next to him, says nothing.

Sometimes Leah finds it hard to navigate Jake's moods. When they had first met, he seemed exuberant, permanently riding along on a wave of optimism. But in these past weeks, since they have moved in together, she has noticed a change in him. A circumspection, a pensive dissociation, that she finds difficult to penetrate.

After a moment, he puts the paint-roller down on the tray, sighs and raises his face to meet her gaze. Something troubled and wary lies behind his expression.

'She wants to move back to Aberdeen, to her parents. She says she's going to take Matthew with her.'

He scratches his head, and she feels a surge of protective love go through her at his obvious distress and confusion. She wants to go to him, offer comfort and reassurance, but anxiety holds her back. That side of his life is threaded with complications, too delicate and strained for her to pull at. Whenever Leah broaches the subject of Jenna, which is not often, she feels the enormous distance opening between her and Jake. An insurmountable wall.

'Is she serious?'

He shrugs in response, not meeting her eye.

'Why does she want to leave?'

'Come on. You've seen where they live. Would you want to raise your kid there?' He catches her eye now and there's something dry in his look, hardness in his words, that makes her draw back a little.

'Those little shits on their bikes, like a pack of fucking baby wolves. Another couple of years and they're the kids he's going to be hanging out with. These are the gangs he'll be joining. And school's no better. The same mindless thugs. The same slack-jawed indifference to anything as nerdy as education. If he stays there, he doesn't stand a chance.'

He picks up his paint-roller to resume his labour, then

changes his mind. Half-heartedly, he tells her: 'If she takes him to Aberdeen, he'll have a decent home with her parents, some stability, go to a good school.'

She considers this for a moment, weighing her words carefully. 'And what about you?'

'I'd visit, of course. Jenna says I could come whenever I want, stay with them and her folks,' he says unhappily. Adding, without much conviction: 'And with technology, I guess it's easier now than it was. We can FaceTime, or whatever.'

'I suppose it's worth considering as an option,' she says.

In response, he throws down the roller, paint splattering in the tray. 'An option! Yeah. Long-distance parenting. Watching him grow up through a computer screen. Seeing him in the flesh once a month, if I'm lucky. And what happens when this baby comes?' He gestures towards her belly, a quick swatting motion that alarms her, her hand moving instinctively to her tummy. A warning starts in her head. 'Am I just going to shuttle between two countries to see my kids? Jesus!'

He hangs his head, puts a hand to his hair, flattening it forward over his brow, a nervous tic that she's noticed whenever he gets deeply agitated. She can tell somehow that he's on the brink of a decision that does not include her but will affect the course of her life and the baby's. Jake and Jenna are committed parents. But it's a commitment that excludes her, a claim on Jake's heart that she cannot be a part of.

Perhaps he reads her thoughts for he bites his lip and brings his eyes up to hers. 'Sorry,' he says. 'I didn't mean to shout.'

She doesn't respond, just waits, needing something more from him than that.

'I just feel like I failed them, you know?' He gives her a quick searching gaze, then looks away again. 'If only there were a way to keep them here. If I could just earn some decent money, I could help out a bit more financially, so they could move somewhere better. It makes me feel so guilty that you and I are living out here while they're stuck in that fucking ghetto.'

In her head she does silent calculations while the unease grows in her chest. Money is tight enough with the rent, and she has recently started thinking about ways they might save, hoping that someday they'll be in a position to buy a place of their own. There will be crèche fees further down the road, unforeseen childcare costs. She can't see where the money is going to come from, with Jake's working life so precarious.

'It'll be okay,' she says. 'We'll find a way to make things work.'

He turns his attention back to the walls, the uneven spread of green. The inadequacy of her response has disappointed him. She wants to comfort and reassure him but doesn't know how.

'And, anyway,' she goes on, pushing forward optimistically, 'once Ian gets the green light for the show, you guys can start filming, and then things will change. You won't look back.'

He puts down the paint-roller, leans back on his haunches. 'I spoke to Ian,' he says quietly. 'He got the green light.'

'But that's terrific!' she cries, confused by the look that comes over him now. Instead of appearing happy about it, he seems sheepish, almost guilty.

'I didn't get the part,' he tells her.

'What? But you and Ian agreed –'

'I know. But they said they needed a big name or it wouldn't fly. Ian fought for me, but they had him over a barrel.'

'Oh, Jake.'

He shrugs. A rush of anger goes through her, a sharp, needling intuition: *how hard did Ian really fight?*

'He said I could try out for one of the small parts, but I said no.'

'How come?'

'Because it would be humiliating!' he cries, roused to anger. 'Everyone knows that part was meant for me!'

'Why don't you think it over? Talk to Ian –'

'No chance.' And then it comes out – the row they'd had. How he'd told Ian to go fuck himself. Bridges burnt. No going back.

She listens to all this, and feels a kernel of anger inside her. This side of him is new to her: the loss of temper, the shouting. What he has done is stupid and short-sighted. She wishes he could be a bit more mature.

'I don't know what to say,' she tells him, holding back on offering words of comfort, like how there'll be other parts, other chances. His childishness worries her, his petulance. She needs him to be a grown-up.

'There's nothing to say,' he replies, quiet and disconsolate.

A noise above their heads draws his attention – the creak of a pipe, the sound of running water. Jake gets to his feet.

'Where's Matthew?' he asks, urgency in his voice.

He leaves the room and she follows him.

He's calling the boy's name, and distantly, in the garden, she can hear the slam of a ball against a wall.

'Matthew!' Jake shouts, charging out through the French windows and striding into the grass.

Leah stays where she is, watching and listening. From the garden, she can hear the boy yelp as if in pain, Jake's voice saying: 'I told you not to come up here. Why don't you listen to me?'

Upstairs, there is no sound. The tap has stopped. The pipes are still. She imagines Anton standing at the window directly above her, also watching.

Jake has the boy by the arm, draws him back to the patio, and she sees him glancing up at the windows of the house, a glance loaded with irritation and suspicion.

She'd told him about Hilary's revelation. She'd had to. His response had been predictable. Shock. Outrage. He'd even rung Mark, demanding to know if it was true. She can still hear Jake's side of that conversation ringing in her ears: 'I have a kid, Mark! Are you telling me I'm bringing him under the roof of a convicted murderer?' His anger barely controlled, trying to keep the tone civil.

Afterwards, he had put his phone down and looked at her uneasily. 'He claims the guy is innocent. Says it was a wrongful conviction. That the real culprit was an intruder who was never caught.'

'Do you believe that?'

Jake had shrugged. 'He was convicted, wasn't he? They must have had something on him. But one thing I do know for sure,' and he had looked out of their bedroom window to the park, where two more tents had joined the first, the ranks of the homeless building in front of them. 'We can't do anything about it. It's not like we can afford to move out. Not in this city.'

They had left it. And since that phone-call, they haven't spoken about Anton. But she's noticed that neither of them goes into the garden now. Their laundry hangs to dry on clothes racks in their bedroom. And whenever there is movement upstairs, the creak of a floorboard, a dry cough, the spill of coins on to the floor, she sees the tension in Jake's face, the tightening of his jaw.

He brings his son through into the flat now.

'Why can't I?' Matthew demands.

'I've told you already. It's not our garden.'

The boy flops on to the couch, sweat making his hair stick to his brow, his arms folded tightly over his chest.

'You can play your Nintendo.'

'I don't want to.'

'Fine. Then sit there and sulk.'

Jake's phone beeps, and he seizes it from the counter, reads the screen, still tense from their exchange. Leah goes to the fridge, pours a glass of juice for Matthew, who accepts it from her, mumbling a moody 'Thanks.'

'I have to go,' Jake tells her.

'What?'

He mentions the courier company, says some jobs have come up while he hunts around for his bag and helmet. She follows him into the hallway.

'But it's Saturday afternoon.'

'Well, shit, Leah,' he snaps. 'We need the money, don't we?'

Hurt rises in her chest. Cut by his words, she feels unnerved by a niggling doubt. 'I didn't mean for this to happen, you know,' she tells him.

He clips on his helmet. 'I know.'

'You are happy about the baby, aren't you?' she asks.

His eyes fly across her face. Then he goes to her, instantly remorseful, and puts his arms around her. 'Of course I'm happy about the baby,' he murmurs. 'Don't ever think otherwise.'

She stays in his arms for a moment, trying to believe him.

He draws back and looks into her eyes, strokes her face lightly with his fingertips. 'We'll find a way to make all of this work,' he tells her. 'I promise.'

After Jake leaves, she sits on the couch with Matthew. On the table-top in front of them *Finding Dory* plays on the laptop. In recent days, the little boy has started to relax more around her. He watches the screen with lazy eyes, half leaning against her, tired, while Leah flicks through her phone.

The browser is still open with the results of her previous search, and now she scrolls through them until she finds an article from the time of Anton's trial. Opening it, she scans the headline, but her attention is caught by a photograph of Charlotte posted beneath the by-line. A colour picture, it shows a woman whose reddish dark hair is threaded with coppery streaks and carefully done, as if for an occasion. Red lipstick to match the red top she wears, a silver heart on a chain around her neck. She gazes into the camera, clear-eyed beneath slender brows, something distant and vague in the way she smiles. Dreamy. Distracted. Everything Leah knows about this woman she has learnt from Anton, whose account can no longer be trusted.

What were you like? she wonders, examining the face on the screen. Brown eyes, heavily lashed. How soon after this picture was taken was she killed? And did she have any idea, any inkling at all, of the violence that was coming?

She was murdered in the kitchen, according to the accounts Leah has read, stabbed to death. Leah cannot imagine Anton doing such a thing, although it is all there in black and white, a conviction and sentence, no appeal. She thinks of the time she has spent with him, the conversations they have had. His presence had felt reassuring, not threatening. She had perceived him to be a kind, lonely man, but more than that, she had felt he understood something about her that she could not easily explain to others.

'Is that you?' Matthew asks, and she glances down at him.

He's peering across her at the picture on her phone.

'Don't be silly,' she says, laughing lightly, but he peers more closely and shrugs.

'It looks like you,' he states, then turns his attention back to the laptop.

Leah examines the picture now, in a different light. The round curve of Charlotte's face, the set of her eyes. The long bow of her smile. A jolt goes through her as she realizes the boy is right. That dreamy expression. Viewed from a certain angle, the resemblance is uncanny.

13

Hilary

'You look nice,' Greg says.

Hilary is just coming in from the garden, her secateurs in one hand, some freshly cut snapdragons in the other. Leah and Jake are due at any minute. She wipes her feet on the mat, then moves to the sink.

'Thank you,' she says, laying down the flowers to fill a vase with water.

She can feel him looking, knows he is taking note of the silver strappy sandals she is wearing, and her new dress – a sedate navy sundress with pleats in the skirt. More sober than her usual colourful outfits but she has noticed that Leah wears simple monochrome, muted shades, and doesn't want to appear garish in the young woman's eyes. At her throat is the necklace Greg had bought for her one Christmas in Weir's – a silver chain with a little pendant heart. She'd picked it out herself. Charlotte had worn something similar.

Greg hovers by the doorway, his hands in his pockets. Glancing at him as she strips off her gardening gloves, she notes that he, too, has changed for the occasion. She takes in the pressed navy chinos and crisp white shirt he is wearing with approval.

For over a year now, Hilary and Greg have occupied

separate bedrooms. It was not something discussed or agreed upon, more an arrangement that came about by chance. A winter flu that turned into a prolonged chest infection had kept Greg awake night after night for weeks, hunched forward as coughing racked his lungs. It was his own idea to remove himself from the marital bed and take the spare room at the back. Hilary didn't object, or suggest he return once his cough had finally disappeared. One afternoon, she had looked in his wardrobe to find it emptied of his possessions and felt a curious finality in the arrangement. A vital change to their marriage executed without a single word spoken on the subject.

It had pained her a little, but the hurt didn't run deep and was soon forgotten. It was natural, she supposed, in the course of a long marriage that eventually that side of things would come to an end. There was an honesty about it, and a relief, to acknowledge – tacitly – that their relationship was more companionable than anything else. It didn't mean she didn't care about him any longer. She still loved him, in her own way. It was a practical step – and Hilary prides herself on being a practical person. Besides, it will make things easier in the long run. Especially now, with Anton's return and what that means for all three of them.

Outside in the garden, the round table is covered with a bright printed cloth and set for four, the Newbridge silverware catching the sunlight, knives shining like cutlasses. She slips the snapdragons into their vase, and turns to take them outdoors, then notes the preoccupied look on Greg's face.

'Everything all right?' she asks, and his eyes flicker towards her.

'An email from Cormac,' he says, referring to his publisher. 'They've heard back from RTÉ.'

'Oh?' she asks hopefully.

'They've passed.'

'Oh, Greg.'

'So have TV3. And Newstalk.'

She puts the vase on the counter and moves towards him. He stands there while she wraps her arms around him, but makes no attempt to take his hands from his pockets and reciprocate the hug.

'That's it,' he says softly. 'Zero publicity.'

'Not zero,' she corrects him, drawing back so her eyes can scour his face. 'You've that *Liffey Sound* interview next week.'

'Community radio doesn't count.'

'And you've the short story in the *RTÉ Guide*.'

'No one reads the stories, Hil. They just get the *Guide* for the celebrity gossip and the TV listings.'

'That's not true. And, anyway,' she says, moving on swiftly, 'it's the reviews that count, and you can be damned sure they'll be good ones. The book is wonderful.'

His head is tilted to one side, giving her a sad little smile. 'You're very loyal, Hil,' he says. 'I don't know what I'd do without you.'

She feels a short stabbing pain in her chest, disturbed by this remark and all the layers within it. She rubs his arm briskly and goes back to her flowers. 'They'll be here any minute.'

'Yes.'

'You can carve the ham, if you like.'

'Right-ho,' he says, in a flat voice, and she carries the vase of flowers out into the garden.

Greg has mown the lawn and the dog is lying in the shade of the rhododendron. At the back of the garden, the hydrangeas are taking over. The rosebushes look a little ragged and the mini-fuchsia has failed to flower again. She wishes Greg would just submit to her suggestions and get a landscape gardener in to dig it all up and plant it anew. It baffles her that he is dead-set against the notion of getting help in the garden yet grumbles any time she prods him to tidy it up. But that is a dilemma for another day.

A warm breeze is ruffling the skirt of the tablecloth. She smooths the fabric, places the vase at the centre, straightens the cutlery and tucks the napkins under the plates, then stands back, pleased with the scene she surveys. As pleased as she can be with that word lodged in her heart.

Loyal. Is that really what he thinks of her? It's true that she has stayed with him. That she held on in the immediate wake of the storm that blew the roof off their marriage, until the days turned to years, birthdays and anniversaries passing so quickly she hardly noticed the time. But sharing a home, sharing a life, taking an interest in the other person, looking out for them – it isn't everything. It doesn't tell the full story. For the truth is she has been waiting, all these years, keeping things ticking over, until the day would come. And now that day is almost upon them, it makes her wonder at his use of that word. *Loyal.* Spoken innocently enough, but the way he had held her gaze made her distrust it.

'They're here,' he calls, from inside the kitchen.

She puts these thoughts aside and goes in to greet them.

'So, come on, then, tell us,' Jake says. 'What actually happened?'

It is late in the afternoon. The food has been eaten, the plates cleared away, and Greg has gone into the kitchen to fetch another bottle of wine from the fridge. In the grass nearby, the little boy lies on his tummy, building up a mound of earth and stones – a bug hotel, he calls it. He's banging it now with a trowel he's alighted upon, savagely beating down the earth, sending little flecks of muck flying. Mona lies in the shade of the tree, half watching the boy with wary interest.

'What do you mean?' Hilary asks, smiling politely, but she knows full well what he means.

'Anton and his wife. I have to know. Is it true he stabbed her in the kitchen?'

'Yes. It's true,' she says, draining the end of her glass just as Greg emerges from the house with the fresh bottle.

'But why?'

She shrugs, unease cutting through the soporific effects of the food, the wine, the heat from the sun.

'But you knew them, right? You were living there at the time it happened, so you must have had some idea, surely.'

Wine has loosened Jake's tongue. When he first came in and sat down he had been all nervous affability. After the food and the wine, which he has been quickly imbibing, he slipped down in his chair, his grin has grown wider, his talk looser and more confident. He's wearing long khaki shorts and a T-shirt emblazoned with a still from the movie *Jaws*. Hilary glances down, notes the tiny blond hairs furring his legs, glinting in the late-afternoon sun.

'Actually,' Greg says, 'we'd just moved out of the flat when Charlotte . . . when it happened.'

'Oh?'

'A few days before, if I remember correctly.'

Hilary watches her husband carefully, notes the manner of his speech — quiet, thoughtful, precise. He pours wine into the three empty glasses. Leah is the only one of them not drinking. Pregnant, Hilary suspects. She casts her eyes over the younger woman — the green print dress, the demure ballet flats, her figure still svelte, no pregnancy showing. Throughout the lunch, as her partner has become ever more garrulous, Leah has remained polite, elusive, reticent. Hilary feels a sudden push of desire to see her lose her cool. To see that pale skin flushed with temper. Yes, she would like that.

Hilary invited Leah and Jake for lunch because she felt guilty. At least, that was what she told Greg, and it was partly true. The look on the young woman's face when Hilary broke the news to her about Anton's history — the shock registering in her eyes, the blood draining from her cheeks — had caused a sharp twinge of regret within her. She almost felt ashamed for revealing it. But, if she's honest with herself, Hilary knows the real reason for her revelation was not to inform or protect the woman. Rather, it was the reaction to a spike of resentment — a little flare of jealous anger.

'But what were they like?' Jake persists. 'I mean, were they at each other's throats all the time? Were there violent rows?'

'No,' Greg answers. 'I mean, there was the odd tiff we'd overhear, but on the whole, they seemed happy.'

'They weren't happy,' Hilary corrects him firmly. 'They were just good at putting up a front. You never know what goes on behind closed doors, do you?'

'Indeed you don't,' Greg says softly.

'And she was difficult. Unpredictable. One minute she would be all charm and affability, the next she was at your throat. And a flirt. My God, when I think of the way she carried on. She tried it on with Greg once – right in front of me!'

'No way!' Jake laughs, enjoying this.

'She had her own problems,' Greg says, something of a warning in his tone.

'Did you see much of them?' Leah asks. 'Anton seems so shy.'

'Well, it's not surprising he's keeping a low profile,' Greg answers, again in the low voice that Hilary can't quite read, 'given his history. But back in the day, he was very sociable. They both were. Forever throwing parties. In fact, we were at one of their parties the night before she died. Weren't we?'

His eyes flick towards her, two hard stones, and there's challenge in them. She thinks of that night, an image quickly summoned, Charlotte's sneering gaze: 'My God, Hilary, whatever are you wearing?' A small shudder passes quickly through her that she attempts to shrug off with a quick shake of her head.

'Really?' Jake asks, sitting up a little now, interested. 'And? Did you notice anything? Any signs of what was to come?'

'Well, Charlotte was drunk, of course,' Hilary states, recovering herself, 'but Charlotte was always drunk, nothing unusual there.'

'She had a drink problem?' Leah asks quietly.

'Oh, yes! Once, when Greg and I were living in that

flat,' she says, warming to the subject, 'there was an after-noon when I was in the garden and I looked up and saw the two children sitting on the windowsill of the bed-room upstairs, their legs dangling out over the edge. Two little ones – younger than Matthew is now. And you've seen the height of those windows. It must be a drop of twenty feet at least.'

'What did you do?'

'I called out to them to get back inside, but they just kept sitting there.'

It had been raining that day, Hilary remembers. She had been outside, her shoulders up around her ears as she hastily unpegged her washing when she had spotted them.

'So I ran up to the back door of the house and started madly banging, trying to get their mother's attention. But nothing.'

'Where was she?' Leah asks.

'In the living room. Asleep.'

'But the children – did you manage to wake her?'

'Eventually. I broke into the house.'

'No way!' Jake says, impressed, and she assures him that, yes, she actually did.

The one and only time in her life she'd ever smashed a window. She still thrills to the memory of taking that rock from the edge of the flower bed and sending it crash-ing through the pane of glass. Then, manoeuvring her hand in to turn the lock and open the kitchen door, crunching over the glass on the floor. She'd gone straight upstairs, her heart in her mouth as she entered that bed-room, praying with every step they wouldn't fall before she got to them.

Afterwards, she had felt rage as she pulled the window shut, the two children scampering away from her downstairs. Such carelessness! People like that didn't deserve to have children.

'I found her afterwards – Charlotte,' she tells them, unable to keep the cold disgust from her voice. 'Laid out on the couch. Drunk. And, my God, the uproar when she found out about the broken window. Accused me of vandalizing her property, claimed I'd made the whole thing up about the kids. Of course, there was no love lost between us, not after she forced me to put my dog down, but I was trying to help her children. You'd think she'd be grateful. If it hadn't been for me they might have fallen.'

She realizes her voice is shaking. The others watch her warily.

'She made you put your dog down?' Jake says, and she sees his eyes flickering to the boy who has abandoned his bug hotel, turning his attention now to Mona stretched out on the lawn.

'Oh, it was just a silly misunderstanding. Our dog, Bella – she was just a puppy, really – snapped at their son. She hardly touched him. A playful little nip. But Charlotte made such a fuss about it – kicked up an absolute storm. And we were their tenants, remember, so I could hardly object too strongly.'

She is surprised to find her heartbeat accelerating in her chest. All these years later, that indignation kicking to life again.

Jake rubs his chin, quietly forming his own opinions.

He must think I'm quite mad, she thinks.

'She was a very unhappy woman,' Greg says. 'I don't

think the suburban life of a south-Dublin housewife suited her. I suppose she felt trapped.'

Hilary finds herself listening carefully. Something thoughtful in his voice. It makes her wonder how often those memories of the past turn over in his head. Do they stir to life inside him as they do in her?

'Trapped by what?' Leah asks.

'By the choices she made. By her marriage. He was very controlling. I've no doubt he was a difficult man to live with.'

Hilary doesn't say anything. She makes no attempt to contradict him. Instead, she sits very still.

'I once overheard her telling someone about how he picked out the clothes she was to wear each morning. He used to write lists for her of the meals she was to prepare, the activities she was to organize for the children, what music she was to practise on the piano. That's how controlling he was.'

'It doesn't sound like Anton.'

Hilary's eyes flick to her. Does she imagine it, or does Leah sound defensive? A cold feeling pools in her stomach. 'Do you see much of him?' she asks, keeping her voice neutral, though her thoughts are racing.

'Not really. He's in his garden sometimes.'

'We hear him upstairs,' Jake says, 'dragging across the floor at all hours of the night. The keys on that bloody piano going plinkity-plonk at three fucking a.m., right above our heads! He's like a crab, scuttling sideways around that house.'

'Jake,' Leah says, a warning in her voice.

'Mark claims the old man is innocent,' Jake continues,

ignoring her, 'but I've my doubts. He gives me the creeps. And now he's started sending Leah love notes.'

'Stop it,' she says, a little more insistent now.

'Love notes?' Hilary asks. It's an effort to keep the smile from falling off her face.

'Not love notes, and there was only one,' the younger woman says.

Two spots of colour have appeared high in Leah's cheeks. Hilary notes them, the tightness of her mouth, that sense of drawing in.

'Oh, come on, all that guff about Greek mythology – the gods and the mortals and their various trysts.'

Hilary sees Leah nudging him with her foot, but Jake just laughs and looks to the others to join him. Greg smiles and Hilary gulps her wine. He cannot know the shot of anguish that's going through her, the harsh abrasion of those words.

'It's just so hard to imagine him doing that,' Leah murmurs now, as if to herself.

'What makes you say that?' Hilary asks. Outwardly, she is calm, smiling in the sun, but she remembers that night in the garden, the way she'd seen Anton leaning forward to touch the young woman's wrist. 'There's something so familiar about you,' he'd said.

'He just seems so sad, I suppose. When he talks of his wife, he still sounds sort of broken about it. Like he misses her.'

'Did he actually say that?' She keeps her voice level, careful not to betray the emotions bubbling inside.

'Yes, he did. I think he's lonely, and sort of lost. I feel sorry for him. And I know that sounds crazy, given what he did, but . . .'

Jake has been listening to all this with a growing sense of unrest. Now, he leans forward, and says to her: 'You haven't been talking to him again, have you?'

'Not lately, no.'

'Good.'

The word is spoken emphatically and Hilary can see the instant effect it has. Leah's face grows solemn, her eyes cold. The glance she gives him is hard, flinty. Then she looks down into her lap, her voice dropping as she says: 'There's just something about him that's very calm. That's all.'

'Cold, I think you mean.' Hilary surprises herself by saying this aloud. Surprises herself with her sharpness. 'That calmness you speak of is really the ice in his veins.'

Leah looks up at her, and for just a split second, Hilary sees the challenge in the woman's eye – a surprising fierceness piercing her expression. But then she blinks, the challenge sinking down within her, and casually turns away.

After they've gone, Hilary pours herself a tumbler of brandy and takes it upstairs. Her bedroom is situated at the front of the house and she pulls the chair from her dressing-table up to the window. She rests her hot feet against the cold radiator as she sips the unfamiliar drink. Brandy doesn't agree with her. The hangovers from it are punishing. But this evening she's feeling a little reckless. She has half a mind to knock back a couple, then march over to Anton's house, demand he let her in.

Instead, she sips slowly and waits.

Hilary is a watchful person, although that was not always the case. Now, when she thinks about it, she realizes the sense of surveillance that forms such a deep part of her had first taken shape in the summer of 1999, and it was because of Anton.

So much of her time, that summer, was devoted to watching out for opportunities for them to be together. Charlotte was always there and, besides, Anton had a day job – some kind of financial position. He never talked about his work, and she wasn't curious about it. That side of him didn't interest her.

She found herself growing alert to the comings and goings upstairs. The sound of their front door closing became familiar to her, as did the noise of their car engine starting. Hilary would peer out of the window and watch Charlotte piling the children into the back seat and driving off, knowing that, minutes later, he would come calling.

Their encounters were erratic and charged. She could not be sure if, taken as a whole, it could even be termed an affair. They had made love only a handful of times, and while the sex was pleasurable, she had enough acuity to realize the pleasure was mainly derived from the sense of transgression rather than from any deep carnal connection. He was affectionate towards her in a way that seemed special – the way he stroked her hair, the way his eyes lingered over her face, taking her in. Sometimes they just talked. And she loved to listen to him. The timbre of his voice hit the perfect note in her ear. There was a lazy quality to the time he took to tell a story. He had a fondness for Greek mythology. Reading between the lines, she knew his wife had lost interest in the stories, if she'd ever had any in the first place. But Hilary loved it. She listened, enraptured.

'Tell me again,' she'd say to him.

And he'd stroke her arm, her head resting against his chest, the two of them sitting together on her couch, or lying in her bed, and he'd say: 'Who will it be today?'

She always picked one of the Greek women. The blighted queens, the avenging goddesses. Hilary had no interest in the men and their battles. So she asked for Circe, Penelope, Elektra, and he would take a lock of her hair and slowly twist it around his finger, his voice reverberating in his chest, her ear against it, and she would feel herself at peace.

'Which one am I?' she asked him, and he thought about it for a moment and smiled.

'Helen.'

'Flatterer.'

Helen, possessed of such beauty it drove men to war. Hilary knew she wasn't that.

'You don't see the correlation?' he asked teasingly. 'Helen, stolen away from her husband, Menelaus, by a man who was enraptured?'

'Are you Paris, then, in this little Greek tragedy?'

He frowned comically, and she laughed, resting her chin against his ribcage. It was mid-afternoon. The sun was shining through the closed curtains. Greg was away at a summer school. Charlotte was shopping in town. Hilary wasn't sure where his children were.

Their time was limited. She had the sense that he was already thinking about returning home.

'What about Charlotte?' she asked tentatively. 'Who is she?'

He didn't like talking about his wife. Hilary had taken to observing Charlotte from a distance. If anything, she thought, Charlotte was Helen. Of the two of them, she was the more beautiful. Her figure was statuesque, her bearing elegant. She had classical features, and it was clear she was careful with her appearance as she was always perfectly turned out. Hilary nursed secret feelings of inadequacy over Charlotte. She couldn't help feeling mousy and small in comparison. But Charlotte had a reputation. She was a flirt who liked a drink. Her beauty turned ugly when she was drunk. And she was a snob. The supercilious manner in which she addressed Hilary lessened any feelings of guilt Hilary might have had about sleeping with the woman's husband. Besides, she still remembered that first evening – Charlotte and Greg on the sofa, her hand resting on his thigh.

Anton's face grew serious and thoughtful. After a minute, he said: 'Clytemnestra.'

'And who was she?'

'Agamemnon's wife.'

While her husband was away at war, he explained, Clytemnestra took another lover. And when Agamemnon returned, she waited until he had sunk into his bath, war-weary, filthy, exhausted, and then she had killed him.

He looked so grave in that moment that Hilary hesitated before teasing him. 'You'd better be careful so,' she said, keeping her eyes on his, 'when you get home. She'll be waiting for you with her net and harpoon.'

It was a sad smile that he gave her. And then he traced the length of her brow with his index finger, and said: 'I do love you, you know.'

And she nodded, then turned her face away, so he couldn't see how much it moved her.

Hilary thinks about it now, all these years later.

What an odd summer it had been, preternatural with the sense of an imminent ending hovering over them all the while. The millennium drawing to a close with all the Doomsday noise it inspired. Y2K was on everyone's lips, the way Brexit seems to have taken over now. It had made her feel . . . reckless.

She knows she was wrong about some things. Charlotte, for instance. With hindsight, she can see that Charlotte was deeply unhappy. The snobbery, the drinking, fooling around with other men, it all stemmed from that place of deep unhappiness.

Still. Hilary is not sorry she's dead.

And one thing she knows she was not wrong about: he did love her. They loved each other deeply. The things they had done just to be together. All they had risked. The secrets they shared. The sacrifices.

No one will ever come between them.

14

Anton

Anton is skimming along the edge of sleep when he feels the touch on his wrist.

Instantly, his eyelids shoot back, and he snatches hold of the hand in a claw-like grip, his heart thumping.

'Dad?'

His vision clears, sleep falling away, and he sees his son's face, eyes filled with alarm. Anton loosens his grip. The hand slithers away.

'Sorry,' Mark mumbles. 'I didn't mean to startle you.'

'That's all right,' he says, struggling to get up. 'Sorry if I frightened you, son. I didn't mean to.'

He says this with real feeling, but Mark is looking at Anton's legs, which are lying outside the bedclothes. One of his trouser legs has ridden up to reveal the electronic ankle bracelet. Mark is staring at it.

Anton swings his feet to the floor and slips them into his shoes. 'I just lay down for five minutes,' he explains, reaching for his watch on the bedside locker. It's mid-afternoon. 'Where has the day gone?'

More of his possessions are lined up neatly – aftershave, glasses, a half-drunk glass of water. On the back of a chair nearby, a pair of slacks is draped. Apparently Mark notices all this because he remarks: 'Have you moved in here, or what?'

'Sort of. You don't mind, do you?'

'No, but wouldn't you prefer your old room?'

He knows what Mark is thinking. After nineteen years' sleeping in a cell, what is he doing bedding down in a child's room at the back of the house? There's still Mr Men paper on the walls, for Christ's sake. But his old room is full of ghosts.

'It's quieter here,' is the explanation he gives.

Mark skulks in the doorway, a bruised look on his face as if he's done something wrong and is now worrying about the punishment. But Mark is no longer a boy and Anton has missed out on most of his childhood. For a moment, he thinks the look Mark is giving him is not anxiety but suspicion. Does Mark think it's true what they say, that he killed Charlotte? Does he believe that conviction? Sometimes the urge to know is so strong that he almost blurts out the question. But Anton is wise enough to hold back, or perhaps he's just frightened of the answer.

'When I came in just now and saw you lying on the bed –' Mark stops, assailed by some hidden emotion.

'What?'

'Just the way you were lying there. I thought you were dead.' He smiles, clearly embarrassed by his admission, but seriousness lies beneath it and touches something inside Anton.

'You thought I'd killed myself?'

Mark shrugs. 'Something I read. About how some people can experience depression, heightened levels of anxiety post-release. Suicide rates are high among ex-cons.'

Anton crosses the room towards him. He would like to hug him, but he doesn't. They haven't hugged since Mark was a small boy. Years of formal prison visits have created a gulf between them. He makes do with taking hold of Mark's wrist again, only this time with tenderness – love, even.

'I'm glad you're here, son,' he says, and Mark nods, made shy by all this tentative emotion, then steps out of the room.

Anton follows him, but instead of taking the stairs, Mark crosses the landing and goes into the front bedroom. Reluctantly, Anton follows.

Mark looks around the room, the furniture, the bed made up in white linen, the rugs on the floor. He surveys it all with a thoughtful air. Then, crossing to the dressing-table, he picks up the bottle of perfume, uncaps it, and raises the neck to his nose. After a few seconds, he puts the bottle back, casts a half-embarrassed smile at Anton.

'They say that smell can be a trigger for memory,' he admits. Looking down at his mother's perfume, the smile dies on his face. 'I don't remember how she smelt.'

'What do you remember?'

Mark shrugs. 'Bits and pieces. Her singing. Fixing ice-cream sundaes for me and Sandy and bringing them out to us in the garden.'

'She loved you dearly,' he says. 'Both of you.'

'Once, I was getting a hard time from this group of kids across the park. I was down at the courts and they started directing their tennis balls in my direction, trying to hit me. Mum saw it and she marched right up to one of them – the ringleader – and grabbed him by the arm. She told him next time that happened she'd break his racquet over his head.'

He laughs suddenly, and Anton allows himself a smile.

'She could be fierce when it came to you two,' he tells Mark. 'A real lioness.'

'Yeah. Like when that dog bit me. Do you remember? Mum went apeshit.' Mark's gaze lifts to the window. 'I wish I could remember more of her.'

From far down below, there's the call of a man's voice: 'Come on, Matthew! I said now!'

Both men fall still, listening. A door slams, and Mark leans forward to look, Anton next to him. At the window, they stand together, watching. Man and boy appear first, and then, after a few seconds' delay, Leah follows. Anton finds himself craning his neck, peering down the better to see her. The sun gleaming in her hair, the swish of her long skirt's green fabric.

It's weeks since they've spoken.

In the garden a few nights ago, he had leant over the railings, a whispered shout through the open French windows, trying to reach her where she sat, upright, on the sofa, listening. 'It's not true,' he had said. 'Whatever it is they've told you about me. Whatever they said I did. I am not a monster.' He had waited and waited for her response, but there had been none.

He feels the time stretching out between them.

'How are you getting on with them?' Mark asks, watching as the man and boy wait on the kerb for her to catch up, then all three cross the road together.

'I keep to myself,' Anton replies.

She is lodged deep inside him, like a stone. These past

170

days, he has become a shell of a man, moving around the ground-floor rooms, following the sounds that echo up from the basement. He has lingered in the back sitting room, holding himself steady while listening to her music. He has sat in the dark on the bottom step of the inner stairs, the trailing sounds of their voices coming to him, snatches of conversation, glimpses of a normal life that has eluded him.

'Sure about that?'

In the early hours, Anton had awoken with tightness in his chest – pain like a hot hand clenched around his heart. A panic attack, but it had left him weepy and shaken. He had gone downstairs and lain on the floor beside the piano, pressed his ear to the gap in the floorboards. Fear had driven him there. All he wanted was to be close to her, to comfort himself with the knowledge that she was nearby so that he wouldn't feel so alone. But what he had heard were sounds of intimacy. The sighs, the private words, the muffled shout, and he had heard the sharp delicacy of her voice as she cried out, he – Anton – a sly witness to their coupling.

Pinned by Mark's question, he feels flustered with shame. 'Of course I'm sure,' he says, but his voice lacks conviction.

He keeps his eyes glued to the three figures on the other side of the road, watching as they turn into Number 43, walking up the path, reaching for the doorbell. What are they doing there? he thinks.

'It's just I had a call from Jake. Asking about you. About what happened to Mum.'

'And what did you tell him?'

The door is drawn back, and he sees Hilary greet them – the reddish frizz of hair, the short, blocky figure. His heart hardens, gives a quick pulse of resentment. He knows that it was Hilary who told Leah. It was the sort of petty thing she would do. Yesterday there was another letter from her, more pleading, more anguish. He had left it with all of the others, ignored.

'I said you didn't do it. That it was a miscarriage of justice,' Mark says.

He catches his eye, and Anton feels it again: the press of a question Mark is neither brave nor reckless enough to ask.

'That's exactly what it was,' he replies.

They walk around to Dunphy's and Anton sits on the banquette, fiddling with a beer mat, while Mark goes to the bar to order. Across from him, an elderly couple are deep in conversation. The man is hooked up to a tank of oxygen, a tube running into his nose. It's quiet in here, dark and gloomy compared to the brightness of the day outside. Anton's thoughts drift back to Number 43 – Hilary's house. It worries him, the thought of Leah inside it. He taps the beer mat against the table, agitated by the thoughts of Hilary pouring poison into her ear.

For weeks now, he has been avoiding Hilary, and still he feels her influence, the force of her determination. When he'd come face to face with her outside his house, he had been shocked by her appearance. The red hair! Jesus, it had thrown him. She was changed, no longer the young woman in his memory. It wasn't that she had aged, it was that she appeared different from how he'd remembered her. Looking down at Hilary the other day, he'd had the weird impression that she'd put herself through one of those transformation programmes, a willing contestant to be taken apart and rebuilt as someone entirely different.

In truth, it's not her appearance that bothers him – it's the weight of her expectations. The letters she has written have been frantic, unhinged. They scare him.

'Have you given any thought to what you'll do?' Mark asks, once he's back with their pints, taking the stool opposite.

'Not really.'

'You have to do something with your time, Dad.'

'You sound like my parole officer,' Anton remarks drily. He's grown used to Jim Buckley carping on at him about finding his role, making the most of his freedom. Once or twice, during Jim's weekly visits, Anton has thought about suggesting they go for a pint. More and more, it feels like his parole officer is the only friend he's got.

'What will you do for money?' Mark asks.

'I've a pension.'

'But that won't kick in for another few years. You're only sixty.'

'I know my age, son. And, besides, I have my tenants downstairs,' Anton says, and Mark shifts his position, begins rummaging in his jacket pocket.

'That reminds me,' he says, producing a wad of notes that he flips on to the table. Something grubby about the act. Anton sees the couple across from them glance over. 'Your rent,' Mark explains, 'only don't start relying on it.'

'Why not?'

'I wouldn't bet on them staying. Jake sounded rightly

pissed off on the phone. I don't think he's too thrilled about you.'

Anton's hand reaches out and takes the money, puts it into his pocket. A quick surge of panic flashes through him – a new urgency.

'Besides, I'm sure it's in breach of your parole. You've got away with it for now, but . . . I don't know. It's probably not a good idea.'

Anton picks up his pint and takes a sip. The froth adheres to his lip. Years he has spent dreaming of this moment – decades – a pint of Guinness with his son. Such a simple thing to desire, but for Anton, it was an image freighted with hope. Now that the moment has arrived, it feels disappointing somehow. The murky gloom of the pub, the old man opposite struggling with his emphysema. Mark seems preoccupied, unhappy, and the beer tastes bitter.

'You know, it might be an idea for you to think about selling the house,' Mark suggests, interrupting his thoughts.

He'd wondered how long it would take for the conversation to come around to this.

'It's too big for one person. The upkeep alone . . . If you sold now, you'd have enough money to live on for the rest of your life.'

Encouraged by Anton's silence, he leans forwards, warming to his subject. 'I've been doing some browsing on property websites. Do you have any idea what a house like that could get?' He lowers his voice, as if someone else might be listening. 'One point two to one point five mil. That's more than enough to set you up in a nice apartment with plenty of change to fund a long retirement.'

Anton puts down his pint. 'Have you spoken to Sandy

about this?' he asks, and watches as Mark's enthusiasm wanes, his face closing off.

'Not really.'

'Not interested in her old man, hmm?' He's shamelessly fishing, and it's unfair of him to put his son on the spot about his sister. 'Not that I blame her.'

She was always the tougher of the two, even though she was the younger. She stopped visiting him in prison when she was fourteen years old. Refused point blank. His letters to her came back unread. As soon as her education was finished, she took herself off to Australia with no plans to return. What little Anton knows of her life there, he has gleaned from conversations with Mark, who is reluctant at the best of times. There's a boyfriend now, and there will in time be children – his grandchildren. But Anton knows he will never meet them. He knows he will never see Cassandra again. It comes to him in a rush – as it so often does – how that one night robbed him of everything. His wife, his children. The rumble of a hard anger starts in his gut.

'That's between you and Sandy, Dad. I'm not getting involved. Just tell me you'll think about selling.'

Something about his son's impatience, the way his features have sharpened with irritation, reminds Anton painfully of Charlotte.

'Mark,' he says quietly. 'All that went on in our house. You were just a child. You couldn't know. How could I possibly give it up?'

'You're right in that I was just a child, but there are still some things I remember about Mum, things I'd forgotten, but lately seem to be coming back.'

There's a pointed manner to the way he says this, and

175

Anton's senses are heightened. He is made nervous by this territory. Danger lurks within these memories. He senses Mark's wariness and knows that he, too, must tread carefully.

'What sort of things?' he asks.

'I dunno. Little things. Like the way she used to put her make-up on. Remember that time I fell off the trampoline and split my knee open, and Mum called for an ambulance? I was talking to a friend about it recently, and I suddenly remembered Mum waiting for the ambulance to arrive and dabbing on face powder, spritzing perfume on her neck, and it came back to me how she used to call it giving herself "a quick going-over".'

Anton smiles and nods. He remembers that, too.

'The only time I've ever been in an ambulance,' Mark says. 'I can still recall the smell of it – ointment and plasters and Chanel No 5.'

Something hard now creeps into Mark's tone. 'You weren't there that day,' he tells Anton.

'No. I was probably at work.'

Mark holds his gaze, his expression unreadable. 'Why did Mum call an ambulance?' he asks now. 'Why didn't she just put me and Sandy in the car and drive to A and E?'

His tone is brittle, and Anton doesn't reply, suspecting that Mark already knows the answer.

'She was drunk, wasn't she?'

'I don't know, son. Perhaps.'

'I remember her drinking. It's another thing that's come back to me. "Just a little tinkle," she used to say to us, and then she'd splash white wine in a glass and take it out into the garden.'

He is half smiling at the memory but Anton gets the feeling that other emotions are just beneath the surface. Something about the manner of his reminiscence feels unsettling, like a dark force threatening to break through from beneath.

'People talk about growing up with an alcoholic parent, how miserable and frightening it was for them, but that's not how I remember it. She didn't slug back vodka with grim determination while we sat festering in our own filth. She seemed perfectly happy. Was she, though?' he asks Anton, a sharpness to the question. 'Happy, I mean?'

'Some of the time, son.'

'But not always.'

'None of us is happy all the time.'

'But there must have been something more,' he persists, 'some deeper unhappiness that made her drink.'

Anton sips his pint, uncomfortable with Mark's tone.

'There's something else I remember. Something about you,' Mark tells him.

Anton puts his glass down, brings his eyes up to meet Mark's, sees the hard, searching look his son gives him. Inwardly, he feels himself shying away from it, afraid.

'I remember a party in the house. I remember going outside when I wasn't supposed to. I saw something. I think I saw you.'

Anton's heart is clamouring in his chest. *He knows. The boy knows.*

'That was the night Mum died, wasn't it?'

'Mark, there were so many parties in our house. You were just a child –'

177

'Why do you keep saying that?'

Mark's eyes furiously search his father's face. Finding nothing there, he lets them fall, then picks up his pint and sinks it. 'I miss her,' he admits. 'Even now, I still do. I wish she hadn't died, okay?' he adds, and the hostility in his voice, with the accusatory look he shoots at Anton, changes things between them. For in that one moment, a realization comes to Anton, the truth he has always dreaded: his son thinks he did it.

Anton walks home alone. Despair has opened inside him. All these years he has pushed back hard against it. But now the last bulwark against it has collapsed: his own son is convinced he's a killer.

All he wants now is to be left in peace. He doesn't look at Hilary's house as he walks up Wyndham Park. Instead he keeps his eyes on the pavement, offering up a silent prayer that he won't meet anyone he knows. He couldn't handle it right now.

He closes the gate behind him, and begins to climb the steps. Up ahead, in front of the door, Anton sees that an old coat or soiled blanket has been kicked in there. But as he gets closer, he notices the snout, the blackened tips of the ears, and the weeping cavity where an eye had been eaten out by insects or birds. He halts his progress, recoiling in horror.

On more than one occasion in the past a vixen had made her home at the back of his garden, parading her progeny across his lawn in the hour before dusk. Anton has no idea where foxes go to die – urban creatures, mangy with disease, seeking out a quiet spot close to human habitation in which to expire. But Anton knows that this dead creature had been *placed* there on his doorstep. It's a message. Over the past few weeks there have been several. Birds, bags of dog shit, and now a fox.

He glances back at the quiet street. The evening sunlight shines strongly through the trees. From hidden gardens come sounds of unseen kids screaming, dogs barking. All that noisy living, it makes him uncomfortable, as if he's trespassing.

Suspicions start to stir to life inside him.

The light is draining from the day when the idea comes to him. It was Mark who planted the seed. An idea so simple there's a kind of purity to it.

He waits until the hour is right. Then he goes upstairs and starts running a bath, leaving the water flowing, while back downstairs, he fixes himself a whisky, counts out the pills. There's a science to it, and he's careful not to go too far. Using a pestle and mortar he crushes the tablets to powder.

The bath is hot. He sinks into it, closes his eyes, feels it all seep from him. Waves of sadness and disappointment and faded dreams. He is a man who has been pushed beyond all endurance and yet still he has survived. The leg with the security bracelet is slung outside the bath. It's a risk, and yet it's worth the gamble. He's got nothing left to lose.

And in those last few moments before consciousness leaves him, he thinks of Agamemnon, returning from Troy. His body weary and used. His soul darkened and bloody and needing to be cleansed. He wonders if Agamemnon welcomed the water as he slipped into his bath. Did he see the shadow of his wife fall over it as she approached with her net and her knife? Or were his eyes closed against the light, locked in the memory of another woman, another girl brought to sacrifice?

15

Leah

Leah wakes to the sound of rain. She listens to its distant patter, a child's cry echoing up from her dream. She knows not to trust this cry. Knows it's not real. For a moment, she lies there, listening to the rain, waiting for her heartbeat to steady itself. If she concentrates on her breathing, the moment will pass.

She is lying on the sofa in the living room, darkness pressing all around her. Her breasts feel heavy and tender, her mouth parched. When she tries to sit up, pain communicates itself through her neck and back, searing through the muddiness of her thoughts.

The flat feels empty around her. Jake's absence confuses her. It's difficult to gauge the time, and she's unsure of where her phone is. Distantly, she remembers him leaving earlier that evening to take Matthew home to his mother. That was when she had lain down on the sofa, exhausted from their afternoon, and from the child's whinnying demands, his petulant sulks, all their efforts to appease him. She must have fallen asleep, sinking far deeper than she had intended. Touching her fingertips to her forehead, she feels the tightness of her skin and recalls, with a groan of regret, the hours spent under the blazing heat of the sun in Hilary and Greg's garden. The feeling of desiccation runs deeply through her, as if every cell in her body is crying out for hydration.

In the darkness, she makes her way to the kitchen sink. She runs the tap and leans over the basin, scooping water with her bare hand into her mouth, lapping like a cat. After a minute, she turns off the tap and leans on the counter, her whole body swamped with tiredness. The little digital clock on the cooker, the numbers normally illuminated green, is dark. And when Leah reaches for the switch on the wall and flicks it, the lights fail to come on.

'Great,' she says aloud. A power cut.

Through the darkness, her eyes are drawn to the moonlight falling on the patio slabs beyond the French windows, pressing up behind it the deep black mass of the garden. Her thoughts run to candles and matches, with no idea of whether they possess these things or where they might be.

By now, her eyes have adjusted to the dark. She seeks out her phone and finds it on the kitchen table. When she presses it, she sees it's well past midnight. Scrolling quickly through, she finds no message from Jake, no WhatsApp to explain his delayed absence, no voicemail to check she's okay. Instinctively, she starts to call him, but before she hits the button, hesitation stays her thumb. Anxiety pulses through her, a niggling doubt. She thinks of him going back to that little house with Matthew, imagines Jenna waiting, sun-kissed from a day in the garden, sipping a cool beer. Perhaps the suggestion is made that he stay a while, just until the boy is asleep. Her imagination tumbles forward, unspooling into dark corners. The two of them – Jake and his ex – sitting alongside each other in the twilit garden, sharing a beer, laughing over something their son has said or done, that old connection announcing itself suddenly, surprising them both. Despite the warmth of the day, Leah feels cold.

They had loved each other once, Jake and Jenna. Leah knows that much. Too young to withstand the pressures of an unplanned pregnancy. But surely there must still be times when he remembers the early days of their love. And when he does remember, perhaps, occasionally, the memories are tinged with regret. The siren song of what might have been.

The steady patter of water continues in the background, as she puts her phone down. The house is so quiet. Apart from the rain, there is no noise from upstairs.

It is only now, as her gaze drifts outside to the garden once more, that she realizes the paving slabs on the patio are dry. Beyond, the trees are still, no dripping leaves, no dusting of raindrops on the furniture outside. There are no rivulets tracking down the French windows. It is perfectly dry outside. Yet she can hear water running – she is sure of it.

Listening acutely, she tries to reorient herself. It seems to be coming from Matthew's room. Using her phone as a torch, Leah pads across the floor, and when she opens the door and shines the light inside, water is streaming down the walls. The little bed is soaked through, the duvet and pillows sodden and dark. Quickly, she pulls it away from the wall, and cries out with alarm to feel the water pooling on the boards beneath her feet. Directing the torchlight of her phone to the ceiling, she sees an ugly brown stain spreading through the plasterwork, small chinks appearing before her eyes as new leaks break through.

Hurrying back into the kitchen, she grabs saucepans from the shelf, and hastens back to the little bedroom, placing them underneath the worst of the leaks, but it's difficult in the darkness to see where the water is coming from and the rapid flow frightens her.

Quickly now, she goes outside, climbs the run of steps that leads up to the back door and starts banging.

'Anton?' she calls, pausing to look up at the house.

All the windows are dark. She hammers again, then presses her face to the glass, trying to see inside, but there are only shadows and the distant sound of running water. It is clear that the source of her leak is within the upstairs rooms of the house.

Back downstairs, she races through the flat, alarmed at the spread of water fanning out across the floor from Matthew's room, and goes out through the front door. But all the windows to the front of the house are dark, too, and when she bangs on the knocker and yells through the letterbox, only silence greets her, the house implacably closed to her.

She is panicking now, unsure of how to proceed. She starts to call Greg but then remembers the door in the inner hall that links the flat to the house upstairs. She has to press her hip against it to slide the bolt, but when she does, the door opens easily.

The staircase is dark, a dank smell invading her nostrils. She moves blindly up the steps until she reaches the door at the top, and it is only now, as she pushes it open, that she feels hesitation. The silence of the house announces itself. The vastness of the space looms in the cavernous hall. Doors open on to rooms dark with unfamiliar furniture. She tries to recall the layout of the space from the one occasion she has been here, at the same time waiting for her eyes to adapt to the gloom.

The steady drip and patter of water calls to her, and she knows that it's coming from upstairs. She puts an unsteady hand to the banister, and begins her ascent.

'Hello?' she calls. 'Anton?' But her voice is less forceful now that she is in his space, cowed by the unfamiliarity, the persistent sense that she is trespassing in the home of a possible killer. Fear fills her chest as she moves blindly up the stairs, alert for sudden movements from the shadows.

As she reaches the top step, the carpet squelches. The floor is saturated, and it stirs an urgency within her, pushing her forward. She follows the noise and gathers her nerves at the door before pushing it open on to the bathroom.

The noise of the water reaches its crescendo here, both taps open as water spills over the lip of the bath, splashing off the tiled floor before running off into corners. Immediately she sees a leg draped over the side of the enamel, skin grey in the dim light, an arm dangling, his head partially submerged. An involuntary cry escapes her lips as she rushes forward, turns off the taps and plunges her hand deep into the water to release the plug. She grapples with the body, trying to haul Anton up beneath his armpits but his skin is slippery and his weight made heavy with water and lifelessness. He slithers from her grasp and she has to plunge her arms in again, trying to gain some kind of purchase.

The water is tepid, and his skin is so cold against hers that she thinks he must surely be dead, yet still she struggles and eventually marshals enough strength to haul him out. The thud of his body on the tiled floor fills her with a new dread.

'Anton!' she screams, looking for signs of life in his face, but there's nothing. She has dropped her phone on the floor in her fright, and when she reaches for it now, she offers up a silent prayer that it will still work.

'Come on, come on,' she says, but as she presses and presses the buttons, the screen fails to light and she lets out a cry of frustration.

He is stretched out on the floor beside her, inert, and when his hand turns and brushes off her knee, she drops the phone and leans over him, saying his name with a new urgency. She presses her head against his chest, the blood pounding in her ears making it difficult to detect any other noise, but then she catches it – the faintest rhythm. A frail unsteady beat.

It spurs a new resolve within her, and she hurries out of the bathroom and into the bedroom, feeling her way through the dark until she finds a phone, an old prayer surfacing in her brain as she punches in three digits and listens to the dial tone.

Suicide. The word makes her shudder. She sits on a plastic chair in the hospital corridor, shivering, and tries hard not to think about the moment she discovered Anton lying there. Leah has found that, over the years, she has had some success with blocking out difficult events from her memory. The tricks she has learnt to stave off an attack of unwanted thoughts whenever she feels it coming upon her. Tricks like focusing on her breathing, or willing her mind to occupy a different thought, a neutral safe place.

Her clothes, she realizes, are soaked. She's shaking like a drunk with delirium tremens. A nurse puts a blanket around her and gives her a plastic cup of milky tea.

'He's in the best place,' the nurse tells Leah. She has a country accent, a rural warmth to her.

There's nothing to do but wait. At Reception, they'd asked her for Anton's details, but there was little she could tell them. She had no contact number for his next of kin, and her own phone was inert, rendered useless by water. They'd allowed her to use their phone, and she'd tried calling Jake, but his mobile was switched off. She wonders where he is, what he's doing.

The tea helps and she closes her eyes, feeling a stillness entering her body, aware of the hard plastic of the chair beneath her. The past is tugging at her, and tonight, as she waits, she allows herself to go back there, to another time, another place, when she was a different person, her whole life ahead of her.

She was fifteen the summer it happened.

'Are you sure, now, Leah?' Mrs Hannigan had asked, and Leah had said, yes, she was sure, then laughed because Mrs Hannigan had already asked her that three times.

'It's just for Saturday. And we'll leave early enough so we'll be back by midnight – one at the latest.'

'There's no rush,' Leah had said. 'Honestly.'

Mrs Hannigan was the music teacher at school, and since she was nine years old, Leah had been going to Mrs Hannigan's house for private piano lessons two after-noons a week. The Hannigans were a youngish couple – he worked for Guinness, a rep for the region – and they had a little boy, Cian, who was eight months old when they asked her if she'd babysit. Yvonne and Jim, as they kept urging her to call them, had been invited to the wedding of one of Jim's college friends in Belfast, a two-hour drive away.

'Any problems, anything at all,' Yvonne had urged her, 'you're to call me.'

They'd left the phone number of the hotel, as well as Jim's mobile, and she'd promised to alert them if anything happened, or if she felt she couldn't cope. But she knew she could. Cian was a sweet baby whom she'd known since he was born, and it wasn't the first time she'd babysat for him. With his fat round face and blond curls, there was a comedy to his sweetness that touched something within her. Even then, in the throes of her adolescence, a victim of hormonal mood swings and irrational rages, something about him reached inside her and brought out softness and affection that were just for him.

'How's everything there?' Yvonne had asked, when she rang that evening, and Leah had held the phone up to the baby's mouth so that his mother could hear him gurgling, making his own sweet, happy noises.

'Listen, we had some trouble with the car on the way here,' Yvonne had told her. 'I'm a bit nervous about travelling back in the dark, in case it breaks down. Would it be too much to ask you to stay over until the morning?'

'Of course not!' Leah had said.

'Just say, now, if you've had enough. I know he can be exhausting and you've already given up so much of your weekend.'

'Honestly. I don't mind.'

And she didn't. Yvonne promised they'd be home first thing in the morning, in time to give Cian his feed. When Leah's mother called in to check she'd be all right for the night, Leah was firm about sending her mother away, determined to do this all by herself.

She began playing a fantasy game. Alone in the house with the baby, she imagined that the Hannigans' home, with its framed old movie posters and shelves full of vinyls, was her own home. When she reached to take Cian from his bouncer, she imagined it was her own child she was lifting, her own son held against her shoulder, the softness of his hair against her face.

He giggled and splashed in the bath, playing with his toys. Afterwards, he lay on the changing table, his flesh all naked and warm, pink and chubby. Kicking his legs and laughing, he pulled his little fat foot towards his gummy mouth, making his high-pitched gurgling sounds. She was laughing and tickling him with one hand, the other reaching for the cotton wool and the baby lotion. It was just there, over by the sink.

Afterwards, she held him close against her chest, rocking him in her arms, saying, 'Shush, there. Shush,' even though he wasn't crying. She kept checking him over, looking for bumps, evidence of bruising, but there was nothing.

He took his bottle and she put him to bed. Twice in the night, she went in to check on him.

She was still asleep on the fold-out couch in the sitting room when Yvonne and Jim got back. Blinking awake, she sat up, embarrassed.

'Morning, Sleeping Beauty,' Jim said, smirking at her bed-head, her sleepy confusion.

For just a moment, she forgot all about the previous evening.

But then Yvonne laughed too and said, 'Where's Cian? Don't tell me he's still sleeping.'

'I wish *I* was,' Jim remarked, a bleary hung-over look about him, and Yvonne slapped him playfully and said she'd go upstairs to rouse the baby.

'How was the wedding?' Leah asked Jim.

She cannot recall his answer. That part of it has become lost to her. All she remembers is folding the duvet over the couch and listening.

That was when, upstairs, the screaming began.

The strip lighting of the fluorescent bulbs in the hospital ceiling burns against her eyes. She opens them a fraction, a hand squeezing her shoulder, bringing her back to the present. The nurse's voice, warm with comfort: 'You can come in and see him now, love.'

Anton, heavily sedated, his stomach pumped, his lungs sucked dry, lies narrow and still in the bed.

It's just the two of them in the room, but Leah feels awkward, as if she's being watched by an unseen third party. She approaches the bed cautiously. After a moment, she reaches out to touch Anton's hand. 'I'm heading off, Anton,' she says. 'You're safe now.'

Anton doesn't react. No flutter of eyelids, no inclination of his head to indicate he's heard. He looks so vulnerable, so alone in that big room.

As she listens to the bleep of the monitor, sees the tag encircling his slender wrist, she remembers the note he sent her earlier that week, words scribbled, the slanting cursive communicating an urgency she felt as she read it.

Haven't you ever done something that you profoundly regret? Aren't you ever tortured by the thought that if you had only done something differently, everything would have turned out right? Do you know what it's like to live with such guilt?

She might have told Yvonne that she was too tired to wait. She might have skipped the baby's bath that night. She might never have taken her hand away from him as he lay on his changing table. She might have reacted instead of just trusting that everything was fine.

In the dimly lit room, she leans forward and kisses Anton's pale cheek. Sudden emotion leaps in her throat. 'Yes,' she whispers. 'I understand what it's like. I know.'

16

Hilary

Hilary is at home when the ambulance arrives. It's late, but neither Greg nor she has been able to sleep. They are in the living room, watching *The Last of the Mohicans* on Netflix, when blue lights flash through the Venetian blinds. Greg hits pause but Hilary's already off the couch, peering through the slats.

'It's Number Fourteen,' she tells him.

A small crowd has gathered by the time they get outside. She spots the Kellys, and Jane and Paul Grant, Will and Maria Bolton both in dressing-gowns. Greg goes to stand beside Martin Cooper – a widower, who lives at Number 38 – while Hilary pulls on a sweater and follows him.

'Any idea who it's for?' Greg asks.

Martin, a small man in his mid-sixties, shrugs. 'I assume it's Anton.'

'Do you know what happened to him?' Hilary asks, trying to push down on the panic rising inside. What if he's dying in there and nobody's with him? What if he's already dead?

Martin stares at her. 'I'm as much in the dark as you are, my dear.'

Murmured conversation ripples through the gathering.

She hears one of the newer residents say: 'Isn't that the guy in the papers? You know – the murderer?'

Idle speculation follows: a revenge attack, some crazed relative of the murder victim seeking atonement, a prison feud that's spilt out into the quiet suburbs. Hilary shifts her weight impatiently from one foot to the other, her jaws clamped together. These people, she thinks, don't have a fucking clue.

While they wait, she scans the crowd, but there's no sign of Leah or Jake.

A door to the house opens, and one of the paramedics emerges – a stocky woman, blonde hair drawn back into a stubby ponytail. A hush falls over the crowd as she comes down the steps and swings open the two rear doors of her vehicle. Without thinking, Hilary moves towards her and asks: 'Is he dead?'

'Please step back, madam,' the paramedic says, before climbing up into the vehicle for some equipment to take into the house.

Hilary feels Greg's hand clasping her upper arm. She doesn't look at him.

When they bring Anton out of the house, there's a ripple of shock through the gathering, everyone craning their necks to see. The street is cast in the orange light thrown from the overhead lamps. Under their sickly glow, Anton looks more dead than alive. Hilary's heart kicks out in fright. Instinctively, she moves towards him, shaking free of Greg's grip.

She hasn't gone two paces when a figure emerges from the door above, and Hilary's eyes flick up towards the young woman descending the steps slowly, carefully, as if at any moment she might slip and lose her footing. Hilary's eyes narrow. Leah's face is white with shock. She's still wearing the patterned green dress she'd had on earlier that day, but Hilary notices now that the sleeves are soaked, a darkened patch of damp spreading through the fabric. The ends of her hair are also wet.

The younger woman doesn't see Hilary, doesn't seem to notice anyone in the crowd as she drifts past. And when the paramedics lift Anton into the back of the ambulance, Hilary feels her chest tighten with resentment as she watches Leah climb up after them. With disbelief, she stares as the young woman – a woman who hardly knows Anton – takes her seat alongside him.

He might die, Hilary thinks. *He might die and I'll never get another chance.*

She moves to approach, but Greg's hand is back around her arm. She feels his grip tighten.

The doors close, and the driver instructs them to move back. The crowd watches as the ambulance executes a three-point turn, and Hilary says to Martin and Greg: 'Where will they take him? Which hospital?'

'Vincent's, I expect,' Martin says.

And then the ambulance disappears around the corner in a flare of blue light and whining sirens.

'Well, that's it,' Martin remarks. 'Drama over.'

The crowd begins to disperse.

'Good to see you, Martin,' Greg says, and Martin claps him on the back and asks when the new book's out.

'Next month.'

'Marvellous. I'll look out for it.'

Vaguely, she's aware of mumbling an invitation – an

afternoon at their house to celebrate the book's publication –
but it's as if the voice is coming from somewhere beyond
her, the words like putty in her mouth.

They are crossing the street to their house when Greg,
a couple of steps ahead of her, stops abruptly and turns
back. He doesn't say anything, just looks at her.

'What?' she says.

'What was that about?' he asks. 'Asking which hospital.
You're not planning on visiting him, are you?'

'Don't be ridiculous,' she says, a stifled huff of a laugh
emerging from her throat. But she keeps her eyes on his
face, the fierceness of his gaze.

He holds her there in his stare for a moment longer, as
if he's considering adding something. In the end, he turns
from her and she follows him into the house.

They take their seats on the sofa and resume watching
Mohicans. But an anxious presence is in the room with
them now, and after a few minutes Greg stands up,
announcing he's going to bed.

Hilary lies in the dark. From the next room, she can hear
gentle snoring. But she's too jittery to close her eyes. She
keeps thinking she can hear a car engine outside. At one
point, she sits up, startled by the scream of mating foxes.
Looking out at the night sky, she tries to read the stars,
but streetlamps blur the darkness and pretty soon she
gives up and lies back against her pillow.

Her eyes close and she thinks about the neighbours
gathered on the street outside, and how it reminded her of
another night many years ago – another gathering.

*

They were coming home from the pizzeria when they saw people standing outside Number 14. It was a Saturday night and music was playing within the house, laughter and high-volume conversation, the tooting of a trumpet pouring out through the open windows and door. There were people on the street with drinks in their hands, leaning against the railings, sitting on cars, an off-spill of the party inside.

'Who are all these people?' Greg asked.

He was holding Hilary's hand, a bottle of wine he'd picked up in the off-licence in the other.

'A party,' Hilary said, before adding drily: 'Our invitation must have been lost in the post.'

This was three days after they had moved out of the flat. Their house, while not quite finished, was habitable, and Greg had been impatient for them to go. Charlotte had been courteous but brisk when they'd handed back the keys, and Hilary had just about managed to be civil. There was no love lost between the two of them – not since they'd fallen out over the dog. Three days of back-breaking work, cleaning and painting and moving furniture around. She had thrown herself into it, careful to hide her doubts from Greg, about the house, about him, and her growing anxiety over the difficulties involved in seeing Anton now that they were no longer living in the same building.

Greg was moving away from the house heaving with people, when the idea came to her, and she pulled him back.

'Come on,' she said, tugging Greg towards the steps. 'Let's check it out.'

She felt his resistance.

'No, Hil.'

'Come on, why not?'

'I'm tired. Can't we just go back to ours? Besides, we weren't even invited.'

'So? They can't have a party like that, right across the road from us, and not expect us to crash it.'

Music and laughter spilt from the open door and windows. His eyes moved between her and the house, the bottle of wine held against his leg.

'All right,' he said, after a moment, and she felt a little zing of pleasure as she thought of Anton, the opportunity this afforded them, and led Greg up the steps.

They entered a sea of noise. Hilary felt like she'd been underwater for hours, and now, coming up for air, she was assaulted by the sensory overload. Women's laughter seemed sharp and piercing. The men were shouting to be heard. A thick pall of cigarette smoke hung in the air, and everywhere she turned there was the press of bodies, people pushing to get past.

'I see Charlotte.' Greg pointed, and Hilary looked past him and saw the hostess coming down the hall holding two plates of finger food aloft. She was wearing a sea-green sleeveless floaty number, hoop earrings gold against her hair. 'We should say hello,' Greg said, already raising his hand in greeting.

'Look who it is!' Charlotte said, her smile broad but not quite reaching her eyes, which flicked with surprised curiosity from Greg to Hilary.

'We're being very cheeky,' Hilary admitted. 'Shameless gatecrashing. But we heard the music so . . .'

'Not at all! It's wonderful to see you both.'

Hilary tried to match her smile, but couldn't quite manage it. She felt uneasy in Charlotte's presence. There was a hardness beneath the hostessy good manners that put her on edge. And then Charlotte's eyes swept over Hilary's body, taking in the jeans, the sandals, the smock shirt she wore when painting and decorating – she hadn't bothered to change when they went out for pizza.

'My God, Hilary, whatever are you wearing?' Charlotte asked, her eyes widening with amusement.

Hilary's cheeks flushed, her temper flaring.

'Here,' Greg said quickly, offering Charlotte the wine. 'A peace-offering.'

Hilary glared at him.

'Oh, now, there's no need for that,' Charlotte said, admonishing him in a mocking way. 'Would you mind putting the wine in the kitchen, darling? I've my hands full!' She held aloft her platters and moved to go past them. 'And help yourselves to a drink!'

In the kitchen, they squeezed past the crowd gathered there to the counter by the sink. Greg put down their bottle and picked up one that was open, poured wine into two paper cups and handed one to her.

'A peace-offering?' she said to him, watching as he gulped his wine. 'Why did you say that?'

'I was being nice.'

He was looking past her now, his head bobbing a little to the syncopated beat of the music. 'Livin' La Vida Loca' was playing.

'If anything, she's the one who should be apologizing to me.'

In the week before they'd left the flat, Hilary had broken into the house to rescue the children from the upstairs window. She'd found Charlotte drunk on the sofa. The row had been fearful, prompting the premature move to their own unfinished house.

'Don't start up with that,' he said gently. 'Look, there's Martin and Vanessa,' he said, holding up a hand and waving.

For a while they chatted with these neighbours, Martin and Greg attempting to discuss Y2K compliance above the din of the crowd, Hilary explaining to Vanessa their latest drama with a building contractor, but her attention was divided, her eyes darting around the room, seeking him out in the crowd.

She felt hyped up and conspicuous. Everyone around her was dressed for the party. The men were casual enough, but the women all teetered in heels and strappy sandals, jewellery flashing. Many seemed to have taken their cue from the *Sex and the City* playbook – sleeveless shift dresses in jewel colours, or frothy delights in cool pastels. In her washed-out grey denims and painting shirt, Hilary felt like a teenager called down to mingle on sufferance with her parents' friends. She thought about slipping out and going home to change quickly, but was afraid if she did she'd lose her nerve and wouldn't come back.

She drank more wine and tried to relax, waiting for him. The reception rooms felt large and beige, light cast from gilt wall sconces shaped like candles, *faux*-wax melting down the sides. Thick-pile carpet underfoot gave off its own particular heat and the stairway swept through the hall in an impressive fashion. The kitchen was a disappointment. Small and poky, it looked unloved and underused. It was clear the lady of the house had little interest in it. The little boy, Mark, sat on the stairs, guarding the upper floor. He wore *Thomas the Tank Engine* pyjamas and sat with his elbows resting on his knees, his chin balanced on his hands.

'Hello there,' she called up to him, but he didn't answer, just stared down at her with a closed-off expression.

She wondered at him being allowed to stay up so late. There was no sign of the little girl.

All the while, she was aware of Anton's presence. Without ever looking directly at him, she tracked him with her peripheral vision, and knew he was keeping tabs on her, too. They worked their way around the rooms of the house, carefully avoiding each other, which lent an erotic charge to the evening – that sense of deliberate withholding. It wasn't until late into the night that he came for her.

The crowd had dwindled but the party was not over, not by a long shot. In the kitchen, one of Charlotte's friends was doing Angel card readings. A karaoke machine was in situ in the living room, drawing most of the crowd. Greg and Martin, their arms slung around each other's necks, were performing 'Personal Jesus', when she felt someone touch the base of her spine, heard Anton's voice in her ear: 'Follow me.'

No one noticed them slipping out. He led her down into the garden, moonlight casting the path in a silvery light cutting through the darkness of the lawn, the lumpy mass of the flower beds. After the thrum of the music and voices of the house, the quiet in the garden felt loaded.

She kept her eyes on the back of his neck above the navy loose-necked shirt he wore.

Hilary knew what was going to happen. She had known it from the moment she had made the decision to gatecrash the party, the possibility shimmering in her imagination for the entire night. And now they were nearing the end of the garden, he reached back for her hand. Opening the door of the little shed, he drew her inside.

At first he just kissed her, deep and slow. But then it became more intense, his hands down the back of her jeans, pressing her to him, his erection straining against her hip.

'Take these off,' he instructed her, tugging gently but insistently at her waistband, and her heart gave a sudden leap. She glanced through the little window, back across the empty garden to where all the windows of the house shone.

It was not the first time they'd had sex, but they had never done anything so risky. And Hilary had never been one of those girls who swapped stories about the weird places they had done it: deserted platforms of late-night railway stations, the women's toilets in the arts block, the stationery cupboard at a part-time office job. Before Anton, the bravest she'd ever been was to have sex with her college boyfriend in his parents' bedroom while they were out at the theatre. And always, with Anton, their coupling had taken place in the privacy of her bedroom, in the quiet of the basement flat, or across the road in her new house when the builders weren't around. There had never been anything like this before.

Anton was unbuckling his belt with urgency so she

swallowed all her doubts and inhibitions and unbuttoned her jeans. She pushed them down to her ankles, along with her knickers, and had barely straightened up when he was upon her, and within seconds he was inside her. So different from their previous encounters, so astonishing, it felt charged with meaning, as if their relationship itself had deepened, grown even more risky and dangerous. Surprise and disbelief went through her that they were actually doing this – it took her a moment to decide to abandon herself to it, free herself from the nagging voice of doubt, unshackle herself from any thought of risk and betrayal and shame. She felt the hard rub of the wooden shed behind her buttocks, and pulled him further into her, as deep as she possibly could. When she came it was with a reckless cry into the dark, and she felt his mouth covering hers as if to suck the cry out of her, killing any noise.

She doesn't like to think of what happened next. One minute it was just the two of them, losing themselves to their passion, and the next Charlotte was there, eyes lit up with fury and disbelief.

Hilary was shaking when she went back into the party. The karaoke was continuing, but there was no sign of Greg. She looked around for him frantically, but when Charlotte returned to the house Hilary sank back into the shadows. A moment later, she slipped out of the front door, the golden ripple of Charlotte Woodbury's laughter following her as she hurried across the street.

All those years she had carried on. She had kept eating and sleeping. She had worked at her friendships. She had been a good neighbour. A good wife. She had shared a bed with her husband, feigning desire and even love. She had allowed him to make love to her while her mind and heart were elsewhere. It shamed her a little, to think of how she kept on living this normal life while Anton rotted in a cell.

But she didn't forget him. She didn't forget what he meant to her. What they meant to each other. Sometimes Hilary lay wide awake, feeling the rushing thrill of that last time together, replaying it in her mind over and over again. She would never forget what he had done for her – his sacrifice had gone unrewarded but for her one act of waiting.

Now, as the sky beyond the window fills with the granular light of dawn, there's a push of feeling inside her – a nasty spike at the futility of it all. All this time she has waited.

She thinks of the way that woman climbed into the ambulance with him. She thinks of the way Leah had looked down upon him, had reached out to touch his face, just as the doors had closed. And a new uneasiness lodges inside her, like a pill just swallowed. It has a bitter taste as it breaks out over her tongue.

17

Anton

A vase of sweet peas adorns the bedside locker. While he has been in hospital, the bedroom has been tidied and aired, the sheets changed. He had not wanted to come home, and now that he sees these kindnesses from his son, Anton feels sad and ashamed. What kind of a father is he? Outside in the hall, the carpets have been ripped up. Discarded, he presumes, although he hasn't asked. He hardly cares.

Downstairs, Mark is busy in the kitchen, making tea. He intends to treat Anton like an invalid – he's said as much already. Passing along the landing on the way to his room, Anton had glanced through the open door to the front bedroom – a room he still thinks of as Charlotte's – and there he had seen a travel bag unzipped and open on the floor, clothes, shoes, books falling out of it, deodorant and aftershave sitting atop the dressing-table. Anton is unhappy about having his son to stay. He doesn't want company, can't bear the thought of being constantly watched. And he feels an accompanying sense of failure and apprehension. Mark should not be here. This house is not good for him.

Anton closes the window in his bedroom, glances outside. The garden is empty: no laundry pinned to the clothes line and fluttering in the breeze; no movement from the patio below. Downstairs feels curiously silent. They must have gone, he surmises. They must have moved on. He can hardly blame them. He had taken his chance, and it had backfired. Anton turns away.

He takes off his shoes and lies down on the bed, closes his eyes. Immediately, he hears Charlotte in his head.

'Have you been a naughty boy, Anton?'

Her voice is sly in the lidded darkness. A hard edge undercutting the playful tone.

In the hospital, his mind had been quiet. But always she waits for him. Biding her time, like a faithful lover – his Penelope – watching for his return.

'Think I don't see, Anton? Do you think I'm thick, or blind?'

An old argument, dusted off, unspooling in his thoughts. His own voice played back at him, weary, disingenuous: 'I don't know what you're talking about, woman.'

'Your little friend downstairs. That plain mouse.'

You cross a line – a word said, a phrase used – and something changes. His heart hardened.

'I've seen you sniffing around her, like a dog in heat. Pathetic.' Eyes narrowed, a plume of smoke coming from her mouth. Half cut and not even lunchtime yet.

'You're drunk,' he'd told her.

'Maybe. But not stupid.'

'You're imagining things. There's nothing going on.'

These words spoken in their bedroom across the hall. Outside, a lawnmower whining. The smell of fresh-cut grass sneaking in through the open window.

'Are you going to tell me about her? Come on, then. I want all the gory details,' she'd demanded, and he'd ignored her, kept

buttoning his shirt under her watchful gaze, his eyes on his reflection in the wardrobe mirror.

He'd tucked in his shirt, paused to run a hand through his hair, examining his hairline in the mirror. Something about that gesture had enraged her, because she was on him then like a cat, clawing at him, plucking and scratching. He felt the burn of her cigarette on the inside of his wrist as he tried to get her under control. Her arm banged on the wardrobe, the mirrored door swinging back, and he saw Mark reflected there, hiding in the hall beyond, eyes wide in his solemn face.

Anton sleeps intermittently through the day, waiting.

His throat is dry and sore. His head hurts. A sour taste in his mouth, his tongue furred and parched. The bed feels lumpy beneath him, the sheets bunched and coming away from the mattress, but he hasn't the energy to tuck them back into place. The Mr Men wallpaper surrounds him and his eyes move over their figures, tracing the repeating pattern, the bright colours dulled with age. Years ago, he had sat in this room, reading bedtime stories to his children. *The Tiger Who Came To Tea*, *Henny Penny*, *Winnie the Pooh*. He sang songs to them, recited nursery rhymes. Cautionary tales couched in childish language. He wonders what lessons they learnt from them.

Will you walk into my parlour? said the spider to the fly.
'Tis the prettiest little parlour that ever you did spy.

Cassandra liked that one, drawn to the macabre, the delicious shudder of horror it brought to her little shoulders. Teddy bears and trains printed over her nightdress.

All so long ago.

A door opens downstairs, and he listens to the footsteps coming up the stairs – slow and deliberate. He knows it's not her. Knows she won't come.

Mark pushes open the door with his elbow. Anton opens his eyes, tries to sit up.

'There,' Mark says, putting the tray on the empty chair. Charlotte's china, neatly arranged. Slices of cake.

He reaches behind Anton, pulls the pillows up so that they're supporting the small of his back. 'How're you feeling?' he asks.

'Tired.'

Mark takes a seat near the end of the bed. 'I've been doing a bit of work in the garden,' he says. 'Jesus, it's a real mess.'

'Yes, I imagine it is.' Anton's head aches. He is too tired for conversation. Longs for the boy to go and leave him in peace. 'Shouldn't you be at work?'

'I've taken some time off.'

'I don't want you clucking around me, like a hen.' He sees the instant hurt in Mark's eyes and is angered by how easy it is to wound him. This feeling is chased by regret. 'Sorry, son. I just need to be on my own for a while.'

'Is that a good idea?'

'I've managed for years without you looking over my shoulder, haven't I?' Words spoken, not unkindly.

'True.'

The question pulses between them, unsaid. *Please don't ask me*, Anton thinks.

'So, then, why now?'

'It was a mistake,' Anton says quickly. He can't bring himself to meet Mark's gaze.

'But –'

'A stupid mistake. I didn't mean it, all right? Now, can we just leave it?' Anger leaking into his tone.

'I need to know you're okay.'

'Why?' Exasperation punching through the word.

The look Mark gives him. It's like the boy is six years old once more, looking for reassurance.

'Because you're my dad.'

Sudden emotion comes as a lump into his throat. He shakes his head. There is nothing he can give him now. His hands are empty. Hoarsely, Anton says: 'Let me rest, son. Please.'

At the door, Mark hesitates, concern in his face as he looks down at Anton. 'Call me if you need anything.'

Days drift by. Anton loses track. People come and go. He hears them from the confines of his room. Builders come to repair the damage. The house reverberates with the sound of hammers and drills, radios tuned to some tinny pop station, the syncopated beat and syrupy love-songs drifting up the stairs to him. He hears Mark talking to them, haggling over prices, instructing them to do the bare minimum. There is strain in his voice – Anton hears it, knows the lad is out of his depth, but he cannot help him. He cannot face anyone. In bed, he turns over and faces the wall.

He thinks about Leah. Somewhere in those fevered hours while he drifted in and out of consciousness, he caught snatches of her presence. The brush of her hair against his temple. The sound of her voice in his ear.

'I know,' she had whispered. 'I understand.'

But this memory cannot be verified or trusted. He'd only wanted to feel close to her, but he'd thrown away his chance.

He doesn't ask Mark about her. Doesn't want to worry his son further. When he hears the hammering downstairs in the basement, he imagines the walls being stripped of plaster, the floors ripped up. The bones of the place exhumed.

'Seven fifty. Eight hundred, if you're lucky.'

A woman's voice downstairs.

Anton pulls back the blankets, swings his legs out of bed.

Opening the door slowly, he hears the voices grow louder, identifies his son's words, his agitation.

'Is that all? I mean, I've looked online. There are houses round here going for way more than that.'

'Let me guess. You thought it would be at least seven figures?'

Anton tiptoes to the stairs, puts a hand to the banister. From where he is standing, if he angles his head he can just glimpse them. Blonde hair arranged into a neat chignon. A black trouser suit, handbag over her shoulder, a clipboard in her hands. He cannot see her face. They stand by the bottom of the stairs, Mark peering down at a sheet of paper, tension in his shoulders.

'The market is slow at the moment,' the woman says. 'Houses like this one – large properties in need of a serious cash injection – are challenging to sell right now. People are worried about Brexit, and the recession is not in the distant past either. Buyers remember. And this house needs at least two hundred thousand pumped into it before you could even move in.'

Anton listens as she reels off all the negatives, needled by a sense of intrusion. Anger stirs to life inside him, caused by her presence, by Mark's presumption. He grips the banister tightly.

'Eight hundred thousand is still a lot of money,' the woman says.

'What if we were to paint it,' Mark says, 'maybe put in an Ikea kitchen?'

'Look, Mr Woodbury – Mark.' She softens a bit. Her voice drops, grows conspiratorial. Anton strains to hear. 'Attracting a buyer would be difficult enough but we have an added problem here. Yours is what we term in the business a *stigmatized property.*'

The sour taste is back in Anton's mouth. He starts softly down the stairs.

'It refers to a property that buyers may shun for reasons unrelated to its features or physical condition,' she goes on, unaware of Anton coming down behind her. 'People are squeamish at the thought of their house having once been the site of a suicide, or a murder.'

'It's not haunted,' Mark says, laughing a little but it's clear she's offended him.

'Listen, I'm just pointing out the facts. Personally, it wouldn't bother me.' Then, her voice changing, losing its edge of professionalism, she asks: 'So your father is out of prison, then?'

Anton bristles at her curiosity. Her prurience.

'That's right,' Mark answers stiffly.

'And you're all right with him?' she asks. 'I mean, it was

your mother he killed, wasn't it? And yet you're living here with him? You've forgiven him?'

'That's really none of your business,' Mark says, and then he looks up and sees Anton.

The woman turns around. Her eyes, heavily fringed with mascaraed lashes, flare with interest and disdain. And Anton sees himself through her gaze: an old man in his pyjamas, wild and bewildered, a dangerous animal on the loose.

The door bangs behind her, and Mark sighs heavily, guilt in the eyes he raises to meet Anton's.

'This is my house,' Anton says, his voice low with anger. 'I say what happens to it. Do you hear?'

'Fine,' Mark answers, moving towards the kitchen, like a sulky teenager. 'But I don't know why you stay here. There's nothing but bad memories and ghosts.'

He sleeps, and when he dreams, images flood through him awash with violence. He dreams of Nigel and Salim, of Fat Eric and Liddy Fitz. He dreams they are back in the prison gym, and that he is on the bench press, trapped beneath barbells that have fallen on his chest. He tries to cry out, but there is just the echo of his own voice, joining the chorus of souls crying out for pity or justice. Fat Eric approaches, and Anton tries to ask for help. In the corner, a small boy plays with his toys, not watching. Fat Eric pushes down on the barbells, bursting Anton's chest. He feels blood rushing into the cavity behind his ribcage, but when he opens his eyes, it's not Eric pushing down on him, but Charlotte, her dress hanging open, revealing the livid wound. Anton's heart is engorged, blood rising into his mouth – he tastes the salt of it on his tongue.

He wakes, his skin cold and slick with sweat. Pressing his tongue gingerly against the inside of his lip, he tastes blood. When he puts his fingers to it, they come away red.

Voices in the hallway. Whispers coming up the stairs.

He cannot cope with this. Cannot cope with Mark's ministrations, his concern. He needs to be alone with his thoughts and his memories.

The voices grow nearer, and he feels his anger bubbling up from within. When the door opens, he turns, eyes wild, ready to pounce.

'I've brought someone to see you,' Mark says gently.

And then she steps into the room behind him, and instantly his anger falls away.

The nursery rhyme in his head again:

> The Spider turned him round about and went into
>   his den,
> For well he knew the silly Fly would soon come back
>   again . . .

The smallest smile pulls at her lips. Shyness in her gaze.

He holds out his hand to her. 'Come a little closer,' he says.

18

Leah

'You're sure you don't mind?' Mark had asked. 'It'll just be for a week or two.'

'It's no problem,' Leah had assured him.

It was only afterwards that she considered what Jake might say about it. How he would react. She knew without having to ask that he wouldn't be happy.

Still, she had made the commitment, and it wasn't much to ask, really. That she keep an eye on Anton, check in on him from time to time. She could easily call up for five minutes after work each day.

Mark would be away, filming a commercial overseas, and he was worried about leaving his father alone. 'Terrible timing,' he had told her. 'What with everything.'

'These things can't be helped.'

The conversation took place in the kitchen of the big house, their tones hushed as though Anton might be listening. Downstairs, in the basement flat, two workmen were re-plastering the rooms at the back where the water damage lay.

'It goes without saying,' Mark said, 'that I won't be charging you rent this month.'

'Oh. Well . . . thank you. Are you sure? I mean . . .'

'How could I in all conscience? The mess of the place – it's hardly habitable.'

In the immediate aftermath of the event, Jake had wanted them to move out.

'But where would we go?' Leah had asked, on her knees picking up bits of detritus and dumping them in a bucket. Between them, they had carried their sofa outside into the garden, along with the mattress from Matthew's bed, hoping that the good weather would hold and they could dry out in the sun.

'We'd find somewhere. I'll send out word. Someone will give us a sofa or a floor.'

But Leah didn't want to go back to that. She would rather stay and face the discomfort and intrusion of the clean-up than subject themselves to the insecurity of sofa-surfing, reliant on the temporary goodwill of friends.

'Besides,' Mark says to her now, 'after what you did for Dad that night, I really owe you.'

'I'm just glad I was there,' she answers truthfully.

'It must have been awful,' Mark says, his eyes fixed on her in a way that made her go very still. 'Finding him like that. It must have been a terrible shock.'

She shrugs, made embarrassed by the sombreness of his tone, but also flushed at the memory of that night.

Yes, it had been shocking. Frightening, even. But there was also something about it that had felt . . . intimate. She had pressed her ear to his bare chest, found the faint heartbeat. In the ambulance, she had stroked his hair.

'And, look, I'm sure he won't try anything again,' Mark tells her. 'He's still a bit low, but he seems quite stable. Remorseful, in fact.'

As he led her up the stairs, she could not help but think back to the previous time she had been there, the confusion of darkness and water, the fear that had drummed in her veins.

And now she stands in the doorway, looking past Mark to where Anton is crouched in his bed. She is shocked by what she sees: how thin and pale and hollow he looks, the skin on his face dry as tissue.

'Ah. It's my saviour,' he croaks when he sees her.

All the colour seems to have drained from him. She watches as he struggles to sit up in his bed, fighting an instinct to rush forward and help him. A flash of memory comes to her – those moments while waiting for the ambulance to come, she had held his hand.

'I've asked Leah to look in on you over the next couple of weeks while I'm away,' Mark explains.

'There's really no need,' Anton says, and there's bewilderment on his face, a pleading in his eyes as he gazes up at his son. She feels the rise of his anxiety, his dignity shredded at being infantilized. 'I don't want to be a burden.'

'It's no trouble,' she says gently. 'Please, Anton. I'd like to visit you.'

His eyes go to hers, the lids half closing in relief or surrender. He manages a weak smile. 'Very well, my dear.'

The first evening, she comes to him straight after work. She is still in her office clothes, her hair pinned back off her face. When she comes up the inner staircase, she is purposefully noisy, her low-heeled shoes clattering on the bare boards. She doesn't want to startle him. When she calls his name, something stirs overhead.

He's in his bed, cheeks sunken, although his expression seems to brighten when she comes into the room.

'It's a beautiful evening,' she tells him. 'Let's go outside.'

She has set up chairs for them on the grass beneath the tree. There is dappled shade, and he walks forward gingerly, his feet in slippers, an old plaid dressing-gown wrapped around him, the drawstring tied at the waist. She brings out mugs of tea and finds him with his face upturned to the sun, eyes closed, the lids shaded purple.

'How kind you are,' he says. But he puts the mug on the grass beside his feet, and Leah watches as it grows cold.

They sit in silence, Anton with his eyes half closed, his face angled towards the house. Leah listens to the distant sounds of tennis being played in the park, the magpies yacking in the trees beyond, and wonders when Jake will be home. More and more, lately, he has been absent in the evenings, taking jobs on the bike when they come up. Often, he meets up with the other couriers for a pint afterwards. There is talk of a new short being filmed in Wicklow before the autumn, a chance of a part. He needs it. Leah knows this. She feels how unsettled he has become, restless and agitated.

'Do you believe it's a sin?' Anton asks, his voice startling her from her thoughts.

'What is?'

'Despair.' His eyes are fixed on hers. There's a faint wheeze in his breathing.

'I don't know.'

'I don't know either.'

He gives a slight shake of his head, a baffled look on his face.

'A priest came to see me when I was in the hospital,' he tells her. 'He said despair was a sin. That turning your back on life was turning away from God.'

'I don't believe in God,' she answers simply, and she is pleased to see the amusement that enters his eye.

'But you did once.'

'I suppose I did.'

'So what changed?'

His voice is soft, measured, but his eye holds her with a look of clear enquiry.

She shifts in her seat. 'I grew up. Started thinking for myself.'

'So you matured and shrugged off the indoctrination,' he remarks, in a way that sounds sceptical. 'It wasn't something that happened to you – some dire circumstance that shook your faith?'

The patient stare – a knowingness to it. She feels the inward squirm, and sips her tea, feels the warm surface of it against her teeth.

'Never cared much for priests myself,' he remarks, looking away now. 'Until my stay in the hotel.'

Released from his gaze, she can breathe again. 'The hotel?'

He grins, as if he's made a little joke.

'The Grand State Hotel. The finest hospitality the Republic has to offer to her most penitent citizens.'

'You mean prison.'

'I prefer to think of it as the hotel.' He crosses his legs. 'The chaplain there was a decent sort. We became friends, I suppose.'

She doesn't know what to say to him. So many questions crowd her thoughts, but shyness and insecurity hold her back.

'He used to tell me I must make my peace with Charlotte, and with God, before I died,' Anton says, 'for it would be too late afterwards and I would regret it for eternity.' A puff of laughter escapes his nose. 'I thought it was nonsense. But . . .'

He looks at her now.

'When I was in the ambulance that night, when I looked across and saw you there, I thought . . . I thought I had died already, and that Charlotte was with me.'

'And what would you have said to her?' Leah asks.

His eyes cloud with consternation. 'I don't know,' he tells her.

The garden around them swells with lush summer greenness. Inside her womb, a baby is growing. How strange it is to be discussing the dead in the midst of all this life.

'Perhaps,' she tries, 'you might have said sorry.'

A brief flash of surprise in his face, before it dissolves into something flatter, harder. 'Yes,' he agrees. 'I would have said sorry. But not for what you think I should.'

His eyes slide away from her, his expression changing as he straightens in his chair, smooths down the front of his dressing-gown.

'Evening,' he says, and Leah turns to see Jake standing in the shadows of the patio, silently removing his cycling gloves, his face unreadable.

'You on the mend, then?' Jake asks, making no attempt to come and join them.

'Yes, thank you,' Anton replies stiffly. Then, getting to his feet, he touches a hand to her shoulder briefly and, softening his voice, he says: 'I'd best go in.'

She watches him retreat back up the steps into the house. Jake has already gone inside.

Leah bends down and picks up Anton's mug, discards the tea into the grass, and steps down into the shadows.

Over dinner, they discuss work, an upcoming audition Jake is preparing for, news at the office that one of the senior partners is leaving. Polite, civil conversation, but Leah feels the strain of all that is left unsaid. A ripple of discontent has been running through their relationship ever since the night she'd found Anton. In the immediate aftermath, there had been a full-scale row – the first of their relationship. Leah is not good at confrontation – she seizes up and becomes monosyllabic or mute – while Jake quivers with nerves and a frantic uneasiness, both of them unable fully to communicate their true feelings.

She had come home from the hospital in a taxi just as he was wandering up Wyndham Park, still puffy-eyed from sleep. He hadn't been home all night – had no idea of where she had been, of the drama that had occurred – and this seemed like a betrayal to her. When she'd needed him, he had been unavailable to her. Quietly, she had said as much, and he had recoiled at the accusation, then reacted. 'Nothing happened!' he had said. 'I fell asleep on Mattie's bed, that's all! I was putting him down for the night, and he asked me to cuddle him for a few minutes, and I fell asleep. All that sun – I just passed out.'

'Your phone was switched off,' she had countered coldly.

'So?'

She had turned away from him, exhaustion creeping through her bones, but waiting for an answer nonetheless.

'So it was switched off. So what? Mattie was falling asleep. I often turn my phone off when I'm with him. Haven't you yourself remarked on how I ought to spend less time looking at the phone when he's there?'

She had waited. His answer was so flimsy. The screechiness of his tone grated on her nerves, fed her suspicions.

'Is this how it's going to be?' he had asked her. 'Every time I'm with them, every time I don't jump to answer the phone to you, you're going to just leap to some ridiculous conclusion?'

'Is it ridiculous?' She had met his gaze with a cold clear one of her own. Her voice was firm and hard. 'If there's something going on between you and Jenna, I'd rather you just told me. I won't fall to pieces, but I do want to know.'

He had stormed out then, muttering under his breath that he wasn't going to stay and listen to that crap. And he had left her with the ceilings still dripping, the power gone, her mind and body reeling from all that had happened.

He was only gone a few minutes. He couldn't have got further than the tennis courts before regret seeped into his self-righteous anger. When he came back through the door minutes later, she was swept up in his storm of apologies, his desperate need for her to understand. She chose to believe him. It was not out of character for him to get lost in his son's company, to forget everything else. And Leah knew that if she allowed doubts and suspicions about Jenna to creep in and take a hold of her this relationship would not stand a chance.

Still, it remained. Like a hair caught at the back of her tongue. An uncomfortable doubt that wouldn't go away.

He has been careful with her since that night, handling her like a piece of fruit that might bruise easily. But now, as they finish their meal, and he is about to gather up their plates, she sees him stop, put his hands on his thighs, and look at her.

'You know, I can go and check on him in the evenings instead,' he says, a small inclination of his head towards the rooms upstairs, and a firmness in his voice that sounds like a challenge.

'Thanks, but it's fine. I don't mind.'

'But I do mind. I mean, aren't you scared?'

'Of course not.' She laughs – it seems absurd to think of Anton as a danger. His vulnerability from the night she'd found him is still so present in her mind. And how can she explain to Jake that she feels comfortable in the older man's company? That she doesn't believe what's said of him. That she likes him.

Jake shakes his head, unhappy.

'You've seen him,' she says, 'how frail he is. Surely you can't think he's any kind of threat.'

He thinks about this for a moment, and she can see the battle inside him over whether to pursue it. The morning after it had happened, when she told him how she had discovered Anton in the bath, Jake had said: 'How come the door was unlocked?'

It hadn't occurred to her to question that, but under his distrustful gaze, she had become flustered. She remembered the time Matthew had locked her out of the flat, and Anton had let her go down the inner staircase. She had unlocked the door then. Perhaps it had remained unlocked. Jake doesn't know about that time. He doesn't know that she had been up there, playing the piano while Matthew was downstairs in the flat alone. So she hadn't mentioned the door. Merely mumbled: 'I don't know.'

'Don't worry,' she says softly now, reaching out to touch his hand. 'Nothing's going to happen.'

But he doesn't look happy. Instead, he appears to be waiting for her to relent, and it is this that makes her resentful. What about all the evenings he's been absent lately, spending time with Jenna and Matthew? Has Leah once pulled him up about it, made a complaint?

'It's not like I'll be staying with him long,' she says, quietly insistent. 'Just checking in on him to make sure he's okay.' It seems reasonable to her, but Jake's unconvinced.

'I don't trust him,' he tells her plainly, and then he gets to his feet and clears away the dishes.

On the second evening, she finds that Anton is out of bed and dressed. He is in the kitchen, two cups and saucers laid out on the table, the kettle on, as if he has been waiting for her.

'You look a little better,' she remarks, and it's true that some colour has returned to his cheeks.

'I feel it,' he replies, pouring tea into the cups.

She has told Jake she won't linger, but when Anton offers her the cup, suggesting they take their tea out to the garden, she thinks: Why not? Jake is not home yet and, besides, she's not a child, but an independent woman capable of making her own decisions.

'I've been doing some thinking,' Anton says. 'With all the work that has been done on the house in recent days, I can't help feeling I should do some work of my own. Clear some things out.'

'Sounds like a good idea,' Leah tells him. 'A spring clean.'

The evening is balmy. The grass is starting to look scorched. It's been weeks since there has been rain of any significance. A hosepipe ban has just been announced.

'I've always been a bit of a hoarder,' Anton goes on, 'but today I found myself looking around my house, all these things I've been holding on to, and wondering why. They're just things – they have no meaning. And it's not as if they have any sentimental value. I mean, I've spent the past nineteen years inhabiting one room, and I managed. The world didn't end. It makes me wonder why I didn't just tackle this when I got out, instead of allowing myself to get holed up in a cave of nostalgia.'

'Perhaps you weren't ready.'

'Perhaps not.' He sips his tea, and when he returns the cup to the saucer, he glances up at her. 'Could I ask something of you, dear? I feel bad, as you've already done so much. It's just . . .'

'What is it?' she asks, her attention caught by the flash of alarm that crosses his gaze, the slight tremor in his hand making the cup rattle on the saucer.

He puts them on the grass, says: 'I want to go through Charlotte's things and I'm afraid. I'm rather dreading it. I wonder . . . Would you mind helping me with it? Not now, obviously. But some evening next week, perhaps.'

The request unsettles her. She puts a hand up to her face, draws a stray strand of hair away from her eyes. 'Wouldn't it be better if Mark helped you with that once he's back? They're his mother's possessions after all.'

His face falls with disappointment, and for just a second she regrets her answer, wishes she could change it. Then he nods quickly, forces a smile. 'Yes. Of course. I shouldn't have asked.'

'No, that's all right. It's just . . .'

'I quite understand.'

Then he says he's getting tired. He picks up his cup and saucer, takes hers from her hands, and she watches as he goes back inside.

It is late in the evening when she gets home on Thursday. She had gone to the shops after work to pick up groceries, taking the trouble to buy a few essentials for Anton. It's unclear to her whether he is ready, yet, for the outside world. Earlier today, she had a text from Mark: 'Everything going okay?' She had responded positively, reassuring him that Anton was fine, improving a little each day, but he didn't reply. She has no idea of when he will be returning.

'I haven't heard you playing,' Anton tells her that evening. 'Not for a long time.'

'I can't, I'm afraid.'

'But why not?'

She offers him a rueful smile. 'My piano got water-damaged.'

He sits forward, his expression changing. He looks as if he's been struck.

'It's no big deal!' she says. 'I'm sure it can be fixed. The tuner is coming the week after next.'

'I'm so sorry,' he says. Then, seeing she's about to shrug it off, he says firmly, more insistently, 'No. I really am. Your piano. My God.'

He closes his eyes, puts his hand to his face. He looks anguished, so much so that she leans forward, touches his knee.

'It's just an old piano,' she says softly, but his eyes fly open.

'Your parents gave it to you. I know what it means to you.'

For a moment, she is too taken aback to speak. How does he know this? Did she tell him? She tries to think.

'You must come upstairs and play mine,' he tells her.

'Oh, no, I couldn't.'

'You must,' he says again, this time forcefully.

Then, softening his tone, he tries again: 'Please, Leah. I would feel so bad if you didn't. I would feel even more guilty than I do already.'

Her eyes glance at the French windows, closed to the flat. Jake isn't home. She has arranged to meet him in town, at a concert in the Button Factory. If she leaves now, she can catch the Dart and make it on time. And yet she feels a wavering inside her.

'Just for a few minutes?' he tries again.

In the evening sunlight, he looks brighter than he has done in days. The lines on his face have diminished, and his skin once more looks tanned and healthy. But it's the

liveliness in his eyes that marks the real difference – a
warmth there that draws her in – from the lifeless body
she'd rescued.

'Please?' he asks, his smile broadening, his expression
fixed on her in a way that is almost flirtatious.

What harm? she thinks. 'Very well,' she tells him, and
follows him up the steps into the house.

19

Anton

How easy it is to reel her in.

Tea in the garden, then watching her unwind at the piano in the front room. After the music they talk, only the talk is different now. More relaxed. Intimate. It's as if when she plays the pieces he sets in front of her the natural barriers between them come down. Communication finds a different level.

Evening after evening, she comes.

'Why don't we go for a walk?' she suggests, and he feels his heart soar.

They don't go far, just across the road to the park. It's quiet at this time of the evening, no one around except the dog-walkers. Anton notices the tents that have appeared in the shade of the trees on the west side. Ireland's homelessness crisis has reached the leafy environs of Wyndham Park, he thinks, with something close to satisfaction.

He tells her about his marriage, the difficulties within it.

'It was not the easiest relationship,' he confesses. 'I had my own weaknesses, and I didn't always understand what she needed from me. But I still loved her.'

'And Charlotte?'

'Oh!' He laughs and looks out across the wide expanse of grass.

At one end of the green a stone plinth holds up the bronzed head of a local playwright, long deceased. The memorial has been there as long as Anton can remember.

'Do you see that?' Anton says, pointing it out for her. 'I once came across Charlotte kissing Ken Tansey from across the road right there, up against that lump of rock.'

She stares at the plinth, then at Anton.

'I can still remember it,' he tells her. 'The Kellys' annual Halloween party, we were all drunk on blood-red punch. I'd staggered out here in search of Charlotte. The bonfire was a smouldering heap at that stage, a few stragglers in fancy-dress weaving through the park. And there they were, Morticia Addams and Rob Roy, locked in a lusty embrace.' He laughs, pleased with the image he's summoned. 'There was Ken wiping away her lipstick with the back of his hand, muttering: "Sorry, mate. I'm shit-faced." But Charlotte just stood there staring at me, a prideful little smile on her face.'

He is warming to the topic now. In the cooling heat of the day, the park almost to themselves, breathing the free air, he lets his imagination roam. 'It was one of the things I found so hard to take about Charlotte,' he tells Leah. 'The lengths she went to in order to rouse my temper.'

'Is that how it happened?' she asks him tentatively. 'Did you come across her with someone? Did something just snap?'

Disappointment is instant. The positive mood that she always brings out in him instantly deflates.

She sees this, and adds, in a quietly defensive manner: 'Even the most temperate man has a breaking point.'

He turns away from her and lets out a sigh. There's a

low wall by the tennis courts, and he goes to it now, drops his weight on to it. It's so hard having constantly to fight this battle.

Wordlessly, she follows him, and he can tell that she is waiting for him to explain. He knows she wants to understand.

Tentatively, he begins to tell her about the day his world fell apart. He recounts it as best he can, willing his mind to travel back.

'It was hot, and I was hung-over,' he admits. 'There had been a party the night before. I had drunk too much – we both had. Charlotte had been up to her usual tricks, drinking too much, flirting,' he says, choosing the word carefully. 'I tried to ignore it. I knew she was only doing it to get my attention – that was how she operated. But she wore me down. Eventually, there was a row between us and I left.'

He remembers Charlotte's voice that night, shivering and vindictive as she made her accusations. Recalling it now, he feels a tightness in his chest, as if he cannot take a deep enough breath into his lungs. He would like them to resume their walk and to drop the subject entirely. But Leah's expression is intent, and he knows he cannot lose her attention now. To pause would be fatal, if he is to convince her.

'I went downstairs to sleep in the flat. It was empty at the time, and Charlotte had made it clear she wished to be alone. Sometime in the night, I heard a noise – it sounded like something falling over upstairs.' He catches her gaze, watchful and wary, tells her: 'I didn't go to investigate.'

'Why not?'

'I don't know. Too drunk, too tired. Weary at the thought of another confrontation. I just turned over and went back to sleep.'

He had slept late. Alcohol made him deeply unconscious.

'When I woke, half the day was gone. I could hear someone upstairs, banging on the front door and ringing the bell. When I went outside to investigate, some of my neighbours were on the top step, trying to get in. I was confused – bewildered. I had no idea what they were doing there, why they had come. It wasn't until later that I was told about Mark . . .'

They'd found her in the kitchen. Blood pooling on the floor. Small footprints tracking blood out into the hallway. A terrible scene.

'I have so many regrets,' he tells Leah. 'That I didn't react to the noises I heard that night. That I slunk off downstairs, like a coward, and didn't stay and face up to her accusations. If I had, she would still be alive.'

He pauses to consider this. Then adds: 'The last words we spoke were in anger. Bitter, hurtful things. We wanted to wound each other, but . . .' and the look he gives her now is pressed with meaning and sincerity '. . . I only ever wounded her with words. With my infidelity. I never caused her physical violence. I swear to you.'

He wonders what bearing it has on anything: the word of a criminal. But it is all he has, and as he speaks it, he hears his voice shake.

'But you were convicted.'

'Wrongfully,' he states, his firmness veering dangerously close to aggression.

'But if it wasn't you, then who?'

'I don't know.' His voice cracks. Tears come to his eyes. 'I kept telling them about the noises I heard, about a possible intruder, but they weren't interested. Instead they kept banging on about the row we'd had, asking me over and over again where I'd hidden the knife.'

'The knife?' Her eyes flare with interest.

'Oh, yes. They never found it, you see? They tore the house apart looking for it, and the garden. They had search teams all over this park,' he adds, his sweeping arm taking in the grass, the trees. 'It never turned up, much is the pity.' He tells her with conviction: 'If they had found that weapon, I would have been in the clear. I'd have been exonerated. That's the great mystery. It never showed up.'

She thinks about this for a moment, then reaches out and tucks her arm into his. They sit companionably on the wall, side by side, and listen to the birdsong in the trees beyond.

Slowly, he gains her trust, a little more each evening.

Like a fish hauled through the water on a hook, not realizing the hook is there, lodged and ready to pull.

She tells him about the baby boy. A shocking truth to admit, made more shocking by the way she just blurts it out, without warning or signal.

They are in his kitchen, and he is sluicing water in their now-empty teacups, telling her about a time when the children were small and he had taken Mark to the shops, and ended up leaving without him. 'I simply forgot for a few minutes that I was a parent. That I even had a child,' he says, with amused recollection. 'It was only for a few minutes, and I went back and got him as soon as I realized. But, my God, the amazement of it! This little boy, entrusted to me, and I'd forgotten all about him! And when I told Charlotte about it, do you know what she said?'

He turns to tell her, but stops when he sees the look on her face. The frozen stillness of it. Shock in the eyes, like she's just witnessed an accident. And then she puts her hands up and covers her face with them, a horrible liquid sound escaping her mouth.

'What? What is it? What's wrong?' he asks, coming and taking her by the shoulders, guiding her to a kitchen chair. It seems such a natural thing for him to do now – touching her in this manner.

He can feel her trembling beneath his fingertips, and is shocked by this naked display of feeling. She is usually so reserved. So graceful and composed. The storm of emotion has come over her without warning. She sits in the chair, and between sobs he hears about the babysitting job, the phone-call asking her to stay on, the parents arriving home, the child dead in his cot.

'My God,' he says, holding her hand across the table. 'It wasn't your fault, my darling,' he says softly, as she sniffs and shudders, struggling to bring her breathing back under control. 'It was a cot death – utterly tragic, but they happen and no one is to blame.'

'No! It wasn't like that. A bleed to the brain, they said.' Her words come out in a rush and he can hardly make them out. Her eyes flicker around the room, unable to settle, her arms hugged tightly around her chest. 'They kept asking me questions, over and over, but I just couldn't say it. I just couldn't!'

She bends over, shaken by fresh sobbing, and he rips a paper towel from the roll and offers it to her. She blows her nose, keeps her eyes on the table-top, her shoulders slumped forward. A picture of misery.

'Is that why you left home?' he asks, and she nods.

'It's a small town. Everyone knew. I couldn't stand people looking at me, talking about it behind my back.'

'You poor darling,' he says again. 'That's a hell of a thing to happen to anyone.'

He is shocked, but feels the pull of the story too. There's something in it. Something that can be used.

She starts crying again, presses the balled-up tissue to her nose. Her eyes are rimmed red, a raw look to the skin on her face.

'Do you know what you need?' he says. 'A brandy.'

And he gets out of his chair, but she shakes her head furiously.

'No, I can't,' she tells him. 'I'm pregnant.'

'Ah.' He sits back down. Her admission knocks the wind out of his sails a little. It muddies the waters. He casts his eyes over her body, as if the signs might reveal themselves to him. Then he steadies himself and reaches for her hand once more. 'That's lovely news, Leah. I'm delighted for you.'

But she doesn't look happy. He is somewhat relieved to see that her face is a mask of despair.

'I don't deserve it,' she says quietly, and he makes a tutting sound of mild disapproval.

'Hush now. None of that.'

'It's true. Not after what I did.'

'You're a good person.'

233

'Am I?' She meets his eyes, and there's something cold in the look she gives him. 'I keep thinking about them, Yvonne and Jim. What they would think if they knew about my pregnancy. They never had any other children, you see.'

He nods, says: 'Well, I'm sure they wouldn't hold it against you. Despite how they might have felt then. Time is a great healer. Take it from one who knows, pet.' He squeezes her hand.

She offers him a sad smile, then draws her hand away, glancing at the clock on the wall. 'I should go,' she tells him. 'Jake will be home soon.'

With the heels of her hands, she presses the last tears from her eyes, then tucks the hair behind her ears. Anton feels the now-familiar flatness of disappointment entering his chest. It's the same every evening when she leaves him alone, with all the hours of the night stretching ahead of him.

At the door, she stops suddenly. 'You won't tell anyone about this, will you?' she says, urgency in her voice.

'Of course not. Who would I tell?'

'Promise me you won't tell Mark? It's just he might tell someone else and then it could get back to Jake . . .'

The realization hits him with force. The boyfriend doesn't know. Her dark secret, and he doesn't know. 'I won't say a word to him,' he assures her, and sits there, staring at the door, for a long time after she has left, turning the knowledge over and over in his mind, like a pebble, considering every plane of its surface, its weight and heft. How to wield it to his own advantage.

She comes to help him with Charlotte's things.

He wants to ask her what changed her mind, but decides

not to. A change has taken place between them – a strengthening of their bond. She has told him things she has not told anyone else.

He's relieved at her offer to help: the task fills him with a degree of dread. Something about Charlotte's clothes seems to call her up from his memory in a way that is far more real than when he is alone in the rooms downstairs. She had loved her clothes, loved the pageantry of them – an outfit for every occasion – and he had indulged her. There was a time when he had thrilled to see her delight in an Hermès scarf brought home from a business trip, or a Furla bag on their anniversary. He recalls waiting outside the little cubicle in Brown Thomas while she tried on the Diane von Furstenburg dress, a little furrow of doubt appearing in her brow as she scanned the price-tag, saying, 'It's a small fortune, Anton,' and the sheer joy that transformed her features when he said, 'Go on. You only live once.' He paid for his pleasure, you might say. How many of those possessions were bought as an appeasement or a distraction? The price of a guilty conscience.

Charlotte would have been fifty-five now, if she'd lived. Hard for him to imagine that. Always, in his mind, she is thirty-seven. Still a young woman, hints of age starting to creep up on her: the grey threading through her hair, swiftly banished; the silvery lines running over the skin of her breasts; the softness of flesh over her belly. He can recall quite clearly the way she'd sat at the dressing-table here in their bedroom, peering at her reflection in the mirror with dissatisfaction, her index fingers pulling taut the skin around her eyes. He'd found magazine cuttings for plastic surgery tucked away in one of her drawers.

'So many dresses,' Leah says, taking each one carefully from the wardrobe and laying it on the bed.

He watches the way she smooths the fabric, reverence in the manner of her touch. She folds the sleeves over the breast of one, and it reminds him of a body laid out on the bed, an image he tries to shake off.

'Clothes were her passion,' he tells her. 'She used to work in a fashion store. Quite upmarket. It's how we met.'

'Oh?'

'I had gone in to buy a gift, and was hopelessly lost, as you can imagine. She came to my aid. Within minutes, I was smitten.'

What he doesn't tell Leah is that the woman whose gift he was purchasing was his fiancée at the time. Even then, it was an affliction he was helpless against. And Charlotte knew. She knew from the very start what kind of man he was. It couldn't be said that she'd gone into it with her eyes closed.

There is a bag open on the floor, and Leah carefully lays each folded item in it, tucking them away with an air of sad finality. He supposes he should feel something more – some deeper pull of emotion. But he wants these things out of his house. As if ditching Charlotte's clothes will exorcize her voice from his head, its insistence haranguing him as he moves through the days.

'Are you sure your daughter wouldn't want some of these?' she asks him.

He shakes his head. 'She's taken her mother's jewellery. I'd be very surprised if she had any interest in the rest.'

'Perhaps you should check before you give these away.'

But he is firm. 'No. Sandy has turned her back on all of

this. Even if she'd speak to me, I still know what her answer would be.'

She stops, a dress looped over her arm. 'Your daughter doesn't speak to you? Not at all?'

'Not for years.' He offers a thin smile. 'I don't blame her. She was so little when it happened. She can't even remember me from the days before the hotel. No matter how I feel, I must accept that I'm just a stranger to her.'

He doesn't tell her about the bitter accusations Cassandra had levelled at him. The poison that had been poured into her ear by her aunt – Charlotte's sister – eager to castigate and condemn. The things his daughter had been led to believe.

She sits down on the bed beside him, says softly, 'It's hard, isn't it?'

And he thinks of what she's told him – those small admissions made in odd moments of candour. 'What of your father?' he tries. 'Surely he doesn't blame you for what happened.'

She smooths the fabric of the dress that rests in her lap. 'He doesn't blame me.'

'Then why the distance? You said you rarely see your parents. That your relationship is difficult. But surely they must miss you terribly. You're their only child. They must worry.'

She is sitting so close to him that he can smell the citrus scent of her perfume, so fresh and youthful. He allows himself to reach out, to put his hand on hers. The smoothness of her skin – a thrill passes through him. He looks down at the paleness of the little hand caught beneath his own. She doesn't try to move away. Hope flames in his heart.

'There's a look that comes into people's eyes,' she tells him, in that quiet, pensive way of hers, 'when they find out what happened. They can't help it. Even people who love you and want to protect you – still, the look is there. The dark curiosity in the backs of their stares, as if they're trying to contemplate what it must be like to have a child in your care die in that manner.'

He loves her voice, its soft timbre, the way it lightly brushes against him.

And he knows all about the look of which she speaks. It's the thing that bonds them – him and Leah. His grip on her hand tightens.

'Even my father had it, when he thought I couldn't see him, but I did. I'd catch him giving me that look, and I couldn't bear it.'

She bites down on her lip. He sees how hard this is for her, how unfamiliar it feels for her to open up in this way. But he also knows she wants to go on. That she feels safe with him: they have a shared understanding.

'It's easier to just cut people off,' she says. 'Not let any-one get too close. I learnt that over time.' A boyfriend she'd opened up to had reacted badly when she'd explained her past to him. 'Not at first,' she tells Anton. 'But I could feel the gradual change. Then one day he told me he couldn't shake it from his head. That it had changed how he saw me, what he felt about me. It made me a different person, in his eyes.'

After that, she'd made a decision. Better to shut that side of herself away, hide it from view. Shove it deep down into a dark corner, and never shed any light upon it. It was the rule that governed her life. And yet she had told him – Anton. She had marked him out in this special way. Surely that means something. Surely it points to some deeper understanding, some fated bond. The pad of his thumb draws across the skin of her palm. Does it send shooting messages through her nerve endings? She is so close to him. Her lips are full, gleaming with a smear of balm. Her perfume is in his nostrils.

'It seems a shame to give these away,' she says, her tone changing abruptly, becoming businesslike, and he watches with dismay as she gets to her feet. 'But the charity shop will be pleased.'

He watches her move away from the bed to resume her task. Outside the evening light is fading. Soon she will go.

'Why don't you keep them?' he suggests, and she laughs suddenly.

'Don't be silly.'

'Why not?' He looks up at her appraisingly. 'You're about Charlotte's height and size. They would fit you.'

He doesn't tell her that at times she is so like his dead wife that it leaves him reeling.

'Right now, they do. But soon I'll be too big. And, any-way,' she says, dismissing the notion with a quiver of discomfort, 'it wouldn't be right.'

'They're just clothes, dear.'

'Jake wouldn't like it,' she says, a warning there.

Her eyes are kept deliberately on the task at hand, avoiding contact with his, and as he watches her folding the Diane von Furstenberg, annoyed by that reference to the meddling boyfriend, Anton is seized with a great longing to see her in it.

'Here,' he says, getting to his feet and taking the dress

from her. 'Allow me to show you. Just for a minute,' he continues, countering the objection that flies up into her face. 'Now, look, it's a wrap dress, you see? Like this.'

He gets her to stand still. Then, taking his place behind her, he guides the dress over her shoulders, her arms slotting into the sleeves. She is wearing a T-shirt and skirt, light, flimsy materials – they barely show beneath the silk of the dress.

Guiding her to the bay window, he positions her in front of the long mirror. Her resistance is still there, but it's waning now, and he can sense that she's captivated by her reflection as he pulls the fabric around her, bending to her hip, then tying a loose bow.

'There,' he says.

He can see the bump now, the low swell of it beneath the patterned silk. His eyes glide over it, to the curve of her hip, the roundness of her buttocks. He is just a little behind her. Were he to take one step forward, he could press himself flat against her back.

'Look how beautiful you are,' he whispers, and he puts a hand to her hair, draws it softly away from her neck.

'What's going on here?'

She jumps away, and he sees the swerve of panic in her face – it corresponds with the sudden pounding of his heart.

Jake is in the doorway, his eyes dark with suspicion.

'Nothing,' she tells him, and Anton hears his own voice explain that Leah was helping him with his wife's things.

'Let's go,' Jake tells her, and obediently, she sheds the dress, and follows.

Anton listens to their footsteps descending, feels the

heat of blood pulsing angrily into his brain. On the floor, the dress lies in a pool of patterned silk.

The boyfriend is a problem.

Even when he's not around, when he's away on his bicycle, or flogging the dead horse of his acting career, still his disapproval and suspicion hover over them.

Sometimes when Leah is with Anton there will come the slam of a door downstairs, and Anton has to watch her scurrying away from him, down into the garden, like a nervous rabbit. And then he is left alone to ponder the empty rooms of his house, the cavernous spaces of his heart, while up through the floorboards come sounds of life downstairs. Music, laughter, voices – it stirs the envy inside him. Sometimes, the child stays over with them, and Anton hears the crash of toys, the electronic noise of video games. He stands at his window and watches them in the garden, father and son, wrestling together, conducting some kind of savage game, yelping and squealing with delight. This boy looks no more than six or seven, he thinks. And when he remembers that this is the age Mark was when Anton was sent to prison, he has to turn away from the window, the scene in the garden too painful to observe.

He tries to occupy himself, begins clearing out the drawers and cupboards in the kitchen. Sheaves of envelopes containing old bills, old bank statements. Progress reports for Mark from kindergarten. Hospital notes from both of Charlotte's pregnancies. Certificates of interest. Investor reports. Scatterings of business cards, yellowed with age. One he finds is crisp and white, the name and numbers embossed in new-looking print. Anton presses the edge of the card to his chin, an idea turning over in his mind.

I wonder, he thinks.

When Anton was in the hospital, Mark had brought him a laptop. 'It's an old one of mine,' his son had said, 'but it still works. I thought maybe you could use it.'

It had lain there, untouched, through the drift of days he had spent in the ward. But since his return home, he's had cause to use it more and more. He's even hooked it up to a little printer, and now, with this new idea gaining heat in his brain, Anton flips it open, clicks on the internet icon. His search does not easily yield a result, and the evening light grows faint as he scrolls down, rethinking the parameters of his search, calculating dates, trying and trying again. He forgets to eat, engrossed in the quest. When at last he finds what he is looking for, selecting the print command, the summertime sounds of evening have all faded, and there is only the distant noise of occasional traffic and the hum of paper feeding through the printer.

When he is done, he takes a blank sheet from the sheaf and sits at the table with the business card in front of him.

You do not know me, he begins to write, *and for my own reasons, I wish to remain anonymous. But there is something I wish to draw your attention to. Something I think might be of interest . . .*

When the letter is finished, he folds it carefully, along with the printout, slides the documents into the envelope, addresses it. In the morning he will send it.

That night, he sleeps soundly for the first time in weeks.

20

Leah

The corridor is stifling, heat trapped between the brown nylon carpet and the white ceiling tiles. Jake is standing some way from her, flicking through his phone. He had offered his seat to an expectant mum. In Leah's lap is the orange file they've given her, along with a laminated sheet of paper containing her number in the queue. Along the corridor, she sees several women using the laminated sheets to fan air into their hot faces. One woman talks loudly into a phone; another discusses curtain samples with her partner. There's a toddler here, a little boy of no more than two years old who runs up in front of the occupied chairs, full of childish energy.

Leah has waited for this day for so long. Excitement and nerves gather in her chest. She has a book with her, but the words blur on the page. She's too distracted by her thoughts to read. Every time a door opens, her eyes flick to the woman who's called, taking note of her bump. Her own pregnancy has become clearly visible. What had been a thickening of flesh around her waistband has moulded itself into a small mound. Instinctively, her hand goes to it, sending waves of reassurance and love through the layers of skin and flesh. Leah knows that in a few minutes, she will get to see her baby for the first time. As part of

243

the consultation, her doctor will perform a brief scan. When she anticipates that moment, a wash of nervy joy goes through her, and she sits up a little straighter.

'*How could you?*'

The words come at her without warning. Yvonne Hannigan, uttering those words with fury, her eyes bright with tears. This was in the church grounds after the funeral, the place heaving with mourners, many who didn't even know the Hannigans but were moved by the awful tragedy. 'There but for the grace of God,' she'd heard one woman mutter to the other. Leah hadn't wanted to go to the funeral. After the interview with the police – all those questions they'd asked her – she dreaded having to face other people, knowing that doubts lingered over the death, questions to which she had failed to provide answers. She had wept and railed against attending the funeral, but her father had been firm. She had to face these people, he'd insisted. She had to show her sorrow, to share their pain. To shirk it would be indecent, unforgivable. So she had gone, kept her head down, felt her parents' protective grip on each arm. She had not expected to be seen, had failed to anticipate the icy rage of the grieving mother. 'How could you?' Yvonne had demanded. 'How could you show your face here?' before being led away. Jim had barely looked at Leah, hostile disgust in his eyes, which was nearly worse.

The baby's face is in her head. The chubby softness of it, a dimple in one cheek, bright blue eyes, like little marbles. Cian. She remembers again the screaming from upstairs. The instant surge of panic, followed by the long, slow sigh of dread that filled out inside her and stayed with her long after that little body was taken away. His mother would once have sat in a corridor just like this one, waiting, full of hope and expectation for the life she was carrying inside her.

'They've called your number,' Jake prompts her. 'Are you okay?' he asks, concern in his voice.

'Fine.' She pushes down hard on all the negative thoughts and feelings, focusing instead on hope for what lies ahead.

Leah is reassured by her obstetrician's age, which she guesses to be early fifties, and by Dr Feeney's quiet manner. A man of few words, he's polite and warm but not over-friendly. Efficient and professional, he looks through her chart and puts some clarifying questions to her, which she answers.

'First baby,' he comments. 'And naturally conceived.'

'That's right.'

'Trying for long?' he asks, and Leah feels herself blush a little.

'Actually, no. It was sort of an accident.'

'A happy accident,' Jake clarifies, and she smiles at him.

Things have been strained between them lately. Distracted by the prospect of his son being taken from him, Jake has been frequently absent from their home over the past few weeks, and when he is there he has seemed distant and preoccupied. He'd made it clear to Leah that he disapproves of her friendship with Anton, and while they have avoided any outright confrontations of late, the atmosphere between them has been prickly with unspoken resentments and anxious uncertainties. At times, it has felt like their relationship might be too precarious to support a new life.

But with the squeeze of Jake's hand around hers, his excitement passing through to her, any lingering doubts she's had about his feelings for this pregnancy evaporate. They are in it together. Whatever happens.

'Right then,' Dr Feeney says. 'Shall we take a look?'

The gel is cold on her belly. He'd warned her it would be but, still, it's a shock. She's stretched out on the examining couch, Dr Feeney on a little stool beside her, one hand pressing the paddle of the ultrasound into her bump, the other hand working the computer beneath the screen, which throws back blurry images in black and white, like interference on an old TV.

Jake stands behind her. He's holding her hand. She feels his excited anticipation communicating with hers, but keeps her eyes on Dr Feeney and that screen, waiting for him to find her baby through the walls of tissue, then turn the screen so she can see.

The silence in the room seems to stretch and grow taut. She watches his face carefully, scouring it for clues. It's a serious and concentrated look, but then she catches a fleeting frown – a barely perceptible tightening of his features. The pressure of Jake's grip around her hand intensifies and she knows he's seen it too.

'Is everything all right?' she asks the doctor, because she's deeply worried now.

He doesn't answer, continues to stare hard at the screen, and she wills him to speak, wills him to tell her that everything is all right. Her baby is safe.

Slowly, he draws his gaze away from the screen and the look he gives her is so full of compassion that she feels it at once: the prick of fear, the puncturing of hope.

She knows what he is going to say before he says it. His voice is soft and she steels herself against it, feeling the imminent return of that old feeling: dread.

'I'm afraid, Leah,' he says gently, 'it's not good news.'

There is no baby.

Even though her belly has become a small mound, there is no baby inside. A molar pregnancy, is the term he gives it. A rare complication, characterized by the abnormal growth of placental tissue. There might, in the early days of her pregnancy, have been a tiny foetus, but if there was, it had been overwhelmed, pushed out, strangled by this abnormal growth – this mole – with its voracious appetite, swelling to fill her womb with its fluid-filled cysts.

A mole. At first, Leah cannot help but think of the small tunnelling creature of *The Wind in the Willows* – all velvety fur and gentleness. But now, in her mind, that creature grows sharp teeth and becomes vicious, a slavering fearsome thing, its tiny eyes flashing with malicious intent.

Jake runs a bath for her. 'Will I bring you a cup of tea?' he asks.

But she says no. His concern – his lovingness – helps, but one part of her simply wants to be left alone. She sinks down into the water, stares at her sunken belly, creases in the skin. It takes a certain amount of courage to do this – as if she has to steel herself to confront her own body. She thinks again of the operating theatre where, yesterday, the procedure took place.

'Just relax there,' the anaesthetist had told her, in his calming voice, and soon she was under in a dreamless sleep.

When she woke, it was with the impression that her eyes had been closed for just an instant – a minute or two. She had the unsettling thought that it hadn't happened yet – that she'd woken up too soon. But then she felt the pad that had been placed between her legs – the wad of it like some awful evidence of the trauma to her insides.

In the ward, Jake had sat by her bed, grey-faced and anxious. He stroked her arm, offered her sympathetic looks, while she lay there waiting. On the opposite side of the room, two women in beds were talking across the space between their cubicles.

'Is this your first miss?' one asked, and the other said: 'Yeah. I've a little fella at home already, though.'

'Ah, that's nice.'

Leah turned over on her side, away from them. Closing her eyes, she felt Jake's kiss pressed to her forehead.

Now, in the bath, there is an ache inside her, like a long, deep pull. She imagines gloved hands delving inside her, surgical tools scraping her out. Blood clots escape into the water. Shaking, she pulls the plug, hauls herself out.

How long will it take? she wonders. How long until this heaviness inside her breaks, like still heat broken by a storm? She hasn't cried yet – not really. A few frightened tears before the surgery, but the shock has a hold on her. She has the feeling that sorrow – grief – has not come upon her yet.

Jake makes her meals, brings her little presents: books, magazines. They lie on the floor unread.

'You should go back to work,' she tells him, worried about all the time he's taking off. He needs to work. They need his earnings.

'I want to take care of you,' he says.

'I'm fine,' she tells him, his arms around her, trying to feel safe in his embrace.

When he draws back, his eyes scour her face, as sharp as a physician looking for evidence of illness or disease. 'You're not fine,' he says gravely.

Leah's mother calls to see her. A tricky one, this. A test. If anyone can cause the emotion to break, it's her mother – always able to reach the tender spot inside her, always able to coax her true feelings out. She sits on the side of Leah's bed, fixes her with a stare that is a complex mix of love, anxiety and maternal warmth. It has some effect. Tears roll. Leah presses a Kleenex to her face.

'You'll have another baby, sweetheart,' her mother says, holding her hand and squeezing it. 'Just give yourself some time. Let your body heal. Be patient, darling. It will happen, and then all of this heartache will be forgotten.'

It is not enough.

Matthew stays away. At weekends, Jake takes his son to the park, the zoo, the cinema, but he doesn't bring the boy back to their flat. It's as if he's anxious Matthew's presence might upset her. Leah feels grateful for this sensitivity, but it worries her too. The weekends, without Jake, are lonely and long. She idles around the flat, half-heartedly re-arranging their possessions, her mind elsewhere. When Jake comes home, she smells the outdoors on his skin. There is a thoughtful air about him on his return, as if his mind is still with the boy. With Jenna. A new and unwelcome thought comes to her: that he is reluctant to come home to her and her pent-up sorrow. That, in his heart, he wishes he were back in his old home with his wife and son. That he is secretly nursing feelings of nostalgia and regret.

'She asked me to give you this,' he tells Leah, handing her a small box.

She opens it and finds a tiny ceramic angel – a brooch pinned to a sheet of card. On the card is printed a poem. Leah reads the first line:

> A butterfly lights beside us like a sunbeam,
> and for a brief moment . . .

She stops and puts it aside. A sudden burn of anger comes up her throat.

Carefully, she returns the brooch to its box, sets it down. 'I wouldn't have thought Jenna'd be into that sort of thing,' she comments. She cannot keep the acidity from her voice.

Jake's eyes flicker over her face. 'She was just trying to be nice,' he says.

Leah picks up the paintbrush she has been using, goes to the bathroom and runs the tap.

'Are you all right?' he asks, following her.

'I'm fine.'

'You don't seem fine.'

She squeezes paint from the bristles, watches the water swirl in the basin.

He runs a hand through his hair, then puts his hands into his jeans pockets, leans against the door frame. 'Is it the pin or the fact that it was Jenna who gave it to you?'

Leah cannot say what is really bothering her. When she

thinks about him having that conversation with Jenna, imagines the confidential tones he used to tell her about the failed pregnancy – about the mole – she feels a rage inside her so strong it makes her shake.

'Have you seen Anton?' she asks, keeping her tone neutral.

'No. Why?'

'I promised Mark I'd keep an eye on him.'

'He's a grown man, Leah. And you've enough to deal with.'

'Could you call up there?' she asks, catching his eye now and holding him with her stare.

'You're kidding.'

'It would just be five minutes. Just call up and see if he's all right.'

Jake shakes his head, an expression of distaste on his face. 'I'm not going anywhere near that man.' Then, softening his stance, he says: 'Besides, it's Mark's problem. Let him take care of it.'

Thinking that's the end of it, he comes towards her and puts his hand to her neck as if he's going to kiss her. She turns away, anger pumping through her. It was such a small thing to ask of him. 'I'm tired,' she says.

He lingers a moment behind her, and when she looks up at the bathroom mirror and catches his reflection there, she sees the expression on his face, full of doubt.

'Fair enough,' he says, in a flat voice, before moving away.

She cannot sleep. At night, she lies in bed, tracing the map of shadows on the ceiling. The window is open, and she can hear the call of night birds, the distant sounds of an occasional car passing on the road. Somewhere nearby she hears a fox barking. There have always been foxes here, Anton had said.

She misses him. Misses the softness of his presence. His undemanding company and the way it soothes her. If she admitted such a feeling to Jake he would be horrified. The world is black and white to Jake. He can pin the label 'murderer' on Anton and dismiss him from his mind. But for Leah, it is not so easy. She has thought long and hard about Anton's account of what happened to Charlotte. She has tried to imagine the frustrations within their marriage, the difficulties involved in living with such a woman. 'I did not kill my wife,' he had told her, and she had felt the resonance of truth in those words, the fierce demand to be believed right there in his eyes.

Leah is not an innocent. Unlike Jake, she knows the world is not black and white. Images come to her unbidden, memories of the little boy who died, all the sorrow and pain she is responsible for. This thing that has happened to her – this mole – it is a type of penance. Even though she doesn't believe in Catholic guilt, she feels it keenly. She is a person who has lied to bereaved parents, lied to the police. *I deserve this*, she thinks, while Jake turns over in his sleep.

Vaguely, she becomes aware of cigarette smoke on the air. It filters through into her bedroom, prodding curiosity inside her. She knows he's out there in the darkness.

Quietly, so as not to disturb Jake, she gets out of bed, tiptoes across the hall.

She finds her cardigan on the back of a kitchen chair,

pulls it around her. She shouldn't do this. She has made promises to Jake. But there is an emptiness inside her that he cannot fill, that he cannot come close to. He doesn't understand what it means to be hollowed out with guilt. He doesn't know what a burden it is.

She steps out on to the patio, feels the warm air against her skin. It seems like an act of recklessness, yet she is drawn on. Her bare foot steps up on to the grass. It crackles under her skin, dry and parched for rain.

The branches of the fruit trees sway gently above her, their leaves silvery under the moonlight. The air smells cleanly of jasmine and lavender, and when she turns to look up at the house, something moves in the garden. Instantly, her attention snaps to it. Through the darkness, she strains to see.

'Hello?' she calls. 'Is someone there?'

No answering voice, no flare of a cigarette glowing through the darkness. The garden is empty – a tangle of weeds and little else.

She thinks of Charlotte, and is surprised the woman has strayed into her head. In the rooms upstairs, there is no framed photograph of her, no wedding-day snap, no tender portrait of mother and children. Leah thinks of the dead woman's clothes, remembers the feel of that silk on her skin, how she had allowed herself, just for a moment, to be wrapped in that woman's dress, in that woman's bedroom, a secret imagining of what it would be like to occupy that woman's life.

A sudden chill in the air, she wraps her cardigan tight around her. Somewhere in the garden she hears the rustling of night creatures. The snap of a branch. Or maybe it's just the thought of the ghost that's been summoned making her cold.

Whatever thoughts she'd had of seeking solace fly past. The garden tonight seems changed. A different presence here. One that is watchful, unfriendly.

Taking fright, Leah hurries back on to the patio. When she closes the French windows behind her, she finds her limbs are trembling, new blood leaking between her legs. In the bathroom, she cleans herself quickly. Someone was watching her in the darkness. Jake doesn't stir when she climbs back into bed.

21

Hilary

Hilary is upstairs one evening when her attention is caught by the windows of Anton's house, her eyes widening in horror and disbelief. For in that moment, she sees Charlotte. Standing right there in the front bedroom, gazing at her reflection in the long, oval mirror that stands by the window. A dead woman in a printed silk dress. Hilary's heart flutters wildly with fear.

But then reality breaks through, and she realizes it is not Charlotte, but Leah, and a new confusion creeps in to replace the fear that slid away. Her attention rapt, she watches as Anton comes and stands behind the young woman – the ingénue – and reaches out to touch her, gathering the swathe of her hair and gently drawing it away from her face. That one gesture makes everything inside Hilary go very still.

Down below, the street is empty, the cars all nestled together in a row against the kerb, a peaceful scene. But here, in her bedroom, a new turmoil has taken hold. They have disappeared from view, and her mind races, wondering what on earth is happening. What can they be doing?

Hilary scratches her upper arms, as if she has a rash, panic taking hold inside her. It's all she can do not to run downstairs and out on to the street, then march across to Number 14 to demand answers.

She doesn't do any such thing. She knows it would be rash – foolish – to draw attention to herself in that manner, blowing the plan with her impatience, her misunderstanding. For that is what it is. Something simple she's misinterpreted that she and Anton will laugh about later when all this is done.

For the next few days, she monitors the situation closely.

Having spent two decades observing the comings and goings on in Wyndham Park – the births and deaths, the divorces, repossessions, feuds and scandals – she sees herself as the custodian of the street's history. Nothing escapes her attention. Sometimes she feels as if she has spent her whole life staring out of her bedroom window.

She remembers the first time she stood in this room, taking in the ancient flocked wallpaper, its ceiling crusted with spreading brown stains, and trying to envisage the two of them – her and Greg – spending their lives there, possibly with children of their own.

'What do you think?' Greg had asked, a breathy bewilderment still in his voice.

He could hardly believe he was in this position, she knew. Barely thirty and already married, getting his hopes up about this house. It was an executor's sale.

'Did he die in this room?' she had asked, and he had laughed, then accused her of being squeamish, coming to stand behind her, his arms wrapped around her waist, his hold firm.

She had married Greg because he was solid, reliable. 'A safe bet,' her father had called him. But that was in the early years of her marriage, before she discovered something vital: that feeling safe can be constricting. It takes all the air out of life. She wanted excitement, a thrill. Something deeper and more profound, something that moved her.

While she waits for a sign from Anton, watching his house carefully, she thinks of all the things that have happened on this street under her surveillance. From this very window, she had borne witness to events that both shocked and moved her. Like the day the police came and took Anton away.

She remembers the morning it happened.

They came for him early, before anyone on the street was awake. Barely forty-eight hours had passed since the discovery of Charlotte's body.

It was summer, so there was a tinge of light through the slats in the blinds even though it wasn't yet six a.m. Hilary doesn't know what it was that woke her. There was no siren blaring. She cannot recall any blue flashing lights. Intuition, perhaps. A deep knowledge of something catastrophic about to happen. At first, she had felt confusion – the unfamiliarity of the room around her, the foreign smell of new carpets and fresh paint. Then she heard the bang of a car door, followed by another, and by the time she was out of bed, struggling into her dressing-gown, he was already coming out of the front door of his house, flanked on either side by uniformed officers. How clearly she can remember the way the guard shielded Anton's head as he ducked in through the car door, and the pang it caused deep in her chest, remembering how she had run her own hands through his hair, how she had felt the hard mass of his skull beneath her fingertips when she had kissed him. And yet there she was, staring at the back of his head through the window of a patrol car, watching helplessly as they sped away with him.

'Where do you think they've taken him?' she had asked Greg, over breakfast, a couple of hours later. A Monday morning, Greg dressed for summer school. She'd tried to keep her tone casual, as if she didn't really care one way or the other. As if it wasn't eating her up inside.

'I imagine he's being interviewed in the local station,' he'd said, scooping out a piece of melon and eating it at the counter.

She tried to imagine the scene – Anton at a table in a windowless room, two slab-faced interrogators opposite, a mirror on the wall screening off the others who were watching.

'Are you really going to work?' she asked, as Greg wiped his face with a napkin, and reached for his brief-case on the table. It exasperated her, the knowledge that he could just carry on as normal while Anton was being interrogated by the police.

'Why wouldn't I?'

'What if the police want to speak to you?'

'Then give them the school's number. Although I can't think what else they'd want from me.'

They had both given statements the day before. Every-one who'd been at the party – all the neighbours – had been questioned.

'I wish you'd stay at home,' she pleaded. 'I just feel so nervous. What if they call around here again? What should I tell them?'

'Tell them the truth,' he'd said simply, then kissed her cheek and left her to stew in her own tormented thoughts.

That same morning, she'd watched from the upstairs window as the little children were taken away. A woman she didn't recognize came and put the boy and the little girl into the back seat of a Toyota Corolla. The police-woman who had been minding the children slammed the car boot closed on the suitcases and bags that had been crammed inside. The little girl was crying. Hilary heard the shrillness of her screaming, the hard, accusatory pitch of it, and for the first time in the forty-eight hours since Charlotte's death she'd felt a cold pang of fear.

What have we done? she thought, her hand held to her mouth.

The police did not return that day, and when she sat down to dinner opposite Greg that evening, she asked him: 'What do you think will happen to those children?'

He was cutting into the lamb chop on his plate, sawing it up into neat little triangles. 'I expect some relative will take care of them.'

'I saw a woman come and take them away. A woman in a red car.'

'Charlotte's sister, I expect.'

Hilary hadn't known Charlotte had a sister. Was briefly surprised to find that Greg did.

'She lives in Cork, I believe,' he added, and this brought a new plunge of guilt, of quavering doubt.

'But that's miles away.'

He didn't answer, just kept pushing meat into his mouth.

It wasn't right – those children being dragged all the way to the other side of the country. What about Anton? Didn't he have a right to have them near? 'You don't suppose,' she began tentatively, 'that we could offer to take them?'

His eyes shot up to meet hers. It made her nervous. Shakily, she went on: 'I mean, just until things are sorted out. Just until he's released.'

It was then that Greg put down his knife and fork and stared hard at her. 'What are you talking about? The man has murdered his wife. By the time the state allows him to take care of his children again, they'll be fully grown.'

She had gone to pieces then. She couldn't help it. Days of sobbing, or thrashing around on her bed in despair, until finally Greg had taken some leave, booked a break at a B-and-B in Wexford and swept her away. Three days' walking on the beach at Curracloe, turning the facts over in her head, trying to tease out every possibility, attempting to make a plan. By the time they returned, she was calm and Anton was in custody. A fact she was forced to accept. A fact she had to try to live with.

Once, when they were together, she had told Anton in a moment of candour: 'I feel like I've waited my whole life for you.'

He had laughed, twirling a lock of her hair around his index finger and thumb. 'Your whole life,' he had said mockingly. 'All twenty-nine years of it.'

She had poked him in the ribs, and he had barked with laughter, then pushed himself on top of her, flattening her against the bed.

'Good things come to those who wait,' he had said. 'Remember that,' he added, smiling into her face before he kissed her, long and deep, calling to life again the desire inside her.

Remember that. The way he had said it had seemed meaningful at the time, although she had no idea what he'd meant. Only later did it start to dawn on her. A message there. An unspoken pact.

And she did remember. When she went to the courthouse almost a whole year later, and sat in the public gallery listening to all the evidence built up against him, those words of his ran in a loop through her brain, keeping her steady and still. Even when sentence was passed and she felt the crushing weight of it – all those years! – it was the one thing that kept her sane. He had looked up at her, briefly, before they led him away. To anyone watching, it would have appeared to be a fleeting glance, but to Hilary it was pointed and personal and weighted with meaning. *Remember*, he seemed to be saying to her. Remember to wait.

I am your Penelope, she had written in one of her letters to him. One of the many she had sent to the prison. Their correspondence had commenced shortly after the sentencing. A correspondence that was, by necessity, carefully coded. And one-sided. That part had surprised and hurt her. But then she thought about how low he must be feeling, how difficult he must be finding it to adjust, and she redoubled her efforts. So what if he didn't reply? He would eventually. And until then she refused to let her devotion waver. It was a test, and she would pass with flying colours.

And then one day he did reply. Her heart crowding her throat as she opened the envelope and took out a single sheet of notepaper. One simple instruction printed on it: *Hilary, please stop.*

Her initial reaction was pain. A wounding rejection when all she had wanted was to reach out and show him she cared. That she loved him. Why on earth would he hurt her like this? But then, once she had taken time to think it through properly, to analyse what it meant, she realized why he had done this. It was painful for him. Of course it was! After all, she was on the outside while he was locked up, paying the ultimate price for their love. And what did it matter if they didn't write to each other? It meant she would have so much more to tell him once he got out and they were together. She would store it all up – her thoughts, her feelings, the little things she knew would move him. She would save them. They would have the rest of their lives to tell each other these things, share all their different experiences, however hard or painful. She would wait.

It has been weeks, and still there has been no word from him. No sign. No indication. It keeps returning to her – that image of Leah in the window, wearing Charlotte's dress. And every time she relives it in memory, she feels the same sucking in of breath, the same tension in her forehead. The way Anton had stood behind that woman, his hand reaching out for her hair. It meant nothing, Hilary tells herself, steeling her thoughts against her own anxiety. Once more she draws on her reserves of patience, feeling, as she does, that those reserves can't last for ever. Very soon, they will run dry.

Now, Hilary looks out on the street, sees the lean figure of their neighbour, Jake, walking up from the tennis courts, a shopping bag in each hand. There's something slumped about the young man's posture. 'Straighten up,' she says quietly, as if he could possibly hear her. His glasses catch the light briefly as he looks up, then turns his gaze to the pavement once more.

Quickly, she slips on her shoes and hurries downstairs. She is across the road, affecting surprise to see him, by the time he reaches his gate.

'Out doing some shopping?' she asks brightly, and he glances up, transferring one of his shopping bags to his other arm and, with his free hand, puts a finger to his eye, presses behind the glasses.

Good God, has he been crying? Hilary wonders.

'Hi, Hilary. Yes. Just getting a few bits and pieces.'

'How is Leah? I haven't seen her around much lately,' she asks lightly, with a smile.

She notes the hesitation in his manner, the uncertainty in his air.

'Actually, she hasn't been very well,' he says. Her attention sharpens. With an air of apology, of sorrow, he adds: 'She lost a baby recently, you see.'

Despite the complicated and negative feelings she's been harbouring towards the young woman, Hilary feels an automatic wash of empathy. She knows that sorrow. She knows that horrible emptiness. 'Oh, no,' she says now, surprised by the genuine feeling in her voice.

'She's okay, but, you know . . .' His voice trails off.

'I do know,' Hilary replies, the force of her tone making him look up. 'I know exactly what it's like, believe me.'

'You've been through it?'

'Many times, I'm afraid.'

'Oh.' He's staring at her now as if making private re-assessments of his opinion of her. 'Look, would it be too much to ask . . . Would you think about talking to her? I've tried, but I just feel like I'm getting nowhere. It might be good for her to talk to someone who's been through it already. What do you think?'

'Of course I will,' she says, smiling, the opportunity presenting itself so easily, a little glow of triumph inside her. 'I'd be happy to.'

She takes flowers with her when she visits the next day – a verdant bunch of hydrangea floribunda, the stems wrapped tightly in paper kitchen towels.

'These are lovely,' Leah says, then leaves them by the sink, instantly forgetting them as she drifts out into the garden.

They sit on hard chairs in the shade of the house, a rickety table between them. The sun burns high in the sky but it doesn't reach them there. From inside the house come playful shouts from the little boy. She hasn't seen him around much lately. He is engaged in some kind of board game with Jake involving hippos and frogs. The noise is distracting, intrusive. Hilary feels needled with annoyance. Can't that young man see how unwell Leah is? Doesn't he realize the yelping and play-acting are painful to her?

And yet Leah doesn't seem pained. Her customary appearance of being slightly distracted has changed somewhat. The hazy, dreamy expression has hardened into preoccupation. It's as if she has forgotten something, and the faraway look in her eyes reflects a quiet desperation inside to remember.

'You're very pale, my dear,' Hilary states, drawing the gaze back to her.

'Am I? Yes. I suppose I have been indoors a lot lately.'

'Why don't we sit in the sun?' Hilary suggests, getting to her feet.

'Oh, no, I –'

'Come on, I insist.' She puts her hand under Leah's elbow to draw her up, is surprised by the thinness of the arm. How slight and delicate the girl is. It's like picking up a loose bag of sticks. The resistance she puts up is feeble enough, and meekly she follows Hilary up into the grass, the older woman carrying their chairs and placing them firmly in a spot that's in the sun.

'A good dose of Vitamin D will do you the power of good,' Hilary says, noting as she sits down that they are fully visible now from the upper storeys of the house. Likewise, behind the shield of her sunglasses, she can cast her gaze up at the windows without it being obvious.

She wonders if he's inside now, witnessing this. Something tells her that he is. They are alike in that way, Anton and Hilary, both keen observers.

'Thank you for calling to see me,' Leah says, in that quiet voice of hers. 'Jake told me he bumped into you. He said you'd had a similar experience.'

'It's true. I know only too well what you're going through right now. That confusion of feelings. One minute you're empty and wrung-out, like there's just nothing left inside you, and the next you're moved to anger at the sheer bloody unfairness of it all.'

Leah nods, her eyes sweeping the grass in front of her.

'Miscarriage is far more common than people realize,' Hilary continues. 'It's just that no one seems to talk about it and I could never figure out why. But it does help to talk.'

She looks at the young woman's face, notes her

complexion has lost all its bloom. There's a dullness to her features now, and Hilary experiences a rise of genuine sympathy. Oh, yes, she can still feel that pain. She remembers acutely what it was like.

'You know, the first time it happened to me –' Hilary stops abruptly. Her attention has been drawn to movement inside the flat, a raised voice, and Leah's head also turns.

'Don't fucking lie to me! It's right there in black and white!'

A woman's voice, shrill with fury.

'I'm telling you – I haven't a clue what you're talking about!'

Through the open French windows, she can see Jake on his feet, the boy still and watchful on the couch, the game forgotten. The woman moves and comes now into view. Small, elfin, in shorts and a T-shirt, her limbs tanned against the ice-cream shades of her clothes.

'I left my son with that woman,' she is saying. 'You told me I could trust her!'

'You're being ridiculous,' Jake says.

'Read that and tell me I'm being ridiculous!' she shrieks, and Hilary watches as she thrusts something at him – a newspaper. Half of it drops to the ground and he bends to reach for it.

'Excuse me,' Leah says to Hilary, in that small, distracted voice.

She's on her feet now, moving cautiously through the grass, but Hilary isn't going to wait in the garden and miss the action. Enthralled by what's unfolding in front of her, she stands and follows.

'Well? Did you know?' the strange woman is demanding.

But Jake is lost to her, his eyes scanning the newsprint. 'What the fuck . . .' he says, and then looks up.

The woman sees them first.

No sooner has Leah stepped down on to the patio than the woman is out of the door, crossing the paving, her small face a tight knot of hostility.

'Jenna,' Leah begins, but before she can say another word, the woman has slapped her hard across the face.

'You bitch! You murdering fucking bitch!' she says, slapping at Leah, whose hands go up to shield her face from the blows.

'Stop it! Stop this at once!' Hilary barks, appalled at the sudden violence. She grabs the woman's wrist and pulls her back.

Leah is crouched on her knees, her hair falling forward over her face. The woman – Jenna – is breathing deeply from her exertions, and it is only now that Jake appears through the doors, walking slowly as if in a daze. The newspaper is still in his hands. Hilary glances down at it. *Murdering bitch* was the accusation the woman had thrown.

'I'm taking Matthew,' Jenna states, wrenching her wrist free from Hilary's grasp, but before she leaves, she takes a step towards Leah, points a finger at her and hisses: 'You are never to come anywhere near my son again – do you understand me?'

Leah lets out a sound like a whimper, but it's response enough for Jenna, who turns on her heel. From inside the flat, they can hear her barking orders at Matthew to gather up his things, quickly. Jake stares down at Leah, a stunned expression on his face. He makes no attempt to help her up. The front door bangs shut and silence surrounds them.

'Is this true?' Jake asks quietly.

Leah is still crouched, but she pushes back her hair, and Hilary can see her face streaked with tears, an angry red mark on her cheek and across her mouth from the blow she'd received. Her eyes, turned to Jake, are round with fear.

'Is this true?' he asks again. 'That baby's death. Were you, in some way, involved?'

The hard thing that is lodged in Hilary's chest seems to collapse, leaking a cold liquid that spreads through her insides.

Leah's small teeth are biting her lower lip, a flash of panic in her face, and then she nods quickly.

Hilary gasps, she cannot help it. Surely that cannot be true.

'Let me see that,' she says, reaching for the newspaper in Jake's hand but he snatches it away before she can take it.

'I think you'd better leave, Hilary,' he tells her, in a voice like ice.

She nods, and glances back at Leah. There is something forlorn and defenceless about her that makes Hilary take a step towards her, but Jake is adamant.

'Now, please,' he says, raising his voice, and she can hear the crack in it. The sharp warning.

She backs away. 'Very well,' she says.

And just as she is turning from them, she sees him. There, in the window gazing down, is Anton, his arms wrapped around his chest, his face pressed right up against the window. All she can manage is a snatched glance at him, but Hilary is sure – she would swear on it – that he is looking down on this scene of disaster, smiling.

22

Leah

'I think you'd better go,' Jake tells Hilary, and Leah watches the swish of her purple skirt disappearing into the gloom of the flat.

Overhead, the day has darkened.

'Come inside,' Jake says. 'I'm not doing this out here.'

He scowls up at the house as he disappears indoors. She follows, weakness in her legs. There's a smeary, indistinct feeling in her head, thoughts muddled, and when she comes inside, the darkness of the flat disorients her. Her face hurts where Jenna struck her, and the memory of that hard slap, all the venom within it, frightens her. She puts a hand out to hold on to the back of a kitchen chair, steadying herself.

Jake is walking around the room, one hand clasped to the back of his neck. He's still holding the newspaper. She's never seen him so agitated.

'Can I please see that?' she asks, pointing to the newspaper, trying to keep calm.

He moves quickly towards her, throws the paper on to the table in front of her. His face is white, a thin-lipped expression of barely controlled rage.

She glances down and sees the headline:

A MATCH MADE IN HELL
Killer's New Love Interest Has Her Own Dark Past

She sits down quickly. Even though one part of her knows she ought to remain standing, face him on her feet, the horrible plunge of nerves going through her has made her weak. Her eyes scan the text.

Convicted killer Anton Woodbury has found love again after serving an eighteen-year sentence for the cold-blooded murder of his wife. Pictured last week leaving Anton's home in the early hours of the morning is sultry twenty-six-year-old Leah Sullivan. Miss Sullivan, who appears to have taken up residence with the newly released killer, has her own dark history. For in 2007 she was at the centre of a case involving the death of a baby that chilled the small midlands town of _____. Eight-month-old Cian Hannigan had been left in the care of Sullivan, his teenage babysitter, when he died under suspicious circumstances. Although never formally charged, rumours continue to swirl around Leah Sullivan's involvement in tragic Cian's wrongful death. When contacted by this newspaper, Cian's parents declined to comment, however several neighbours we spoke to confirmed that the babysitter had sole charge of the child in the crucial twenty-four hours leading up to his death.

She reads the words on the page, white noise filling her head, a loosening happening deep in her bowels. A surge is beginning inside her — all those dark feelings she has kept down for years are clamouring now to be heard, threatening to rise and overwhelm her.

'Well?' Jake asks. 'Were you ever going to tell me?'

'Yes.'

'Yeah, right!'

'I wanted to. I knew that I should, but –'

'But what, Leah? I mean, what the hell was stopping you? Were you going to wait until after our baby had been born? Was that it? Wait until I was fully trapped before revealing the truth to me?'

'It's not like that. And I wasn't trying to trap you!'

'Well, tell me, then. What is it like? Come on, I'm all ears.'

He's shaking with rage and she knows she must tell him, but not like this.

'If you could just calm down,' she begins.

'Calm down?' His voice screeches against the side of her head. The veins threading through his neck are pumped to the surface, his eyes bulging. 'I thought you loved me,' he says. 'I believed you trusted me. But you've been lying to me the whole time.'

'I haven't been lying.'

'Withholding the truth, then. It's the same thing.'

'I wanted to tell you, but I was afraid.'

'Of what? I'm not a monster, Leah. What did you think I'd do?'

'I thought if you knew you wouldn't want me any more.'

He stares at her, then shakes his head, his shoulders slumping forward. His voice drops, a note of bewilderment entering it. 'I don't know what I want.'

Fear is alive in her chest. She tries to control it. 'What this article says,' she starts quietly, 'what it suggests, is false. I took care of Cian, but I never hurt him.'

'Then why the suspicion? Look – what about this?' He grabs the newspaper, finds the line he's looking for and reads it to her: *'Another local tells us that Miss Sullivan was spotted in Supervalu with the baby late on the Friday afternoon before his death. The child was crying, and the babysitter appeared to grow impatient, rocking him in a way that alarmed onlookers. "I told her that she should put the child back in his pram, that she was rocking him too hard, but she didn't listen. Just turned away and ignored my advice."'* He puts the newspaper down and looks at her.

'It wasn't like that.'

'You didn't rock that baby?'

'No! Not in the way they're suggesting. I didn't shake him. I didn't damage him. He was upset, I picked him up out of the pram to comfort him. And most of the time that weekend he was fine – he was perfectly happy! Just that one time, in the shops, with everyone around. I got flustered.'

'And?'

'And nothing! I paid for the shopping, and then when we were outside, I put him in the pram and by the time we got home he was calm. The same thing that happens every day of the week with women and babies, but the only reason people talked about it – the only reason they pounced on that one little thing – was because of what happened afterwards. I swear to you, Jake. I didn't do it.'

'So what happened to him, then?'

He's giving her a flat stare, and she cannot tell how deep his suspicion goes. She's aware of rain outside in the garden, the patter of it on the stone paving, foreign-sounding after weeks of drought. But all she can think about is the baby, the soft weight of him in her arms.

'I don't know,' she says, in a small voice.

'It says here the cause of death was a bleed to the brain.'

'Yes.'

'But you don't know anything about that?'

She wavers and, for a moment, she is back in the police station of her hometown, facing a detective asking her the same question. Her father had been sitting alongside her, gently coaxing her to answer. And when the question had come, as she had known it would, *Did you see Cian fall, or bang his head?*, she had stumbled over her reply. The same reply she gives Jake now:

'No.' She has never said any different. Nor will she, ever.

Jake is silent. Leah can tell he is unsure of what to believe and wishes there was some way of reassuring him, of drawing him back to her, but he seems so distant, as if he's speaking to her from behind a wall of glass. Instinctively, she has sealed herself off, allowed herself to be paralysed by fear.

Instead, she looks down at the paper once more. Two photographs accompany the article. The larger one shows Anton on the steps outside his house, half turned towards the camera, his expression caught in a grimace of irritation. An unflattering shot, something vaguely reptilian about the cast of his features, the slicked-back hair and suspicious gaze – nothing like the Anton she knows. The picture of Leah is blurry and out of focus, but the impression it gives is quite different. The diaphanous dress, the sunglasses, the way her hair is lifted around her face, caught in a sudden breeze – it depicts youth and beauty and a certain blitheness of spirit. She has no recollection of the photograph being taken. A distance shot, captured on camera by a photographer hidden across the road in the park. It must have happened as she was leaving for work one morning.

She tries to think back, but her brain is muddled and confused, her feelings too anxious and troubled to remember. The idea of someone spying on her like that, a hidden presence watchful of her movements, brings a shudder of fear. She remembers the journalist outside Anton's front door, calling through his letterbox in a wheedling tone.

The thought crosses her mind: how did he find out?

'This thing they're implying about you and him – this love affair,' Jake says, his voice snarling around the term. 'Where did they get that impression?'

'Oh, Jake, I don't know,' she says, wearily. 'They made it up. Put two and two together and made seventeen.'

'You have been seeing a lot of him,' he tells her, in a voice made quiet by a new suspicion.

'Because he's been unwell. I felt sorry for him.'

'Even though I told you I was unhappy about you spending time with him. Even though you knew I had my doubts.'

A challenge.

'You don't seriously believe what's printed here? That I'm having some kind of a romance with him? Come on!' Despite the gravity of the situation, the thought is so absurd she cannot help but poke fun at it.

'Do you think it's funny?' he snaps. 'This isn't some little domestic tiff between you and me. It's printed in the fucking paper! Everyone can read it! My parents will probably see it. Jesus Christ, my ex has read it. How am I supposed to square it with her?'

'You'll talk to her,' she says calmly. 'Explain that all of this has been taken out of context, misrepresented. These are lies – deliberate falsehoods.'

But Jake doesn't appear to be listening. He's over in the kitchen now, plucking an apple from the fruit bowl, then putting it back and pacing to the sink. He's like a wind-up toy ready to rattle off in a new direction. His agitation scares her a little.

'Bad enough that I kept it from Jenna about Anton. That our landlord who lives right above us, with whom we share a garden, has a criminal record. I didn't tell her because I thought there would be no point in worrying her. That we wouldn't be staying here all that long, probably, just until things improved and we could move somewhere else. And I figured that Matthew would never be left on his own here, anyway, because either you or I would be on hand to keep an eye on him. But how the fuck am I going to explain away both of these things, Leah? Not just about Anton, but about you?' His voice cracks, and she can see that he is close to tears. 'Why didn't you tell me? Why?'

Leah gets out of her chair and goes to him. It's a risk, but she feels compelled to put her arms around him and draw him close. He lets himself be pulled into her embrace, and she reaches a hand up to his head, strokes his hair back, runs her fingertips down over the crevice at the base of his skull where it meets his neck. Only this morning, she had lain in bed beside him, his body spooned into hers, and she had kissed him there in that tender place. Now, everything is different.

'Why?' he says again, whispering it into her hair.

'Because I was ashamed,' she answers truthfully. 'Because I didn't want anyone to know.'

She draws back so she can look him in the eye while she says these things. 'It was the worst thing that ever happened to me, Jake, and for a long time, I thought it would destroy me. But then I learnt that if I could just put it behind me, if I could force it deep down into a dark corner of my past – try to forget about it – I could survive. That was the only way. I had a choice, and I chose to live, even though that meant cutting myself off from my home, my parents, all my old friends. I had to start over. To take that second chance. And when I met you it suddenly seemed possible that I really could begin again. A clean sheet, a fresh start – all those stupid clichés were real. I love you, Jake. I'm still the same person. This terrible thing happened to me ten years ago, when I was just a teenager. It doesn't define me. It doesn't change how I feel about you. But the question is,' and here her voice falters a little, 'does it change how you feel about me?'

She lets her arms fall, a little pocket of air coming between their bodies, and waits. Her eyes pass over his face, see the seriousness in his frown. His skin is ashen, and he looks thin and grey in the gloom. Outside, the rain is coming down heavily now, but she doesn't turn to look at it. Instead, she tracks the changing expression on his face. He opens his mouth to speak, but pauses, his frown deepening into a question.

'How did the newspaper find out? About what happened to you all those years ago.'

Her heart gives a hard beat. 'I don't know.'

'Did you tell anyone?'

'No.'

'Then who knows about it?'

'My parents. And the people of our town, but –'

'And no one else? Anyone at work? The girls you used to share with?'

'No.' But her voice is tapering off, a new suspicion entering it, and immediately he picks up on it.

'I just don't understand how they could put you with Anton, then somehow dig up this thing from your past.'

She turns from him, pulls at her lip.

'Leah?'

Her thoughts are turning over rapidly.

'Did you tell Anton?' he asks, the sharpness of the question pulling her up suddenly.

'Did you?' he asks again, when she doesn't answer, incredulity leaking into his tone.

She doesn't speak for a moment. Sinking back against the wall, she closes her eyes. 'I didn't mean to,' she says quietly. 'It just sort of slipped out.'

When she opens her eyes again, Jake is staring at her, his face made impassive with shock.

'Please don't be angry with me,' she tells him, although he looks beyond anger now. 'Something he said just triggered it in me. I was upset and he sort of coaxed it out.'

'Coaxed it out?' His voice is a low croak, his lips bloodless and pale.

'I was upset,' she says again, a tremble in her voice. 'I felt he understood something.'

'What did he understand?'

'What it's like to carry this guilt and shame around

277

inside you all the time. What it's like to be judged for something you didn't do. To carry the burden of a person's death even though you're not responsible for it. It's hard for people to understand – to really know what that's like. The awful weight of it. But he just –'

'Unbelievable,' he says, cutting across her. An ugly smirk has appeared on his face that confuses her. 'You think he didn't do it, don't you? Nineteen years in prison and you think he's some downy innocent.'

'Jake, I –'

'Un-fucking-believable. You keep this secret from me, and yet you confide in *him*?'

He's pushed himself away from the kitchen now and is hurrying around the room with a new urgency, gathering up his bag, his helmet, his coat.

'What are you doing?' she asks, but he doesn't answer.

He's leaving me, she thinks, and the idea makes her panic. The thought of living without love in her life sets off a range of new emotions inside her. She cannot bear the return of loneliness, not again, not after all she has been through.

She follows him out into the hall, watches him slinging the bag over his shoulder, and clipping the clasp of his helmet beneath his chin.

'It's pouring with rain,' she tells him. 'You'll get soaked.'

But he ignores her, wheeling his bike to the door.

'At least tell me where you're going,' she pleads, panic entering her voice. This stony silence is worse than his wound-up agitation. It feeds the certainty inside her that this is an ending between them. He's leaving her.

'Jake?'

He opens the door, cold air cutting through the little hallway, rain spattering over the threshold. His eyes are fixed on the handlebars of his bicycle, avoiding all contact with her.

'I need to think,' he tells her quietly.

He wheels the bike outside and she watches him carrying it up the steps, rain falling on him, darkening his clothes.

Then he is gone, and she stands listening to the loud patter of drops bouncing off the leaves of the magnolia, falling fatly and noisily on to the steps and all the hard surfaces around her.

After a minute, she steps back and draws the door closed.

It rains all night. She lies awake, listening to the patter of it on the window, on the concrete path outside. The wind moves through the magnolia, the tips of the branches brushing against the walls of the house. Overhead there are creaks and groans and she knows that it's Anton, awake and moving around. This reminder of him arouses suspicion within her – did he betray her secret? Did he deliberately break his promise? Reason tells her he couldn't have. Why would he? She has witnessed his contempt for those tabloid hacks so bent on twisting his own story. She has seen him cowering from them, frightened of being exposed to their vicious lack of scruples, their limitless appetite for gossip. No, it must be some other source. And then she remembers how they swarmed to the town after Cian's death – the same tribe of hacks, bent on digging the dirt. Because of her age, they couldn't print her name. But was it unreasonable to think that her details might still be on record, sitting in some database held by these people, for future use, the provision of context in future stories?

The night passes without word from Jake, and in the morning, she dresses herself and goes to work. At the office, several people remark on how pale and unwell she looks, but she is glad of the opportunity to lose her mind within the rigours of the familiar for just those few hours. On the train journey home, the doubts come flooding back.

She eats alone in the kitchen. The flat shrinks around her. Dampness in the walls, the tang of mould in her nostrils. She cannot seem to get warm.

When she tries calling Jake again, his phone is switched off. The message she leaves sounds weak to her ears, feeble, but she is running out of energy, disheartened by his silence, his refusal to speak to her. She tries to remember the last time she felt close to him, and what comes to her is the memory of a kiss when she lay in the hospital bed, scraped out and empty. She recalls the press of his lips against her forehead, the way he held her there. But the memory provokes a knot of grief, so she pushes the thought from her mind.

That night, sleep sweeps down over her and Leah dreams again of Cian. It's always the same dream. He's lying on the changing table after his bath, his flesh all naked and warm, pink and chubby. He's kicking his legs and laughing, making his high-pitched gurgling sounds. She's laughing, too, and tickling him with one hand, the other reaching for the cotton wool and the baby lotion. In these dreams, she is half turned when she feels him begin to roll. The padded cushion beneath him slips to one side. In these dreams, she turns just in time and catches him, holds him to her chest. 'Where d'you think you're going?' she tells him, smelling the baby shampoo in the fine threads of his hair, his little pounding fists at her neck, the sudden wriggle and bounce of him in her arms. That's what she usually dreams.

But tonight it's different. In the dream, she half turns and reaches for the sink. The baby lotion is just there by the tap. Reaching for it, her fingers knock it over and it falls to the floor. Quickly, she leans away and bends down to pick it up – it takes an instant. And as she reaches, she feels the rush of air behind her, and then the soft thud, like china wrapped in cloth, hitting the cold surface of the tiles. The baby is sprawled on the floor. He doesn't cry. He just lies there, his limbs outspread, staring up at the distant ceiling in amazement. Fear pounds in her chest and then she sweeps him up in her arms. In takes a minute or two before he starts to cry. He doesn't wail or scream, but rather there is uncertainty within his distress, as if he's not quite sure of the root of it.

She holds him in her arms, and rocks him back and forth. 'It's okay, it's okay, it's okay,' she tells him, her heart thudding through her chest and into his little body. Wetness against her blouse when he pees suddenly. She puts the padded mat back on the changing table and lays the baby down, holds him there with one hand on his belly. It takes a minute for her hands to stop shaking enough for her to fix his nappy on.

'Hey,' a voice says.

Leah blinks her eyes open and starts to sit up.

It's dark in the room and, without consulting the clock, she knows it's the middle of the night. Jake sits on the bed, his hand on her chest, gently but firmly, so it's like he's holding her down, preventing her from sitting up.

'Jake?' she says, her tongue thick in her mouth, the remnants of the dream disconcerting her.

'I'm going now,' he tells her.

'What? But you've just come back.'

She pulls herself up a little more and looks past him. There's a light on in the hall and, through the open bedroom door, she sees a rucksack and a sports bag, both packed and waiting, a laundry bag bulging with Matthew's toys. It's all coming at her too fast. How long has she been asleep? How long has he been here, sneaking around packing up his things while she slept?

'But where are you going?'

'My parents' house.'

'But . . .' She scrabbles to think. The pressure of his hand on her is lessening and then, abruptly, he gets up and goes into the hall.

'But for how long?' she asks. She's out there with him now, pulling her dressing-gown around her, covering the long T-shirt of his she's wearing.

Jake doesn't answer. He picks up the bags and heads outside to where the van waits. The ends of her dressing-gown flap about her and she feels the cold around her legs, the sting of it coming up through the soles of her bare feet as she follows him, panic making her blind to the manner of her dress.

'You are coming back, though,' she says, as he slams the back door, then climbs into the front seat.

'Jake? You are coming back?'

He doesn't look at her, just turns the key in the ignition

and pulls the van away, and she's left there, staring at the red tail-lights travelling up the street until they disappear around the corner.

It's so quiet now. The windows in the houses opposite are blank. The park is a dense black mass pushing up against the night.

Hurrying back inside the flat, she shuts the door behind her, goes into the kitchen, her movements blind with panic, and as she crosses the floor sudden pain shoots up through her foot. She lifts it and sees a stray piece of Lego embedded in her sole. And as she picks it out, she thinks of Jake hurriedly packing his son's things, and then she thinks of Matthew chattering to himself as he played, and this somehow gets woven into her memories of Cian. The thought that all of this is behind her now, that happiness has been wrenched from her, causes a howl of anguish to rise through her and escape into the night air. All the pain she has kept suppressed for so long rushes to the surface. Here in her kitchen, she cannot control it any longer. She cries and cries, so loudly that, at first, she doesn't hear the knocking. The gentle but firm tap-tapping on the glass.

She wipes her eyes and turns, and then she sees him. His face pressed against the glass. And as she steps towards him, it's not fear she feels but relief. Because she cannot carry the burden alone any more.

He's waiting with his arms held wide as she opens the door. Wordlessly, she steps into them.

'Oh, my darling,' Anton says softly, folding her into his embrace. 'Oh, my poor sweet darling.'

August

23

Anton

Intimacy.

That is the word, Anton decides. The word he has been hunting around his brain for, the word to describe it.

He stands in a queue, waiting. Ahead of him, a woman is sampling olives while a young bearded man in a long apron stands poised for her decision. There's a breeze ruffling the awning overhead and a little dog keeps sniffing around Anton's ankles – a tiny brown slinky thing, like a rodent on a lead. Anton smiles at the dog's owner. 'Busy today,' he remarks.

'It's the good weather. Everybody flocks here.'

The woman goes for the Kalamatas, picking through her purse for coins as the young man weighs and prices them.

Anton looks at the wooden troughs glistening with various olives sweating in the heat of the August Sunday morning, and wonders whether Leah might prefer the Kalamatas or the stuffed Cerignolas. A thrill goes through him, like a volt of electricity, when he thinks of her, at this very moment lying in bed in his house, waiting for him.

'Have you tried their salted almonds?' the dog-owner asks him now. 'Amazing. Very moreish, do you know?'

Anton makes a vague humming sound of approval, then turns back to the counter.

Moreish. A word he's not familiar with. A word that seems to have sprung into existence during his years inside. Moments like this feel extraordinary to Anton, where he finds himself vividly present in the normal world once more, all his senses engaged, after so long starved in the darkness. Having a conversation with a stranger, being among these crowds of normal people, with this cornucopia of exotic foods spread in front of him, knowing that she is at home, right now maybe sitting up in bed, stretching.

He buys Kalamata olives, anchovies, a Barolo salami, some salted almonds, puts them all in the cloth bag slung over his forearm, then drifts into the crowd. For weeks, he has been avoiding situations like this, shying away from the masses for fear of being overwhelmed, consumed. It's something he hadn't expected – how even after you'd left your cell behind, still you carried the confines within you. That cell, meant to keep the law-abiding public safe from you, becomes over time the thing that protects you from the outside world, a curious reversal. The very confinement you dreaded at the start becomes a need, a vital limitation. A few weeks ago, visiting the Sunday market would have been an impossibility for him. But now everything is different.

There is a space free on one of the benches looking on to the spouting fountain, and Anton sits and opens the bag of olives, savouring the salty tang of juices as the fruit's flesh bursts in his mouth. Nothing like this on offer at the hotel. But he doesn't want to think of that now. Instead, he retreats into the quiet reserve of his imagination, replaying the events of the night he rescued her.

He had been biding his time. That was the hard part.

Keeping his distance until the time was right. Tricky enough, trying to judge it, but he knew, deep down, it was best to let her stew in her anxiety while she wondered if her young man would return. Best to let her hollow herself out with sleeplessness and doubt, the feverish going-over of past events in her mind, as if better to understand what the future might hold. Anton had experienced a single plunging moment of regret when he had heard the young man's return in the middle of the night. Fearing a re-union, he had scuttled down the inner stairs to that private space that has become as familiar to him now as his own bed. He had listened anxiously, silently berating himself for not having made his move sooner, for having left it too late. He need not have worried. The fickleness of that foolish youth meant Anton was safe. And when the young man left with his bags that night, Anton had felt an unmistakable swell of triumph in his chest. Minutes later, the howling had started.

He had not anticipated the level of her distress. The way she just fell apart like that. It was like witnessing a collapsing building, the nauseating plunge, the inevitable dropping away. She had fallen into his arms in defeat.

'Oh, my darling. Oh, my poor sweet darling,' he had said, aware of the flimsy dressing-gown she was wearing – why, she was almost naked.

She had offered not the slightest resistance when he coaxed her upstairs, sinking weakly on to the sofa and staring blindly into the middle distance while he fixed her a brandy, and one for himself. A light had been turned off inside her, and he couldn't be sure if she was actually hearing the words of comfort he spoke, if she was aware of him in the room at all. When he put out his hand to touch hers, she didn't even blink.

Anton finds himself remembering that touch. The coolness of her skin beneath his fingertips, like alabaster. Her bare feet on the rug – long and slender and pale, one toe crooked, an imperfection he found strangely endearing.

'I'm afraid for you, sweetheart,' he'd said. 'You're in a terrible state. I don't like to think of you being alone.'

She had put her hand to her forehead then, as if pained. Her brandy remained untouched.

'I know what it's like when those feelings come. The desolation. The awful emptiness inside.' He'd kept his voice low and steady. 'It's not good to be alone with those kinds of thoughts. A slippery slope. Who knows where they might lead?'

Both of them had been down that path before. Their own separate journeys along that forlorn stretch of road. Weeks now since his own mishap, and in those days afterwards, when she'd come to him, coaxing him from the darkness of his depression, there was a moment when she'd revealed her own despair. It had happened when she was fifteen, shortly after the child's death. Pills. She had panicked after swallowing them and told her parents moments later. A disaster swerved but not completely averted. Something like that stays with you.

'I couldn't have it on my conscience, sweetheart, if you did something to harm yourself, knowing I might have helped.' He watched as the tears came, falling soundlessly. The heaving sobs had abated, replaced now by silence and a stillness within her that did, in fact, worry him a little.

'Take a sip, love,' he said softly, moving the glass towards her. She drank obediently, which pleased him, pushed him to say, 'You need to rest. To get some sleep. But I hate the thought of you going back down there to that gloomy apartment, especially after what's just happened. You there all alone, with no one looking after you. I'm not sure it's a good idea, Leah,' his voice silky with concern.

He watched as a tear slipped down her cheek, falling on to the sleeve of her dressing-gown, making a little spreading stain through the fabric – some kind of nylon, it was. It had crackled with static electricity when he'd put his arms around her earlier.

'There is, of course, the room upstairs,' he offered, keeping his voice light while the blood thumped thickly through his chest. 'Charlotte's room. It would put my mind at ease, Leah, knowing you were not downstairs maybe doing something terrible. You would be welcome to rest there for the night, if you'd like.'

Two nights now, as it happens.

Anton puts the olives back in the cloth bag, and gets to his feet, moving in the direction of the park gates. He stops to buy bread at the One In the Oven stall, then continues, taking his time, a leisurely stroll. He knows she'll still be there when he gets back, and half the pleasure is in the anticipation.

Anton is a patient man. And there is an art to this sort of thing – a method. He recalls his approach from years gone by, how so much of it involved hanging back and waiting, always leaving the door open for an experience. The initial connection made, the pilot light of desire lit, he would hold himself back from acting upon it, knowing that this was the way to fan the flames. Sometimes it would happen by chance. He had met Gail before a flight from London, idling in the airport lounge when it was delayed. Maria worked for a telecoms company and had called to the office to try to sell him a new communications package. Louise and then Anne-Marie, both babysitters for his children. Hilary had rented the flat downstairs.

In each of them, he'd seen a want, like a small hunger, they kept hidden inside them. Good girls who secretly yearned to transgress but needed persuasion. And that was half the fun – the game they made of it. The way he had to coax and cajole, deploying his classical education to good effect – all those Greek myths, coming in handy in a way he hadn't considered as a boy. How they lapped it up when he likened them to Helen and Persephone. To Artemis and Demeter and Ariadne. Perfect pleasure to watch them wilt and surrender themselves to him. Fun while it lasted, but he always went back to Charlotte. That was a given. A non-negotiable.

For two days Leah has been in his house, her sleeping form occupying the room upstairs. On that first morning, he had gone down to the basement flat for her toothbrush and some of her things. A laundry basket with neatly folded fresh clothes was on the floor beside her bed, and he had carried it up all those flights of stairs to Charlotte's bedroom, not saying a word, just leaving it in the curve of the bay window, the toothbrush in a glass on the nightstand. She hardly stirred. Tea trays were brought up during the day and left untouched. In the evening, he had stood in the shadowy darkness behind the door left ajar, watchful of her movements, her breathing. Sometime in the night, a noise like a whimper, but when he tiptoed across the landing to check, there was only silence.

She is a broken bird, Anton thinks, as he turns now on to Wyndham Park. A bird fallen from the nest, and he has picked her up and taken her into his home. Gently, he will wait on her, slowly nursing her back to health. But a bird like that won't ever return to the wild from which she came. Those injured creatures we take into our homes grow dependent, he thinks, putting his key into the lock, their natures changed by the very fact of our nurturing, our care, so that they become tied to us. Without us, and he pushes the door open, they cannot survive.

He closes the door behind him, pauses to listen, to judge the air. Silence fills the hall. Since she has become ensconced in the room upstairs, the atmosphere in the house has changed, grown peaceful. For the first time in months, he cannot hear Charlotte's voice. He resolves to go upstairs and check on her, but first he will put together a tray with his purchases from the market. A smorgasbord to tempt and delight her. He has a half-bottle of Viognier cooling in the fridge and thinks about persuading her outside into the garden. Anton carries his shopping into the kitchen and stops dead.

'Hi, Dad.'

Mark looks up from where he is sitting, and Anton feels a sharp announcement of nerves, like acid rising from his stomach. This is quickly followed by a rush of concern. 'What happened to you?' he asks, putting the cloth bag on the counter and coming closer, the better to see his son's face.

There's a crust of blood around Mark's nostrils, a bulbous look to his nose and cheek. A bruise blooms over his left eye, the lid puffy and swollen. And, from the way he is sitting in the chair, a hangdog look about him, a guilty air.

'You should see the other guy,' he says, with a feeble laugh that quickly falls away.

'You'll need ice on that,' Anton tells him, then opens the freezer and takes out a bag of frozen peas, wraps it in a tea-towel. 'How long have you been here?' he asks, keeping his voice light. His mind is upstairs in the bedroom with Leah, wondering whether she is awake and listening. How will he explain her presence if Mark finds out?

'I got here a few minutes ago. You don't mind me letting myself in, do you?'

'Of course not. This is your home too.' Words said without much conviction, for in truth he is irritated by Mark's intrusion. Anxiety flickers within him. What if she comes downstairs? What then?

Mark watches impassively, accepting the bag of peas and placing it against the side of his face.

'Who did this to you, son?'

'Jason.'

A quick calculation in Anton's head – Jason is Mark's flatmate.

'Why on earth –'

'I deserved it, okay?' The defiance in his voice dies, a shame-filled tone slinking in as he admits: 'He caught me on the couch with his girlfriend.'

'Oh, for God's sake!'

'I know, I know. Stupid, right? But I just –'

He breaks off, shaking his head, and Anton sees how close to tears he is, and softens towards the boy. How lost and confused he looks.

'Let me make some tea,' Anton says gently.

As the kettle boils, it all comes spilling out: how Mark

had stupidly, recklessly fallen for Katya with her Slavic beauty, her shrugging coolness, her unattainability. Unrequited love was bad enough but it was agony when the object of your desire was sleeping with your flatmate. He described the mornings, after Jason had gone to work, how he'd loiter in the kitchen waiting for her to appear, talking for a few minutes over coffee and then she'd leave. Those few minutes were all he had to feed his desire and sustain him through the cold loneliness of his one-sided romance.

'I felt she understood something,' he tells Anton now. 'Like I could talk to her about anything, stuff I never shared with anyone.'

'What kind of stuff?' Anton asks, wary of the answer.

'About you. About where you've been.'

They are dangerously close to touching upon Anton's years of incarceration, a no-go area for both of them. It has been an unspoken contract between them – a tacit agreement not to discuss prison, or the reason why Anton was put there. Without ever articulating this need, it was nonetheless agreed that both of them would maintain the fallacy that his prison stay was without violence or personal danger. A fallacy bolstered by Anton's insistence on substituting 'hotel' for 'prison'. Whatever nightmare scenarios Mark had dreamed up over the years about prison brutality, they never discussed them. In the same way, they avoided discussing Mark's mother. What happened to her.

'I told Katya I was the one who found Mum that morning,' Mark says now, and Anton can hear him fighting the emotion that's rising in his voice. 'But the thing is I can't actually remember it. The memory is just gone. Have you any idea how frustrating that is?'

'Son –'

'It kills me to think that I was there but I just can't remember. Katya suggested I try hypnotherapy to try to access that memory, and do you know what? I did. I went to see this hypnotist, told him I wanted to try to get back to that moment so that I might understand it better – accept it, even. But when he brought me back there, that point evaded me.'

Anton listens to this, full of fear. He doesn't trust himself to speak, frightened of what he might blurt out.

'I was trying to find Mum in my memories, but instead I kept finding you.' Mark's tone is weighted with accusation. 'Every time, I'd go under and he'd bring me back to that night, I kept seeing you in your shed at the end of the garden, and I was locked out, looking in. You were with a woman, but it wasn't Mum. It was someone else. I don't remember much more, but I remember that feeling of being locked out – like I couldn't get to you. Like I was shut out.'

'Oh, Mark.' It's too much. All of this is too much.

'They asked me afterwards whether you had any special hiding place. That's one of the things I do remember – some detective crouching beside me, asking me to point out anywhere in the house or garden where you might tuck things away to keep them hidden.' Mark's eyes shine too brightly in the gloom of the kitchen. 'I thought of your shed. I thought of you and that woman and what you were doing in the shed. So I didn't tell them. I thought I was protecting you.'

Anton cannot look at his son as he says these things.

'It was only later – years later – that I realized they were looking for the knife. They wanted to know where you had hidden the knife.'

The air between them has grown very still. In the silence, Anton knows that Mark is waiting, and when he looks up, he sees the expectation in his son's face.

'Well?' Mark asks, impatience, desperation in his voice, which trembles now as he adds: 'Where did you hide it?'

'I didn't . . . You couldn't possibly think –'

There's a sudden bang from above their heads.

Mark's eyes move towards the ceiling. 'Is there some-one upstairs?' he asks, incredulous.

Anton watches with alarm as Mark gets to his feet. 'Just hang on a second, son!'

But Mark is already out in the hall, taking the stairs two at a time. He stops at the return and stares up. 'What are *you* doing here?' he asks.

Anton listens, hears her hesitation. Then her voice comes weakly: 'I'm so sorry. I didn't mean to disturb.'

And there she is, stepping quickly and lightly past Mark, her dressing-gown clutched tightly about her chest. Her hair looks dull and messy, her face gaunt. He catches the look Mark gives her, the way he takes in her bare feet, her pale legs.

'Please. Now just wait,' Anton says, panic coming into his voice as she moves past him. 'You're not well, my dear. Please.' Then, looking up the stairs, he adopts a firm tone: 'Mark, I can explain all this.'

But Leah is opening the door now that leads to the inner stairs.

297

'You've been very kind,' she murmurs, 'but I can't stay here.' And then she hurries away from him, down into the darkness.

There is silence in the hall. Anton thinks of the olives and the salted almonds and the wine. He thinks of the soft cadences of her voice, the cool alabaster skin. He thinks of her wrapped in Charlotte's dress, the shy manner in which she'd looked at him in the mirror. Such furious disappointment curdles in his stomach that his fists clench and the blood rushes to his head.

Behind him, Mark stands, waiting, by the bottom step. When Anton turns, the boy is staring at him, his face blank of expression, his eyes two hollows in his face.

'Son,' Anton says, but Mark doesn't want to listen. He's had enough excuses and lies.

He turns away his bruised and swollen face in disgust. The front door slams behind him.

24

Leah

Leah lies still in the bed, listening. In the course of the past few days, she has grown accustomed to the sounds of the house – the creak of a door opening and closing, the splutter of water from the tap in the bathroom, the gentle shushing of Anton's leather slippers across the wooden boards. Sometimes, he sings lightly as he moves about the house, tunes she doesn't recognize, his voice surprisingly sweet and low. When he makes tea, she hears the ding of the kettle and the clatter of china on the tray. There is something comforting about these sounds, about his presence, about the quiet tenderness of his care of her. Leah knows that she ought to return to the basement flat, to try to piece her life back together. She's aware of the strangeness of their arrangement. But, right now, she's just so tired. It's all she can do to cross the landing to the bathroom and back again. She cannot face eating, and sleeps fitfully. Days have passed since she showered, and she's aware of the bodily smells that thicken the air of the room. But something is holding her back. A deep fear keeps her trapped.

She listens to the footsteps crossing the hall down-stairs, hears the pause at the bottom, and then a voice calling: 'Dad?'

She pulls the covers up, stays very still. Her thoughts, so muddy and unfocused over the past few days, now sharpen and draw in. All at once the oddness of her presence in this room – in his mother's bed – seems blatant. Obscene, almost. What if Mark comes up here? She cannot imagine how she would explain it, and part of her knows that explanations would be futile. A woman in her nightdress, the bed in disarray. The conclusion he would draw is obvious. And yet she does not think of Anton in that way. While not exactly fatherly, there's a reassurance in his maturity linked to an understanding of her. It feels as if he, more than anyone else in the world, can fully understand what it's like to be her.

She pulls the bedclothes tight around her, slowly sits up. Her eyes scan the room, taking in the handsome dresser, the heavy mahogany wardrobe. She recalls a basket of clothes on the floor by the window, but when she looks for it now, she cannot find it.

Mark has gone into the kitchen. From her eyrie upstairs, she hears the scrape of a chair drawn out from the table. Moments later, the front door opens and closes again, and she hears Anton's familiar tread across the hall, then his voice in the kitchen, raised in surprise.

Sunlight falls at a slant through the curtains. It hits the side of her face, trapping her with its heat. Her mouth is dry, her eyelids heavy, a crust of hardened tears clinging to the lashes. Fragments of thoughts and dreams stick to her – a muddied mass drifting and crowding her weary brain. She keeps thinking of her father in the car, taking her home after the police had interviewed her and she'd given her account of what had happened. The way he'd glanced at her in the rearview mirror. 'Are you sure now, Leah, that there's nothing else?' Doubt in his eyes – a brief flash, but she'd caught it. Enough to pierce her heart. The same way that Jake had looked at her. A quick blaze of disbelief, followed by doubt, like a sort of shyness. Like he couldn't bring himself to look at her properly, afraid of what he might see.

She wonders where he is now. He had told her he was going to his parents' house, but she is convinced he's gone back to Jenna and Matthew. Already what Leah and Jake had shared together has vanished, disintegrated under the heat of these revelations. He would never trust another word she said.

'These things happen,' Anton had told her, in the soft, gentle way he had. 'It doesn't always help to look for a reason.'

She feels the truth in that. She has driven herself close to madness in the past, hunting for some deeper meaning behind events in her life over which she had no control.

She puts her hands to her belly now, feels the sagging skin beneath the flimsy cotton of her nightdress. She thinks of Cian, the moment of that hard *thunk* on the floor. Her stomach contracts, nausea rising up her throat. Downstairs, a door closes. She knows she must prepare to leave.

Slowly now, she eases herself out of bed. It's an effort to move, her whole body weighted, as if it is drenched with water. The temptation to sink back into the bedclothes pulls at her, but she knows she cannot be found like this. Already, her mind is running to ways of escape. If she tiptoes downstairs, and if the kitchen door is closed, she could slip down the inner stairs to her flat without being noticed. But what if he were to come out of the kitchen and see her like this, clad in only her long T-shirt? She looks around for her dressing-gown but it's not there.

Opening the door carefully, she goes slowly, tiptoeing across the landing. In the bathroom, she checks for her dressing-gown. Frustrated, she returns to the landing. A murmur of voices rises up through the floorboards, and as she stands there, biting the edge of a nail, made anxious by the thought of being caught, her eyes find the open door to Anton's bedroom, and there, on the floor by his bed, a laundry basket with her clothes. Quickly and quietly, she hurries over to it. It feels strange to be in there – in his private space – dressed only in Jake's T-shirt. She rummages in the basket and finds her dressing-gown.

She is slipping it around her shoulders, her gaze on the floor, when she spies the corner of a box peeping out from under the bed. A shoebox missing its cover. She leans forward to push it back under the bed, when her eye is caught by the vividness of colour – a small bright splash of reddish-pink. Drawn to it, she reaches into the box and takes out the flower. It's a snap-dragon, pressed and dry with age, but still a wash of bright cerise. The paper within which it had nestled is blue and dense with writing. Leah takes it out, meaning to place the flower within it, then return the letter to the box unread, but her eye is caught.

My darling, my only love,

My thoughts are with you constantly, imagining where you are at this moment, what you are doing. I am consumed by you – every

meal I eat, every conversation I have, every place I go, it's always
you there with me in my heart. I feel you inside me, my love. I
carry you around with me always, and in that way I can keep you
with me. I can keep you free.

Leah looks at the tight cursive, the letters small and wiry, the press of them through the paper, like braille. She wonders at what point in their marriage it was written. 'We loved each other deeply,' Anton had told her, and here is the evidence. She holds the flower to her face, feels the dry tickle of it against her skin, tries to imagine Charlotte pressing it within her note. What thoughts were flowing through her as she wrote this? Reading those words on paper, Leah is struck by the urgency – the pulse of life – within them.

Curiosity has been growing inside her for some time, and in recent days, lying in this woman's room, Leah has felt her questions about Charlotte moving to the surface. The space is alive with indications of a life lived – everything from the scent of her perfume still sitting on the dressing-table to the walls papered with a bright print of primroses and narcissi intertwining and spreading around the room. There is not a single photograph of Charlotte in the whole house, yet her presence is pervasive. She is there in every room.

Leah's eyes tip in the direction of the box. It is stuffed full of letters, documents and scraps of things. A box of nostalgia. She can see a painting done by a child, the paper hard and crinkled with ancient poster paint, daubs of yellow and brown. But she can feel her gaze being drawn to the blue sheets that lie deeper within the box. An opportunity there to discover something of the woman who was once mistress of this house. Curiosity unfurls within her, compelling her fingers to touch the blue paper and slide another letter from the box.

My darling, my precious one,

I am writing this letter to you in the corner of the staff-room – can you imagine it? Beyond the window, there are whoops and screams from the girls on their lunchbreaks, and in here, in this room, there is the usual heavy Tuesday-afternoon dreariness. All around me, my colleagues are correcting essays, making lesson plans, eating their sandwiches, gossiping, none of them aware that I am writing to my lover. This page is slotted within a manila file so that I am ready to flip it over should anyone draw near. How adept I have become at the art of deception! That's because of you, my love, and because of you I will maintain the deception for as long as necessary. I have given you my solemn promise.

Besides, I dare not write from home. Greg lingers in the house constantly. He has been watchful of me since the trial, hovering like a gnat, observing my every move. Sometimes I think I just won't be able to stand it any longer. That I'll have to leave him. But then I remember our plan, and all you have sacrificed. Above all else, we must not raise suspicion and draw attention to ourselves. I have caught him, at odd moments, looking at me in such a way that makes me think he must know – he must have worked it out, about us. The thought frightens me but at the same time I am thrilled by it too.

Leah's heart kicks out with sudden fright. *We must not raise suspicion.* The words leap at her from the page. All this time, she had believed him when he told her of Charlotte's flirtation, her drinking, her affairs. He had cast himself in the light of wronged husband, silently suffering through each indignity, every humiliation, and she had accepted this without ever questioning the truth of his account. And Hilary – her words return to Leah now. That day in the garden: what had she said? That Charlotte was a difficult woman, an outrageous flirt. And all the while it was Anton who was the faithless one.

The truth comes over her now, like the prickling flow of blood into a limb that has fallen asleep. She has been crouched on the floor by the bed, and now leans sideways, needing to support herself. Her weight falls against it, unsettling the duvet. A book that has been lying there slips off. It clatters on to the varnished floorboards. The sound it makes seems to echo loudly around the room. She stares at it for a moment, feeling her whole body tense and still. Another noise from downstairs and, quickly now, she is on her feet. She can hear him coming out into the hall, and hastily, before she has any time to think on the consequences, she reaches into the box and grabs the blue pages, as many as she can see, and stuffs them into the pocket of her dressing-gown.

'What are you doing here?' Mark asks, on the landing. His eyes flicker over her, taking in her bare feet, her dishevelled hair.

It's an effort to keep her voice steady, her breathing clear. 'I'm so sorry. I didn't mean to disturb,' she tells him, feeling the smooth grain of paper in her hand, hidden in the pocket.

She keeps her eyes on the stairs, moving quickly now.

Anton attempts to stop her, but she is powered by a new urgency, all her feelings about him washed away in a tide of fear. The knowledge that has started seeping in at the corners of her consciousness. She knows she must not stay here.

'You've been very kind,' she murmurs.

And then she is past him, down in the shadows of the stairway, her heart pumping painfully in her chest, the letters scratching through the thin material of her dressing-gown. She can feel the abrasion of them, like damning evidence, burning a hole against the skin of her thigh.

25

Hilary

Hilary is in her bedroom, preparing herself for the party, when she sees Anton ascending the steps to his house. She's already changed into her dress: the poppy-red Diane von Furstenburg she'd bought years ago now, her first big-splash sartorial purchase. Now, watching him approaching his front door, she pauses in brushing her hair to watch him. There's a spring in his step, a brisk optimism about his movements, that provokes a sudden impatience inside her. She wills him to turn and see her, but he doesn't look. She goes to the window and throws open the sash, putting her hands on the sill so that she's leaning out, but still he doesn't turn. He twists the key in the lock and then the house swallows him. Disappointed, Hilary turns back to her preparations, continues fixing her hair. But then the anger cascades over her and she throws the hairbrush on to the dressing-table, sending an array of cosmetics clattering across the surface.

She sits down hard on the edge of the bed, a surge of agitated feelings travelling through her. And that's when she smells it: meat grilling on a barbecue in the park. From outside, she can hear the screaming of children on the green, and it is that, along with the scent of meat cooking, which strikes a deep chord of memory, the day of Charlotte's death ringing up from the past.

Greg was outside that morning, planting his new purchases from the garden centre. She had watched him unloading them from the car – rosebushes and fuchsias, hydrangeas and clematis – then carrying them through to the back. She had no idea where his sudden desire had sprung from to tackle the wasteland out there.

It was over between them, although Greg didn't know it yet. There could be no going back. Not after the party last night. Not after what had happened. She loved Anton in a way that couldn't be replicated or denied. She was sitting on her bed, trying to summon the courage to go downstairs and explain this to her husband, but when she thought of the stricken look that would surely appear on Greg's face when she told him, her stomach clenched into a tight knot and she had to lean forward and wait for it to pass. Anton was probably over there right now, breaking the news to Charlotte. Hadn't he said as much to her in those brief moments after Charlotte had discovered them together? Hilary couldn't remember the exact words he'd used, but that was the impression he'd left her with: that they couldn't wait any longer. It would be better for everyone this way. Quick and painful, like ripping off a plaster. Then they could all figure out a way to heal.

She was sitting on the edge of her bed, gathering herself, when she heard the screaming begin. All morning, there had been noise from the park. The neighbours gathering for the bank-holiday barbecue. There were bags of sausages in her fridge, a coleslaw prepared in a china bowl – her contributions, which would remain untouched. Everything had changed last night, once Charlotte had discovered them together. But the screams that rose from the park were different from the shouts and tantrums of children. Amidst the noise, there was the shrill cry of an adult voice, panic within it. And then a strange hush. It drew Hilary to her feet, and when she looked out of her window, she saw some of her neighbours, Martin Cooper and Will Bolton with a couple of others, striding across and up the steps to Number 14. Her heart had clenched, her thoughts confused. The battering on the door, an urgency within it, reached her all the way from across the street, and then she saw Anton emerging from down below, coming up the outdoor steps from the basement flat, his movements slow and heavy, as if he'd just been dragged from sleep.

The men all disappeared into the house, and there was a moment of calm, the front door left open, the absence of movement, and then Will Bolton came rushing out and down the steps, calling instructions to his wife, who was crossing towards him now, a high note of panic in his voice. Hilary watched him say something to her, saw the woman raise both hands to her mouth. Then her eyes went back to the front door where another neighbour emerged – Martin Cooper – and Hilary watched him gripping the railings that lined the steps, taking deep gulps of air, like he'd just surfaced from underwater. She watched as he bent over suddenly and threw up, right there on the steps. Only then did she move.

'Something's going on,' she'd said to Greg, as he came in from the garden and met her at the bottom of the stairs. 'Aren't you coming?'

Without waiting for him, she'd hurried outside and run across the street to where a small crowd had gathered.

'What is it? What's happened?' she asked, and Maria

Bolton had turned to her, eyes round in her small pale face, saying: 'Oh, Hilary, you won't believe it. Charlotte's dead.'

The word hit her. That was what it felt like – as if the word itself were a cool hard pellet slapping against the centre of her forehead. She didn't yet fully understand.

'But how?' she asked, her thoughts tending automatically to some sort of accident. Memories of Charlotte drunk came sliding up, nursing to life a suspicion of an intoxicated fall, the slam of her head against a sharp corner, a hard surface, but when Maria said, 'She's been murdered,' the street seemed to tilt, the row of houses all falling away.

It jolted something within her, and she started up the steps, but Martin Cooper caught hold of her and drew her back.

'Don't, love. It's a bloodbath in there.'

The words made Hilary start, like she'd been slapped.

'But . . .' she began, craning past Martin to look up at the open door, wanting Anton to come out – needing to set eyes on him for some kind of reassurance.

'*You must be patient*,' he had told her only the previous night. '*We will find a way.*'

Was this what he'd meant?

He didn't appear, and her thoughts beat around her head, like a frightened pigeon trapped in a room, and the more she turned the idea over in her head, the more real it became. He had done this for her? For them? Had she known he would? Did this make her complicit? Bloodbath, Martin had said, and the violence of the act – the depravity of it – pushed her thoughts out of shape, as if her mind was melting and being rewelded into an unfamiliar shape. She thought of Anton wielding a knife – she envisaged the scene: Charlotte disbelieving right up until the last, the awful plunge of the blade through flesh, the terror. Distantly, she heard Maria Bolton saying her name, and then the sun flashed brightly overhead, and the sky loomed. She heard the crack of her head meeting the pavement and then nothing.

A shiver goes through her now as she sits on her bed, remembering. Nineteen years ago, and still the memory has the power to reduce her to this. She wonders about Anton and whether he, too, is thinking back on that morning, his memories twisting and intertwining with hers. The morning that marked the start of their long period of waiting.

But Hilary has grown tired of waiting. Tired of staying away. Throughout the burning heat of the summer, she has watched and waited for Anton's signal, the nod to set things in motion, and still it hasn't come. Her letters to him have all gone unanswered and she is sick of writing, fed up of the written word and the hold it has over her life.

'Enough,' she tells herself, powered by a sudden impatience. Enough waiting. Something needs to be done.

She hurries downstairs and into the kitchen, but there is no sign of Greg. No doubt he's off licking his wounds somewhere. It's been three days since his book was published. Three days of gritting her teeth against his anguish and reproach. Her house has fallen silent, the rooms echoing with unspoken disappointments. No reviews, little traction from the press, a handful of mediocre online comments. 'What does it matter about any of that?' she'd said to him last night, when he'd appeared in the kitchen, eyes red-rimmed and haunted. It had startled her how wild he'd looked. 'Let's throw this party and enjoy ourselves. Who cares what anyone else thinks? Let's you and I celebrate your achievement with our friends. Surely that can be enough.'

In an hour's time their guests will start arriving, all gathering to celebrate the publication of a book that has become loaded with anxiety and resentment. Hilary glances around her kitchen: trays of lasagne defrosting on the countertops, hors d'oeuvres ready to be popped into the oven, salad bowls covered with cellophane, silverware individually blanketed in paper napkins, an army of glassware lined up on trays, jugs waiting to be filled, wine bottles as yet still corked.

'Oh, to hell with it,' she says to herself, turning on her heel and flouncing from the room.

The dog, roused by her sudden movement, jumps to life and skitters across the kitchen, following her out into the hall with a yipping excitement as she grabs her keys. But she has no intention of taking Mona with her. This is something she must face alone. She locks the door behind her, and marches out on to the street baking in the sun.

The park is jammed with people, summer in full-throated cry. Even with the usual August bank-holiday exodus from the city, still they throng here. Hilary's insides leap with excitement and alarm as she crosses the street. Going to his house in broad daylight, after months of stealing around in the dark, like a ghost, calls up within her a shiver of nerves at her own brazenness. What if Greg were to return right now and catch her there with Anton? How would that confrontation play out?

She's at the entrance to Number 14 when she hears her name being called. There's a blood-rush in her face as she turns and sees her neighbour, Martin Cooper, striding up Wyndham Park, a shopping bag in each hand. 'Just picking up a few bits and bobs,' he says cheerily. 'All set for the party?'

'Oh, yes,' Hilary says, grinning like a fool.

'What time is it?' Martin asks, checking his watch. 'You want us there for midday?'

'That's right.'

'Best get my skates on so!' He smiles at her, then glances sideways at Number 14.

She can see the thoughts turning over in his mind. In a rush, she says: 'I'm just calling down to Leah and Jake. Do you know them?'

'Not really. I've seen them but –'

'I was going to ask if they'd like to join us today.'

'Ah, I see.'

He stands there nodding and smiling, while she slips past the gate and down the steps, half turning to wave goodbye.

Down in the hollow by the door to the flat, she feels a tremble of nerves going through her legs. For a moment, she just stands there, waiting until Martin has gone and her composure has returned. It's cooler down here and she welcomes the opportunity to calm herself, to think this through.

The window to the bedroom is situated at the front of the flat, and Hilary goes to it now, presses her face to the glass. She sees the unmade bed, the wardrobe, the door standing ajar. There is an air of desertion to the place – a profound emptiness.

Emotions stir inside her when she thinks of how she

once lived here, once slept in the room she now peers into from the other side of the glass. And then she remembers the last time they lay together – her and Anton – in that bed. How he'd held her against his chest, running his hand over her bare shoulder and freckled upper arm.

'This is all that matters,' he'd told her. 'The time we're together. Everything else is just a blur.'

She'd been crying. It was their last day before the move to the new house. Her last day in Number 14. What would happen once she left? How would they see each other? She couldn't bear the thought of not being near him. Couldn't countenance what they had shared coming to an abrupt end.

Light had filtered through the heavy curtains into the bedroom, and in the dimness of the room, she could see the outline of the little wardrobe lying open, displaying its emptiness. Everything had been packed up and taken to the new house. Even the bed had been stripped. They were lying on the bare mattress in a tangle of limbs, his thigh pressed between her legs. Her dress lay on the floor alongside his shirt and trousers. She'd told Greg she was going to Nolan's to look for fabric samples, and instead she'd come creeping around the back lane and snuck up through the garden to where Anton waited in the basement. Hilary had no idea where Charlotte was, nor did she care. Probably upstairs, drinking herself into a stupor, and Hilary could not find it in herself to feel remorse or guilt, let alone pity for the woman.

'I just want us to be together,' she told him. 'If only there was some way, without all this sneaking about.'

'There's always a way,' he'd answered lazily, his fingertips running over her skin.

314

'What do you mean?'

'Things happen. Unexpected things. Who's to say? Something unexpected might happen to make things possible for us.'

'But what will people think when they find out?' she had asked him, frightened and excited now by the prospect he was dangling in front of her.

His hand had paused in its stroking. 'It doesn't matter what people think. All that matters is us two, together.'

She'd held him closer. 'I've never felt like this before you,' she told him. 'It's not like this with Greg. It never was. That's an awful thing to admit, isn't it?'

'Not awful. Just honest.'

'I feel I can be honest with you. That what we have between us is honest and true, no hidden meanings, no pretences. Don't you feel that too?'

She had moved so that she could look down on to his face, leaning her weight on her elbows and forearms.

'I do. You are extraordinary to me, little one.'

His leg moved then, his thigh nudging between hers and she felt her arousal come alive.

'I want us to be together always,' she told him then.

'We will find a way,' he said, kissing her neck, a shiver passing through her as his tongue ran along her collarbone.

'But Charlotte –'

'Don't worry about Charlotte.'

'But I do. I don't want to share you.' His mouth was reaching for her breast now, and she moved so that he could find it. 'If only I could have you all to myself.'

'You will,' he whispered. 'Be patient.'

And then she was kneeling over him, feeling nervous

and dissolute and heavy with desire. His eyes gleamed –
she could see his pupils dilated in the dimly lit room – and
he reached for her and pulled her to him, their bodies
continuing the conversation long after words had flown.

She should go back, retreat into the safety of her house,
but the memory has a strong hold over her, keeping her
rooted to the spot, her fingertips pressed to the window
pane of that basement bedroom, staring in, bewildered.

At that moment the front door opens above, and a man
emerges. He bangs the door shut behind him, and stands
there for a moment, as if catching his breath.

Anton, she thinks, her heart clenching in her chest. But
when she hurries up the steps, she sees that it is not Anton
but a younger man, still tall with a youthful head of hair,
zipping up his jacket and staring out over the park with a
narrowed gaze.

She knows who he is. His face is bruised and swollen,
but she still recognizes him. The boy she wanted to take
in. The boy she wanted to raise as her own. A grown man
now, and so like his father that it disarms her.

'Mark,' she says, her voice fluttering with nerves. 'You
probably don't remember me . . .'

'I remember you.'

There's harshness in his tone. The look he gives her is
cold and assessing, layers of meaning within it. Her insides
curdle beneath the weight of his stare.

'I didn't know you were here. It's been so many years
since –'

But he is already moving past her, hurrying away, as if
he can't escape the place fast enough. Her eyes go back to
the house and she sees that the front door remains open.

Quickly now, without giving it thought, she runs up the steps and inside, closing the door behind her.

It takes a moment for her to reorient herself to the gloom after the bright sunlight of the street. She leans against the door, breathing heavily. This is the house where her life had changed. The house where Charlotte died. The house where Anton killed her.

Blood rushes through her veins – she can hear the thrum of it in her head. Beyond the workings of her heart, she listens for noises in the house. The creak of woodwork expanding in the heat of a summer's day. The call of bird-song through an open window at the back of the house. But apart from that, it is silent. The house feels empty.

Hilary takes a step forward into the hall, calls hesi-tantly: 'Hello?'

Another step towards the staircase.

'Anton?'

His name echoes around the hall. She puts a hand to the banister and looks up, feeling uncertain, trying to locate within her some courage. A noise overhead points to his presence, making her bold. She moves up the stairs quickly, her resolve recovered by the time she reaches the return. On the last step, the bedroom door opens, and there he is, a tray in his hands. He sees her and his mouth opens, but no words come out, his face registering astonishment, and something else – a flash of confusion, perhaps.

Her heart, which had been fluttering wildly, now grows still.

'I couldn't wait any longer,' she tells him. 'Why didn't you reach out to me? Why didn't you come?'

26

Anton

'What are you doing here?' he asks, as the frown on her face softens, her eyes lighting with a new intensity.

'I couldn't wait any longer,' she tells him. She reaches out and touches his arm. He looks down and sees her hand clasped around his wrist. 'Anton, I had to come.'

Briefly, he wonders how she got in. His thoughts are frustrated and confused. They keep bending towards Leah, and the way she wouldn't look at him as she was leaving – the way her eyes refused to be drawn to his, as if she was embarrassed or ashamed.

'Anton,' Hilary says, drawing his attention back to her face, two spots of high colour in her cheeks. She's staring at him intently, but her eyes are darting about, as if they cannot find a feature to settle on. Her grip around his wrist is clammy and hot.

'What is it? What do you want?' he asks, sounding irritable but really it is confusion that is blurring his thoughts, obscuring clarity.

Perhaps it was not shame or embarrassment he had glimpsed in Leah, but fear.

'What do I want?' Hilary asks, and the smile on her face falters. He is surprised to see shyness coming over her, as she says, almost coquettishly, 'Why, you, of course. What else did you think?'

He pulls his hand free of her grasp and, still clutching Leah's tray, he hurries down the stairs. She follows him, hot on his heels.

'I've waited and waited,' she tells him. 'Why didn't you send for me? Why didn't you give me the sign?'

'I don't know what you're talking about,' he declares, panic starting to spread through him. There is an intensity about her that he wants to draw back from. It's like standing too close to a fire.

'We agreed that we would wait until you were free. Until the time was right. And it is right.'

He wants her out of his house, but balks at the idea of manhandling her out of the door. This woman was once his lover, yet the thought of touching her now makes him feel queasy and unclean.

She follows him into the sitting room, babbling about letters and promises, about recompense for deeds done, sacrifices made. He puts the tray down on the coffee-table while his mind races. He feels fenced in, cornered, and even though the room is large, the ceilings lofty, somehow the space shrinks with her in it, such is the force of her presence. The way she keeps coming at him with her words, her smile, those eyes hungry for something from him, but it's hard to decipher just what she wants.

'Hilary, please. I think you should leave.'

'No,' she tells him firmly. 'We've waited nineteen years for each other. We cannot wait any longer.'

Despite the purpose in her voice, he hears the under-current of nerves. He looks at her now, properly, for the first time since his release, taking her in fully. Her hair, which he remembered as brown and gleaming, is shorter now – a shingled bob, like a 1920s flapper's – and coloured orange. She is still small, her figure beneath the silk wrap dress has remained trim, although there is something stoutish about her now, as if the softness of her flesh has hardened over the years, grown tough and sinewy. Her bare arms are wild with freckles, a sort of joined-up mass of them making her look tanned, her legs too, cerise-pink toenails peeping out through silver sandals. In this brown-ish room, she is a blaze of colour – her red dress, her copper hair – but there is something artificial about it, like a flower too vividly bright to be real or lasting. Just as the expression in her eyes seems falsely bright.

'We promised we'd wait for each other,' she's telling him now. 'Don't you remember? "Good things come to those who wait." That's what you said to me. "Be patient," you said, and I have been. All these years, your words have sustained me. The memory of them, of what we had, of all we shared. The love between us made it worth every day spent apart, every month, every year.'

'What are you talking about?' he asks, bewildered.

'Our last night together, your parting words to me. You told me you would find a way for us to be together. You said there was no obstacle that could not be moved. You told me that, no matter what happened, I was to hold firm and be patient. I have kept faith with that, Anton, through-out that night, and everything that happened since.'

Her loud and vivid presence makes it impossible for him

to think straight. With her words, she's dragging him back into the past, back to a night he does not want to return to.

'I cannot . . .' he begins, but she steps forward suddenly and presses her mouth to his.

For that instant, he feels the firm mass of her body against his, the sticky sweetness of her lips on his mouth, her nose pressed into his cheek. This sudden onslaught of sensation overwhelms him, as if she's pushing through his skin, her breath invading his lungs.

A wave of revulsion comes up through him and he shoves her away, disturbed by the violence roused in him. She stumbles backwards, her eyes widening with shock.

'No!' he shouts at her. 'Christ, what are you thinking?'

Her hair has fallen forward, a flap of it partially covering one eye, but the other is on him, filling with tears. He sees her chin tremble, but it doesn't arouse any compassion within him. And when she tells him now that she loves him, that she's never loved anyone else, he turns away from her, and moves to the armchair by the fireplace, sinks into it, exhausted.

'You've got the wrong end of the stick,' he says, leaning forward so that his elbows rest on his knees, his face dropping into his cupped hands. It seems amazing to him that hardly more than an hour ago he was sitting in the park amid the busy Sunday-market commerce, eating olives, full of hope. All that energy and enthusiasm has drained away. His son has marched off in despair, and Leah has retreated from him, like a nervous rabbit. He is left alone with this woman and her unfathomable hopes, her reckless fantasies.

She comes to him now and, to his horror, she kneels in

front of him, placing her hands on his knees. Her face is watery, her certainty having wavered under the blow of his rejection, but there is still a stubborn persistence: he sees it in her flushed cheeks, her dilated pupils.

'I know the sacrifice you made,' she tells him, her voice shaky and barely controlled. 'And I have kept faith with it all these years. I never breathed a word. I have kept your secret, my darling, and I have waited.' Her face breaks into a wavering smile. She appears unhinged, and then she adds with a hopeful raise of her eyebrows: 'Haven't I proven beyond all doubt that I am your Penelope?'

Her hands are still on his knees, and he grabs hold of them now.

'I don't know what it is you thought would happen between us,' he tells her, forcefully, 'but this love affair you've conjured up is just a fantasy.'

She twitches her head, still wearing her hopeful smile that seems maddeningly complacent to him and makes him tighten his grip on her hands, shaking them.

'I never asked you to wait for me, or – or lie for me or keep secrets! I don't love you – I never did! It was just supposed to be a bit of fun, that's all. The odd shag here and there. It was nineteen years ago, for Christ's sake! You're the one who constructed this ridiculous notion of romance around it.'

Her smile falters, the gleam in her eye dims. When she speaks, her voice has weakened with doubt. 'My letters. All those years I wrote to you. You knew what I –'

'Dear God, Hilary! I told you to stop sending them! In the same way I wouldn't have you visit me. Those letters were nonsense, like some lovesick teenager's!'

He remembers reading them with a sort of ghastly amazement. The flowery prose, the sickly sentiments expressed. For the most part, he felt embarrassed for her when those missives arrived. And it was true that they sometimes amused him, provided a spark of distraction from the dreary accumulation of his days. He'd even gone so far as to keep some for sentimental reasons: a reminder of what it had been like for him, some sort of touchstone to his old life. And it heartened him, sometimes, when his son neglected to write and his daughter set her mind against him, to think that there was someone out there who retained a spark of feeling for him, even if she was a crazed love-starved lunatic who needed these fantasies to punctuate the boredom of staid middle-class life.

'You told me they kept you going,' she says, wounded but still doggedly following her course.

'I never . . . When did I –'

'When I visited you in prison. During the third year, when you were at such a low ebb. You told me my letters were the only thing keeping you alive in there. That with-out them you didn't know how you'd manage.'

He scrambles back through memory, shuffling to find an occasion when he might have uttered such a thing, but those early years are blurred and faded, like old sepia prints, mildewed and creased.

'I remember the evening we met,' she tells him now, her face and voice softening with recollection. 'When Greg and I went upstairs to your house and Charlotte made that awful pass at Greg. We were so shocked, poor Greg not knowing what to do, how to disentangle himself without causing offence. I couldn't believe she would do something so brazen, so cruel, right there in front of you. And I remember how still and quiet you were, and I knew – I just knew – that, despite your stoicism, she had cut you to the quick. There was something so pained within you, my love, something crying out to be healed. I wanted so much to comfort you – oh, yes, I wanted that. Even though I hardly knew you, I still felt this connection, like something ancient between us, waiting to be unearthed. So when you came to me that day, when you kissed me – you attempting to be a salve to my pain – I knew that really it was every bit as much about me healing your wound, my love easing your pain. You needed to be loved, and I wanted so much to love you. That hasn't changed, Anton. It's only got stronger.'

He's mesmerized by her in one way, even though there's a sickness in his stomach. There's a kind of purity to her dogged belief, this trail of gibberish coming out of her with such fervour. It inspires pity and remorse.

'Look, I'm sorry if you've been waiting for . . . well, for some kind of grand reunion but, honestly, that's never entered my head. I liked you back then,' he says tenderly, 'but I loved Charlotte.'

'How could you say that?' she asks, and he's surprised by the disgust that creeps into her tone.

'Because it's true. I mean, yes, I was unfaithful. God knows I tested her sorely on that point. I like women,' he admits. 'I always have.'

'No,' she tells him firmly. 'No, that's not how it was. You're mistaken. What we had was special. It was unique.'

The colour in her cheeks has flared and spread. Her face is blotchy and flushed. Beneath the calm, controlled exterior, her passions are running close to the surface — he can see that clearly. 'Hilary —'

'We came together because we recognized something missing in each other that only we could fill. I am your missing piece and you are mine,' she insists.

'It was a casual fuck!' he shouts, exasperated. 'That's all! Enough of this madness about missing pieces and being special. There was nothing special about it! You want to know what I saw in you back then? Convenience. You were right there beneath my doorstep. It was easy. No inventions, no elaborate excuses for where I'd been. A bit of fun — a distraction to break up the boredom. I didn't love you, Hilary — if anything, I felt sorry for you. When you told me you couldn't have children, and then Charlotte insisting the dog be put down and afterwards, realizing that the dog was like your child or something . . . It was sympathy, but it wasn't love.' His voice changes, growing hard once more. 'I pitied you, Hilary. Your sad, pathetic yearning, your ridiculous romantic sensibility. Anyone could see that your husband — that dull, unimaginative drip — would never be enough to satisfy you. Easy pickings, that's what you were. That's all you were.'

Exasperation has made him cruel, pushed him beyond the point to which he had wanted to go. And now, looking up, he sees that his words have tipped the balance. The light of conviction has died in her eyes. They are dull and dry, her mouth a thin line. She is still kneeling on the floor looking up at him, and it is only now, in the awkward silence that descends, that it seems to hit her — the wildly inappropriate nature of this exchange, how she has demeaned herself with her admissions, her actions. It is almost unbearable, the way she draws herself in, getting to her feet awkwardly, one foot and then the other, tucks the wing of hair back behind her ear. He can hardly bring himself to look at her, but when he does, he sees that same flat stillness in her face. The high colour is gone from her cheeks. Instead she seems jaundiced, unwell.

'I just want you to know,' she says quietly, 'that despite what you've said, I still trust in what we had.'

She is exhausting.

'Please. Just go,' he tells her.

Relief sweeps over him when he hears the front door bang shut.

In the silence that follows, he leans back into the arm-chair, feels the weight of his limbs, the heaviness in his chest. The house whispers around him, the air unsettled in the wake of Hilary's manic presence. She has stirred something to life, and he closes his eyes, thinks back.

His affair with Janice was coming to an end when Charlotte found tenants for the flat.

'A short lease,' she'd told him, over the children's heads at dinner, 'three or four months. Just until the work on their house is complete.'

A young couple who'd bought the house across the street, teachers, she told him, with an air of forbearance. He'd spied them in the garden, the day they came to view the flat, Charlotte turning on the charm as she showed them around: the husband with his pudgy features and serious expression looked every bit the geography teacher; the wife was small and animated, a mousy little thing, who tittered at Charlotte's jokes, eager to please. He watched for a minute, then turned away, instantly forgetting them. He was, at that time, consumed by other things – he'd hit a road-bump with one of his bigger investments, and Janice had become tearful and needy, the whole thing tiresome as they played out its bitter ending.

He gave no further thought to the young couple who were taking the flat, until one Thursday evening, he came through the front door from work, dread lodged in his chest, and heard voices in the living room.

'Ah, here he is!' Charlotte said, as he came into the room. 'The man of the house.'

Her tone was falsely bright, as was the mobile smile on her face.

'Come and meet Greg and Hilary,' she cried gaily, putting a gin-and-tonic into his hand without meeting his eye.

In the early hours of that morning, Janice had telephoned their house. Drunk and tearful, she had spoken to Charlotte. The scene that erupted was awful. So while Anton observed his wife perform the role of charming and animated hostess, he knew it was just that: a performance, in front of an unwitting audience. There was a dangerous edge to her laughter and he watched her carefully.

When she put her hand on that poor fool's thigh, Anton didn't react. Even when he read the young man's discomfort, his little wife squirming with unvoiced outrage on the opposite armchair, still Anton remained calm and quiet, not rising to the challenge. Charlotte wanted a scene but he would not give it to her.

The young couple made their excuses, then hurried away downstairs. He imagined them turning to each other with muffled hilarity, falling into one another's arms, delighted and aghast at the awful behaviour of that odd couple upstairs.

After they'd left, Charlotte had held his gaze, raising her eyebrow in an arch expression, saying, 'What?' like some bratty teenager. He knew it was his fault, and when he attempted to apologize, she stormed past him. He could hear her crying upstairs but, like a coward, he remained in the living room, drinking his gin and watching the light fade from the window. When he finally went upstairs, their room was empty. He found her asleep in Mark's bed, the little boy wrapped around her, his arm slung across her neck.

The first time he met Hilary – so, a bad start. Almost immediately, Charlotte took against her.

'She's a dull sort, don't you think?' she would say to Anton. 'Not even you would be tempted.'

They had a little dog, which drove Charlotte mad with its constant yipping.

She complained that they left their washing on the line for too long. That the dog fouled the garden and they were lazy about cleaning it up. The wife was always hanging around, staring after her – it gave Charlotte the creeps.

Anton knew that none of this was real or, rather, that it had nothing to do with Hilary but stemmed from Charlotte's deep unhappiness over his betrayal. It was always the same after she'd discovered one of his affairs – the drinking and the carping began. He knew it wouldn't last. In the same way he knew that it was best for him to hold his tongue. But when the dog snapped at Mark, and Charlotte insisted it be destroyed, he felt the guilt of letting things get so far.

Hilary was different from the other women. Different

because he hadn't pursued her in the way he had the others. There was no need to. He sort of stumbled into their affair, and engaged in it half-heartedly. It was lazy and foolish, but in the heat-haze of that summer, it served as a distraction.

They said stupid things to each other in the way that all lovers do – lavish praise and excessive sentiment, but it was all just part of the game. It wasn't serious.

Mostly they came together in the basement flat in the mornings while Greg was at summer school and Charlotte was out with the children. Sometimes they snuck across the road to Hilary's house on days that the builders weren't there, rutting on the floors of those bare, echoey rooms, the smell of paint and sawdust lingering in the air. They were coupling in his shed at the end of the garden the night Charlotte found out. The party was in full swing back at the house; no one had noticed them slipping away. Earlier in the evening, he had done two lines of cocaine with Steve, a friend from the golf club. It had made him feel reckless and invincible. Hilary, compliant as ever, had followed eagerly when he'd suggested it. He hadn't spotted Charlotte until she'd found them among the shovels and bags of compost and potted seedlings, his slacks around his ankles, the small mounds of Hilary's breasts exposed.

Charlotte's face was white; she looked but said nothing. She'd never caught him in the act before.

'Wait,' he'd said, but she'd withdrawn into the darkness, and somehow that made it worse – her silence. Better if she'd cursed them, spat out her fury and hurt. But that silent withdrawal sent a chill through him – the air of finality.

Hilary fell apart then. Pulling her clothes back on, she'd snivelled and prattled on about being caught out and what they should do next. He'd tried to calm her but his mind was addled. God knew what he'd said, what promises or concessions he'd made.

When he'd gone back to the house, everything was as it had been. The rooms still alive with music and drunken chatter. People sitting on the stairs, talking, the party spilling on to the street outside. And Charlotte leaning against the railings, a drink in one hand, a cigarette in the other, throwing back her head and laughing at something Will Bolton was telling her. He marvelled at her ability to act in such a manner – as if nothing had come between them. And when she passed him later in the hall on her way to the kitchen to refill her glass, she had said the words so casually, he almost didn't catch them: 'You're to sleep downstairs in the basement flat tonight, Anton. I don't want you in the house.'

And that was it. The last time he would ever hear her voice.

A chill comes over him now, a shiver of cold air, as he remembers.

The memory has left him weak. He blinks and looks to the window, sees it is open a fraction, the air passing through it a chill draught against his neck. He gets up and crosses the room, reaches up to pull the sash closed, and as he does so, his eye snags on the flash of colour.

Across the road, at the entrance to her own house, Hilary stands staring at him. He cannot read her gaze, too far to make out her expression, though her presence – the act of staring – brings on a lunge in his chest. He lets go

of the window and steps back into the safety of the shadows. But as he does so, he recalls a line from one of her
letters – the frenzied scrawl across the page, spelling out
her dark threat: *I want you to get rid of her, Anton, or I swear I
don't know what I'll do!*

He'd dismissed the letter when first he'd read it. But
now the words crowd his thoughts and he feels behind
him for the coolness of the wall, needing to steady himself against the heat of those words, the dread rising
within him at what he has unleashed.

27

Leah

She reads quickly, her eyes passing over the tight weave of sentences. The letters are in no particular order, the information coming at her jumbled and confused, but still she understands. The truth of the past comes at her through these secret missives.

Anton and Hilary were lovers. The shock of that knowledge transcends the feelings described on the page. A love that was strong, obsessive.

I yearn for you. I feel you in me. Without you I am an empty vessel, my heart a wasted organ uselessly pumping blood around a body that is dry and parched for your touch.

Leah thinks of Hilary, her primness, her manners. She recalls that lunch in Hilary and Greg's garden: the silver cutlery, the starched linen napkins. Everything just so. Hard to imagine her writing such a letter. Hard to envisage a heart bursting with such passion encased within Hilary's stout bosom.

Leah sits on her bed as she reads the letters, one leg curled underneath her. Two days have passed since she occupied this room, and there is a stale abandoned atmosphere inside it. The smells that have become trapped here

invade her nostrils: the musty dankness of the partially
subterranean walls, the decaying sweetness of wilting
flowers on her bedside table, slimy stems visible in brackish water through the glass vase. She is still in Jake's
T-shirt, her feet bare, her dressing-gown falling open as
she puts one letter down and moves on to another.

*I think of what it must have been like for you, my darling, faced
with that horrible task. You made the decision for both of us.
And when I think of your bravery in executing that task, my
passion for you is renewed, strengthened ten times over. 'A crime
of passion' is how they described it during the trial, that term
splashed across the pages of all the newspapers. And they were
right, in one way, but they were also mistaken. You didn't kill
Charlotte because she drove you into a passionate rage. You did it
for me. Because of your love for me. Driven by that desire for us to
be together, you plunged your knife. Agamemnon turning the
blade on Clytemnestra.*

Outside, a cloud is passing over the sun and the room
around Leah darkens. Her feet are cold, her hands and
face numb. She thinks of Anton and his tenderness towards
her, his gentle care. The soft melodic sweetness of his voice
as he sings while he goes about the house. The kindness
of his eyes. The way he holds her gaze and listens – really
listens. There has been a bond between them, a deep
connection that she can no longer trust. When he told her
that he had been wrongly convicted, she had believed
him. When he had maintained that his conviction had
rested on unsound and circumstantial evidence, she had
allowed herself to be persuaded that he was an innocent

333

man. People judge cruelly – she knows this – and he had responded to her own dark past with compassion, a feeling she had reciprocated. Over the past few weeks, she has come to think of him warmly, tenderly even.

But now, with the coldness of these letters invading her mind, he becomes recast in a new light. She pictures them together: Anton and Hilary. Lovers whispering in the dark, making their plans, Charlotte oblivious to what lay ahead. Words come at Leah now: Greg telling her that Charlotte was an unhappy woman, misunderstood. 'He was very controlling,' Greg had told them, that day in the garden, but she had dismissed those words, preferring to rely on her own version of Anton. It was easier to think of Charlotte as a drunk and a flirt, who made his life a misery but still he loved her. Easier to think that a terrible injustice had been done to him than confront the hard truth of his capacity for violence. But now, when she recalls him telling her how he loved his wife, how deep was their connection, she feels the hollowness of those words, knows them to be untrue. Jake hadn't trusted him and now Jake is gone and she is alone.

Upstairs, there are voices, the creak of floorboards as someone crosses the room above.

Leah picks up another letter, and immediately her own name jumps out at her from the page.

We had them over for lunch today, your tenants. Jake's a bit of a bore, but there is something intriguing about Leah. I can understand your interest – your fascination, my love. But I have to tell you how it pained me to hear her speak of you with barely disguised affection, your little defender. Don't you know how it

334

hurts me to think of you engaging with her, the young woman in your basement flat, knowing I was that young woman once? Surely you can understand how easy it would be for me to jump to the wrong conclusions, conjure up images of romance between the two of you, even though, in my heart, I know you would never betray me. I know that you're just testing me, that she means nothing to you really. All of this would be so much easier, my love, if you would just reach out to me. Give me the sign. We agreed to wait but for how long? When will enough time have passed for you to deem it safe for us to reveal our love?

Leah reads quickly, putting the page down and snatching up another, scanning the text for her own name, a dark feeling opening inside her at her own presence within these letters.

I saw you tonight, in your garden — the two of you. Caught together in your cosy corner. This has to stop, my love. She needs to go.

The next letter then:

I saw you, Anton! I saw you and her in the window of your bedroom. For one horrible moment, I thought it was Charlotte up there, back from the dead, and that you were being tender towards her, like you actually cared for her instead of hating her! But then I realized it was Leah, your little friend, your little ingénue! Parading her in your dead wife's clothes in the window of your bedroom! You knew I could see, didn't you? Why are you torturing me like this? Why are you punishing me, after all I've done for you, after all I've given up? I want you to get rid of her, Anton, or I swear I don't know what I'll do!

The numbness has spread up Leah's arms and legs, as if all the nerves are frozen. She looks at the letter, the way the biro has bitten into the page, imagines the force and frenzy involved in the writing. She puts it down and stares sightlessly about her.

For the first time, she feels frightened. Her heart hurts with scared feelings. She puts her hand to her chest, feels the thin cotton sticking to her skin. Even though she's cold, her body is clammy with sweat. It comes to her then that she must leave. Right now, there's not a moment to waste. She reaches for the suitcase on top of the wardrobe, dropping it on to the unmade bed next to the letters. She empties the wardrobe of her clothes, dumping them haphazardly on the bed, then pulls out drawer after drawer, their contents spilling, a snaking mass of legs and sleeves. Stuffing the clothes in, she shuts the case and carries it out into the hall. Then she goes back into the kitchen and finds her phone. It's been days since she checked it, and the power is dead. She plugs it in and decides to shower quickly while waiting for the phone to come back to life.

In the bathroom, she turns the taps on, sets the temperature to high. When she steps under the shower, the water on her skin feels shocking. It scalds her flesh, reviving some spark of energy inside her. After days of wallowing in her depression, the skin on her body disgusts her. She scrubs vigorously, her nails clawing through her scalp as she shampoos her hair. She wants to get clean and away. She wants to wash these past few days and weeks from her body. She turns the water's heat higher, needing to be cleansed to the bone. A plan forms in her head: she will call Jake and ask him to meet her, and then she will take only what she can carry and walk away. Later, they can return together for their furniture, her piano. Or perhaps not. Perhaps it's best to leave it all behind – a scorched-earth policy – and start anew somewhere else.

The towel is rough on her skin. In the mirror, she sees her reflection – pink-skinned and puffy-eyed. She pulls on her underwear and then a loose-fitting cotton dress. Her hair drips on to the fabric as she steps into her shoes. She opens the door and there is Anton, right in front of her. The breath catches in her throat.

The door behind him is open to the flight of stairs he has just descended. Her suitcase lies at his feet and he looks at it now before bringing his eyes up to meet hers.

'You're leaving?' he asks, his voice low. It makes the silence that surrounds them feel deeper, more profound. She realizes she cannot hear any sounds from outside: no birdsong, no kids in the park, no traffic humming from the streets beyond. Despite the recent heat from her shower, the skin over her neck and the backs of her arms prickles with goosebumps.

'I'm going to stay with my parents for a few days,' she answers, her voice level. She knows, somehow, that it's important not to betray her nerves.

'Your parents.'

His eyes are on hers, and even though he seems calm, unperturbed, an undercurrent of quivering doubt is there beneath it. He knows that she never goes home. He knows her reasons for staying away.

'Jake is coming to pick me up,' she says, the lie slipping awkwardly from her tongue. 'He'll be here soon.'

Anton nods, never once releasing her from his gaze.

The door to her bedroom lies open. She remembers that the letters are right there on the bed. Has he seen them? How long has he been down here? She doesn't ask – or question him on the liberty he has taken in walking down here, entering her private space without first seeking permission. She doesn't ask because she's afraid, and somehow not asking draws attention to that fear.

'You're not coming back, are you?' he asks, and she catches the forlorn note that is barely there in his voice.

She shakes her head. There is something shameful about her plan to run away. After all they had shared, all that he has done for her in the past few days. But those letters . . . Now that she's read them, now that she knows . . .

'Could I ask one thing of you?'

She looks up, sees the shyly perturbed look on his face.

'Would you come upstairs and have one last drink with me before you leave?'

'Oh.'

Fear jumps along her nerves. She knows she should not go back up those stairs.

'I get the feeling that after today we will not see each other again,' he tells her, his voice a silky ribbon. 'I would so like for us to sit down this one last time, just like we did at the start of the summer. A cold glass of white wine, a little company. You have no idea how that was a lifeline to me, Leah. How that saved me. Please. Just until Jake comes for you. Let's part as good friends. What do you say?'

She thinks of their conversations in the garden, the soft warm night air, the consolation of talk. He had been kind to her. He's standing there, waiting for an answer, and she thinks about her phone charging in the kitchen, the front door locked, just the two of them alone together in this house. A whisper of nerves passes over the back of her neck. Somehow she cannot think of a way to say no.

She takes her seat on the edge of the sofa near the door. From the kitchen, she can hear the clink of glasses, the gentle pop of the cork leaving a bottle. The tread of his slippers comes slowly down the hall, and when he enters the room, he gives her a melancholy smile, then hands her a glass. He has brought the bottle with him and places it on the coffee-table, then steps forward so that they can clink glasses.

'Your health, my dear,' he says, with benevolence, and she takes a cautious sip, leaning back a little into the sofa.

She expects him to sit in the armchair closest to her, but instead he stays on his feet, moving slowly to the marble mantelpiece. She watches as he reaches out to put his wine down on it. Through the foxed glass of the ancient mirror, she sees the reflection of his face. He looks tired, the lines running through his tan like deep grooves, harsher, more permanent than she remembers.

'What made you decide to leave?' he asks, in a speculative tone, still with his back to her, his gaze fixed on the wine glass, his fingers stroking the stem.

'I don't know. I just thought I should. I've been feeling so down. Maybe it might help.'

'I thought I was helping,' he tells her softly, and she hurries to reassure him.

'Yes, of course you were. You've been amazing. But I don't want to intrude on your kindness any longer. I can't stay here indefinitely.'

'Why not?'

'Anton . . . I just can't . . .'

He nods, still smiling, still not looking at her. There is an inwardness about his behaviour, a quiet containment, that does not feel quite right.

'I went to the market this morning,' he tells her, 'while you were sleeping. I bought olives and salami, treats to tempt you. I had it all planned, that I was going to set up the table in the garden and spread out our little feast. In my head, it was perfect.'

'I'm sorry.'

Her nerves are back again and she takes a sip of wine but it tastes sharp, too fruity and acidic.

'What time are your parents expecting you?' he asks lightly.

'I said I'd get the evening bus.'

'Ah.'

She glances towards the window. From the way the light falls through the glass, she can tell it is almost evening now, although with her phone downstairs, she cannot be sure of the time. The day seems stretched and elongated, as if time is passing too slowly for her to measure it accurately.

'Actually, I should really get going, if I'm to make my bus,' she says, putting her glass on the coffee-table.

'But aren't you waiting for Jake to come for you?' He's looking at her now, but still with that unnerving calm.

'Yes, he said he would. But perhaps I should start walking down to the station anyway,' she says, wiping her hands on the fabric of her dress covering her thighs. 'Just in case he's delayed.'

'Leah,' Anton says then, and the smile he gives her doesn't reach his eyes, 'you're lying.'

The words land softly and coolly between them. A new fear uncurls inside her.

'I'm not,' she tells him, in a small voice, but he keeps giving her that pitying smile and shakes his head in gentle admonishment.

'Yes, you are.'

She watches as he reaches into his pocket and withdraws from it something tiny and blue. He leans forward and places it gently on the coffee-table in front of her. A SIM card from a mobile phone. She stares at it, her heart kicking out in fright.

'You didn't call your parents,' he tells her, in that same calm voice. 'You didn't contact Jake. No one is expecting you. No one is coming for you.'

Her mind is running furiously through different calculations. The door to the sitting room is right beside her – he closed it on his way in. If she's quick, she can make it to the door and fling it open, but he has the advantage of remaining standing – he would easily catch her before she made it to the hall. Her best bet is to stay calm and alert, to reason with him – appeal to his compassion, his humanity.

'You read the letters, didn't you?'

'I'm sorry. I didn't mean to pry.'

'I just wanted to take care of you, Leah. To look after you.'

'I know. You've been so kind.'

'And now you know my little secret,' he tells her, his eyes widening a fraction. 'My little misdemeanour. It turns out I was not the best husband in the world.'

She moves her gaze, brings her focus to the glass on the table in front of her. The way he looms above her makes her feel intimidated, fearful.

'It doesn't matter,' she says falteringly. 'It's in the past.'

'But it changes things. You can hardly bring yourself to meet my gaze, can you?'

She forces herself to look. The smile is gone from his face. A hard expression replaces it.

'You shouldn't have gone through my things. Not after everything I've done for you. The kindness I've shown. Don't you see how this changes everything?'

'Please, Anton,' she says, her legs trembling as she slowly gets to her feet. 'I'm sorry for looking. I didn't mean any harm.'

'But the harm has been done.'

'I won't tell anyone what I read. No one needs to know.'

His face creases with confusion. 'Who would you tell?'

'No one,' she says again, but just for an instant Mark comes into her head. She thinks of their conversations about Anton, his concern when asking her to look out for his father. Does he know? she wonders.

His eyes flicker over her face, narrowing with suspicion. As if reading her thoughts, he says: 'My son.'

Alarmed now, she takes a step sideways. 'I need to go,' she says softly, nerves in her mouth.

'We could have been so close, Leah. I would have given you everything.'

The door is right there beside her, but she dare not turn away from him. A woman died in this house. *Get rid of her*, Hilary had said.

'I'm sorry,' she tells him, 'I need to go now,' her hand

fluttering behind her back, in a panic as she feels for the cool brass of the doorknob in her hand, but he shakes his head sadly.

'No, dear. You've got it all wrong.' His voice is low, his stare cool and direct. 'I'm the one who's sorry. And you're not going anywhere.'

28

Hilary

'Where have you been?' Greg asks, as soon as she steps into the hall.

Hilary closes the door behind her, glances at him, and says: 'I needed some air.'

Her voice sounds strange to her, weirdly disembodied, not her own. She sees Greg's gaze, the oddness in it, the wariness, and feels herself inwardly squirming away from his scrutiny.

'Has something happened, Hilary? You look awful.'

She feels awful, as if she's been in a car crash, as if she's just witnessed some horrendous event. As if she's been stripped naked in public, all her hair shorn, like those French women after the Second World War, punished for sleeping with the enemy. Shocked and humiliated, right now she would like to die.

'Too much sun,' she says, in her new false voice, keeping her gaze averted from her husband as she moves towards the foot of the stairs. 'I'll just go and freshen up. I'll be right as rain in a few minutes.'

Her legs are trembling as she starts climbing up past him, and she's sure he can see it in her – how stricken she is, her inner scaffolding poised to collapse.

'The Boltons are here already,' he hisses, as she passes. 'Everyone's arriving – you can't just disappear.'

Disappear. That's exactly what she would like to do. Vanish in a puff of smoke.

'Five minutes,' she croaks, the strain about to break.

She hurries up the last few steps, slams the bathroom door behind her, then leans against it, relieved to be alone at last, shut away from Greg's scrutiny, his demands. But no sooner is she alone than it all comes crashing back at her.

'It was a casual fuck! That's all!'

Anton's words coming at her again with violence, bringing with them a wash of nausea and shame. She limps across to the toilet, flips open the lid and leans over the bowl, waiting for the retching to start, but nothing comes. Her insides are in turmoil, her thoughts tumbling over each other, like clothes in a washing-machine, the dizzying swirl of accusations and misunderstandings, his account against hers in violent opposition.

A distraction, he'd said. Easy pickings, he'd called her. She slumps to the floor, thinking of the long ribbon of her correspondence stretching back over all those years, the charting of her eternal hope, her blind faithfulness, her unquestioning devotion. She had gone to him full of love and he had responded with bitterness and cruelty. She still recalls the way his lip curled in disgust as he pushed her away – abhorrence washed all over his face.

From downstairs come sounds of the front door opening, voices in the hall, among them Greg's raised in greeting. She listens to the flow of people passing through into the kitchen, more arriving, and somehow drags herself to her feet, her responsibilities tightening around her neck, like a noose.

In the bathroom mirror, she stares aghast at her reflection. Her cheeks appear scalded, as if boiling water has been flung into her face. Her eyes have shrunk back into their sockets, the skin around them loose and bruised-looking. Quickly now, she applies make-up, dabs at her face with brushes, paints colour on to her chapped lips, draws a comb through her hair. She sprays her underarms with perfume – Chanel No 5 – then straightens her dress, gives herself a little shake.

I can do this, she thinks, as she descends the stairs, her heart like lead in her chest. She has always prided herself on her ability to cope, but with each step she feels her confidence crumbling, the prospect of having to play the smiling hostess for hours to come making her weak with exhaustion.

The guests have congregated in the garden where Greg has erected the canopy. In the kitchen, she sees he has already put the food to warm in the oven, and she sets about laying out the salads, needing to focus on a task. Activity will pull her through. Straight away she is swept into the storm of talk, greeting friends, receiving kisses on the cheek, hearing her voice telling people how delighted they are about the book and how proud she is of Greg, repeating these things *ad nauseam* until the phrases feel worn thin.

Keeping busy is the key to warding off the horrors of the afternoon. Movement keeps at bay the awful finality of the encounter, the searing pain of his rejection. For the last nineteen years, her focus has been singular, her life moving forward with one purpose, one future, and now that it's been shattered she doesn't quite know what to do. If she stops to think about it, though, there is every chance that she will come completely undone. So she doesn't stop: she stays busy and maintains the veneer of easy sociability. Even when there's a hush as Greg makes a little speech, thanking her for her unwavering support, still her resolve stays rigid. After the applause, she darts into the kitchen and gets the desserts going, pressing Martin Cooper into service, tasking him with refilling people's glasses.

It's late in the afternoon when Maria Bolton comes up to her, putting her hand to the small of Hilary's back and saying: 'You've been running around like the Duracell bunny all afternoon, Hil. Come and have a glass of wine in the garden, take the weight off your feet for five minutes.'

She allows Maria to drag her outside, the two of them sloshing Cabernet Sauvignon into large glasses and perching on the bench at the edge of the lawn. The sun is dropping down behind the hornbeams that line the perimeter wall, and Hilary feels an ache in her limbs, and a stiffness in her neck. She takes a deep slug of wine and closes her eyes for a moment.

'You're worn out, Hil,' Maria comments kindly. She's one of those warmly frank people, never afraid to speak her mind. 'You look like you're about to collapse.'

'I feel it.'

'I'll bet you've been up since dawn, eh? Probably been preparing all week.'

'Something like that.'

'Well, I hope he appreciates it,' Maria adds, nodding towards Greg, who is standing a little way off in conversation

347

with Martin and one of the men from the tennis club. He's probably within earshot of their conversation, but if he hears he gives no indication.

'He does.'

'A good turnout,' Maria remarks, and Hilary agrees, drinking again from her glass. The wine is helping, but still she feels the shock sticking to her, like a shadow.

For a moment, they comment on all the people who have come, and then Maria nudges her arm and says: 'No sign of Anton, though.'

Hilary puts down her glass and looks cautiously at her friend. Maria is smiling, her eyes alight with mischief. 'No. Why do you ask?'

'I saw you today, leaving his house. I said to Will: "She's gone in there to invite Anton to the party." And Will said: "Christ, I hope not!"' She laughs, and elbows Hilary again, dropping her voice to add: 'Will can't stand Anton. Never could.'

'No. I suppose, after what happened . . .' Her voice trails off. She's on shaky ground here. Looking towards the men standing nearby, she imagines she sees a stiffening in Greg's features, a thoughtful seriousness entering his pose. She wonders whether he's heard what Maria said.

'No, it wasn't that,' Maria continues. 'Even before what happened to Charlotte, Will was dead set against him. It was because of what happened between Anton and me.'

Hilary feels the words coming at her as a sort of physical shock. She blinks and stares at Maria, whose manner has grown conspiratorial, gossipy.

'He rang me one morning – this is years ago, back when

Jason and Sadie were still in kindergarten. Rang me up out of the blue and asked me if I'd meet him that day for lunch. Such an odd request. I mean, I knew him socially, of course – Jason and Mark were pals, in and out of each other's houses – and I'd chatted to Anton at Christmas drinks or the tennis-club social, same as I chat to everyone. But, still, it was weird when he rang me. And he sounded so serious. "Is everything all right?" I asked him, thinking that something had happened to him, or to Charlotte, and he told me it was delicate and that he couldn't discuss it over the phone. Well! I arranged to meet him, hurried down to the Royal Marine that lunchtime, expecting to find him all ashen-faced with news that Charlotte was leaving him, or he'd been given some horrible diagnosis, or that he'd gone bankrupt, something like that. But when I got there, he was all smiles, wine already ordered, not a care in the world. I'm there expecting to hear some sob story, and instead he starts spouting all this nonsense about Greek goddesses and mythological queens!'

Hilary's heart goes cold. The glass in her hand feels heavy. She looks at Maria, taking her in properly – the wide blue eyes, the ski-jump nose. She's blonde and pretty in an obvious way. 'Pert' is the word that comes to Hilary – pert and chatty. She will not stop talking.

'Eventually, I said to him: "Anton, what is this about?" And that was when he put his hand on mine and told me he was mad about me, that he had been for ages, and then he suggested we go somewhere private to explore things further – those were the words he used! Well! You can imagine how shocked I was, Hilary. Getting propositioned like that in broad daylight! When I told Will he hit

349

the roof, of course. It was all I could do to stop him going around there and punching Anton in the face!'

Maria gives her little tinkly laugh, and Hilary can see her delight in telling this story, unaware of the effect it's having.

'You know, at his trial it was all talk of Charlotte and what a flirt she was but, really, he was far worse. Charlotte was harmless. All that behaviour was just her way of look-ing for attention. But Anton? The way he went after women was single-minded and focused. Later I found out he'd tried it on with half the ladies in the tennis club. Kathy Fairfax had an affair with him, apparently. And rumour has it there were one or two ladies around Wyndham Park who succumbed to his charms.' She shudders. 'I'll never forget his eyes that day of our lunch, the way they zeroed in on me when he laid out what he wanted. So serious and intent. No shame at all. Later, when I heard what he'd done to Charlotte, I wasn't all that surprised. Something icy about that man. Something twisted. Did he ever try it on with you?'

The question comes at Hilary suddenly and, flustered, she swallows her wine and quickly shakes her head, no. Tears jump into her eyes with this denial. For years she has disowned their love, and now here she is, denying it again, only this time the denial is real. He doesn't love me, she thinks. He never did.

'Are you all right?' Maria asks, putting her hand out to grasp the crook of Hilary's elbow. 'My God, Hil, you're crying. What is it? What's the matter?'

Hilary cannot speak. The grief she has been keeping at bay surges up inside her. She gets up from the bench, the grass a green blur through her tears as she staggers across the lawn, like some blind Minotaur. Behind her, she hears Maria saying loudly: 'Poor thing – she must have worn herself out.' And even though she knows she will feel embarrassed by her own behaviour, right now all she can feel is a great sense of loss rampaging through her. The life she has conceived, the future she had constructed so carefully over the years, has all been ripped asunder.

In the kitchen, guests crowd around the island, clogging her route. She has to push through to the hall, her high-heeled sandals clattering up the stairs. She can feel them watching, senses the hush that falls as she passes, her distraught state observed. It's unbearable the way they look at her, unbearable the way this hurt presses through her chest, harsh and unrelenting. She is a fool, a stupid, vacuous idiot, and when she reaches her bedroom and slams the door, she doesn't throw herself on the bed and start bawling: instead she goes straight to the corner by the radiator and slides down so that she's curled up against the wall, shaking like a distressed animal, wanting so badly to hide herself away, such is the shame that slices through her.

When she hears footsteps on the stairs, she knows it's Greg and that he's angry. His face, when it appears around the bedroom door, is flushed and bewildered.

'What is wrong with you?' he asks, sounding angry rather than concerned, and she turns her face away and opens her mouth, crying into the wall.

'Jesus Christ, Hilary. What is this? What's the matter?'

He's come around the bed and is hunkering down on the floor beside her. She's still crying soundlessly. He takes her hand – she can feel the panic in him, uncertain of what to do.

'Did something happen?'

She shakes her head, unable to speak. How to tell him that it's over – her life as she'd seen it is over. And in such a way! Now that she's broken down, it's started to come at her: a cascade of memories, the letters she'd written, the past she had constructed, the future she had hoped for. She sees now, with horrifying clarity, how Anton is right: how the great love of her life was a fantasy, a cheap romance that she'd magnified to become a grand affair. She'd thought she was special to him, that she was the one. Christ, she thought he'd killed for her! When all the time she was just one of a string of women, a blip in his consciousness – a casual fuck, as he had called it. Her humiliation is devastating.

'Is this about Anton?' Greg asks, and her eyes slide to his.

He lets go of her hand, confusion clearing, replaced by coldness.

'You went over there, didn't you? Maria said . . .' He is shaking his head, his jaw clenching, anger quickening inside him, and then he leans forward so that his face is close to hers and hisses: 'Why the fuck can't you stay away from that man? I mean, *today*? You had to go and see him today? Even though we were having guests over to celebrate my book, Hilary. My book! Doesn't that mean anything to you? Does he always have to take precedence?'

'I know, and I'm sorry. I can't help it.'

Back on his feet, he moves away from her. He walks towards the door. She thinks he's going to leave, but then he turns and comes back to her, his face blotched with anger.

'Do you think it's been easy for me all these years? Watching you with your ridiculous daydreams, your foolish hopes? Your letters and your little prison visits? Oh, yes, I knew all about it. I didn't say anything because I knew it wouldn't last. And then when you stopped going to see him, I thought, There! You see? She's over it. She'll return to me now. But still you held back from me, Hilary. Always keeping me at arm's length.'

'Well, if you were so unhappy, why didn't you say something?' she finds herself yelling.

'I did! Or at least I tried. But you just wouldn't listen. The same way you never listen.' He's clearly appalled, as if he cannot fathom how they have come to this. 'You get these ideas in your head and they just stick – they won't budge. Notions you nurse that grow inside you with no basis in reality. You're a fantasist, Hilary. And you're just so fucking obsessive!'

She's crying again, silently now, the pain blooming in her chest.

'My heart is broken,' she tells him.

He's standing above her, and for just a fleeting moment, the look on his face turns to pity. 'Let me guess,' he says softly, 'you threw yourself at him and he knocked you back.'

She sniffs, and she hears him exhale.

He goes to the window, puts two hands to the sill to steady himself. 'Well, let that be an end to it, then.'

His words are breathed out at the glass, and she looks up. He meets her gaze, his voice hardening: 'Do you hear me? Just let it go!'

'I can't! I can't just turn it off. Love doesn't just end like that!'

'Love?' He is aghast. 'That isn't love! It's a twisted obsession with a dead woman!'

It takes a moment for the words to sink in.

He moves to the bed, collapses on to it, exhausted.

'A dead woman?' she asks, confused. 'Charlotte?'

'Of course Charlotte. Who else?'

'I'm not obsessed with her!'

'Dear God, you've been obsessed with her from the moment you first met!'

She's too startled to speak. If there was any obsession, it was with Anton. But Greg is talking again and she struggles to follow, listening as he details those few months they'd spent living in the basement of Number 14.

'You couldn't stop talking about her. Always going on about some dress she was wearing and how much it must have cost. Or the way she allowed the kids to run around the garden screaming without intervening. Or how she idled away the hours reading magazines or playing the piano. It was non-stop.'

Hilary doesn't answer. Too bewildered to speak, her mind racing. Was it true what he said?

'And all the questions – Jesus! Did I think she was attractive? Would I call her beautiful or just pretty? If I met her at a party and I wasn't married, would I fancy my chances? When she put her hand on my knee that evening, was I tempted?' His voice gains strength as he runs through the litany of questions she had plagued him with. Distantly, they ring a bell, a chime of recognition. A cold feeling is crawling up and over her neck and shoulders.

'And then you started emulating her,' Greg says, snapping her attention back to him.

'No, I didn't!'

'You did. The smoking, for instance. I never saw you smoke a cigarette in your life until that summer. Then you were smoking Marlboro Lights – Charlotte's brand of choice. You began to dress like her.'

'What?'

'You never wore dresses when we first met. Or hardly ever. Apart from school and the odd formal occasion, you were always in jeans and T-shirts – you were kind of grungy, Hilary, and I liked that about you. But then you started wearing dresses, chiffony numbers, or little tight sleeveless things. All of a sudden, you were wearing red and pink and orange – a riot of colours – spending a fortune on designer clothes. Christ, to this day you still dress like her. You dyed your hair the same colour as hers. And why? There was nothing wrong with your brown hair. It was lovely the way it was.'

His voice has lost its power. There's a melancholy note in it now. Indistinctly, she thinks she hears him say: 'Sometimes I think you just do it to punish me.'

She absorbs the implication of his words – that she is a fraud, a cheap fake, her whole life built on a persona that is not her own, and now she feels the cracks running through it, the surface about to break.

'This thing with Anton,' he says now. 'What did you think was going to happen?'

Biting her lip, she shrugs. 'I thought he loved me. I thought that, once he was released from prison, we would be together.'

'I see.' He runs a hand over his mouth, leaning forward. 'But he's been out for over two months now.'

'I know, but we had to wait, you see? So as not to arouse suspicion.'

'What suspicion?' A frown appears on his face as he gazes at her intently.

'That I knew about it. So that I couldn't be charged with conspiracy.'

He's staring at her, nonplussed. 'You knew about what?'

She whispers it. 'About Charlotte. That he was going to kill her.'

The look he gives her is awful. And it's only then as she says it out loud that she realizes how dreadful her admission is. How profoundly wrong.

His manner changes. Hilary sees him drawing himself in, growing guarded. He gets up from the bed. 'Greg?' she asks.

But he won't meet her eyes. Instead he moves away from the bed, warily casting a glance at her as he reaches the door. It's as if he's afraid of me, Hilary thinks, amazed. And then she finds herself alone, a crumpled mess in the corner of the room.

She presses her hands to her eyes, her thoughts coming at her in a panicky rush. She wishes she hadn't left her glass of wine downstairs. Right now, she needs a crutch.

Her cigarettes are in her bedside locker, and she takes one and goes to smoke it by the window. But Greg's words come at her – Charlotte's brand – and she stubs it out angrily. What should she do? Everything is such a mess. There's no way she can go back downstairs and face that crowd. Then she remembers how Greg had looked as he departed – disgust mingling with fear of her. The memory twitches something inside her, an awful self-loathing that she needs to shake off. If only she could talk to Anton. If only she could make him understand. Perhaps she could write to him . . .

But then it comes to her again in a sweep of fresh pain. She cannot write to him or ever speak to him. The thought is terrible. It makes her feel shivery and deranged, as if her mind is tilting away from her.

Slowly now, she brings her eyes up, trains them on the house she has watched for almost twenty years. The yearning inside her is a bottomless thing – a great black hole she cannot fathom. She stares at the house, at the panes of glass in the windows glittering in the evening sun. And something hardens inside her. A feeling comes over her – the inevitable pull of Fate. She has felt it before.

Dry-eyed, the blood beating coolly in her veins, she moves away. When she descends the stairs, she is perfectly calm. She knows what she must do. Comfort – that's all she ever wanted. To comfort and be comforted in return. Happiness is an act of will, or so she has always thought. Now, pulling the front door open, she steps outside, no longer knowing what might be possible.

29

Anton

He is not a bad man. That is what Anton has always told himself.

Not bad in the way of Salim, who bludgeoned his flat-mate to death over a dispute in a game of Scrabble. Or Fat Eric, who sent his own mother to her grave by slicing through her carotid artery while she watched *EastEnders*. Even wise, gentle Nigel had caused the fatal collapse in the major organs of his wife by poisoning her slowly over the course of several months. Dark deeds and evil thoughts. By comparison, Anton's soul is relatively unblemished. But when he picks up the wine bottle from the coffee-table and swings it at Leah's head, it occurs to him that he is both bad and dangerous. He is what they have always claimed him to be: a cold-blooded killer.

She is bolting for the door when he strikes her. It seems to happen in one fluid motion, as if her sudden turn towards the door triggers his reach for the neck of the bottle. She has her back to him when his arm swings through the air – he both feels and hears the smack of thickened glass as it makes contact with her skull. The breath is knocked from her in a single gurgling cry. Instantly she goes down.

A terrible calm descends on the room. Anton stands, the bottle still grasped in his hand, breath heaving in and out of his lungs as he stares down on her. She has fallen awkwardly, one leg half curled under the other, her arms pinned beneath her torso. Her head lies against the door, and he notices now that her hair is darkened and wet from her shower. She lies completely still.

It was the thought of Mark that did it. The unbearable prospect of his son discovering the tawdry nature of his deceit through those letters, the certainty of this information being distorted into some kind of motive for Charlotte's death and Mark actually believing it. 'Everyone has a tipping point,' Nigel had said to him once, explaining his own dark journey into the abyss. And now Anton has found his.

In the silence that follows her fall, he realizes what he has done. He half expects her to move slowly, push herself up into a sitting position, rubbing her head. But her body lies inert. He is still panting but, cautiously now, he approaches her. He says her name, breaking the silence, but it hangs there unanswered. Warily, he goes closer, leaning down, his heart racing. Her eyes are closed and her hair has fallen over her face. He can smell the citrus tang of her shampoo. Instinctively, he puts his hand out to draw the hair back and recoils when he feels something sticky. His fingers come away glistening with blood. It seeps from a wound he cannot see, and he leans down again and listens carefully. At first, he can only hear the pounding of his own pulse in his ears, but then it comes: a liquid breath, low and shallow. He peers into her face but it's completely still, her eyes shut fast. He remembers then the look on her face when he'd told her she could not leave, the flash of terror as she understood what he meant by that, the dark finality of his firm intent.

He sits back on his heels. The hem of her dress has ridden up her thigh from the fall, and he reaches to draw it down delicately, protecting her modesty. It was one of the things that had troubled him about Charlotte's death – the indignity of it and how he couldn't protect her from it. Easy for him to make the connection between the two events. He recalls now the morning when they'd found her. Will Bolton and Martin Cooper banging at the door, rousing Anton from his drunken slumber in the basement. He'd climbed the steps towards them, blinking in the daylight, the blaze of the sun calling his hangover to life. They'd found her in the kitchen, her throat slashed, lying in a pool of her own blood. He remembers the smell of the room – like meat left out too long, already on the turn. It was hot, the sun burning down on the roofs of the houses. Every surface was littered with the detritus of the party from the previous night. Beer cans, half-empty bottles, overflowing ashtrays, crumbs littering the countertops, a few stray sandwiches, the bread hardening and curled at the edges. There were flies everywhere – on the food, hovering over sticky puddles of spilt booze, buzzing around her, crawling in the wound. The amount of blood on the floor was astonishing. There was no doubt that she was dead, and that her death had occurred some hours before. The air in the room declared it – the staleness, the stench.

Martin reached to open the window, all the while making little hacking noises in his throat, as if he was gagging. 'Jesus Christ,' Will kept saying, while Anton just stood there, staring down at the body collapsed on the floor in a jumble of limbs and green chiffon. Her dress had fallen open, revealing her left breast, and the indignity of it rose up in him suddenly. It cut through his shock, like a blade, propelled him towards her. All he intended was to pull her dress closed, give her some dignity in death, but he felt Will Bolton grabbing his arm and pulling him back.

'Have a heart, Will,' Martin had exclaimed, but Will's grip didn't loosen.

'We can't touch her. Not until the police come.'

It took four minutes for the police to arrive. Anton knows this because it was stated during the course of his trial. But that short interval seemed to stretch far, far beyond four minutes, and while he waited, he looked down at her – his Charlotte – and he tried to recognize within that twisted mass of unmoving flesh the woman he had known and loved for more than a decade. There seemed to be nothing of her in that room – no trace of her throaty laugh that was deep for a woman's, no spark of humour or malice, both of which jumped quickly and easily into her gaze. No liquid sway of hips, no languid pull on a cigarette, no slow but steady smile to challenge or arouse. A woman who loved her clothes, a woman so stylish and carefully put together that the shamefully revealing disarray of her dress seemed like violence in itself. There was nothing of her left. Only ruined flesh and indignity, and as he gazed down at her, he felt sadness and anger start to coalesce, threatening to push up and explode through the wall of his shock.

By the time the police arrived, the muscles of his body had grown rigid, so great was the pressure of keeping those emotions at bay.

At least he can do that much for Leah now. Preserve the dignity of her flesh. The hem pulled down, his fingers trail along the smooth skin of her leg, tracing down to her ankles, the knob of bone above her shoe. One of those shoes has slipped off, and he runs his fingertip over the sole of her foot, but there is no answering twitch. He cradles her toes tenderly in his hand. *We could have been happy*, he thinks.

Fat Eric sat down and watched the rest of *EastEnders* after he'd murdered his mother. Salim had left his flatmate slumped on the floor, Scrabble tiles scattered around him, then gone to the nearest boozer for a stiff drink to quell the shake in his hands. Nigel hadn't been there when his victim died, and that seemed to Anton the worst of all – an abandonment. He will not leave Leah. It's clear to him what he must do and, in a way, he is horrified at the point he has reached. It's like staring at his own self but from a distance, realizing the monstrous nature of his actions but helpless to stop himself.

Slowly he gets to his feet, then crouches next to her. He turns her over on to her back, like a rag-doll, slots his arms beneath her body and lifts her. She is small and slight – a bird – but his body is tired, left weakened now the surge of adrenalin has worn off. Her weight feels heavy in his arms. An ache runs down his spine and through his hips. Each step is difficult, trying to keep steady, trying not to lose his balance. As he climbs the stairs, he talks to her.

'It's all right, my darling. I'm going to take care of you now.'

Her eyelids remain closed, her mouth has fallen slightly open, but no voice escapes her lips. In his head, he counts the steps – a habit formed in childhood. He has always loved numbers. As he counts, he thinks of the years he spent in prison – how the weight of the number oppressed him when the sentencing happened. In the dock, with the judge's words still ringing in his ears, he had quickly calculated the months, the weeks, the number of days and nights he was facing into. He felt them falling on him, obliterating his indignation – the fury he had been forced to suppress and keep hidden throughout the trial.

From the start, he had protested his innocence, but the police had made up their minds. His denials throughout their investigation became an annoyance and a frustration; in the same way the missing murder weapon was an open sore. At the time, he was incensed by their refusals to believe him, but now he just feels tired. Tired of being misunderstood. Tired of having to fight to explain himself. And what's the point of it any more?

His life is finally yielding to inevitability. For the past few weeks he has been sustained by the promise of love and comfort that she held out to him. The way his heart had quickened when he first saw her move through the garden. Her likeness to Charlotte was there from the start, in her carriage, the bow of her mouth, the slant of her eyes, the steadiness of her gaze. It had unnerved him, as if his wife had somehow returned to him – and then later, it had provided that sliver of hope: the chance of redemption. He had failed Charlotte in life. His faithlessness, his philandering. He had been helpless to it then, but the years in prison had suppressed that side of him. An older man, now, he wanted comfort and affection and the chance of something extraordinary. For weeks, she has been a buffer against advancing dread. But now, with the sun descending behind the houses, he feels the sense of inevitability rising in him. He knows now what is called for. What is required. A beautiful ending. The kind denied to Charlotte, but at least he can do something about this one.

At the top of the stairs, he crosses into the bedroom, lays Leah gently on the crumpled sheets. The stillness in her conveys a sense of peace and he feels himself longing for it too.

'Not long, my darling. Almost there,' he tells her.

He smooths the bedclothes around her, fixes her head on the pillow. Blood seeps through the cotton pillowcase, spreading quickly. He arranges her hair to hide it. There are things that need to be done, but for just a moment he stands and gazes at her, his eyes passing over her prone body, so small and helpless in the drift of the big bed. Her face is peaceful, her breathing calm.

He thinks of Agamemnon, when the gods had demanded his daughter, Iphigenia – how Agamemnon must have felt in those moments before the sacrifice, how the pain and fear of the prospect must have been eased by her serenity, her acceptance. And that is what he feels from Leah. Acceptance. Equanimity. With this act, he will take away her suffering. No more will she be tortured by thoughts of that child. No more will she have to strive to overcome her guilt, her fears. There is nothing for her on this earth, only judgement and pain. Together, they can leave it all behind.

With purpose gathering inside him, he hurries to the bathroom. In the cabinet, he finds the pills, grinds them up and stirs them into a cup of water that he fills at the bathroom tap. Next, he sees to the letters. There is paper in the cabinet beside his bed and he takes out two sheets and writes quickly. A note for Mark, and another for Cassandra.

They will not understand and he won't try to explain. Cursory missives telling them that he loves them and that he's sorry. That he wants to be with their mother now. He makes no reference to Leah, cannot begin to explain why she must come with him. He stuffs the letters into envelopes, offering up a silent apology with the foresight of anguished questions to which there will never be answers.

He takes the letters and the glass of powdered water, then crosses the landing back to the front bedroom. On the dressing-table in front of the bay window, he leaves the letters for Mark and Cassandra propped against the mirror. Then, taking the glass, he turns back to the bed and sees her lying there with her eyes wide open, staring at him.

His heart stumbles, then rights itself, beating quickly now. Her gaze is clear and direct, her body unmoving, so that, for a moment, he thinks she must be dead. But then her brow wrinkles with sudden pain, and her limbs start to move. She draws her gaze from his and tries to roll over on to her front, a groan of anguish or pain emerging from her throat.

He has been standing rigid, but now springs into action and hurries around to her side of the bed, leaving his glass on the floor and perching on the mattress so that he can feel the press of her hip against him. She is still moving, but with the slow unsteadiness of someone seriously intoxicated. The sounds that are coming out of her mouth are unformed grunts.

'It's all right,' he says to her. 'Everything's going to be all right, you'll see. Just lie back now, my dear. It will all be over soon.'

He reaches for her arms, but she resists him, her

shoulders rising defensively as she attempts to roll across the mattress away from him. The grunts become words.

'No, no,' she says, her voice low and nasal, but there's urgency in it.

This same urgency communicates itself into his body. He's feeling panicked now. This is not how he wanted it to be. Not the way he'd planned it. He has to climb on to the bed and lean across her, pinning one of her arms beneath his knee so that he can reach for the pillow and bring it over her face. She thrashes beneath him, finding some last reserves of strength, but he is stronger than she is, and is able to hold the pillow in place, pressing down, all the while saying, 'Sssh, sssh, my dear,' in a cooing voice. 'It will all be over soon. Be calm, my love, calm.'

These words are meant as much for him as for her, for his heart is beating madly with fear. The atmosphere in the room, which had been peaceful, now feels charged with violence and disorder. Her legs are kicking out against the mattress, scrabbling over the sheets, and the duvet slips off the other side of the bed and falls to the floor. He knows this is all for the best, but is shocked at how hard she struggles against it – as if she wants to live.

'Please, Leah,' he says.

But then there's a hand in his hair, the scrape of nails over his scalp and the sharp pain as his head is yanked back. His thoughts scramble in confusion, trying to understand how she has managed to grab hold of his hair and tug him backwards, while both hands are pinned to the bed. A fleeting thought, chased away by a new terror, as an arm goes around his neck and he feels himself drawn backwards off the bed. The heat of another body presses through him, and he can feel laboured breathing close to his ear. As he is dragged off the bed, his feet scramble for their footing, almost slipping beneath him, but somehow he remains upright, and it is this one triumph that turns things to his advantage. He is taller than his assailant, and as he stands to his full height, their grasp around his neck breaks in a sudden cry of pain. A high-pitched yelp.

He turns and she throws herself against him, fists pummelling ineffectually at his chest, and for a moment, he is so astonished, he can hardly react. Red hair falling forward, freckled limbs, her dress a riot of colour. Hilary. She is clawing at him now, like a wildcat, and he grabs her wrists, wrenching them away from his face. Fury rises in him, like a seething ball of irritation. What is she doing here? Why must she always stick her nose into his business? He's sick of her interference, her demands. She's a pest and he wants to be rid of her, once and for all.

He's easily stronger than her and, after a quick scuffle, he's able to twist her around so that her back is to him, his hands groping for purchase on her flesh, grasping her beneath her breasts. He's holding her so close, as close as lovers, and he feels her braced against him.

'Let me go!' she cries, plucking at his sleeve, one hand reaching back to claw his face.

But he's intent now on his task. As he drags her from the room, his eyes go to Leah, her body lying still on the bed. Not long now, my love, he thinks, but his breath is labouring in his chest and he cannot speak. Hilary is small but she has a wiry strength, and is fighting hard against him, kicking out at his ankles and shins, scratching at the skin of his arms, his face.

Together, they lurch through the doorway, out into the hall. His mind is on the staircase – it's right there to the left. If he can just get her there, get her down the stairs . . . Then he can get back to the business at hand. The business of dying.

All the while he's been dragging her backwards, she's been pulling away from him in the opposite direction. But now, without warning, her resistance stops. Instead of bracing herself against him, she's going with him – not just surrendering to him, but actively pushing in the direction he's been dragging. This change of force is astonishing, and suddenly he finds himself flung backwards. His spine cracks against the banister that skirts the landing, and he feels the sudden splintering of that old wood, those ancient spindles. There is the briefest sensation of hair in his face – the perfumed scent of it in his nostrils, a red swish across his eyes – and then there is a rush of air around him and beneath him, the distortion of walls and ceilings racing past. His arms and legs kick out at nothing, and as he flies down through the house, he feels the wind leave his lungs in a single astonished breath before the floor crashes through him. His limbs twitch briefly. Darkness falls.

October

30

Hilary

On a dull Thursday morning in October a *Sale Agreed* sign appears outside Number 14. Hilary sees it as soon as she draws back the curtains in her bedroom.

For a moment, she just stands there, her hand to her chest as if there's pain. It's not pain, but a different sensation – unexpected. Relief. As if she's been holding something tightly in her chest and now can let it go. Relief that this is all about to be over.

Downstairs, she finds Greg in the kitchen finishing his breakfast and tells him.

'That was quick,' is his response.

The house has been on the market for barely a month, and for the past three weekends, Hilary has stood at her bedroom window and watched as dozens of people – prospective buyers as well as the curious and the prurient – disappeared inside Number 14 for the open house viewing.

'It's not all that surprising, I suppose,' Hilary says, as Greg sets a mug of tea in front of her at the table. 'It's priced very low.'

'I expect he wants a quick sale.'

'Probably,' she says thoughtfully, watching as he gulps his tea while checking his watch.

It's almost eight fifteen. Only half an hour until school starts.

'I wonder who the buyer is,' she says, and Greg snorts.

'Whoever they are, I hope they know an exorcist.'

Placing his mug in the sink, he comes towards her. 'Any plans for the day?'

She shakes her head and asks what he'd like for dinner that evening.

Sweeping aside her question, he says: 'I'm cooking, remember? You're to take it easy. Do something nice for yourself.' He leans down, brushes her cheek with his lips, and then he is gone.

It is ten weeks since Anton died. Ten weeks since that awful day, and Hilary is still recovering. The cuts have healed, the bruising faded, the muscles of her shoulder, torn during the struggle, have knitted themselves back together. Most days, she feels fine – stunned but lucky. On bad days, she feels the scarring inside, deep wounds slashed across her thoughts, her heart. Some nights, she awakens from her dreams, sweating and crying, and Greg has to hold her close against him until the panic subsides.

She has not gone back to school this term. A leave of absence was hastily arranged in the last days of August. Officially, her leave is to last until the new year, but lately Hilary has questioned whether she will ever return to teaching.

There is a sense about her, these days, of needing to start over. She yearns for renewal of some sort. A second act. She's only forty-nine. Much of her life remains to be lived. Some days she spends hours on the internet, perusing different third-level courses, browsing speculatively through websites for adult education, life-coaching; occasionally she checks out recruitment sites. Greg thinks it's too early for her to make any big decisions.

'Take your time,' he says. 'Wait until you're ready.'

His kindness to her in these past weeks is the one true thing that's kept her going. It feels like a small miracle, the way they have drawn close again after all these years. Small gestures of consideration, like Greg's new-found enthusiasm for cooking, his need to nourish and protect her, encourage her to seek out new challenges for herself – these things fill her with hope. For so long, she had planned a future without him. Now she shrinks from the prospect. She has survived, and she intends to make the most of the rest of her life.

Over the next few weeks, she watches the comings and goings across the street. Estate agents, valuers, surveyors. A removal truck sits outside Number 14 for an entire afternoon while three men carry furniture out of the house. She watches as they struggle with the piano until eventually it disappears into the dark cavern of the truck.

Maria Bolton tells her that a young family have bought the house. 'He's in the tech industry, she works in finance,' Maria says. 'Four kids between the ages of two and ten – all boys. They've an au pair, too, so they'll need the space. Money to burn, apparently. They plan to gut the place *and* build on some glass-box extension – as if the house wasn't big enough already. That's if they get the planning.'

'I hope they do,' she responds.

Maria gives her shoulders a little shudder, her eyes widening. 'Four boys, though! Can you imagine?'

'I'm glad,' Hilary says, surprised at the conviction she feels, so strong it brings a lump to her throat. 'It's just what that house needs. To be filled with the joyous, raucous noise of young boys.'

As her energy returns, she starts to look closely at her own surroundings. A desire has been growing inside her to make more of her home, to make it feel loved once more. Little things, like freshening the paint on the woodwork, buying some new scatter cushions for the sofa in the sitting room, finally getting a plumber to fix the slow leak under the kitchen sink. The garden doesn't escape her attention either. The final flourish of summer has bloomed and faded, and even though it has always been Greg's domain in terms of maintenance, Hilary finds herself relishing the opportunity to cut back and to prune. The outdoor work makes her feel enlivened, vigorous. She slices away the dead and dying, plants spring bulbs, considers new growth – renewal. In her new-found enthusiasm, she resolves to dig up the dying mini-fuchsia and replace it with something: a rosebush, or perhaps another hydrangea.

In the end she chooses a camellia. She is just returning from the garden centre in her car, the camellia on the back seat ready to be unpotted and planted, when she sees the couple climbing the steps to Number 14. For a moment, she sits in the car, the engine still running, and watches as they unlock the front door and go inside. The young man is Mark, and the woman with him – she's sure of it – is Leah.

Hilary switches off the engine and gets out. After a moment's hesitation, she crosses the road and climbs the steps. That same hesitation is there when she reaches for the door-knocker, trepidation running through her at the prospect of returning to a place she had sworn off for ever.

'Oh, hello,' she says to Mark, when he opens the door. 'I hope you don't mind, but I just saw you there and thought I'd come over.'

His face loses some of its wariness, and he opens the door wider. Behind him, Leah is standing with her hands in the pockets of her raincoat, her eyes wide and watchful amid the bones of her thin face.

'Hilary,' she says softly. Then the blankness disappears from her stare and her mouth broadens slowly into a smile. 'It's so good to see you.'

Mark closes the door behind her and steps past. Hilary sees him touching Leah's sleeve, hears him say: 'I'll just go and check out the back. Will you be okay?'

'Sure. I'm fine.'

Once he's gone, Leah's attention turns back to Hilary. She reads the speculation in Hilary's expression and smiles shyly. 'It's not what you think. We're just friends.'

There's a softness to her voice, and an imbalance to her features that wasn't there before. Her smile extends on only one side of her face; the other seems frozen. Nerve damage, Hilary concludes. Partial paralysis.

'It's weird being back here,' Leah remarks, looking around at the walls and ceiling before her gaze comes to rest near the bottom of the stairs, the place where Anton fell. 'I thought I would feel frightened. But it's as if nothing ever happened here.'

Hilary nods. She has the same feeling. Something momentous happened in this space, and yet on this

Thursday morning, the street quiet outside, it feels so ordinary and benign.

'I kept thinking about this house, about what happened here, what he did to me,' Leah tells her, 'and every time I thought of it, I felt frightened. Don't get me wrong – most of the time, I'm just so grateful to you that the outcome wasn't different. The very fact that I'm alive, well, that's what matters. But still.' Her gaze flickers again around the stairs and hall. 'This place has been haunting my thoughts, and I wondered if I came back here – if I saw it now without him in it – maybe I wouldn't feel scared any more. Does that make sense?'

There's an earnestness about her that Hilary finds moving. 'Yes. Yes, it does,' she says, and Leah nods, still serious.

Despite the delicacy of her features and the notable pallor of the convalescent, Hilary identifies a new steeliness in the young woman, a determination that wasn't there before.

'Will you come upstairs?' Leah asks, already half turned, her foot on the bottom step.

'All right.'

'You'll have to forgive the limp,' Leah explains, climbing slowly and stiffly upwards. 'I'm told it probably won't be permanent, but it's taking some getting used to.'

'How are you doing, otherwise?'

'I have some nerve damage in my back, my leg and my face, but you probably noticed that.' She turns and offers her lopsided smile. 'I get headaches, dizziness, but the blurred vision is gone, thank God. As for long-term damage, I don't know. My doctor is noncommittal when I ask. For now, I'm just trying to take one day at a time.'

They have reached the top of the stairs, and Leah moves towards the bedroom door, but Hilary stops. Where the banister had once wrapped around the stairwell, there is now a piece of plywood nailed into place. Seeing it there, it all comes flooding back: the moment he fell. One second he was firmly clasped against her and the next she was twisting free, her face turning just in time to catch the look in his eyes – that mute stare. She cannot remember any sound coming from him, no shout or cry, just an expression of sheer surprise and the movement of air, followed by that terrible thud. She leans over the plywood now and looks down, as if she can once more glimpse those open eyes staring up at her, the light of recognition dwindling from them. A vertiginous view.

It is too much. She takes a step back, turns away quickly.

Leah is inside the bedroom and Hilary goes to join her, not wanting to be alone on the landing with its memories, its ghosts. The bed is gone, as are the wardrobe and the dressing-table. All that remains is the carpet, faded and marked in places with deep grooves and indentations where the heavy furniture once stood.

'Can I ask you something?' Leah says. 'Why did you come back here that day? What made you come? I mean, how did you even get in?'

Hilary smiles. 'I know where the key is hidden, remember?' She goes to the window, looks out across the road to her own house. How small it looks from here. Small but safe.

'For a long time,' she tells Leah, 'I thought I was in love with Anton. I did love him, in fact, very deeply, and I thought that he loved me. It broke my heart when I found out otherwise. I came back here that day because I thought ... Oh, I don't know what I thought – that I could have it out with him. Demand to know how he could have used me in that way. And, if I'm honest, deep down I still hoped he felt something for me.'

'But did you know . . . did you believe he'd killed his wife?'

'Yes.'

'And you still loved him?'

Hilary turns back to the room, sees the blend of curiosity and disbelief in Leah's expression. 'I don't know what that says about me,' she admits, and she hears her own voice – the wistfulness in it. 'I thought it didn't matter. I just kept focusing on all the reasons why he did it – his unhappiness, what a difficult and troubled person she was, all the complexities within their marriage. And me, I suppose. I felt that he did it so that he'd be free to be with me. I was stupid and selfish and deluded. It was a fantasy. And it wasn't until I came up here and saw what he was doing to you – saw that violence within him with my own two eyes – it wasn't until then that I realized the true horror of it. The monster he was.'

She thinks she sees a small flash of terror in Leah's eyes, but then the young woman gives herself a shake, that steeliness coming back into her resolve.

'Jake never trusted him. But I . . . I felt something for him – something platonic,' she adds quickly. 'Friendship. I felt he understood something about me.'

'What about Jake?' Hilary asks, and Leah puts her hand to her hair, sweeps it back off her face.

'He's gone,' she says plainly. 'It turns out he wasn't the one for me after all.'

She meets Hilary's gaze with a smile touched by defiance, and goes on: 'I'm fine. I really am. It feels right – inevitable, I suppose. He's gone to Scotland. His son is there and he wanted to be close to him. And there was nothing really keeping him here.'

'Except you.'

'Yes. But that wasn't enough. And I think both of us knew that. Even before Anton ... what happened ...' Her words die away, and Hilary sees her expression grow thoughtful, introspective.

'Years ago,' Leah says, 'I told a lie about something that happened. A serious lie. While I was in hospital, I kept thinking about it, about all the people I'd hurt because of that lie – the damage I'd done. I thought about how I'd lived for years with this shadow hovering over me. I lived like I was afraid the whole time of being found out.' She fixes Hilary with her clear-eyed stare. 'I can't do that any more. When Anton put that pillow over my face, I thought I was going to die and I wanted so badly to live. I don't like thinking about what would have happened if you hadn't come into the room. All I know now is that I've been given this second chance and I don't want to mess it up. I want things to be different now. Do you know what I mean?'

Hilary says yes. She understands. A second act. A renewal.

Leah glances once more around the room, and then says: 'I think that's enough now. Will we go down?'

It's different now out in the hall. As if by saying those words aloud in the bedroom, Hilary has released some tension that was within her. Leah's voice also sounds

379

lighter, less tense, as she walks towards the door. She tells Hilary how Mark came to visit her in hospital. How he'd felt guilty for renting the flat to them, for inadvertently putting her in harm's way.

'He didn't really believe it, you see, that his father was guilty of the crime. But now . . .'

'I think we all know now.'

They've reached the front door and Leah draws it open.

'Well, goodbye, then,' Hilary says, and to her great surprise, Leah steps forward and puts her arms around her, drawing her into a firm hug. There is real warmth in that embrace, and Hilary hears the deep chime of sincerity in Leah's voice when she says, 'Thank you,' close to her ear.

She is taking the camellia from the back seat of the car when she sees the two of them leave the house. Leah gives her a little wave, and Hilary responds, watching as they walk slowly down the street. Leah's limp looks more pronounced out in the daylight, and Hilary watches as Mark offers her his arm and she leans on him – something courtly and romantic about the gesture – a closeness between them as they disappear around the corner.

Clouds are gathering in the sky. Rain is forecast for later in the afternoon, and Hilary would like to get the camellia into the ground before the downpour. She carries it out into the back garden, smiling to herself as she imagines Greg's surprise when he comes home from school and sees her handiwork. With the new plant waiting in its pot on the grass, Hilary fetches the spade and begins digging.

It's hard work. The fuchsia has been in the ground for

close to twenty years. It was one of the first things they planted after moving here. Its roots are deep and spreading. Hilary works with dogged determination, the spade slicing through the earth. At intervals, she pauses in her digging and pushes hard against the main trunk, then pulls it, trying to loosen it from its mooring. Eventually, she feels it give. She puts down her spade and grabs hold of the bush with both hands, braces her feet against the earth, heaving with all her strength. Her body aches with the effort, but she feels it come. Moments later, the bush leaves the ground, its roots clogged with soil. Hilary drags it to one side. Then, with her spade, she begins to hack at the roots in a bid to free the clay that's lodged there, a great ball of it. She hits it with the blade and something comes loose and falls out.

At first, she thinks it's a rock covered with muck, but when she prods it with the spade, she feels the softness of it. Putting down her tool, she lifts the bundle and is surprised by how light it is, lighter still after she shakes some more hardened clay from it, using her hands to sweep off the dirt. It's a bundle of cloth – what might be a blue stripe runs through the ruined fabric. Shaking it out, something drops to the earth with a small thud. Hilary's eyes go to the ground.

She looks down, and it's as if she's staring down a long, silent tunnel. The garden falls away. A great stillness comes over her.

It's a knife. A kitchen knife, no more than eight inches long. It is caked with dirt, but she can clearly make out the shape of it, the heft of the handle, the long, thin blade.

Her limbs don't shake when she bends down slowly to

pick it up. A dead calm has come over her, a simple understanding. The long slow 'ah', like a last release of breath.

She sits at the kitchen table and waits.

Everything inside her has slowed, grown still. She is
sitting there, perfectly calm – almost serene – when he
arrives home from work.

The energy of his busy day is brought into the house
with him as he comes into the kitchen, slings his bag on
to the countertop. 'Hey there, how are you?' he says, at the
sink, filling a glass with water and putting it on the table.
'Good day? God, I'm starving. I stopped off at Supervalu,
picked us up a couple of steaks . . .'

He has come forward to kiss her when his words
trail off.

On the table in front of her is the knife, still caked with
mud. The ancient T-shirt in which it had been wrapped
and concealed sits alongside it. Hilary's hands are folded
neatly in her lap. She watches her husband's face, the initial spark of confusion clearing, replaced by the shock of
understanding. The blood drains from his face.

'Jesus,' he says hoarsely, the word a croak.

He pulls out a chair quickly and collapses on to it, his
eyes fixed on the knife, staring at it with disbelief.

She doesn't say anything, just watches as he leans his
elbows on the table, rubs his nose and mouth with the
back of his hand. Still he can't drag his gaze from the
knife, as if fearful it might, at any moment, jump up of its
own accord and attack him. She can hear him taking
quick, short breaths, and in a voice that is immeasurably
calm, she tells him: 'Have a drink of water.'

He does as she instructs, grabs the glass, like a lifeline, gulps the water. He closes his eyes briefly as he sets the glass down, and when he opens them, he is looking at her. A fearful look.

'Did you know?' he asks quietly.

She shakes her head.

'Sometimes I thought you might have guessed.'

He looks again at the knife, squeezes his eyes shut, and whispers, 'Christ,' under his breath. She watches as he exhales – a long, slow breath to calm himself – and then, when he is ready, he starts to tell her.

'The strange thing is, I liked Charlotte,' he begins. 'I know you thought she was trouble, but she was always nice to me. A flirt, yes, but she could be funny as well, and attentive. Whenever we'd talk, I always felt she was genuinely interested in what I was saying. She was nice – far nicer than her husband.' Hilary notes the change in his tone, wistfulness giving way to hardness. 'He was a creep. Chasing other women – not even trying to conceal it. He thought he was God's gift. I couldn't understand what she saw in him. And the mind-games they played with each other – it was head-wrecking. I felt sorry for her.'

He kneads his hands above the table. She sees the whiteness of his knuckles.

'I knew you liked him, but I told myself it was nothing, just some stupid crush. You were all over the place after we'd lost the baby, so I let it go, presuming it wasn't serious, just some stupid infatuation that you'd get over once we'd moved into our own place. But then at the party –'

He breaks off suddenly, and she sees the emotion springing up inside him.

'Go on,' she tells him, in her quiet, firm voice.

'I just wanted to let off steam. It had been a hard summer for me. I'm not sure if you even realized that at the time. Trying to get this place done, dealing with builders who knew I didn't have a fucking clue ... And you, Hilary. You were so upset after the baby. I didn't know how to deal with you. It was like treading on eggshells all that summer. I wanted to protect you – to comfort you – but you just kept holding me at arm's length.' He shakes his head, as if annoyed with himself. 'That night, when we went to the party, I just wanted to get drunk and forget about things for a while. So I laid into the booze, and got lost in the party. It was not until well into it that I realized you weren't there.'

Understanding is coming to her now, returning to that night, her mind reeling backwards.

'I was looking for you when I found Charlotte. She was coming in from the garden with her little boy, and it was clear she was worked up. "Looking for your wife?" she asked me, in a catty kind of way. And then she told me to look for you in her husband's shed.'

Hilary feels the breath drawing into her lungs, the cold rattle of it. Her feelings colour with shame as she listens to him tell of how he'd gone down into the garden, how it was dark, how he'd seen them emerge from the shed, watching from the shadows while Anton helped her fix her clothing, the two of them clinging together for one last embrace. The thought that he was there in the darkness of the garden witnessing that – not the sex, but the attempt at concealment, the way they separated from each other, him going back in first, followed a minute later by her, each of them shaking themselves off, trying to look 'normal' ... Nineteen years ago but the memory feels vivid and fresh.

'What then?' she asks softly, needing to draw him on, not wanting him to lose the story now when they are so close to the truth.

He shrugs sadly, his eyes inward-looking, weary with remembering.

'I pretended nothing'd happened. Rejoined the party, kept on drinking. I couldn't look at you, though.' His eyes flick to hers, something sharp in his gaze. 'So when you told me you were going home, I said I'd stay on. Somehow I felt you were relieved at that.'

She holds his gaze, heavy with accusation. 'Please go on,' she urges softly.

The hardness in his stare fades.

'I stayed on, even when the party dwindled. At one point, Charlotte came over to me and asked me if I was okay. I said yeah, even though it was clear I wasn't. She suggested I stay on until everyone else had left. I knew what she meant, so I asked, "What about Anton?" She told me not to worry. That she'd got rid of him. We'd be alone and free to enact our revenge, she said. I knew full well what she wanted and part of me wanted it too. I was so shocked by what you'd done. I couldn't believe it. It was stupid, but I thought, Why not? Why shouldn't I, if that was the way you were carrying on?'

A certain bullishness has entered his tone, an angry self-righteousness. She does not challenge him. She knows that if she is patient, if she is calm, the truth will come out.

'I pretended to leave,' he says next. 'Drunk as I was, I

knew that I didn't want any of our neighbours to suspect. I hid in the bathroom until the last person left, and then I went and found Charlotte. She was in the kitchen, cleaning up. "I thought you'd gone," she said.'

He stops, a wary look coming over his face. 'Well, I think you know what happened next,' he says.

'Tell me.' Her voice has lost its softness. She is calm, but her tone is hard, her gaze steely.

'We started kissing. Things were getting a bit out of hand. I mean, I thought that was what I'd wanted. She was a good-looking woman and I wanted to get my own back on him – and punish you too. But somehow, when it came to it . . . It was weird being with her, like it just wasn't right. She smelt different from you, she felt different. When I kissed her, rather than feeling aroused, I felt kind of . . . intimidated. It was embarrassing. We were both there together with one aim in mind, and I just couldn't . . .'

His hand goes up to cover his eyes. It's like he has to shield himself from her gaze as he tells her what happened. Hilary listens without saying a word. She imagines the scene: the two of them entwined in that kitchen, Charlotte fumbling with the buttons of his jeans, reaching inside to find . . . What? Shyness. Softness. Humiliation.

'She kept laughing at me. Thought it was hilarious. I tried to walk out and leave her, but she kept pulling at me, stood in front of me, barring my way out into the hall. And all the while she's laughing and mocking me, saying stuff – lewd, disgusting stuff. I just wanted to get away from her. "Perhaps, if I act more like your stupid little wife," she said. And then – then she starts putting on this voice, this whiny little voice, like she was trying to mimic you but in the worst possible way. Saying those disgusting things in that ugly voice – I just wanted her to *shut up*!' His eyes bulge, his voice lowered to an angry hiss. And then his gaze drops, falls to the knife sitting between them on the polished surface of the table.

'There'd been a cake,' he says forlornly. 'She'd used the knife to slice it.'

The work of an instant. A rush of blood to the head. One swift movement of the hand.

'I couldn't believe what I'd done,' he says, his voice small and astonished. 'She just went down. I didn't know what to do – there was so much blood. Everything just happened so fast. A few seconds – a minute. I was afraid to touch her, even to feel for a pulse. Not that I needed to. I could see she was dead.'

His T-shirt was covered with blood, and his hand. His mind was racing, chasing through all sorts of permutations of how he might be caught.

'I just took the knife and ran,' he tells her. 'And it's funny the things that occur to you, even in a situation as shocking and stressful as that. Like how I took care not to step in the blood, how I thought to cover my fingers with a clean corner of my T-shirt when I opened the front door, and the same when I pulled it shut behind me. That I would have the presence of mind not to leave fingerprints . . . I still thought they'd come for me, though. It was a miracle there was no one on the street. It was so late at that point – past three a.m. A miracle that no one was looking out of their window or driving past in their car.'

It was only when he reached his own house that he

realized he had no clue of what to do with the knife. That was when the idea came to him.

Their garden was a mess after the builders. Scrubby grass grew in tufts among the debris left behind after the renovation. They'd had vague plans to clear it up, perhaps put in a patio once they had the money. But neither of them had much interest in gardening. Their focus was all on the house.

'I picked a spot near the back. It was difficult to see anything in the darkness, but I just pulled at this weed that was as big as a shrub. It came out, leaving a hole that was large enough until I could sort out something later. I pulled off my T-shirt, which was spattered with blood, and wrapped the knife in it.'

He'd covered it over, replacing the weed, then let himself quietly into the house, stripping off the rest of his clothes in the kitchen and putting them into the washing-machine. Then he'd stood at the sink scrubbing his hands, his arms, his face, his torso – scrubbed his skin raw.

'I stayed on the sofa that night. I was afraid of waking you. Afraid that you'd ask me something and then somehow know what was wrong, what I'd done.'

He lay awake all that night, thinking over various options, all the while alert to noises outside. He kept expecting to hear the whine of sirens, the screeching of brakes outside. But the police never came, and by the time the sun had risen, he had a plan.

'As soon as it was light, I got up and showered. Then I went outside and began working on the garden, digging it over, like it was a regular Sunday-morning thing to do.

Which it was. People are always doing their gardens on Sundays.'

He'd made sure that the knife was hidden, and then he'd gone to the garden centre, with his crippling hangover, and bought a range of different plants. It seemed important that he make it look like a big project – like he'd decided to landscape the whole back garden. He spent a fortune, he tells her now, just to conceal the reason for planting that single fuchsia bush.

'I kept thinking they were going to come for me,' he says now. 'When they interviewed each of us – all the guests from the party – I was sure I'd let something slip or that someone else's account would point the finger in my direction. For weeks, I hardly slept, so sure they would find something – some trace of evidence that would link me to her death.'

In the end, the party saved him. After the number of people who had been present, trampling through the house, the place was a mess of fingerprints and forensics. The door-to-door questions, the trawling through differing accounts, never turned up the murder weapon or indeed the murderer himself.

Except for Anton.

'I felt conflicted,' Greg tells her now. 'I knew it was wrong – an innocent man going to prison. But then I thought, Well, how innocent is he? His behaviour towards her was terrible. And he was fucking my wife!' His indignation bursts through, then recedes. 'Sorry,' he tells her. 'I'm sorry.'

He shakes his head. 'For years, I thought it would be

okay. That I had put it all behind me. That I was safe. But then when Anton came back, and I could see you obsessing all over again . . . I just wanted him to go away. To leave us in peace. I thought if I could just scare him away, but . . .'

His eyes come to rest on the knife sitting on the table between them.

'Hilary,' he says. 'What are we going to do?'

Clouds are gathering overhead in thick, tight bunches. The sky has darkened, and in the garden now a chill wind blows. All traces of summer heat have fled. Autumn is finally here.

The camellia bush she has bought lies on its side in the grass, and Hilary kneels beside it, easing the root-ball from the plastic pot. Gently, she loosens the feathery roots from the potting earth they're moulded to.

She thinks of all the seasons that have passed here. The summer evenings dining out on the patio. The winter days while the garden slept beneath a blanket of snow. And all the while it kept its secret concealed within the dark heavy earth.

The hole they have made waits, like an open grave, and there is a degree of reverence in the manner in which Greg places the bundle in it. Hilary watches him push some loose earth over the lip of the hole. And then he stands up and reaches for his spade while she carries the camellia forward, carefully manoeuvring the root-ball down into place.

She steps back while her husband fills in the hole around it. There is a rhythm to his movements, a gentle shush of earth joining earth. She watches as he puts aside the spade and, with the sole of his shoe, tamps the soil, firming it down. It is all done, sealed in place, by the time the rain begins to fall.

Acknowledgements

This book began as a conversation with my friend Lydia Dickson outside the school gates, and I must thank her for planting the seed of an idea. Others helped it to grow by providing me with space, time, encouragement, and a listening ear, as well as the occasional glass of wine, and for that I thank Kitty Martin, Catherine and Paul Sweeney, Rachel Conway, Tana French, Emma Murphy, Rowena Walsh, Alison Weatherby, and the ladies of the Exclusive EU Book Club. Thanks also to Ciara McGowan for giving me that extra-special push to find an ending! Huge thanks to my wonderful agent, Jonathan Lloyd, and all the team at Curtis Brown who take such good care of me, in particular Luke Speed and Melissa Pimentel. This book was a team effort in many ways and I am so grateful to my amazing publishers, Michael Joseph, for their talent, professionalism and support, in particular Maxine Hitchcock, Joel Richardson, Jennifer Porter, Beth Cockeram and Sarah Kennedy. Thanks to Hazel Orme for smoothing the edges, and thanks also to Cliona Lewis at Penguin Ireland. Special thanks to Matilda McDonald for her guidance and support while working closely with me on this book. Once again, I am grateful to the Tyrone Guthrie Centre for yet another fantastic residency where part of this book was written.

Biggest thanks of all and much love to my peeps: Conor, Rowan and Freya Sweeney.